THE HERO SLAYERS

THE HERO SLAYERS

O. S. Marrow

Podium

ISBN: 978-1-0394-8781-9

Published in 2025 by Podium Publishing
www.podiumentertainment.com

THE HERO SLAYERS

CHAPTER ONE

What a Waste of a Perfectly Good Town

(Like all great stories, it begins with a slaughter.

I take no joy in starting at this point—it hardly sets the tone for events still to come—but it's where my journey truly began. To gloss over it would be to remove a core part of my being, the very motivation that set me upon this path. What do you want me to do, lie about it?

So we'll start with the slaughter, yes, but . . . bear with me.)

I was in attendance at a dinner party. The people were merry, singing songs and trading anecdotes, and our host—the much renowned Collector of Plainside, who brought much tourism and wealth to this small coastal town—had plenty to do with that. She was truly generous, both with her food and her company, and for that reason I really wished I wasn't there to rob her.

Raising a goblet, I locked eyes with the host at the far end of the ornate table, across towering candlesticks, and I celebrated her with a silent toast—one that she received with a raised goblet of her own, and a smile that existed not just in her mouth, but in her purple irises. Perhaps, in another world, I was there under my own name, and we might have celebrated one another in more intimate ways.

The merriment couldn't only be explained by the generosity of the Collector, however. The bottles of wine placed intermittently around the table had been supplied by myself, brewed by my very hand using an ability I'd only recently found value in.

> **Brewing**: Level 18
> **Floral Notes (Brewing)**: Disguise the strength of your vine-based creations by nurturing and bringing forth the underlying floral notes present in the fruit.

Looking around at the other guests, at their glazed eyes and hearing their slurred words, I swirled the—still entirely full—goblet in my hand. It was funny how even the most seemingly useless ability choices could prove invaluable in the right situation—the tricky part was manipulating yourself *into* that situation. But a forged invitation handed over, a fake name given, and a crate of homemade wines had done just that. Once the guests were drunk enough, I could slip off into the basement, where the Collector kept her—

"You're not d-drinking," the man at my left said, managing to communicate more with the stench of his breath than with his words.

"I assure you, sir, I am," I replied.

"You're not! I been . . ." He put a hand to his face, and hiccupped. "Been watching you. You know, I been to parties before—"

"Yes, I'm quite sure that you have."

"—where someone wasn't drinking that which he brought, and it was because it was poisoned. Is your wine poisoned, sir?"

I forced a smile to my face. It was, of course, but not in the way that this man was jokingly suggesting. It would not cause their flesh to rot away, or their minds to dissolve, or whatever manner of creative and cruel inflictions alchemists were inventing these days. It would only make them very, very drunk.

"I assure you, sir," I said again, "I wouldn't know how to do so. I'm a simple . . ." I paused, forgetting my cover story just for a moment, "merchant, and have no time for developing skills such as . . ."

I trailed off when I realized that the man's feigned accusation had drawn some attention. Two elven women sat opposite had turned to face me, and were notably no longer drinking.

"Be that as it may," one of the women said, "it would not do for us to consume such a gift without its creator partaking. You would not force such ill manners onto us, would you? Poison or otherwise?"

The tone of the woman's voice was harsh enough that more guests turned their attention to me—when all I wanted was the distinct *lack* of attention. Only one action would swiftly divert their attentions away, and it would make the job . . . slightly more difficult.

The woman raised her own wine-filled goblet, beckoning me to drink.

With a polite smile, I did so, taking a perhaps needlessly large gulp before placing the goblet back down atop the table. My stamina bar drained before my eyes, a good quarter or so depleted just from that amount of wine. It really was strong stuff, though perhaps my underinvestment in Dexterity—the stat that governed my stamina reserves—was partially to blame. My other two power bars, Health and Mana, were—thankfully—unaffected. I hadn't overdone it *too* much on the wine, then.

Satisfied, the two women resumed their shrill conversation, and the man at my left passed out onto the table. I tried to blink the table back into focus as the two women opposite continued their loud conversation.

"She did say there would be a Player in attendance."

"And it would be a rare honor indeed, to have such a hero dine with us! Yet where are they?"

"Has the Collector ever given us reason to doubt her, dear cousin? I do believe . . ."

"Gods, I'm already drunk," I mumbled aloud, then prayed a silent prayer to Dionysus, willing that He sober me up some. The act was fruitless, though—I would need to raid my host's collection . . . in this state.

"Excuse me," I said to nobody in particular, then stood from my seat at the table, swaying. Blinking my cloudy vision back into focus, I made for the bathroom, resisting the urge to gulp as I passed between two of the Collector's guards at the doorway of the feasting hall.

Thankfully, their heads didn't turn to follow me; they thought me not a threat in my current, alcohol-fueled state, just as I'd planned. Of course, I hadn't expected to *actually* be drunk, but that was the hand I'd been dealt.

I strolled slowly, casually, down the long corridor toward the bathroom, but as I reached the door, I didn't enter. Instead, I continued onward, to the door at the end of the hallway, where my sources had reported that the entrance to the basement was located.

Stepping inside, I took one last look at the—thankfully *empty*—corridor behind me, and closed the door gently, doing my best to disguise the creaking. Unfortunately, my *Stealth* tree investment had never yielded the option for abilities that dealt with creaky doors; you wouldn't believe how often this was an issue in my line of work. *Why can't people oil their door hinges? Won't someone think of the thieves!*

Slowly, I pressed on, down a winding stone staircase, until I came to a grand cellar, lit by flickering candles, filled with loot the likes of which I'd rarely seen before. My every instinct was to hoard all the valuable items I could find, but I forced myself to concentrate; I was here for one object, and only one.

I scoured display case after display case—necklaces and blades and glowing stones, each with powers and abilities of which most could only dream. Some were so high in level requirement that my *Identification* skill couldn't even tell me what they did, and that only made me want them more. To my drink-addled mind, they were almost worth gambling with whatever traps the Collector had surely laid down here.

And then, I saw it. Against the far wall, surrounded by gold and jewels and ornamental blades—the artifact. It was just as my client had described: an octahedron—*yes, I'd had to ask what that was, too*—of pure silver, seven of its eight sides polished to perfection, the last inlaid with an emerald larger than any I'd set my eyes upon before. Even if it didn't have any power, the raw material itself would sell for quite the price.

I crouched by the artifact, making sure not to touch it, and I *identified* it. You know, just to make sure I wasn't being distracted by a fake—it'd been known to happen.

> **Identification:** Level 29
> **Advanced Identification (Identification):** Discover more detailed attributes for a particular object or person, and basic attributes for higher-level objects and persons. Ability scales with [WIS] + [INT].

My skill check passed, and the item's name appeared before me. *The Sisyphus Artifact*, it read. *Power: [unknown]. Charges remaining: (1 / 7)*. This was it, then. I had it. Weeks of hard work and planning had finally got me to this point, and all I had to do was reach out and—

I stopped my hand in midair, remembering myself. That wine had made a fool of me, had made me throw all my usual expertise out the window. Before I picked up this item, I had to, of course . . .

> **Stealth:** Level 43
> **Identify Traps (Stealth):** Search for traps in an area limited to eyesight range. Scales with [WIS].

By itself, I'd learned, this *Identify Traps* ability wasn't all that. Only when you scaled up your Wisdom stat did it start to work reliably, which was why I'd never invested much in my Dexterity—when the choice was there, Wisdom was the base stat I'd invested in. Not just *traps* scaled up based on Wisdom, either; many of the abilities relevant to my . . . *job* were related to this stat, or at least the ones I'd selected out of my lists of options.

> **Stealth:** +80XP

Activating this ability did, indeed, identify a trap. The artifact was sitting atop a hex rune; surely nothing that the Collector had created herself, being that she had a social class, rather than a magick class. This would have been a contractor's doing.

I'd lucked out. Not a week ago, I'd had a lovely conversation at knifepoint with the most renowned magick-based trapper in all the Eastern Tundras, based on information that this was the Collector's preferred method of security. They'd revealed to me—after, admittedly, an impressive amount of "convincing"—that they built themselves a backdoor into all their hexes, in case they ever needed to deactivate them. To do so, all you had to do was speak a simple code word, though no doubt they had changed this phrase for all traps crafted *since* our little conversation.

I leaned close to the artifact to speak this code. "Mihi templus—" I stopped, finding myself slurring and stumbling over the words. *Damn wine!* "Mihi tempus v-venit. Venit." Nothing. I sighed, and tried once more. "Mihi tempus venit!"

A turquoise glow illuminated the otherwise candlelit dungeon for just a moment as the hex faded away, and in my excitement, I threw my hands into the air . . . and knocked a vase from a pedestal.

Before I could think to react, it collided with the stone floor with an almighty crash, sending fragments of ceramic skittering into all corners of the dark room. I cringed, paused, and waited for a sign of movement upstairs. *Maybe it wouldn't come*, I thought. Maybe the guards were distracted with the dinner guests. Maybe—

"Who's down there?" someone shouted from the top of the stairs—from the top of my only way out.

"Erm . . ." came the involuntary reaction from my mouth.

Thinking quickly, or at least as quickly as I could with my mind in its current drunken state, I grabbed the artifact and shoved it into my jacket pocket, then dove for cover.

In a shadowed corner of the room I hid, clutching a thin steel dagger that had served me oh so well in the last few years, since I'd gotten the level to wield it effectively. It would need to serve me well again, now.

The two guards entered the basement quietly, their footsteps soft on the stone floor. From my corner of the room, I could see swords glinting in the candlelight—they would have reach, so I would need to rely on my agility. No matter; it had worked out for me before.

As the pair of guards reached the shattered pottery—no small curses uttered at the sight—I took advantage of the shadows to scuttle along the perimeter of the room. With any luck, I could slip up the stairs without alerting—

I tripped on an uneven tile, tumbling to the ground with an "oomph," followed by a "hmm."

Two glimmering blades turned toward me as I scrambled back to my feet. I met the eyes of the orc guard, and then both pairs in turn glanced at the exit.

"Hulm," the orc said to the other guard, nodding him toward the stairs.

I and the human guard both bolted for the door, and in normal circumstances I would've put good money on me making it to the exit long before him, but with this strong wine in my system . . .

We arrived at the stairs at the same time, a blade coming down to block my path—one that I instinctively reacted to with a raised dagger of my own. A metallic clang rang out as metal hit metal, and I staggered backward at the force of the hit.

Stumbling, I fell into a display case, causing the guard to freeze for a moment, his eyes wide with fear—would his employer be about to lose a few more items from her collection?

Seizing the opportunity of the man's hesitation, I swung forward with my right fist, knocking the guard squarely in the temple. With just this one hit, he collapsed to the ground, unconscious.

Level 25 Guard defeated!

Knifework: +1,000XP
Bareknuckle: +1,500XP
Bareknuckle increased to Level 14!
Base Points Gained: +1 VIT, +1 DEX, +1 STR, +3 Free Points (VIT/DEX/STR)

"Huh," I muttered.

At my right, the orc guard growled, beginning to pace angrily toward me.

"Right. Yes," I said, minimizing the notification. "Time for that later."

I steadied myself and raised my dagger, ready to strike quickly before the orc could swing his blade. For once, this went according to plan, and my dagger met the guard's hand as he swung, causing him to cry with pain and drop the sword to the ground with another almighty clatter. *Hopefully, all this noise won't attract too much attention . . .*

But even bare-handed, the orc's innate race boons meant that he would put up quite a fight—especially against a weapon as short-ranged as a dagger.

I slashed at the orcish guard's swinging arms, flailing the tip of my blade near blindly in an attempt to defend myself. But the orc had both height and strength on his side, and soon I found myself pacing backward, losing ground with every—

I crashed to the floor hard, the stone ground knocking the wind from my lungs before I'd even known what'd hit me. With the orc towering over me, I looked around for something . . . *anything* that might get me out of this mess. I saw only one thing that might just work.

"I'm too drunk for this," I garbled as I lashed out with my right foot for a nearby pedestal. With one sharp kick, the unit was toppling, and the great collection of enchanted glassware began falling to the ground.

"You little—" The guard scrambled to prevent as many of the collected items as possible from shattering on the hard stone floor. He held out the front of his tunic into a makeshift bag, and I didn't stop to find out just how successful this strategy was.

Instead, I staggered to my feet, colliding with another pedestal in the process and causing the armor thereon to fall to the ground, too—though at least this was surely less fragile than glassware.

I dunno, though, I've had some particularly terrible Light Armor in the past . . .

I hurried for the door, hopping clumsily over the other guard's unconscious body, and stretched my left leg out to begin bounding up to the ground floor . . . and to freedom.

But it was only at this point, somehow, that the real trouble began.

An almighty boom echoed around the underground chamber, reflecting an incredible release of power coming from somewhere above. Against my better judgement, I paused at the bottom of the stairwell and turned to face the orc guard.

Screams, ear-pinching and heartrending, erupted above.

The guard stood, empty tunic in hand, hundreds of shards of glassware on the floor around him, and his eyes grew wide. Both the guard and I gulped, and in that moment we both understood that we were allies, not enemies, in whatever battle brewed above.

We charged up the stairs to find a world aflame.

Half of the Collector's manor was missing, as though disintegrated from reality itself by the fire that still raged around it. I could see the rest of the town of Plainside from the top of the stairs—being that the wall that had once hidden it from view was now gone. At the bottom of the gentle hill, this town had suffered no less than the Collector; its buildings were aflame, its people were screaming, fleeing, or dead.

Nothing could have sobered me more.

Fresh screams pierced my right ear, and I spun my head to the source of the noise. A young girl, clutching a stuffed toy, stood facing a mahogany dinner table that was engulfed by flame, those who had sat at it only halfway out of their seats before the destruction could end them.

And there, through the flames, I saw three figures. Though only silhouettes to me, I could see that one was a burly orc, clutching a great battleaxe. Another was a blade-wielding tiefling, her wispy tail twisting and turning like the flames themselves, her eyes glowing a horrifying red. And in the center, ahead of them, was a human clutching no weapon at all.

These three did not scream, nor did they panic. They only strode silently, almost floating, toward me, the guard, and the young girl. I knew, deep down, that this trio was the source of the destruction, even before I *identified* their apparent leader.

Level 42 Pyroknight
Race: Human
System Note: Player

At my side, the orc guard gasped. He, too, had seemingly *identified* the man ahead of us, and I knew this for one simple reason. The guard hadn't gasped at the sight of the destruction of his employer's home, nor at the screams and cries of the pyroknight's victims. He had gasped later, and there was only one thing in Alterra more surprising than a massacre of such scale: that a Player might be behind it.

"No," the orc mumbled. "No, no, I . . . It can't . . ."

In front of us, the young girl turned, and she gazed at me with wide, distinctively purple eyes. "Where's my mummy?" she asked.

Before I could answer—though I do not know what my answer could've been, considering that an unmoving host still occupied the seat at the head of the table—a voice boomed from the flames.

The Player.

"Where is it?" he demanded, and with the raise of his hand a great sword formed of flame darted for my throat.

I couldn't have moved to avoid it, not in the state of shock I was in, but its creator stopped it an inch away from piercing skin. The heat still licked at my neck.

"I . . ." was the only word I could muster.

"The artifact," he said. "Where is it?"

Of course, I knew in that moment exactly what the Player meant. My every instinct was to hand it over, to beg for mercy, that he might save my life if nobody else's. I knew that all I needed to do was to reach into my coat pocket and pull the Sisyphus Artifact out, but . . . then I caught sight again of the wide purple eyes of the newly orphaned daughter of the Collector.

And a rage erupted inside my heart of an intensity to rival the surrounding flames.

"To Tartarus with you," I spat.

The Player stepped out of the flames, and a snarl twisted its way onto his face. "I see," he said. With the raise of his hand, a pillar of fire formed ahead of him, and a moment later it was hurtling toward the three of us—thief, guard, orphan.

I had just enough Dexterity to both dive out of the attack's way and grab the young girl as I did so. We fell hard toward the ground, and I heard a bone snap beneath me. It wasn't, I soon realized, any of mine.

At my left, the vicious flames engulfed the orc guard in his entirety, and his scream lasted little more than a second before there was no life left to feel terror.

I grabbed at the wailing young girl, seizing her shoulders as she cradled her arm. "You must . . ."

"But he was a *Player*," the girl cried. "He's supposed to *help* us."

"Listen, you need—"

"He's supposed to be—"

"Listen!" I snapped, shaking the girl hard. "You have to run."

"I don't—"

"Run!" I roared, and I pushed the Collector's daughter through a gap in the crumbling wall of her home. Only once I saw that she was following my instruction did I turn to face our attackers, to buy this innocent seconds more in order that she might escape.

I stood, reaching into my pocket not for the artifact, but for the throwing knives I kept back for tight spots. After all, where I seemed to be going, I wouldn't need them.

With a glance at the current location of the trio, as well as at one of the last remaining pillars ahead of me, I activated a *Knifework* ability that I'd only used once before.

> **Ricochet (Knifework):** Throw blades at a hard surface for half your stamina power to ricochet. Thrown blades retain 70 percent of speed with each bounce. Damage dealt scales with [DEX].

It was a last-ditch effort.

The three blades soared through the air, bouncing off the side of the pillar with a metallic clink, then flew toward my targets. I thought, if this plan failed, that the flames might melt the knives, or one of the Player's two bodyguards might protect them. But the truth was worse. Each of the three blades hit true, landing in the Player's torso.

The failure was simply that he didn't care.

The Player only glanced down at the knives protruding from his chest, furrowed his brow, and then cast a spell with the telltale yellow-white hue of a healing enchantment. Each of my three throwing knives hit the tiles below with another—far more pathetic, to my ear—clink.

"You'll have to do better than that," the Player said.

Silently agreeing, I took a deep breath, then stepped out in sight of the enemy.

"You'll never find it. The artifact you wanted? It's far from—" I started.

"He has it," said the tiefling from the cover of the flames, her eyes glowing brighter.

"Ah," I said.

"Yeah," agreed the Player. "'Ah' is right."

I swallowed, forcing myself to stand firm. If this was how I went out—trying the save the life of an innocent young girl—I was fine with that. I could've died doing something far less noble, perhaps springing a deadly trap or being beaten by guards. Maybe even rotting in a jail cell. It hadn't occurred to me, ever, that I might actually die doing something *good*. I took some comfort in that as I opened my mouth to taunt the man in front of me. "If you want it, you'll have to—"

Fire engulfed me.

Pain. Searing, at first, and then . . . nothing. Nothing that I could feel, at least. My vision faded fast, but my hearing . . . that remained longer. Long enough to hear the trio step closer, looming over me.

"Him?" the Player asked. "He's a petty crook."

"*Lightfinger* class, boss," the orc corrected him.

I felt something grow cold at my side. Cold?

"Innuendo, Lev. It means he's a thief."

A notification popped up in front of me, but there wasn't enough life left within me to read it. I swallowed, in vain hope of understanding it, but found myself choking.

"Where?"

"Inside his coat pocket," the other bodyguard said.

Someone rolled me over, and I felt the cold sensation abruptly end. Instead, the heat returned, growing stronger with every passing moment.

A shout. From the Player. Not one of words, but of frustration.

"What is it, boss?" the orc asked.

"It's . . . *spent*." He spat the last word.

No. That . . . wasn't true. I remembered. One charge left, of seven. That's what it'd said.

"We'll find another."

"There is only one," the Player replied.

"Another way. No artifact. Another way to get what you seek."

With that, three sets of footsteps paced away, fading into the distance, leaving me to die on the tiled floor of the burning manor.

As my life force drained from me, I found one last rush of energy within me, and with it, I brought up the notification that was waiting for me.

HP Depleted
Sisyphus Artifact Activated
Charges Remaining: (0 / 7)
Respawning at Level 0 . . .

CHAPTER TWO

A Life in Ashes

I gasped as the power of the artifact wrenched me back to life, the burning ruins of Plainside flickering in my blurry vision. I was lying just where I'd been before, specks of ash scattered over my body. I was just where . . . just where I'd . . . died?

I found that my memories were hazy. There'd been a dinner party, an attack, I'd . . . Yes, I'd died, hadn't I?

And yet here I was, lying on the dirty ground, surrounded by flames, with a headache bad enough to put any hangover to shame. *Must be Meterday.*

I pressed my hands to the ground beneath me, attempting to push myself upright, but found myself weak. The effort generated a fresh wave of nausea and my vision grew blurrier once more, and before I knew it, my head was hard against the ground. I'd passed out. Again.

Why was this so hard?

I brought up my stamina bar, making sure I wasn't simply completely drained.

Stamina: 10 / 10

Ten out of *what* now? Out of *ten*? That wasn't right. I'd underinvested in Dexterity, sure, but it wasn't like I'd *never* put any points into it. My stamina was in the four hundreds. It was—

And then I remembered the artifact. The one I'd been sent to retrieve. The one that had exhausted its last charge on me, in order to . . .

Respawning at Level 0 . . .

That's what the notification had said. But that couldn't be. Saving someone from death was one thing, but to reset a life's worth of progression? *I must have imagined it*, I thought. I must have been delirious. But if my maximum stamina was only ten now, then . . . I swallowed back the fear, breathed deeply, and brought up my stat screen.

Level 0 Peasant
Race: Human

No! This couldn't be! This—

Power Bars:
Health: 10 / 10
Mana: 10 / 10
Stamina: 10 / 10

Gods damn it! No! Death might have been better than—

Base Stats:
Vitality: 0
Intelligence: 0
Dexterity: 0
Strength: 0
Wisdom: 0
Charisma: 0

Gods, this hurt. Particularly that Charisma reset; I'd prided myself on a high Charisma, had worked hard at it over the years, because it was so important to the abilities relevant to my job. And what would happen now, with it so low? Would my charlatan abilities ever function? Would I be able to tell even the most innocent of lies? Would my skills—

Prostrate on the floor, surrounded by burning buildings, I gasped. My skills— surely not them, too? Surely not all the abilities that I'd unlocked over the years?

I bit my tongue, finding it harder than I ever had before to open my skills menu, and pressed my eyes closed as I found the brief moment of courage required to do so.

Skills Menu:
[None]

If I'd had the energy, I might have cried. Or screamed. Probably I would've screamed, to be honest; that was more my speed. But as it was, with my stats so low, I was . . . weak. Too weak to stand, too weak even to scream.

I passed out once more.

When I next awoke, I was being dragged by the arms by two soldiers in shining heavy armor. I tried to speak, to ask them just what they thought they were doing, but upon opening my mouth, I found myself passing out again.

As I finally came to—with more energy, this time, than before—I found myself in a small, damp, dingy room. The floor was dusty stone, and there was a rickety bed in the corner, and bars across one wall.

No. I wasn't in a room. I was in a *jail.*

I groaned with effort as I swung one leg over the side of the—actually ridiculously uncomfortable—bed, and then the other, before pushing myself upright. I sat still for a moment, willing myself to believe that this was just a bad dream, that this was just some horrific nightmare caused by the strength of that wine I'd crafted.

But the world around me was too real, and the headache somehow realer. And the bed beneath me? Even at my worst, I wouldn't imagine a bed so uncomfortable. Honestly, it was like whoever had made it had gone out of their way to *make* it uncomfortable. But perhaps that was just the reality of jails; I'd spent little time in them.

"Hey!" I tried calling out, but found that the words escaped as little more than a whisper. I coughed, finding my mouth and throat dry, before trying again.

It made little difference.

That being a bust, I tried a different strategy instead, banging on the metal bars with the base of my palm. Again. And again.

"Let me out!" I tried to cry, but again managed only a croak.

Finally, I got a reaction—but not from whoever was in charge of these cells. A woman in a cell opposite rolled out of bed and glared at me with deep brown eyes. "Will you cut that out? Some of us are trying to sleep."

"On these beds?" I croaked back, but my voice was quiet enough that the woman didn't hear.

I sank back into bed, and tried, fruitlessly, to get comfortable.

Soldiers finally arrived a good few hours later, silently pulling me to my feet and dragging me toward the door—much as I remembered being dragged from the ruins of Plainside.

They pulled me up a flight of steps, my legs struggling to keep up, and into a room somehow both darker and dingier than the jail cell. A bright oil lantern hung overhead. The pair of soldiers dumped—or practically *threw*—me into a wooden chair, and then stood over me, arms crossed. On their armor was a familiar badge—the golden sun of the Baron of Umlok.

"Think you got some explaining to do, eh?" one of the soldiers asked. A dwarf, though tall for his kind, and with muscles bulging enough that most taller races would avoid picking a fight with him.

"I . . ." I started.

The other guard, a human woman with a kind smile on her face, crouched down in front of me. "What's your name? Let's start with that."

"Styk."

"Styk? Styk what?" the dwarf asked.

"I just go by Styk." With every word I spoke, my voice returned an ounce more to me.

The dwarf blinked. "Fine."

"Tell us, Styk," the human said. "What happened back in Plainside?"

"It wasn't anything to do with me! I was just . . ." What was I doing there? I searched my spotty memories. "I was just at a dinner party. With the Collector."

At this, the dwarf laughed, and even the kinder soldier had a smirk cross her face. "Yes, mate," the dwarf said, "We didn't think it was *you*."

"Just tell us who it was," the woman said. "*What* it was."

"It was . . . it was . . ." But the words got lost in my throat. They wouldn't believe my answer. If I hadn't seen it for myself, I wouldn't believe it, either. But what other choice did I have than to tell the truth?

"Yes?" the kind woman prompted.

I gulped. "It was a Player."

The male soldier shook his head, rubbing his temple with his hand. "He's an idiot," he muttered, turning away.

The woman licked her lips as she searched for the correct words. "Well, that can't be, can it?"

"Why not?"

"Because a Player would never—"

"Yes," I said. "I know how it sounds. And most Players wouldn't, I know. Most of them are honorable. I'm just saying that *this* Player. This particular one . . . they're a monster."

The kinder soldier looked back at me, her eyes glazing over.

"You don't believe me, do you?" I asked.

"I believe that *you* believe it," came the reply.

The rest of the interrogation went much along these lines, but as time passed, the human soldier revealed her true colors more and more, the kind smile fading from her face and being replaced by an expression of frustration. But I stuck to my story—was it still a "story" when it was the truth?—despite any attempts to lead me to blame something or someone else, and eventually the pair grew tired of me.

They threw me back into my cell, where exhaustion soon overcame me, and I found that the bed wasn't quite so uncomfortable after all.

* * *

I awoke to a wooden bowl being shoved through the gaps in my cell's bars, a bowl that contained a white substance of suspicious texture. Without thinking about my current lack of skills, I tried to engage my *Identification* skill to understand just how much eating this gruel would make me want to throw up. I narrowed my eyes, bringing the strange foodstuff into focus, and realized what it was— offcuts of meat mixed with old oats. Pet food, practically.

Identification unlocked!

This latest notification brought on the despair once more, acting as a reminder that all my skills were gone. Well, all my skills but the most cursory of *Identification*. At level 0—not really a level in its own right—it didn't even come with an ability.

I was about the only person alive who was both level 0 *and* had had their fourth birthday party. No, that wasn't fair—even a four-year-old would have leveled *Identification* up a few times.

If anyone *identified* me, I was screwed. Anyone would be able to see that I was only level 0. That I was easy pickings. While most people out there wouldn't take advantage of this power imbalance, a small handful would. And it wouldn't be too long before I ran into one of them.

If I was ever released from this jail cell, at least.

Why was I even in here? The soldiers had made it perfectly clear that they didn't think I did it. So surely, I was just a witness. A *victim*, even. Surely not someone suitable for a jail cell.

Unless they thought me complicit, somehow.

At that moment, the penny dropped. Of course they didn't think I'd done it—they would have *identified* me the moment they set their eyes on me. And they would've seen just what I had: a Level 0 Peasant.

What a fool I'd looked. No wonder they'd laughed.

I'd had everything taken from me but my life. Escaping death was all well and good—how many had dreamed of such a thing?—but losing twenty-four years of progression was about as good as dying. I was screwed. I was—

At that moment, I noticed I had one more notification still waiting for me, glowing in the corner of my vision. With a frown, I brought it up.

My frown quickly faded.

Active Effect: Legacy of Sisyphus
Days remaining: 999 / 1,000
XP gain increased by +400 percent

"Huh," I said. Maybe I wasn't quite so screwed after all.

CHAPTER THREE

Not Quite so Screwed After All

"You need to let me go," I said to the guard on duty. Unfortunately, it was the burly dwarf soldier at this particular moment—the one who hadn't even *pretended* to give me the benefit of the doubt.

"The baron requests you as a witness," he replied, voice gruff.

"And they usually imprison their witnesses, do they?"

The guard smiled that same mocking smile that I'd seen in the interrogation chamber. "They ain't normally level zero."

"And that makes a difference why?"

"We let you go, there isn't any guarantee you don't get killed by a bandit. Or a stray cow. Or a . . ."

". . . particularly strong gust of wind?" the woman in the cell opposite suggested.

The dwarf pointed his thumb at her, as if to say "yeah, or that."

"I'll be fine!" I protested. "I'll take it slow. I'll go after some starter beasts— I'll go kill some wolves or whatever is in fashion these days. Easy. I'll be fine."

"Even most twelve-year-olds have a couple of levels of combat skills under their belt, though, don't they? Not sure I'd fancy *your* chances against a wolf. Might be some rats in these dungeons, though?"

"Oh good," I mumbled, casting a quick glance at the floor.

The guard turned to leave, opening the door to return to his post outside.

"You have no right to keep me here!"

The dwarf responded only by raising his arms in a shrug, then closed the dungeon's door behind him.

"Very compelling," the woman opposite said.

"Thanks."

The woman's dark brown eyes remained on me.

"Can I help you with something?" I asked.

"How'd you get to this age without leveling up a single skill? You some rich noble or something?"

"I'm . . ." I started, then sighed. "It's a long story."

The woman gestured to the bars of the cell. "I got time."

"Well, I don't."

"No?"

"No. I gotta figure out a way out of here."

The other prisoner smirked—I was getting really sick of these mocking smiles that people couldn't seem to resist. "Mm-hmm? Let me know how that goes, yeah?"

I rolled my eyes and turned away, but couldn't help but feel like the prisoner's own eyes were still upon me. Not that I could blame her; there wasn't much else to look at around here. Certainly nothing prettier.

Right. What could I do?

Without skills, escape was going to be . . . I didn't want to say "impossible," so I went with "very difficult" instead. The only thing I had going for me? Five times experience gain—something that might just afford me an advantage. But I'd have to gain it from within this cell.

Once I got out of here, I figured, it'd be easy. I could level up my skills in no time, and I'd have the tools on hand to do so. And now that I knew the system—or rather, knew what I wanted from it—I'd make better choices. I wouldn't underinvest in Dexterity, for one; that low stamina was always a pain. And when I got the choice of abilities—every time I gain five levels in any skill—I'd be able to make smarter choices. Better ones.

Maybe this was a blessing in disguise.

As long as I could, you know, get out of here.

I looked around. One skill I could level up in any situation was *Identification*—all I needed were people or objects to study. It might not help very much in my escape, but it was a start.

Beginning with the most mundane object I could find, I stared at a stone wedged into the wall beside my bed. I forced myself to activate my *Identification* skill even though I knew exactly what it was—I'd seen a good few of these so-called "stones" in my time on Alterra. It took a moment of concentration before the notification popped up.

Identification: +50XP

The subsequent notification informed me that it was, in fact, a stone. The type of stone, alas, remained a mystery to me at this level. I concentrated on another object—the bed beneath me—and activated the skill in exactly the same way.

> **Identification:** +50XP
> *Identification increased to Level 1!*
> **Base Points Gained:** +1 WIS, +1 INT, +1 Free Point (WIS/INT)
> **Ability Unlocked:** Basic Identification
> **Basic Identification (Identification):** Discover basic attributes for a particular object or person. Ability scales with [WIS] + [INT].

> *Level up!*
> *You increased to Level 1!*

And there we had it! My first level. I was officially comparable to a two-year-old—Dad would be so proud. I felt a rush of exhilaration as these notifications appeared and my levels increased—one that wasn't really comparable to, well, *anything.*

I'd forgotten, over the years, just how easy it was to level up entirely new skills. It took only 100XP for that first level, whereas the incremental XP requirement for each subsequent level increased by another 100XP each time. By the time you got a skill to level 50, you were looking at, oh, 150,000 or so until you got to the next level? Maybe a little less; math was never my strong suit.

And I'd reached the skill requirements for my overall level to increase to level 1; I supposed that was very slightly less embarrassing. Only two more skill increases until I was level 2, as well!

With an increase to my skill, I'd gotten a few base points to invest. Not many, for such a minor skill, but it was something—one added to my Wisdom stat by default, and another to Intelligence. And then, of course, I had one free point to invest into either of them—I selected Wisdom, as the Intelligence-led boon to mana didn't exactly interest me. Not that this was the only reason to invest in this Base stat, of course.

I breathed a sigh of relief; it was small progress, but it was progress nonetheless. If I just kept *identifying* as much around me as I could, I'd be leveling up before I knew it.

When I'd finally exhausted every object in my tiny cell, I had leveled up *Identification* to level 4, put five points into my Intelligence and seven into my Wisdom, and even leveled myself up to level 2.

And I'd done it all under the curious gaze of the prisoner opposite.

"Having fun over there?" she asked.

I ignored her, scouring every corner of my cell for a new object to interrogate. I found nothing.

"Can see you're level two now," the woman said. "You must be very pleased with yourself."

I couldn't resist shooting her a dirty look.

"Could *identify* me, if you like?"

Oops. I'd been spending so much time thinking about the objects inside my cell that I'd forgotten I could identify *people*, too. I turned my attention to the irritating prisoner.

Level 27 ???
Race: ???

Gods damn it. I wasn't high enough a level to *identify* her. Of course I wasn't. Not if she was level 27 and I was still level 2. And the worst part? She would've known that.

A smile stretched across the woman's face. "What did you get? Nothing?"

"Nothing," I grunted.

"Thought not." She stared me down for a few moments longer, then stuck her hand through the bars of her cell. "Name's Val, by the way."

"Wish I could say it was good to meet you, but . . ."

"You could tell me your name, at least."

"Styk," I replied.

The woman looked fit to break into a smile once more. "Funny name."

"Coming from someone named 'Val.'"

At this, the prisoner only shrugged. "You ready to tell me why you're here, yet? Figure it has something to do with that low level of yours."

I sighed, taking a seat on the edge of my bed, still in full view of the woman across the corridor. "Dunno if you'd believe me. Them up there"—I gestured to the ceiling—"sure as hells don't."

"Try me."

I wiped my hands down my face. What was there to lose in telling the truth? Just another person who'd think me crazy, as well as weak. "A Player killed me."

Val sat forward. "Sorry?"

"I know, I know," I said, waving the woman down. "Players don't do that. Players are honorable. Blah blah blah. I know all that. And yet . . . one of them killed me. Burned down a whole town while he was at it, too."

Val studied me with narrowed eyes. "Are you messing with me?"

"It's not much of a joke, is it? Where's the killer punch line?"

The silence that followed was strangely eerie; already I'd established that this 'Val' had trouble keeping her mouth shut, so to see her do so without struggling . . .

"Where?" she asked, and all mirth was gone from her tone.

"Plainside," I replied. "You . . . believe me?"

At this, Val smiled. "Oh yes, I believe you. After what I've seen . . . yes. At least, I believe that a Player is capable of killing—I don't know about the whole 'coming back to life' bit." Val rose, dusting down her slim-fitting light armor, and then shifted over to the bars of her cell, staring through them. "I need you to tell me everything you know about this Player."

"I'd tell you everything I know about *everything* if you could get me out of here . . ."

"Deal," Val said, sticking her hand through the bars once more.

I looked down at the outstretched hand. "You know I can't reach that, right?"

"It's symbolic. Is it a deal or what?"

"Is what a deal?"

Val looked at me like I was stupid. "I get you out of here, and you tell me about this Player."

I scrunched up my face, blinking at this peculiar woman. "If you could break out of here, you'd be gone already."

"Not if I was hiding from someone."

"I . . ." I put my head in my hands for a moment, not believing in this woman for a second. "Fine. Deal."

"Great!" Val said, and twisted her outstretched hand so that the palm was facing upward.

Moments later, the ground started to shake, and the stone around the bars of my cell began to crumble.

CHAPTER FOUR

A Matter of Knife and Death

I stepped back from the shaking iron bars, eyes wide. "What are you *doing*?" I shouted.

Val furrowed her brow. "I thought you wanted to get out of here?"

"I didn't know you meant *now*!"

"What, do you have a spa treatment booked in that I don't know about?"

"I . . . I . . ." My head spun to the door. "What about the guards?"

Val shrugged. "Dunno."

"What do you mean 'dunno'?"

She shrugged again. "Haven't planned that far ahead."

"You haven't . . ." I began to repeat. "That's literally the *next* step!"

As the two sets of iron railings crashed to the ground, the dungeon's heavy wooden door swung open. The dwarven guard stood on the threshold to the room, eyes wide, clutching an axe. "*How?*" he demanded of us. "Those cells are warded against sorcery. How can you . . ." He shook his head, fixed his gaze on Val, and then stepped into the room.

"Right, what's next?" Val asked me.

"What! Why are you asking *me*?"

She shrugged. "Just thought you might want to have some input at some point."

The guard, correctly assessing Val as the biggest threat and not myself, made for her, swinging his axe high.

With another twist of her hand, the room began to shake once more, before the stone walls cracked, giving way to long, winding tendrils. No, not tendrils. Roots.

The plant roots grabbed the dwarf's hands in midswing, bringing the axe to a halt.

"Well?" Val asked, looking at me and nodding to the bound guard.

"Honestly, unless you want me to *identify* him, I got nothing."

"Fair enough," came the response, and Val turned her attention back to the guard, yanking his hand against the tendrils that bound it. Another root split through the wall and looped around the ring of keys on the dwarf's belt. "I got more where that came from. Enough to tie you up from now till the end of days. So, the way I see it, you got two options: get in this idiot's cell, let us lock you in, and remain quiet, or . . ." Val looked to me.

"Or we kill you," I said.

Val furrowed her brow for a moment, then shrugged. "I was looking for a little more artistry of imagination, but, sure, that."

The guard looked from Val, to me, and back to Val again. "I'll get in the cell," he mumbled.

"An excellent choice." Without giving the dwarf any option, Val's roots lifted him off the ground and placed him in my old cell. One of the tendrils threw the ring of keys to me, which I managed to catch after only a few seconds of frantic fumbling. Val raised an eyebrow at the sight, but gracefully did not verbally comment on it.

"Alright," I said, finally finding the correct key for this cell and locking the door. "That's one guard. What's next?"

"What's next is I get my stuff."

Val led us out of the dungeons and into a long stone corridor, which was, thankfully, devoid of any further guards. We kept low, crouching, as we gently made our way down this room, making sure not to make a sound with each step of our—

I tripped, tumbling into Val's back, and she blinked at me as I used her shoulders to recover. "What was that?" she whispered. "Are you literally a child?"

"I'm level two right now; you're going to need to cut me some slack," I whispered back.

"Oh, and next week you'll be, what? Level fifty?"

"If everything goes according to plan, I won't be far off it." That was a ridiculous act of hyperbole, of course; even with the Legacy of Sisyphus status effect, I wouldn't be growing anywhere near that quickly. But in a few months? Maybe my level wouldn't be quite so embarrassing.

We reached the end of the corridor with no further issues, and I hung back while Val poked her eyes around it.

Stealth: +40XP

"Ooh, nice," I mumbled, receiving an irritated glance from Val as a result.

We waited for a few moments longer, and finally my new acquaintance turned to me. "Alright. I think we're clear." She led us down the winding, turning corridors of the castle like she either had a skill assisting her, or like she knew this building already—I couldn't tell which—and finally brought us to a storage room.

Val's eyes lit up as they landed upon a silver necklace inlaid with a gemstone as black as night—one that glowed with a gentle green aura.

"Is that—" I started, but then I was distracted by a sight of my own. "My stuff!" I hurried for the pile on a rickety wooden shelf, one that held my trusty ornate dagger, my remaining throwing knives, and a small glass vial which may or may not have contained poison.

"Good," the supposed sorcerer said. "I suppose you're gonna be a tad more useful now?"

I ignored the jab and strode across the room for my dagger, picking it up with one hand.

Item Equipped: Blade of Samal

Blade of Samal: +70 percent to damage when unnoticed by an enemy. Suitable for poison coating.

Warning: you do not meet level requirements to wield this item effectively! Requirement: Knifework—Level 22

"Gods," I spat.

"What now, peasant boy?" Val asked. "Someone scratch your fancy blade?"

". . . I can't wield it," I eventually said, relenting and embracing the wave of mockery that was sure to follow.

"You can't . . ." Val started, then her eyes widened with mirth. "You can't wield it!" She laughed, stopped, and then laughed again, this time with tears leaking from the corners of her eyes. "What did they *do* to you?"

I pressed my lips together. Hard. "I said I'd tell you when we got out."

Val held up her palms in surrender, and didn't press the matter further—but this didn't stop her from getting a little more of a chuckle out of it.

I wedged the blade back into its sheath and wrapped the belt around me; even if I couldn't use it right now, I would be able to soon, with any luck. And few blades had served me as well as this one.

At least I'd been wearing party clothes, I supposed. If I'd been wearing my light armor, I would barely have been able to move, being that I wouldn't have the level requirements for it. I'd be walking around naked in this moment, and I suspected that would've tipped Val from pitiful aid to absolute despair at my existence. Not that the light armor had found a better fate, being that I'd left it at an inn in Plainside—one that had almost certainly been burned to the ground.

"You good?" Val asked, adding the last of her possessions to her person.

I shrugged. "Good as I'm gonna get. Would've liked a weapon, though, if we're breaking out of here."

The sorcerer nodded to the door. "There's a kitchen across the corridor. You know, if knives are your thing."

I stuck my head back out into the hallway, and—content that there was nobody around to spot me—dashed across into the kitchen. It was a small room, clearly meant for preparing servants' meals rather than those for the baron himself, and as such was kept in—I imagined—a condition much less fussed over. Pots and pans were drying on the counter, alongside, helpfully, a wide selection of cutlery.

I picked up the largest knife—one with a long, deep blade.

Item Equipped: Basic Cooking Knife
Basic Cooking Knife (Blunt): +2 percent to quality of prepared food.
Warning: you do not meet level requirements to wield this item effectively!
Requirement: Knifework—Level 3 or Cooking—Level 3

"Gods *damn* it," I hissed again, and thanked my lucky stars that Val wasn't in the room to witness this. I was level 36! 36! I . . . But there was no use despairing; what was done was done, and I couldn't change a moment of it.

Maybe not wielding an item effectively wasn't the end of the world, I figured, and tried waving the cooking knife around. The *basic* cooking knife. It was surprisingly end-heavy to my touch, and waving it around—

I dropped the knife.

It fell quicker than I was able to react to, and it shot toward my shoes. I braced for pain as the knife pierced them, then released a sigh of relief as the blade happened to slide between my first and second toes.

Well, that was that question answered, at least. Best find another weapon for now. I searched the rest of the cutlery on offer for another knife. For something that I might be able to wield. For something—

And then I saw it: a humiliation to end all humiliations. A butter knife.

I picked it up.

Item Equipped: Basic Butter Knife
Basic Butter Knife: +2 to quality of prepared food. -85 percent damage when used as a weapon.

My heart sank. Was this what I'd been reduced to? Wielding a butter knife? Hardly something that was going to stop another guard, once we ran into one. Maybe I could play it off, I figured—make them believe I was so effective with a knife that all I needed to wield was a butter knife. "You couldn't *dream* of what I can do with one of these," I tried aloud, and then was mortified to find that Val was standing at the door.

She looked from me, to the butter knife, and back to me again, then opened her mouth as if to say something. But no words came out; apparently the sight before her was too ridiculous for even *her* to comment on. And then, just as I thought that Val maybe *wasn't* the kind of person who would kick a man when he was down, she burst into laughter.

"Don't," I said.

This only seemed to make her laugh harder.

"*Don't.* I went through a very traumatic—"

This seemed to be doing no good.

"Stop laughing!"

But all I could do was wait for her to tire herself out—which, as it happened, took a great deal longer than I expected.

"Time we got going?" the sorcerer finally asked, wiping tears from her eyes, and then muttering something about butter knives under her breath.

Keen to move on from this horrifically embarrassing incident, I nodded. Maybe I could find a way to level up my *Knifework* in all this.

Butter knife firmly in grasp, I followed Val out into the corridor. Hooray.

CHAPTER FIVE

The OK-ish Escape

The hallways of the Baron of Umlok's main fort were surprisingly empty, considering they were owned by, you know, a *baron*. You'd think they'd splash out for some personnel to roam such a grand estate. It was only good news for us, though, as we made it up out of the dungeons and servants' quarters without so much as seeing another soul.

That all changed, however, when we found our way out. We got overconfident, I'd say, but that was as much Val's fault as my own. We hurried up the stairs to the ground level, rushing around a corner toward what I noted as natural light, and Val came to a sudden halt in front of me.

Not quite as athletic as I was a few days ago, I wasn't able to stop in time, and I crashed into the sorcerer's rear, eliciting an unintentional *oomph* from each of us. In front of us, a hulking woman in light armor stood from a chair and table, and put her hand on her sword.

As if that wasn't problem enough, the guard stood between us and our exit—the door to the castle yards at the far corner of the room, next to a thick stone wall lined with ornate tapestries.

"Err . . ." I started, staring at the woman.

As if completely lacking in awareness of my hesitation, Val shoved me forward. "Your turn!"

Brow furrowed, I turned back to her and mouthed, *"Mine?"*

When I turned back, the guard was upon me, but with her sword still sheathed. She looked like she was in no rush to attack, so I could only assume that she'd done a quick *identification* of me and deemed me no threat.

Well, I decided, it was time to show her what I could do with a knife. Even if it was a butter knife.

I raised the blunt blade, causing the guard to raise an eyebrow, and then I struck blindly forward. I remembered, in that moment, a time when my knife strikes were highly targeted and highly specific, where I could both aim at and hit a quarter-inch segment without much trouble. Without all my *Knifework* skill possession, though, I felt clumsy—and the slice reflected that.

The guard didn't react as the butter knife struck her chest armor, though her eyebrow remained raised. It was almost like I hadn't attacked her at all.

"You know you just did . . . one . . . point of damage, right?" Val asked.

I looked at her, then back at the woman in front of me. All I could do was force an apologetic smile to my face, then shrug.

The guard . . . did not look impressed.

I gripped the butter knife tighter, and slashed again, once more barely leaving a scratch in the woman's armor.

"Did you just try . . ." Val started.

I flung my hands into the air. "I don't know!"

The guard with the slightly indented leather chest armor glared at me, and one hand began to draw a long, shining sword from the sheath at her hips.

"Err . . . Styk?"

"Yes?"

"Duck."

Maybe combat wasn't my thing right at this minute, but falling? Yes, I could do that. My chest hit the floor before I'd really had a chance to register what I was doing, and I felt a great wind pass over me.

Glancing upward, I saw a cloud of dust—punctuated by the odd small stone—pummeling into the guard. She staggered backward with every hit of rock, and she held her hands over her eyes to keep them unharmed.

Feeling uncomfortably close to this magick cloud, I hugged the floor tighter, allowing myself just enough room to keep an eye on the woman who'd accosted us.

She grunted as her back hit the far stone wall, allowing her to retreat no further. I waited for Val to up the attack, to press the guard while she was routed, but instead the gust faded away.

The guard growled. "Now you're—"

Another magically created gust of wind sprang to life, flinging the door open and smashing the guard in the face. She had just enough time to mumble something that began with "What . . ." before tumbling, unconscious, to the ground.

Level 17 Guard defeated!

Knifework unlocked!

> **Knifework:** +100XP
> *Knifework increased to Level 1!*
> **Base Points Gained:** +1 DEX, +1 STR, +2 Free Points (VIT/DEX/STR)
> **Ability Unlocked:** Slice
> **Slice (Knifework):** Slice the enemy for physical damage worth weapon's base damage and additional damage scaling on [STR].

I pulled myself back to my feet, staggered across the room, and looked down at the unconscious body of the guard. There must have been a smug smile on my face, because Val was soon to call me out on it.

"What's got you looking so happy all of a sudden?"

I held up the butter knife. "Gonna be rid of this before I know it."

"You . . . you got XP? For that? The system recognized *that* as contributing to the fight?"

"You said it yourself: I did one point of damage."

"Two, actually."

"*Two* points of damage!" I supported this point with two raised fingers, just in case Val had forgotten how to count in the past few seconds.

Val shook her head in wide-eyed exasperation. "Maybe you'll be able to wield a soup spoon next." With that, she pressed through the door and out into the castle yard.

I followed, keeping—as she had—to the shadows at the perimeter of the yard, this particular area apparently used as a stable. We paused at the castle's exterior wall, and as there was no obvious way to climb it, we instead looked for a ground-level exit.

Across the yard, inconveniently located at the very far side, was the gate. But between us and it? A good half dozen guards, standing—admittedly rather disinterestedly—at their posts.

"Got any bright ideas?" Val asked.

I looked at our surroundings—at the three guards who would easily spot us if we continued on our path around the perimeter, at the bows hanging on two of the further guards, and at the handful of horses watching us while lazily chewing on dirty hay. I might have lost my skills, but that didn't mean I'd lost my brains—and I had a good head for strategy.

"You know?" I replied. "I think I just might."

Before Val could respond, I picked up the last few strands of hay, and the three nearest horses immediately stopped chewing. Midmouthful. They got as worried as I did when someone got between them and their food, then.

"Shh," I said to the nearest one, brushing its face gently. "Here you go." I dropped some of the hay in front of it, leading it ever so slightly away from the wall—and closer to the gate.

Val remained crouched in the shadows, her eyes narrowed.

"Well?" I asked. "You coming?"

She sighed. "Suppose I am."

We kept well hidden behind the massive beasts as I led them forward, dropping small bunches of hay every few paces. I directed them ever so slowly across the stable yard, keeping my breath shallow, willing that none of the guards spotted us.

Two prisoners and three horses reached the far side of the horses' yard just as I ran out of hay, and—after a quick scan over the horses' back from Val—we dived over the fence for the cover of a low wall. From here, it was easy; we'd made it through the eyelines of the guards on the ground floor, so from here we scuttled for the gate, slipping through it.

As we reached a hay bale in the surrounding farmlands, I felt a notification or two pop up.

Stealth: +80XP

Stealth increased to Level 1!

Base Points Gained: +1 DEX, +1 WIS, +2 Free Points (DEX/WIS)

Ability Unlocked: Basic Stealth Attack

Basic Stealth Attack (Stealth): *Passive.* 10 percent boost to damage when unnoticed by an enemy.

Level up!

You increased to Level 3!

Level 3 already—and I wasn't even out of here. Suddenly I was feeling a little more optimistic about my chances of surviving in the outside world long enough to return to a respectable level. And that was quite the number of base points I was building up, too.

I looked to Val, who was waiting with hands raised, a look on her face that said something like "what the hells are you waiting for?"

"What the hells are you waiting for?" she asked.

"Sorry," I mumbled, hurrying after her—but not before putting two of my four free points into Vitality and the other two into Dexterity. At this point, both those stats were safe bets, as they'd boost my health and my stamina, respectively—both of which I needed . . . desperately.

We ran for the safety of the woods, not looking back until the castle of the Baron of Umlok was long behind us. Finally we came to a rest, out of breath, though Val looking in a much better state than low-stamina me. We took a moment in silence, catching our breaths, and it was the sorcerer who finally spoke.

"Well, that was fun, huh?" she said.

CHAPTER SIX

The Hound & Hound

I'd insisted on getting well clear of the barony before even beginning to think about fulfilling my end of the bargain. I'd tell Val what I knew about the Player only once I was sure she wasn't about to abandon me to be recaptured—the gods knew I needed all the help I could get.

Val had thought about this for only a moment before she'd announced that she knew "just the place"—a place which, as it turned out, was an inn with "really bloody good beer." It had taken me some time to get even this tidbit of information out of her, and I couldn't help but think this was some form of revenge for me holding back information of my own.

When we'd finally reached the inn—a quaint, freshly painted building which seemed to appear from between the trees in little more than a blink of an eye— Val had hurried us inside, under a creaking, swinging sign that announced the establishment as The Hound & Hound. She swiftly traversed over the typical inn ground floor to the bar, ordering two ales from the barkeep.

"I don't have any money, Val," I said.

"Oh, did you want one?" came the response.

I, of course, wanted one, but I wasn't about to indebt myself to this strange woman any more than I had to.

"I'm gonna hit the big girls' room," Val announced for all the—admittedly sparsely populated—inn to hear, slamming her coppers down atop the bar. "You'll grab us a table, yeah?"

I pressed my lips into a polite smile and nodded, returning my attention to the barkeep as she poured the second of the dark, murky ales. "So why *The Hound and Hound?*" I ventured. "Why not *The Two Hounds?*"

The woman looked at me as though I was lacking in the brains department—though my low level might have gone some way toward implying such. "Because there's one hound, right?"

"Yes, I'm with you so far."

"And then, right, there's another one." She plonked the second pint glass down on the counter to punctuate this point.

I thought about arguing, but quickly caught myself; this conversation, I reckoned, was going nowhere. Flashing another polite smile, this time to the woman who thought me dim, I collected the two ales and placed them on a table in the corner—away from prying eyes and open ears.

Val soon returned from her trip to the toilet, and she flicked wet hands over me as she took her seat at the table.

"Thanks for that," I said, but the woman ignored it.

"So," Val said. "About time you held up your end of the bargain, isn't it?"

I glanced around at the inn's other patrons. The small groups all seemed to be deep in conversations of their own; that they might eavesdrop on ours was unlikely, but not impossible.

"Oh," Val said, waving a hand dismissively, "they ain't listening. Why d'you think I brought you here?"

"I thought it was for the beer."

"That too." Val stared at me while she gulped down a good quarter of the first pint. "Well? Go on. What happened?"

I sighed; this was it, then. Time to tell the truth. What was the worst that could happen? That this woman would laugh at me? That she would think I was lying. No, I realized—the worst that could happen was that she'd pity me. "I was in Plainside. On a . . . work assignment."

"Oh? What sort of work?"

"It's not relevant to the story."

"Something illegal, sure, got it." She took another swig of beer, which I found myself eyeing jealously.

She sighed an exasperated, exaggerated sigh, then pushed the other pint toward me.

"I can't—" I started.

"It's on me."

I raised it in toast—one that was returned impatiently.

"Plainside?" Val prompted.

"Yes. I was at a dinner party. With the Collector, if you've heard of her?" The sorcerer nodded.

"And I went downstairs to see her collection."

"For a . . . *private viewing*, I imagine?" Val didn't seem able to suppress a smile.

"Something like that. I picked up one of the Collector's items—an eight-sided shape. Formed of silver. Had a—"

Val leaned forward, across the table. "How'd you get past her traps?"

"I—the traps? That's what you're interested in?"

"At this point, yes."

I furrowed my brow. "Well, I'd had a word with the man who'd created them."

"Small man? Speckly skin? Wears a stupid hat?"

"I . . . yes. How can you know that?"

Val pressed her lips together. Hard. "Steve . . ." she grumbled.

I shook my head, *very* happy to be in ignorance about all that, and continued the story. "So I had it in my pocket, this device. For . . . safekeeping. And then, up above, I heard a rumbling. An almighty rumbling. Like the world was ending, you know? So I rushed upstairs, and I found myself . . . outside. But the entrance to the basement hadn't been outside a moment earlier—it was more that half the Collector's manor had been incinerated. And I saw them, then—"

"*Them?*" Val asked. "You didn't tell me they were working together. You said *Player*. One of them."

I begged for her patience by raising my hands with downward-facing palms. "Only one of them was a Player. The second was an orc, and the third . . . a tiefling? I think? And it turned out they were after the same thing I'd been employed to . . . *rehome*. But I couldn't have that—a Styk guarantee is a good guarantee—so I faced them down, using all the combat skills I had before that I no longer possess, and I very nearly had them"—One look at Val's face told me she wasn't convinced by this lie, but she let it pass—"but, ultimately, they won. And the Player? He killed me."

The pair of us took a large sip of beer each. It *was* good beer; Val hadn't been lying about that.

"Yet here you stand."

"I do."

"Wanna explain how?" Val asked.

I pulled the exhausted artifact from my pocket, having collected my coat from the storage room in the baron's dungeons, and I passed it to Val. "Ever seen anything like it?"

"A . . . *Sisyphus Artifact?* Can't say that I have." Val threw the device back to me haphazardly, with no thoughts for what it might be worth to the right customer.

"Well, it saved me. Brought me back to life."

"But there was a catch," Val continued, filling in the rest. "Back to level zero?"

"Exactly. Except . . . I got a status condition from it. The Legacy of Sisyphus, it's called."

"And?" Val prompted me. "What's it do?"

"+400 percent XP gain for the next . . . 998 and a bit days."

Val raised her eyebrows. "Not bad."

"Well, I still lost my life's work."

"Sure, but that's a pretty decent way to get it back, isn't it? And, you know, you're *alive*, aren't you?"

Val was gracious enough to buy me a room at the Hound for the night, though I couldn't help but think maybe she'd bought me the cheapest room, considering that the heavy rain was dripping on me through the ceiling. I couldn't imagine she would be suffering such an unpleasantry.

But it wasn't just for this reason that I spent hours staring at the roof, unable to speak. Val wasn't wrong; if you had to start over, a boon to experience gain was a good way to go about it. And I still had my old client list. I could still work, but I'd need to do so remotely for the time being, so that they couldn't *identify* me. I could start with a small job, get the basic *Stealth* skill leveled up again, and I could grow. It wouldn't be so bad; I knew what I was doing now—with age came wisdom, and all that—and I could make better ability choices this time around, once I started getting them at level 5 for each skill.

With that reassuring thought, I finally drifted off to sleep.

. . . And then was awoken moments later by an intensely cool bucket of water being tossed over my head. "Wake up, sleepyhead!"

I gasped as I sat bolt upright, finding Val standing over me in front of the small window, through which the warm light of the morning sun was pouring. Not moments later, then, but hours.

"And what in the *hells* was that?"

"A cooling spell," Val answered. "Cool, right? If you'll forgive the pun."

"No, not what was *that*. What was that *for*?" I demanded.

Val shrugged. "Well, we've got work to do, haven't we?"

"*I* have work to do, sure. I don't know what it has to do with *you*, though."

"I figured we'd be traveling together."

"Traveling—"

"To Plainside," Val finished.

If the bucket of magically cooled water wasn't enough to wake me up, *that* certainly was. "To *Plainside*? What? I don't want to go back there. Why would we want to go back there!" I couldn't help but notice that my voice had become rather squeaky.

"The way I see it," Val said, "our first step is to find out why the Player wanted that artifact."

"I don't care why he wanted it!"

"What, you're not the least bit curious?"

I blinked. "No! All I want is to get back to my life, start building up skills again, and—"

"Well, I care," Val said, crossing her arms with irritation.

"Why! Why on the gods' green lands could you possibly care?"

For the second time in a handful of hours, a woman looked at me like I was stupid. "Because we're gonna kill him," she said.

CHAPTER SEVEN

Killing a God with a Butter Knife

"Kill him?" I repeated. "You want to *kill him*? You can't kill a Player, they're basically gods! Even back when I had all my skills, I wouldn't've stood a chance. And now? Armed with a gods-forsaken *butter knife*? Just how am I gonna do something like that?"

Val stood with an artificially patient expression as I spoke. "Are you quite done?"

"That wasn't a rant, that was a perfectly reasonable summary of the situation. So don't look at me like that."

The sorcerer continued to look at me like that. "Well, you're not going to be using a butter knife, are you? Or did you think we weren't gonna train you up before we go do some a-Player-slaying?"

"Oh good. So I'll be using, what, a chef's knife? Maybe even a short sword?"

"I was thinking a greatsword, but . . . sure, whatever floats your boat."

I raised my hands in the air in mock defeat. "Ah! A greatsword. A greatsword versus a spawn of the Architects. That'll do it!"

"I mean, I can teach you some spellwork if that's more your—"

"I think you're fixating on the wrong thing!" I said. "It's the lack of experience that's the issue here. Even with this buff I got going on, I don't think that's gonna be changing any time soon—not enough to kill a Player!"

Val's artificially patient expression began to wane. "Yes, you said that."

"I've got no skin in this fight! I don't want—"

"Woah," Val said, begging for me to stop with raised palms. "Woah, woah, woah. Did he not try to kill you?"

"Yes, but—"

"Do you not want revenge?"

"Revenge?" I repeated.

"Yeah, revenge. Vengeance. Justice. Whatever you wanna call it."

"Sure, I want justice. But I'm not suicidal! I know what happens if we go down this path. We—"

"OK," Val cut in. "Here's the deal. You're gonna come with me, back to Plainside. On the way, we'll fight some monsters. Together. We'll get you sorted with some basic skills. And I reckon that by the time we get there, I'll be able to convince you."

"And when you don't?"

"Then you're free to go. What, you think I was gonna hold you prisoner?"

I hesitated. There wasn't a chance in any of the many hells that she was going to convince me, but I didn't mind the idea of getting some help while I got my first few skills leveled up; that'd come in handy.

"What's there to lose?" Val prompted me. "You're gonna need someone to hunt with if you're gonna get those combat skills back up. Tell me, what did you use? You strike me as an archery sorta guy. Or *One-Handed.*" She paused. "*Two-Handed?*"

"*Knifework,*" I replied.

Val raised her eyebrows. "*Knifework.*"

"Something wrong with that?"

"No, it's just—"

"I was in a very specific line of business."

"You were . . ." Val started, ". . . a hitman?" Something changed behind her eyes; whereas before there'd always been this joy in them, there was now something else. Not fear, not quite, but . . .

"What?" I replied. "Gods, no. I was a thief. And a pretty good one, at that."

"So you didn't kill people?"

"Nobody that didn't deserve it."

"And how many *did* deserve it?" Val asked.

"At last count? Twenty-two."

We departed The Hound & Hound later in the morning, after a hearty breakfast—paid for by Val—over which she spoke enthusiastically about how she was going to have my mind changed by lunchtime. I'd nodded along, not really listening, instead thinking about my path to regrowth. There were so many abilities I'd not chosen over the years, only to never get another chance to unlock them whenever I reached another 5-level increment in the associated skill. Now, I had a do-over—I could make the right choices.

Our stomachs full of oily, fried goodness, we set out southeast, toward

Plainside and the just-about-still-rising sun. There was no danger of traveling in silence, not with Val's perpetually open mouth, and I zoned out while she spoke about a bear she'd once known or something along those lines—the details escaped me.

There was something different about the air on this morning. It was almost supernaturally crisp, it seemed, the low autumn sun having boiled off the last of the most recent rains. The—

"Are you listening?" Val asked.

"Yes."

"What was I talking about?"

I hesitated for a moment. "A bear?"

Val's eyes grew wide. "That was almost an hour ago! Is this what traveling with you is going to be like? Trying to draw blood from a golem?"

"I've got a lot on my mind!"

"Yeah, or too small a mind, I think," came the snappy response. "Not enough capacity."

I remained silent; I was beginning to realize it was simpler this way, as it didn't give her anything to retort to.

"What you thinking about, then?" she asked. "Tell us."

"The weather," I started, and then—realizing this was only going to lead Val to believe I *did* have a tiny mind—added, "and my progression choices."

"Oh yeah? You decided on a combat skill yet?"

"Is that all you care about? Combat?"

Val made a noise as if she was offended, placing a hand to her chest. "Of course not! But it's what's gonna keep you, you know, *alive*, isn't it? We can work on your *Needlework* and *Baking* skills later, yeah?"

"I didn't ever mention either of those," I replied. "Or did you think I was the sort to settle down in a quiet village, begin a slow-burn romance, and maybe open a . . . a . . ."

"A cafe?"

"Sure," I said, flinging my hands up with exasperation. "No, I'm a thief by trade and that's always gonna be the case."

Val smiled. "You know, when some people go through traumatic events, they rethink their life choices."

"Oh, I've rethought them, alright. I'm gonna make some real big changes, and be a far better thief than I *ever* was before. I'll work hard, I'll pick better abilities, I'll level up *multiple* combat skills—not just one. You know how many times I got in situations where there were no daggers handy? Plenty of swords, bows, and what-have-you, though. But I hadn't leveled any of those up, had I, so I was useless."

Val held a knowing smile on her face.

"No, I'm gonna have a broader skill set this time around. Maybe pick up a bow, or figure out some *Bareknuckle* abilities. I don't know yet."

"Not *too* broad, though, eh?" Val said. "Don't want you spreading yourself too thin, get yourself to level fifty and be barely able to handle a level twenty enemy."

"Sure. Two of them. Maybe three. That's what I was thinking about, while you were talking about your bear pals."

"I didn't say they were my pals. Or that there was more than one of them. You really weren't listening at all, were you?"

I waved a hand at the sorcerer dismissively. "Whatever, then. The point is, I got a lot to work out, so . . . sorry if I wasn't paying enough attention."

Val paused midopening her mouth, as though the apology had completely derailed whatever retort was coming. Instead, she only mumbled, "It's OK."

The pair of us continued in silence for a minute or two—only a minute or two—before Val spoke once more, and I was beginning to think that was the closest I'd get to peace with her around.

"So you decided on any of those combat skills yet?"

"Yes," I replied, hand touching the dagger at my belt, "*Knifework.*"

"Hardly pushing the boat out, is it?"

I shrugged. "It's what I know. I don't wanna change too much; the way I see it, being able to make better ability selections is a gift—if I level up different skills, then I'm just going in blind again."

"I keenly await your next, more interesting, decision."

". . . Thank you?" This wasn't the first backhanded compliment I'd received from Val, but still I didn't yet quite know how to respond to them.

"No problem."

Again, silence fell, and more comfortable this time, too. I was beginning to think my earlier assessment was incorrect, that I would get more peace traveling with Val than I'd thought.

"So . . ." Val finally said, shattering any illusions I had about this period of peace and quiet lasting. "When do you think you wanna get training?"

I gestured an upturned palm to the quiet woodlands around us. "Do you see anything I could fight?"

"Well, no, but I'm sure we could—"

"Exactly. Soon as we find something—something I'm *able* to fight—I'll get right on that."

"Styk . . ."

"And no, I won't get ahead of myself. Like I said back in the dungeons, I'm gonna take it slow."

"*Styk* . . ." Val tried again.

"I'm thinking really slow; even the weakest enemy should give me plenty of experience points what with this *Sisyphus*—"

"Styk!" the sorcerer cried out.

"What!"

In the rare silence that followed, my ears pricked up. Coming from behind me—*close* behind me—was a growl.

CHAPTER EIGHT

The Traditional Wolf Fight

I turned slowly, painfully slowly, so as not to scare the growling creature into pouncing. It was one thing knowing that I was weak, but a whole other thing entirely now that I was faced with actual danger. This beast, whatever it was, could potentially rip me limb from limb in my current state. I gripped my knife—yes, my butter knife—firmly as I turned to face down the . . .

Wolf.

Of course it was. A small, scrawny, wide-yellow-eyed wolf. The classic start to learning a combat skill; it was almost like the Architects themselves were watching out for me. And a weaker one, at that. As it bared its teeth and continued to growl, I risked a cheeky *identification* on the creature.

> **Level 2 Wolf**
> *Variant: Basic*
> **Identification:** +100XP

A Level 2 Wolf with no power variants? The Architects really *were* smiling down on me—maybe there was a side effect of this *Legacy of Sisyphus* that I wasn't yet aware of, because I really couldn't have done any better with my first opponent. Particularly that it was a basic variant. Not that you'd expect much variance on a creature like a wolf, but if it was, say, one of the elemental variants or—my least favorite—armored, I might have had a little more difficulty.

But a basic? Honestly, even a butter knife might have been overkill. Suddenly I felt a whole lot more confident about this whole thing.

I held a hand out behind me, toward Val. "Stand back," I said. "I got this one."

"Are you sure, Mr. Butter Knife?" she replied. "There's no shame in asking for help; that's the agreement, after all—you come with me, I help."

"I got it," I repeated, stressing the words maybe an ounce more than was polite, creeping into "stroppy" territory. I didn't think myself a stroppy man.

"What you gonna do, *slice* 'em to death? With *that?*"

It was too late to relent now. I whipped my head to face Val, and said, again, "I got it!"

Unfortunately, this was the moment the wolf pounced.

A blow to my back knocked me to the floor at Val's feet, and though I was fortunate that the wolf was low enough a level that its claws struggled to break even *my* skin, I was unfortunate in that I got to see my new sorcerer acquaintance smirking down at me.

"Got it, huh?" she asked.

I had no choice but to focus on, you know, the rabid beast on top of me, and so I could not continue verbally sparring. Engaging my stamina bar, I pulled my knife from its sheath and *sliced* down the length of the wolf's body—but, just as the wolf's claws failed to break my skin, the knife failed to break the beast's. I brought my knee up into its rib cage instead, and the wolf staggered off me.

"Alright," I said, pumping my shoulders. "New strategy."

"Good idea."

I held my blade high as the wolf and I began to circle one another. This blade wasn't gonna cut it—pun not intended—in its current state. I was going to need to either put a hell of a lot of weight behind it, or . . .

"Come on, then," I called to the beast, hoping that the tone of voice would be enough to communicate it as a taunt.

"I don't think it speaks the Common . . ."

The wolf pounced again, but this time I was ready for it. I raised the knife the moment it moved, engaging my stamina once again and waiting to *slice*. This time, though, I positioned the blade high, aiming it toward the wolf's snapping jaw.

I thrust the blade forward as the beast was in midair, and instead of *slicing* at its thick hide, I struck at the inside of its mouth. Even with the damage reduction accompanying my equipped butter knife, a blade to the skull . . . had to hurt.

The wolf cried out in pain, landing heavily on the ground before staggering back to its feet, my knife still buried deep in the roof of its mouth.

"So now you've let yourself be disarmed," Val said. "Nice—"

The beast fell to the ground, lifeless.

"You were saying?" I asked.

Level 2 Wolf defeated!

> **Knifework:** +500XP
> *Knifework increased to Level 2!*
> *Knifework increased to Level 3!*
> **Base Points Gained:** +2 DEX, +2 STR, +4 Free Points (VIT/DEX/STR)

I sighed, breathless, placing my hands atop my knees and taking a moment to recover. "Whew," I said, wiping my brow. "Don't remember it ever being this hard."

"You're like an old man. Or a newborn baby."

"Thanks."

"How many XP?" Val asked.

"Five hundred."

The sorcerer shrugged. "Not bad, for what it was. Guess that's your status effect you got going on. So you still need, what, a thousand more, before you get to level five?"

"Before I get my first ability selection, yeah. A thousand."

"So two more wolves, then?" Val asked.

"Yeah, but one was enough for—"

And just like that, I heard growling behind me. Louder, this time.

As I turned to face the source of the noise, I realized I was mistaken—it wasn't just louder. It was . . . two of them. ". . . Huh."

"A lovely coincidence," Val said, echoing my own thoughts—though mine had been followed up by "but I wish they hadn't both come along at once."

I jumped to the body of the first wolf, wrenching the blade from its mouth just in time to turn and use it to protect myself against the next to pounce. The force of the leaping beast was enough that my instinctual *slice* did cut into its hide some, but not enough to do any reasonable damage.

"Alright," I muttered, "two on one. I can do this."

"You can always ask for help if you need it!" Val called out, musically, from her position sitting on a nearby fallen tree.

"I got it!" I said once more, and leaped toward the closer wolf. If one of them leaping at me was enough to give my knife a reasonable chance of *slicing* flesh, then me leaping at *them*, hopefully, would do much the same.

Swinging the blade down, I jammed it into the first wolf's head, and though it cut the thinner flesh on its scalp, I failed—obviously—to pierce the skull. The beast was enraged, but still alive.

I yanked my arm back as the growling beast snapped at it, almost pulling my flesh entirely clear.

Almost.

Fangs clipped at my skin, ripping a pair of thin slices in my forearm and spraying a gentle coating of red over the wolf's gray fur.

I wasted no time in *slicing* once more, aiming the butter knife again for the beast's gums—as nowhere else could I do the damage required to fell it—and draining my stamina bar a not-insignificant amount in the process. But lightning didn't strike twice, as they say, and my attempt to jam the knife between the snapping jaw only ended up with me catching the wolf's fang and my weapon being knocked from my hand.

I staggered backward, putting some quick space between me and my two opponents, for what little good it'd do me. At this moment, I considered calling for Val's help—what chance did I have, *Bareknuckle* style, against these creatures. What I really needed was a—

"You leveled up, right?" Val said. "Cos you dropped something back in Umlok—thought it might come in handy." I glimpsed her raise a deep, shining knife in the air, then toss it toward me.

I made no attempt to catch the knife in midair—I'd learnt by now just what I was and wasn't capable of—and instead let it fall to the ground. Only once it had clattered to a stop on the dirt did I leap for it.

Item Equipped: Basic Cooking Knife
Basic Cooking Knife (Blunt): +2 percent to quality of prepared food.

I flashed the sorcerer a smile. "Thanks."

New blade in hand—and one that didn't suffer an 85 percent damage reduction; such a novelty!—it was time to deal some *real* damage.

I spun on the spot, flailing my knife toward the nearest of the wolves, slicing at whatever part of its body was closest to me. This, as it turned out, was its snapping maw, and the blade slashed at the edges of its lips. The beast recoiled, squealing, and I pressed the advantage before the other could swoop in. I charged forward, *slicing* again, and watched as my stamina bar dipped below the halfway point—another few *slices* and I'd be drained.

Fortunately, this swing of the blade caught the wolf by the throat, spilling more blood than it could afford to lose. As this beast fought its rapidly incoming fate, I turned my attention to the other. I eyed my stamina bar. By the speed at which it was draining, I only had another three or four good *slices* before it was finished. Once my stamina was drained completely, I'd need Val to swoop in to save me. And I didn't exactly like the idea of it coming to that.

I stared down the other wolf, flexing my fingers around the handle of the cooking knife, and then we both moved at once. I *sliced* forward with my blade while this wolf lashed out with its claws.

Neither of us hit our target, and instead we collided with one another, the stench of filthy fur filling my nostrils. I rolled onward with my momentum, using it to spring back upright—but the wolf was spry, too.

Two *slices* left. Better make them count.

The beast growled at me, and I stared back. I couldn't risk lashing out blindly, I needed to be damn sure that blade met flesh—and met it well. I needed to wait for the beast to pounce once more, and this time—

It leaped.

Before I knew it, I was rolling forward once more, back toward it, and reaching out my knife in an arc in the process. I *sliced*, leaving myself with just a smidgen left in my stamina bar, and as I completed my roll, I plunged the blade upward into the jumping beast above me. It sliced stomach, and it sliced it deep.

Val followed this move up by standing from her log and offering a round of applause—though I couldn't tell if she meant it sincerely or not.

---

2 x Level 2 Wolves defeated!

Knifework: +1,100XP
Knifework increased to Level 4!
Knifework increased to Level 5!
Base Points Gained: +2 DEX, +2 STR, +4 Free Points (VIT/DEX/STR)

Level up!
You increased to Level 4!
Ability Selection Unlocked . . .

"A couple more for you!" Val cried out.

I looked up at her, pained, and eyed my remaining stamina supply. It was . . . low. But I didn't want to lose face now.

"Alright . . ." I told myself. "Two more. You can—" I was cut off by one of my legs buckling beneath me. That was what happened when your stamina got as low as mine was—things stopped working. Maybe it was time to admit defeat. "Alright!" I cried out. "I admit it. I need help."

With a wave of Val's hand, the wolves seemed to suddenly . . . lose interest. The remaining pair ambled back into the woods, stopping only briefly to lick at their wounds.

I looked from Val's waved hand, to the retreating wolves, and back to her hand again. "That was *you?*"

"You said you wanted a wolf fight."

"When!"

"Back in Umlok."

"I . . ." I shook my head. "I . . . suppose I did?"

"I'll take that as a 'thanks,' shall I?" Val asked me.

I ignored the jab—I'd had quite enough of those—and went instead to a question that was weighing on my mind. "How'd I get 1,100XP from the first pair, back there?"

Val shrugged. "I threw a level three in the mix. Wanted to see if you'd notice. You didn't."

"Well I didn't exactly have time to hang about *identifying* them, did I? And . . . wait. Those weren't spirits, they were wolves."

"Well observed."

I held up a finger to indicate that I wasn't finished. "What I mean is, that's not like any sorcery—any *conjuration*—I've ever heard of. Spirits, sure. Specters, demons, revenants . . . yeah. All normal conjuration stuff, as much as certain administrations don't like it. But wolves?"

"And you have lots of experience in advanced magicks, do you, knife guy?"

Before I could respond, the sorcerer opened her mouth once more.

"Come on. Plainside is another few hours away. And I wanna get there by sundown."

With nothing else for it, I cradled my wounds and limped after her.

CHAPTER NINE

The Ruins of Plainside

Three paces later, Val came to an abrupt halt. "Why are you limping?"

I stared blankly back at her, then gestured to the three wolf carcasses behind me.

Val's furrowed brow suggested that the confusion remained.

"They . . . *attacked* me? Dug their claws in?"

"And that hurt?"

"Hello? Level three? Well, level four now. Yeah, wolf claws are gonna hurt."

"Ugggh . . ." Val said, dropping her shoulders and rolling her head backward like a sulky teenager. "Come on, then."

"What?"

"Come on, then," she said again. "Let me sort you out."

"Oh, so you can heal, too, can you?"

"What, jealous?" Val replied, and continued before I had a chance to deny it. "Healing? Sure. A little. Just enough to get rid of a bad hangover, really, but good enough for some light wounds, too." She placed her hands on me, her touch surprisingly soft for someone who didn't seem to worry about getting into scraps.

A warm, light-yellow glow spread around my wounds, and through the mild itchiness I could feel the gashes close, and the skin regrow.

She tapped the nearest wound—or rather where the wound had been. "Very nice work."

"If you do say so yourself."

"I do."

With that, she continued walking, leading us onward to Plainside, and away from the setting sun. I let the unseasonably warm breeze wash over me, lifting with it the aromas of the region's forest, and then concentrated my attention to the minimized notifications.

> *Knifework increased to Level 4!*
> *Knifework increased to Level 5!*
> **Base Points Gained:** +2 DEX, +2 STR, +4 Free Points (VIT/DEX/STR)

These four free points I would come back to later. Normally, I'd invest them straightaway, but in this particular circumstance there was something else worth doing first—to know exactly where my points would be best invested.

> **Ability Selection Unlocked**
> *Select an ability from the list below:*

> **Option 1: Stab (Knifework)**—Put your weight behind your wielded blade and force the tip through tougher hides and armor. Damage scales on [STR].

It was a basic skill, sure, but that would have been more than handy in that fight with the wolves. And it was another ability that scaled on *Strength*, too, as well as *Slice*. If I chose to focus my base point investment into this stat, then this might be the way to go, but I couldn't shake the idea that I wanted to focus on *Dexterity* more this time around, and build up my stamina more. I minimized this option and moved on to the next.

> **Option 2: Throw (Knifework)**—Throw blades at great speed toward your enemy. Damage scales with [DEX].

It was another uninspiring one—I was secretly hoping at this point that I'd have fulfilled some special condition to unlock a hidden, more advanced, ability. But when would that have happened? The only other skill I really had was *Identification*, with *Stealth* also barely unlocked. At least this one scaled with *Dexterity*, and if I wanted to go this route, it might be an option. It'd give me some range, too, meaning that I wouldn't have to get right in my enemies' faces. That would have kept me well out of reach of those wolves' snapping jaws, at least for a few moments . . .

I turned my attention back to the notifications and brought up the third and final option.

> *Hidden condition met! Alternative ability choice unlocked.*

> **Option 3: Execution (Knifework)** [Requires: Stealth skill unlocked]—Attack a target while undetected for +100 percent damage.

Oh hey! I did get one hidden option after all. It wasn't like it wasn't one that I hadn't been given the choice of last time around—*Stealth* and *Knifework* did go hand in hand, to an extent, after all—but it was a nice option. It didn't scale with any of my base points, which was the downside, and after a while even that +100 percent bonus wouldn't be enough to counter that . . . Besides, it was an ability I'd unlocked last time around, and in order for it to be useful, I'd had to upgrade it to *Execution II* and *Execution III* at future ability selection points. Did I really want to miss out on other abilities because I was constantly upgrading this one?

Though my gut reaction was to pick the hidden ability choice—it often was the most exciting—I pulled up the first two options instead. If I was going to train up from scratch, then chances were that I was going to be fighting a lot of low-level beasts. There was only one of these ability choices that gave me a larger advantage in those circumstances. With some hesitation, I picked option one.

> **Ability Unlocked:** Stab
> **Stab (Knifework):** Put your weight behind your wielded blade and force the tip through tougher hides and armor. Damage scales on [STR].

And then, there were the base points to accept. Now that I knew I was picking *Stab*, there was an obvious choice out of Vitality, Dexterity, and Strength. I placed all four free points into Strength.

This was a whole new me indeed—the last me would've gone hard into *execute*, adding the free points into Vitality on the basis that more health points were always good. But what was the point in surviving for longer if you couldn't do any meaningful damage? I might have gotten out of some fights with fewer scrapes if I'd thought this way in the past . . .

With a new ability registered, I closed the notifications and concentrated on keeping up with a hurrying Val. At the speed she was going, we'd get to Plainside before nightfall, no problem.

It was nightfall by the time we reached Plainside.

I don't really know how that happened; I thought we had plenty of time. I might have slowed us down some. Val didn't seem too upset about this, though—all I received was a dirty look as the sun faded, and no cutting remark—but perhaps that had much to do with the sight before us.

Plainside was charred.

Charred might have been an understatement. I knew that the Player and his two accomplices had set the town alight, but I hadn't until now realized the sheer scale of the devastation. Not a building was untouched—those at the outskirts of town were just as leveled as those around the Collector's mansion; the fire had spared nothing. Plainside, once a bustling stop on the journey to the Badlands in the east, was truly quiet for the first time in living memory. Not a single being stirred amongst the remnants.

"Where are . . ." Val started.

"The bodies," I finished; the question had been weighing on my mind, too.

Brow furrowed, we trudged further into town, and the answer soon became clear.

In the center of the town square was a large patch of freshly patched dirt, two shovels stuck into the ground at one side as though forming a makeshift gravestone.

"Survivors?" Val asked.

"Or noble adventurers," I replied. "Plenty of people pass through here on the way to the Badlands. Used to, at least."

Val nodded thoughtfully, staring on at the unpacked dirt of the mass grave. I felt my legs begin to buckle beneath me as I watched her, and I took a seat on what had once been the town square's low stone wall.

"Do you remember those wolves back there?" Val said.

"It was literally this morning. Yeah, I remember."

"How guilty do you feel for killing them?"

This question caught me by surprise, wrenching my attention from the mass grave. "They were wild animals, Val. I have sympathies, sure, but I'm not gonna wrestle with some grand moral quandary over whether I have a right to defend myself. If I'd sought them out, maybe that's even a question, but in that scenario . . ."

"Wild animals," Val repeated.

"Am I wrong to call them that?"

"Not at all. They're animals. They're undomesticated. The definition fits. But what you're really saying with that label is that they're below you. On the food chain, or in society, or in the great hierarchy of existence. Right?"

". . . Sure?"

"Look at the ground. How many bodies do you think are in there? How big a town was Plainside?"

It wasn't a matter I wanted to dwell on, and I answered quickly. "A hundred people. Maybe two. Where are you going with this?"

"Your Player slaughtered two hundred wild animals."

I felt my blood boil. Couldn't help it. To compare what the Player had done to what—

"That's how this Player sees them," Val hurried to clarify. "How they see us. As lower than them. As 'wild animals.' As pests. That's how they see us, whether they act like it or not."

The town's eerie silence was shattered by the howls of distant wolves.

Val was right, of course. Though the social contract of Alterra meant that nobody—nobody *normal*—would ever say such a thing, the Players had rights that none of the rest of us did. They'd descended from the great Architects themselves, the creators and gods of our domain. We treated them as our saviors because, often, they were—slaying dragons and crumbling evil empires and disbanding terrifying cults. But even when they did such things—even when they were heroes—we knew they did it for themselves. To advance their skills. To collect their rewards. When was the last time a Player ever failed to accept a reward for such missions? These Players, they thought us lower than them, and it was only a matter of time before we grew too insignificant to each and every one of them.

"Are you in?" Val asked, without pulling her attention away from the grave.

I nodded, though she couldn't see me. "I'm in. Let's kill this monster."

Lambkin

"I hope you realize I cannot allow you to marry my daughter, after this," the Baron of Umlok said. "Third daughter or otherwise, even one so low down the line of inheritance should not marry someone of your . . . your social status. I endured the thought to keep my family happy—the gods know this to be an impossible task—but after the escape . . . Well, you see how it must be."

Lambkin blinked lamely at the baron, hearing the words but somehow also not quite understanding them. They stood in an otherwise empty chamber in the castle, the baron sat upon a throne far too grand for anyone but a monarch, and Lambkin staring up at him from the bottom of a tall set of stairs. The baron did enjoy looming over people, Lambkin knew, but he'd never before been on this end of it. "But, my liege, we are in love. We are meant to be. We are—"

"*I* say what is meant to be, when it comes to my land and my family, Lambkin."

"It was one escape, I—"

"Two," the baron replied.

"Two *escapees*," Lambkin clarified, "but one escape."

When the baron didn't reply, he realized this detail was lost on his employer.

"I appreciate an escape isn't ideal," Lambkin continued, and the baron raised his eyebrows at the descriptor *ideal*, "and that the blame must land at the feet of your head guard—me—but—"

"There is to be no more *but*s, Lambkin. A tragedy has occurred—a slaughter of a town *under my supervision*. Do you see how this makes me look? The one saving grace was that we had a suspect in custody. Someone that we might point to and say, 'It is under control. The threat is over.' Yet *somebody* let them escape."

"If it's any consolation, sir, I don't think this 'Styk' fellow could've been the one to do it. He—"

The baron waved Lambkin down. "I'm not interested in your facts, Lambkin. Only results. Do you understand?"

"I—"

"And this is one bad result too many. I have to ask you to turn in your bow and your badge."

"I don't have a badge, sir," Lambkin replied, "and I brought my own bow from home."

The baron raised his eyebrows once more. "You weren't provided equipment by the armorer?"

"No, sir." Before the baron could speak once more, Lambkin continued, "If I may, sir, there must be some other way this can all turn out. I've done good work before. Do you remember when your second cousin—the farmer—had his sheep stolen? I found them, didn't I? I returned them to him?"

"Except for their heads, yes."

"And I know there is a certain status that comes along with employing one of the highest-leveled archers in the Gentle Tundras, sir."

"The *second*-highest-leveled, Lambkin. Let us not dance around that point."

"First or second, it matters not; I could still shoot an apple off a sheep's head at one hundred yards."

"Is *that* what happened to those sheep's . . ." The baron trailed off, apparently not wanting an answer. "Look, Lambkin. It's over. There's nothing left to say."

But the previous head guard wouldn't give up so easily. "And there is—"

"Lambkin!" the baron shouted, "I've spoken, Lambkin. I've spoken." He sighed, deeply, and this was the only suggestion the baron gave that he didn't relish making this decision. The two men stood in silence, not making eye contact, for a moment longer, until the baron's mouth twisted as something occurred to him.

"What kind of name is Lambkin, anyway?" the baron asked. "Friend of Lambs? Do you have witch blood in your veins, Lambkin?"

The ex-head guard held up his hands to protest his innocence. "No, sir. My family were farmers, sir. Lamb farmers. That's all. I—"

"It isn't very *friendly* to the lambs, though, is it? Farming them? I mean, you do slaughter them at the end of that process?"

"After being kind to them, sir, I assure you."

The baron narrowed his eyes, pressing his lips together. "Perhaps I should have sent a man to the archives earlier. Perhaps I should have pulled out your family history."

"Please do, sir, if it would make you feel more comfortable about me marrying Sae. I have nothing—"

But the baron interrupted. "We have discussed that already, I thought? You will not be marrying her, no matter the result. This only decides whether or not you are burned at the stake."

"Sir, please, I—"

"I think this conversation has gone on long enough, don't you?" The baron turned to the other end of the chamber. "Guards!" he called out, and the doors swung open. "If you will please escort Captain Lamb— Sorry, *Mister* Lambkin out of the castle."

"Sir!" Lambkin cried. "There must be something I can do!" Two of his once employees grabbed him by an arm each, dragging him across the stone floor. "Anything! You want results? I'll give you results! Any results you want, I'll—"

But the doors to the baron's reception room slammed closed behind them, and the guards continued dragging him until they reached the front gate.

"Noz, Bart," Lambkin tried. "You're good men. You know you don't want to do this to me. You know—"

"I'm sorry, boss," Noz said, averting his eyes before dropping Lambkin to the ground.

"Yeah," the other guard echoed. "Sorry, boss. We don't . . . It's just orders, you know?"

The two guards returned to the gate, then stopped for one last look at their former captain, lying on the wet dirt. Noz opened his mouth as if to say something, then thought better of it. He shook his head, and they disappeared back into the barony, leaving the ex-captain truly alone for the first time in years.

Lambkin wasn't the kind of man to give up so easily. He was a good man. He would be good to Sae. She would be good for him. And they *would* marry, someday. All he needed to do was redeem himself. To find the man the baron thought responsible for Plainside.

He needed to hunt down the man known to him only as 'Styk.'

If that *was* his real name.

CHAPTER TEN

It Tracks

We'd spent the better part of the last few days tracking. The Butcher of Plainside, as Val and I had taken to calling him, had made precisely no effort to cover his tracks, and neither, it seemed, had his two accomplices. Charred footsteps had journeyed northwest from the leveled town, and even once the soot had faded from the trio's shoes, broken branches snapped underfoot gave Val and me a pretty clear picture of where they'd headed.

They'd joined up with a main road, traveling west, and though there were no visual signals that we were still on the right track, the locals of the small towns and inns on this road well remembered the "great" Player they'd set their eyes upon—and were all too eager to talk about it. I'd had to remind myself that they didn't know what the Butcher had done, that they'd be speaking differently of him if they did. Or . . . I hoped they would, anyway.

The best part of a week later, we found ourselves in the quaint town of Tath. This town, formed of a good four dozen buildings, sat in the lower foothills of the Bladerocks, the great mountain range that separated the Gentle Tundras from the (definitely *not* gentle) Badlands. But despite being so close to this intimidating region, Tath seemed to boast all the charmingly eccentric qualities of many remote towns in the region—the people wore permanent smiles, the street merchants began their pitches with friendly jokes, and the buildings were roofed with straw rather than slate, which was an intentional preference for beauty over practicality.

Everyone knew that the best place in a town to hear gossip was an inn, but I couldn't rid myself of the feeling that this wasn't why we were going there; Val had mentioned feeling thirsty for ale even more than normal in the past few hours. Me? Well, I wasn't one to shy away from a good beer, either, so I went along with it.

The inn was larger than you'd normally expect in a town the size of Tath, though that had much to do with its positioning on one of the main roads between the regions. And there was custom enough to warrant this size, judging by the gentle good-natured murmuring that washed over me as we entered, putting me immediately at ease.

"I'll start with the barmaid," Val said, already hurrying out of earshot before I had a chance to reply. I'd just need to hope she'd assume my order was the same as hers.

I made the rounds by myself, prying into group conversations and approaching those surly customers drinking alone, asking them about a certain trio who passed through town a few days back. Those who knew who I was talking about were only too eager to say that they'd met them, spoken with them, been named the guardian of their future children, and so on; it was hard to believe every word coming out of their mouths.

At some point—I wasn't quite aware when—Val shoved a pint in my hand, and it was already a good quarter gone before I realized I was drinking it. She was right; it wasn't half bad.

Midinterrogation with an older, very drunk, woman—one who had more grandmotherly vibes than "getting sloshed at the inn" vibes—I caught sight of a man staring at me, over the woman's shoulder. I glanced at him, and the man's eyes seemed focused elsewhere, but I was sure he'd been staring . . .

Shaking my head, I moved on, looking for more information on the future whereabouts of the Player and his two cronies. I'd heard plenty of where he'd *been*, but nobody so far had had any idea where he was *going*.

Val seemed to have had more luck, though. "Got him," she said, grabbing me by the arm and wrenching me away from an attractive elf—or human, I couldn't quite tell what she'd *identify* as—who I'd been intending to get to know a little better. But there were other priorities, I told myself, with one last glance at her.

"Got him? The Player? You know where he's headed?"

Val shook her head.

"Then why did you drag me away from—"

The sorcerer raised an eyebrow, glancing at the woman I'd just been speaking with. "You weren't her type."

Of course, Val had only seen me in my . . . well, in my powerless state, at this point. Let's not mince words here, *powerless* was about the most apt descriptor for me. But back when I knew who I was, I considered myself actually quite an attractive man, if that wasn't arrogant to say. It's not like that came from me; there was a healthy handful of women out there who'd described me as handsome, and no, not a single one of them was my mother. Though maybe she'd have added a voice to that choir if she'd hung about for longer than it'd taken to give birth to me.

Before I could interject, Val continued, "I don't know where the Player's headed, no. But I have a line on the orc."

"Where?"

"Heading northwest. Back toward Rose Fort. Not with the Player we're after, from the sounds of it, but I figure he'll know where to find him."

I considered this, licking my lips, then nodded. "OK. Good. Sounds like a plan. We'll head off now, then?"

"In the morning," Val replied, stifling a yawn. "I'm beat, and I already got us a room."

"A?" I asked. "One room?"

"They only had one."

"We're not sharing a . . ."

Val's eyes widened, blinking at me. "What? No. Two single beds, don't you worry."

"Good, because I—"

The sorcerer drew in close. "Do you see that guy over there?" she whispered into my ear, apparently trying to make this interaction look like something other than what it was.

"Who?"

"Over my left shoulder. Corner of the room."

I glanced, not quite in the direction Val had specified, but close enough to see with my peripherals. It was the same man I'd seen earlier—the one staring at me, but not. "I see him. Thought I saw him staring earlier."

"He probably was. You see the mark on his wrist?"

"You want me to look now?"

"No. Don't draw attention. If you didn't see it, you'll have to trust me—it was a circle with a line through it. A broken sun."

Val paused, but if this was supposed to mean anything to me . . .

"It's the mark of the Cult of Ascendancy. We've encountered them before."

"We?"

The sorcerer shook her head. "I. I meant *I*. They're a dangerous bunch. And if they think we mean the Player harm . . ."

"What's Players got to do with Ascendancy? Ascend to where?"

Val only shook her head, pulling her face away from my ear. "Best not to talk about it here." She turned back to the bar and ordered another couple of ales. "What'd you think of the first?"

"The beer?" I asked.

"Yeah, what else would I be—"

"It was nice, yeah."

"They use rosemary in the brewing," Val said. "Rumor is—and I can't confirm it's true—there was a witch in these parts who used rosemary to disguise the taste of her poisons. One day, she poisons the product of a local pub. Not one like this, but one that caters to bandits. The nasty kind of bandits, too. They notice the rosemary—who wouldn't?—but they like it. Adds a nice extra element to the taste profile of the—"

"Taste profile?" I repeated. "What are you, a food critic?"

"If the fates had been kinder, I would be. But I'm trying to tell a story, so stop interrupting."

"Sorry."

"So they like the beer, even with the rosemary, and they drink enough that night that the poison—powerless in small doses—is in their systems enough to kill 'em. A whole bandit clan, wiped out in one night. Courtesy of one small-town witch. So this"—she passed another glass of deep red ale—"is called the Witch's Brew. A re-creation, all the rosemary, none of the poison."

"Huh," I said.

"Yeah, cool, right?"

"Yeah, almost makes me hate witches a little less."

The smile faded from Val's face some. "Oh, Hecate's torch, don't tell me you believe all that stuff."

I damned well did. Witches? These were the types of people even *I* tried to avoid; there was no knowing what one might do to you, for the simple crime of existing in their presence. "When they stop being evil, I'll stop hating them."

"I'd come to expect a little more nuance from you," she said. "Clearly I was mistaken."

Val's mood seemed to have turned, so we drank the rest of the pints in near silence, sat at the bar of the bustling inn. Val downed the last of hers, having drunk it far more quickly than I had, then stood abruptly. "We should sleep; we'll need to leave early in the morning."

As we left the basement for the stairs, I couldn't help but feel like there were eyes bearing into the back of my head. Though sleep grabbed Val quickly, I remained awake, staring at the ceiling, unable to shake the idea that we hadn't escaped the attention of dangerous factions. As the night grew into its darkness, I was just beginning to think that it might have been paranoia, caused perhaps by my insanely low level. But that's when our room's wooden door began to creak open.

CHAPTER ELEVEN

Reality Is What You Make It

The light of a hallway lantern shimmered in the reflective surface of the raised metal blade, and I prepared to pounce.

I wasn't exactly unfamiliar with the sort of dagger our attacker wielded, but I have to say: I'm usually far more comfortable on the other end of it. Still, I knew that its range was short, and I would need to wait until the last moment to fling myself from the bed and tackle him to the floor.

Floorboards creaked gently under the attacker's feet as he paced slowly across the room. I held my breath—not just to remain silent, but in anticipation of the fight to come. These things were always worse in anticipation, as they say.

It was to Val's bed, on the other side of the—admittedly very small—room that the attacker paced, offering me the cover of his shoulder, somewhat obscuring me from view. I'd need every advantage I could get, what with my low level.

The attacker stepped into the small stream of moonlight that seeped in through the window, and I caught sight of their face. The cultist from the inn. I wasn't exactly surprised by his identity, but there was an intensity in his gaze that I hadn't quite expected. A fury, perhaps. A passion. No, a fervor.

The cultist arrived at the side of Val's bed; the creaking floorboards disguised by Val's intense snoring. It was a wonder I managed to get any sleep at all, with her around—though I suppose the last few days truly had been exhausting. Beneath the bed covers, I tensed my legs, and as the cultist raised his dagger, I sprang from my position.

. . . And found my legs caught in the surprisingly heavy quilt.

A heavy thunk announced my arrival on the wooden floor—there would be bruises in the morning, for the record—and two heads turned to face me. The cultist turned, alarmed, still holding the dagger in midair, and Val, wrenched from unconsciousness, blinked over at me.

I really needed to get my *Stealth* skill leveled up.

"What are you . . ." she mumbled, trailing off when she noticed the man standing over her. Val looked from him, to me, and then back to him again. There was a moment—seemingly an eternity—where nobody moved. Then, Val muttered simply, "Hades's fork," then we all moved at once.

Our attacker correctly guessed that the person not currently on the floor was the greater threat, and concentrated his efforts on Val, instead. The dagger flashed before her as she ducked, eyes scanning the room, presumably to find some way of using her skills—whatever they were—to her advantage.

As I sprang back to my feet, my own blade in hand, dust whipped toward me. Or rather, it whipped toward the cultist, and I was just collateral damage.

I staggered backward, blinking my eyes aggressively to clear them of grit, then pressed forward once more. I slashed near blindly with my dagger, aiming for the blurry unfamiliar shape and hoping I wasn't about to slice up my new friend. *See? I cared more about collateral damage than she did!*

The tip of my dagger caught flesh, and I knew I'd hit my target only because the resulting groan came from an unfamiliar voice. I risked pressing my eyes closed for a second, ridding them of the worst of the dust, and when I opened them . . .

The ground gave way beneath us.

Around us—me, Val, and our attacker—was nothing but an infinite void. A darkness, black only due to the absence of light, but the void itself surely color-less. I had a familiar yet unfamiliar sensation in my stomach as I plummeted; one of momentary weightlessness, as though I was a child falling from a tree. *Or a grown man falling from a bed*, I thought.

The attacker shifted his weight, and in doing so he created a space between him and my dagger as we plummeted. The blade fell free, my grip having loos-ened for the obvious reason of astonishment at falling through nothingness. I reached out to grab it and succeeded only in knocking it further from me.

Only now thinking to glance at Val, I saw that her eyes were wide; her shock at current circumstances was near as much as mine. "How do we stop this?" I called to her, but she only responded with a shrug. Big help.

I turned my attention back to our attacker, who'd created more distance still, by holding his limbs closer to his body, streamlining his form like a bird falling from the heavens. His apparent comfort suggested that he'd been in this situation many a time before.

Copying the man below me, I pushed my legs together and held my hands flat at my sides, and closed on the dagger spinning through the void ahead of me. When I was close enough that I was in danger of accidentally slicing my face with my own blade—for a second time, and the first wasn't enjoyable enough that I was in any rush to repeat it—I whipped an arm forward, and snatched the dagger out of midair.

I caught it by the blade, of course.

"Argh!" I groaned, then pressed my lips together and concentrated on ignoring the pain of my slashed palm. There'd be plenty of time to complain about it later. That was, if we ever got out of this one.

Right. How *did* we get out of this?

I fixed my eyes on the cultist—who was getting no further ahead of us now that I'd gotten the hang of this whole flying business—and activated my *Basic Identification* ability.

> **Identification:** +50XP
> **Level 22 Ascendent Worldbender**
> *Race: Human, Elf*

". . . Worldbender?" I repeated, loud enough that Val could hear. "What in the hells is a Worldbender?"

Val gestured to the void around us, the nothingness through which we plummeted. "Look around, idiot," she replied, then ripped off her cloak, pulled her limbs tight, and soared ahead of me, closing in on the cultist. Her smaller frame allowed her to near our attacker quickly, but when she reached him, she attacked only with her fists.

The cultist made little attempt to block them, and it soon became clear why—he was strong enough that Val could only do minor damage with hands alone. A few blows in, the Worldbender grabbed at Val's wrist, twisted it, and soon had her tumbling away once more.

"Use your magicks!" I shouted.

"We're in a void!" came the response. "I've got nothing to work with in here. My abilities . . . they work by altering that which is already there. But there's—"

"Then summon something. I've seen you do *that*, at least."

Though Val's mouth moved, I didn't hear a response, and could only assume she was grumbling. So her solving this wasn't an option, it seemed. I was going to need to do this myself—a pitiful Level 4 Peasant against a Level 22 Magick User. They were certainly long odds; I was going to need to get creative if we were going to escape this infinity of falling.

What did I have to play with? *Basic Stealth Attack* was out, obviously, being that the cultist knew full well that we were both here, and there wasn't exactly much to hide behind; the void wasn't known for having, you know, *stuff* in it. And of my remaining abilities, only two were combat-related: *slice* and *stab*.

I sighed. With no other options available to me, I figured I'd give them a go.

Closing the distance between myself and the cultist once more, I reached out and *sliced* with the dagger. But our opponent was quicker, and instead of moving to escape the attack, he altered his skin into thick scaled hide—just for a moment, just for long enough to negate the attack. It made sense now, why he'd not been worried about Val punching him, either; if a knife couldn't hope to hurt that hide, then fists definitely couldn't.

I pulled away, giving myself some space to evade any attacks forthcoming from the cultist. Neither of my *Knifework* abilities, in their current form, could hope to pierce that hide. It was useless. How could I think I'd be able to help take down a *Player*, of all things, when I couldn't even take down someone at level 22? What had Val done to my ego to make me think this was a viable route? What did—

I caught myself. I was spiraling. Mentally, that is—that I was spiraling physically, too, was obvious.

There was, perhaps, one option. My abilities, at the moment, didn't have enough force to pierce this magick-bent hide. Of course they didn't; I was level 4. But that didn't mean I couldn't find additional force from elsewhere . . .

"Val," I called out. "Can you stop his magicks?"

"Why?"

"Gods, Val, just answer the question! Can you do it?"

Val seemed to weigh this up, tilting her head from side to side. "For a second, maybe?"

I nodded, then repositioned myself above the cultist, knife held out, tip pointed downward. "Do it," I said.

Val outstretched her trembling hands, reaching them toward the cultist in a clawlike shape, a snarl revealing clenched teeth. Though I couldn't see her magicks, not these, it certainly seemed like there was some great exertion on her part.

And, a moment later, the floor of the inn's bedroom hurtled toward us.

The sorcerer and the cultist hit the wooden floorboards first, each grunting with pain at the impact—I could only imagine the shin splints—as I gripped the dagger tightly, and activated my *Stab* skill.

I'd been on a few dates, a while back, with an academic. She was a quiet sort, most of the time, but when you directed the conversation onto her field of study—the physics of our world—there was no putting a cork in it. Her eyes lit up, and word after word after word tumbled from her mouth. You could only settle down and enjoy the show. I mention this now only to explain how I know the phrase *terminal velocity*.

Thanks to the cultist's worldbending powers, the three of us had been falling for, oh, five minutes or so? And as a result, we'd all reached the maximum speed possible, I suspected—or at least thereabouts.

While I was still traveling this speed—at *terminal velocity*—for moments longer, the cultist had already come to a stop beneath me. Our relative velocity—yes, that phrase came from the physicist too—was extreme.

It was extreme enough, even, that my *Stab* ability had force enough behind it to pierce even the thickest of hides.

When the tip of my dagger hit the cultist's thick flesh, it pierced, this time. But it did more than that. In fact, blood splattered everywhere.

Level 22 Ascendent Worldbender defeated!

Knifework: +2,200XP
Knifework increased to Level 6!
Knifework increased to Level 7!
Knifework increased to Level 8!
Base Points Gained: +3 DEX, +3 STR, +6 Free Points (VIT/DEX/STR)

Level up!
You increased to Level 5!

CHAPTER TWELVE

Blood on Your Hands

"Ah," I said, drenched in blood.

"Ah," Val echoed, also drenched in blood.

We looked from the disintegrated body, up to one another, and then at the room around us. Which was . . . well, you know, *also* drenched in blood.

I found myself frozen to the spot, unable to move. This crime scene was horrific on a scale to rival the tragedy of Plainside, if a little more of the victim's making. Still, that didn't seem to matter too much to my brain, which was at the time screaming something along the lines of "Aaaaaaaaahhhhhhhhh!"

"We . . ." I started.

"Should get out of here," Val finished.

"Before more cultists arrive?"

Val shook her head. "Before the boardmistress sees what we've done to her room. She scares me."

"Agreed." I paced toward the door and found that my feet squelched with every step. "We should . . ." I started, gesturing to the pail of water in the corner of the room, next to a rusty old mirror.

"Yes."

Silently, Val and I shared the small bucket of water, washing the worst of the red from our faces, hair, and arms, only to realize quickly that it was going to take a lot more doing than one bucket. We looked to one another, shrugged, and then faced the door once more.

"Ready?" Val asked.

"Ready."

We bolted through the door, squelched our way down the stairs, ran from the inn, and never looked back.

We camped, instead, under the stars.

We'd found a nice spot next to a shallow river, just far enough away from the town of Tath that we wouldn't be tracked down and told to pay a cleaning fee, while not so far that we were exhausted before we got there. Our skin stained as red as it was, we were lucky we didn't encounter anyone on the roads at this late hour, as someone might take one look at us and think we were wearing the blood of an entire army. It really was something, how much blood could fit in one person.

As soon as we reached the riverbank, both of us stripped down to our undergarments, neither of us apparently worried about the other seeing. For me—and likely Val as well—I would have paid any price to wash, at this point. We both hopped in, squealing and gasping as we plunged into the cold water, and set about scrubbing ourselves from head to toe.

Only once we were clean did we turn in the water to make eye contact, at which point there was a brief, awkward pause, before Val splashed water over me. "I'm getting out. No looking."

I held my hands up in the air to protest my innocence, to say that I had no intention of doing so, but I suspected that a woman as arrogant as Val wouldn't believe me. Instead, I only ground my teeth together, bearing the cold a moment longer, and turned to face away.

Behind me, I heard an "urgh," then a couple of snaps of wood, and then a soft orange light washed over me. At this cue, I turned to find a dressed Val huddling by a fire.

"Were you gonna tell me you were done?" I asked through shivering teeth.

Val shrugged. "It looked like you were enjoying yourself. Who am I to get in the way of that?"

I shook my head. "No looking."

"You aren't the boss of me," came the reply.

"But you just . . . You just said—"

"Calm down, drippy boy. I won't look. I have better things to look at than your wet arse."

There really was no winning with women sometimes. I pulled myself out of the water, hurried back to my clothes, and sat opposite Val at the fire. There was an almost unnatural warmth to it, one that didn't seem to fit a fire of this fairly pathetic size, but I wasn't exactly going to complain. Here, still in the foothills of the Bladerocks, the breeze had a mighty bite to it; any warmth would have done just fine.

"Sleep," I eventually said as my skin and clothes grew dry enough to not be grossly uncomfortable.

"Yes."

"Who's on first watch?"

The sorcerer looked across at me with a raised eyebrow. ". . . Neither of us?"

"We're in the middle of the woods, Val. What if we get attacked? Wolves and such?"

Val smiled. "Trust me. With me around, your days of worrying about wolves nibbling your toes while you sleep are long behind you."

"They don't 'nibble toes,' they—"

"Eat faces, yes. Can we sleep now?"

I shook my head to myself—a habit I'd learned quickly in the few days since meeting Val—and looked around for a flat patch of ground. "Where'd you learn this stuff, anyway? Were you one of them fancy academy students?"

"For a time, sure," Val replied, and the answer caught me by surprise; this was the first real time she'd volunteered any information about herself. "I was at Managlass Academy. But I had some abilities under my belt already, at that point."

"I'm not sure I can imagine you at an academy."

"And why not?" The question had a snap to it, but I suspected Val was toying with me.

"Did they have you wearing uniform robes? Doing morning prayers? Writing spells over and over on chalkboards? None of this really screams 'Val' to me."

"Oh, and you know me so well already, do you?" Val retorted, but this time a small smile broke through. "No, you're right. Me and the academics . . . we didn't get on all that much."

"Why? Too fusty for you?"

"Too theoretical."

"Ah."

"Yeah. I suppose I wanted to prove them all wrong about me, about what they suspected I was."

I suppressed a laugh. "What did they think you were? A rogue? A cheat?"

"Something like that."

"Why'd you leave, then?"

The small smile on Val's face faded; something about this particular question brought forth painful memories. "A story for another time, maybe." Before I could get a word in, she continued, "What about you, knife boy? How did you get into your line of work?"

"Procurement?"

"Sure, if you want to call it that. Most people call it theft, though."

I raised my eyebrows; I'd been caught out. Yet Val didn't seem all that worried about what I'd really been doing with my life. "Same as all of us crooks, really, I think. Came from a poor background. Didn't have much education, many skills. Society didn't seem like it had a place for me, so I . . . fell into it, I suppose?"

"And just who did you 'fall into it' with? A friend? A brother?"

"My father. It's what he'd done as long as I could remember. I was better at it than him, though. In my prime. By which I mean . . ."

"Before your death."

I nodded.

"Do you still see him?" Val asked.

"My dad? Nah. He's dead. Spent his last moments surrounded by dozens of his old acquaintances."

"Comforting him?"

"Stabbing him."

Val raised an eyebrow. "Oh."

"I suppose that's the fate that most in my line of work meet. Me included."

"What about your mother? Is she still around?"

I shook my head. "Never met her. From what Dad always told me, it was only one night. She passed through town, they . . . you know, did that thing people don't want to talk about their parents doing, and then she left on her next adventure. Came back nine months later and dropped a child on his doorstep."

"Thief blood *and* adventurer blood in you. We might make a slayer of you yet."

I tried a smile in response, but nothing came. All this talk of parents—or lack thereof—had formed a pit in my stomach. I tried to shift the conversation along. "What about you?"

"My parents?"

"Yeah."

Val shrugged. "Don't have any, either."

"They've passed? I'm sorry, I—"

"No, they're not dead," she responded. "At least, not as far as I know. They just . . . didn't want me. Didn't like how I turned out."

"Oh, that's . . . that's worse. I'm sorry. When did you last . . . see them?"

"When I was seven. When I first . . ." Val trailed off, her eyes fixed intensely on the fire. "Do you mind if we don't talk about this?"

I paused. "Of course. Sorry. I didn't mean to pry. I just—"

"No, it's not that. It's just . . . a sore spot for me. That's all. You weren't to know." She offered me a sad smile—one that I returned in kind.

This vulnerability didn't seem to fit with the Val I knew; it didn't seem her style at all. But maybe all this ego and humor was just a—

"I think it's time I go to sleep, now," Val said, interrupting my pattern of thought. "Night." She lay down where she was, turning away from me and the fire.

I spent the next few minutes staring into the fire, thinking of my father. It had been a few years since he'd passed, and these days I didn't think of him all that much. I wondered what that said about me—whether I'd moved on, and whether this was the sort of thing you *should* move on from.

As Val drifted off to sleep, as announced by triumphant snores, I brought up my notifications once more—the one good thing that had happened as a result of the cultist assaulting us.

> *Knifework increased to Level 8!*
> **Base Points Gained**: +3 DEX, +3 STR, +6 Free Points (VIT/DEX/STR)

With my current *Knifework* abilities, *Stab* and *Slice*, both leveling with Strength, the choice was obvious, and I put all six of my free points into this base stat. In future, as I gained new abilities, both in *Knifework* and otherwise, this choice might not be so clear-cut. For now, however, it was simple, and I took some kind of pleasure in that.

CHAPTER THIRTEEN

Welcome to Murderpost

WELCOME TO MURDERPOST, the sign at the perimeter read. *DO NOT BE ALARMED BY THE NAME.*

We'd been tracking the orc for the best part of a week, by this point, and judging by what little intelligence we could gather, he'd long since parted ways with the Player and the other accomplice. But that was no matter, according to Val; you don't massacre a town with someone and not keep in touch. The logic was: we track down this orc fellow, and we interrogate him for information on the Player's whereabouts. "Cos he'll know," Val had said. "He'll know."

It had brought us to Murderpost, the only orcish outpost this far east in the Gentle Tundras, which orcs tended to visit when they needed access to materials they couldn't get in the other outposts. It made sense, then, that the orc had passed through here. We could trust the intel.

Val grabbed the arm of a passing orc—one of few, really, considering that this was a supposed orcish post. "The blacksmith," she said. "Tunrok."

"Northern gate," the orc grunted back. "He close soon."

"Much obliged, mister," Val responded, and waved me on.

It was the only piece of information—other than where he'd been—that we'd been able to gather on the orc. It was a throwaway comment, really. Someone who'd been drinking in the same inn as the mysterious orc had happened to get a look at his battle-axe, and just so happened to be in the blacksmithing trade himself. As a result, he recognized a sigil on its hilt—one that marked it as being produced by one of the Clan Tunrok, an orcish family known for their high-level *metalworking*.

Only one such clan member could be found this far east, and it happened that they were at this outpost. Surely, if the orc in question had passed through here, it was to do business with this trusted blacksmith.

We passed through the small outpost, between ramshackle huts and along roads lined with stuff that really should have been in a sewer system, should one have existed.

"Nice place," I mumbled.

"Snob," Val replied, though she flashed me a smile to show that she was just teasing. "You know, I passed through here once before, looking for something."

"What were you looking for? To be assaulted?"

Val ignored the remark, though a nearby satyr flashed me a dirty look.

"Just a talisman. Something to help channel my changeling abilities."

"Oh, right," I started, then . . . "Wait, what? Changeling?"

Val stopped suddenly, but didn't turn to make eye contact. "A quarter, yeah. My grandad on my mother's side. You got a problem with that?"

"No, I just . . . I just didn't know. You hadn't mentioned it."

"And it changes how you see me, does it?"

"No!" I cried. "I didn't say that. There's no judgement here. This is a judgement-free zone, alright?"

Finally, Val made a nervous kind of eye contact. "Fine. Sorry. I'm just . . . I'm just sick of people judging me for who I am."

"If it makes you feel any better, I'm a quarter ogre, on my mum's side."

"Really?"

"No," I said. "Well, maybe. Isn't like I ever got much contact with that side of the family, is it? But when I said it, you didn't judge me for it, did you?"

Val shook her head. "No. I was just surprised."

I remained silent.

"Ah, right. Gotcha."

"See?"

"Yes, I told you I got it."

Val happy once more, we continued across town—though "town" was a bit of a stretch of a label—until we reached a tent with a small but consistent plume of smoke rising from it.

"I think this is the blacksmith," I said, having to shout over the noise of hammer upon anvil.

"Oh yeah? You think?" Val led us inside.

An orc wearing an amulet with a familiar sigil etched on it looked up from a glowing blade, rested upon his anvil. "Yes? You want sword or armor?" he asked.

"Information."

"I can't smith that."

"Yes, we know," Val said. "You made a battle-axe, recently. For an orc by name of Lev. Has your sigil on its leather hilt."

"I know of this, yes."

"We want to know where he might've got to," I said.

The old blacksmith raised his eyebrows, then glared at me. "You think I give information about my customers? Not good way to do business. Not without . . . something to sweeten this deal."

Val sighed, reaching into her pocket. "What is it, money? That what you want? If you're looking for sexual favors, then . . ." she trailed off and looked over to me.

"I don't do sexual favors, Val," I clarified.

The sorcerer shrugged. "No judgements here."

"I want rock," the blacksmith said.

"You want . . . a rock?" Val asked. "Just any rock?"

"No! Not just *any* rock. Particular rock. Rock I love."

"You want us to get you a particular rock," Val repeated. "Like . . . granite? Or sandstone? What?"

"No. You not understand. Not particular *type* of rock. *Particular* rock."

Val glanced to me, then back at the blacksmith. I opted to take a seat on a stool in the corner of the room; it seemed like this was going to take some time.

"What rock, then?"

"Crystal."

"You want us to get you a crystal?"

The blacksmith slumped his shoulders back. "No! Her *name* is Crystal!"

"Whose name? I thought we were talking about a rock."

The member of Clan Tunrok sighed, then placed his hammer down. "OK. We do story time. Sit." He turned to me and narrowed his eyes. "Oh. You already sit."

"You were gonna tell us a story?" I prompted him. "Maybe a quick one? Time's a factor here."

"I am member of Clan Tunrok."

"We're aware," both Val and I responded at once.

"Yes, good. Then you know: I have great *metalwork*. Very high. One of highest in the tundras. At high level, very strange abilities. Good, yes. Strange, also yes. I have choices: locate ore, talk to metals, fine detailing . . . All these kinds of thing."

"'Talk to metals'?" I repeated. "Who'd pick—"

The blacksmith's face soured.

Val smiled at me, pointing to the orc as if to say "Him. He would pick that."

"You have problem? Maybe you have other source of information, hmm?"

I held up my hands in the air, palms facing forward in surrender.

"I cut long story short, yes? Avoid . . . judgements. I speak to metals. Many metals. A surprising number of them like poetry. And one . . . one beautiful geode, she is purple in daylight, pink in nighttime, very generous with her affection. I fall in love with."

"I—" I started, but Val threw me a glance that cut me short.

"Then my brother . . ." The blacksmith made a noise that was something like a raspberry, but hindered by his long tusks. Or were they fangs? It felt rude to ask. "*Borosz*. Not good brother. Not in family trade, either. He sell her away. For money? No. Not even for money. For a pony. He is *farmer* class, yes? And he get ability to speak with animals. He fall—"

"I don't think we need to hear where this is going," Val cut in. "What's the job?"

"Steal back geode for me."

Val slapped her legs, standing up. "Great. We can do that. Tell us where it is, and we'll—"

"No. I come with. I want Crystal see me as gallant knight. Saving her, yes?"

Val threw her hands in the air. "Fine. Makes no odds to me, cos I'm not seeking the affections of a rock."

"Geode," the blacksmith corrected her.

"*You're* the one who called her a—" I started, but Val shot me a look.

"Geode," she corrected herself. "Where is she, then, this geode? Who are we stealing her from?"

"From most despicable evil in this land. From people with quick tongue and faster mind. From people who use tools to cast spell over others, make them happy, sad, make them pay up. From people who get rich with not single day of hard work done in their lives." The blacksmith paused. "We steal Crystal from Bard's College of Eastern Tundras."

CHAPTER FOURTEEN

A Rock and a Bard Place

The Bard's College of the Eastern Tundras was a fairly pathetic affair, considering it was owned by a guild. Out here, in this region of Alterra, there was never much investment—the lack of a true central government will do that—so perhaps it shouldn't have surprised me, but . . . Well, I guess I just thought that bards thought themselves too fancy to live in places like this.

The college was more of a campus, really, with several small buildings dotted around a makeshift square, all surrounded by a wall that was . . . not *low*, by any means, but easily scalable. Especially with a more-than-seven-foot-tall orc at our side.

"What do you see?" Val asked me, while the blacksmith held me up to peek over the wall.

"You see Crystal?"

"Just people milling about, really," I replied. "Lots of lyres. Why do bards like lyres so much?"

"Pretty sounds," Val said, and the blacksmith grunted his agreement.

"Do you have any idea where she might be?" I asked. "Or who might have her?"

"Borosz sell her to guildmaster. Small man, no hair, wear long robes. You see?"

I scoured the people in the courtyard. "Only person I can see wearing robes is over six feet tall. He's bald, though."

"Yes. Is him. Small man."

"That's taller than me!" I cried.

"And I help you look over wall, yes?"

I opened my mouth to argue some more, but a cry of laughter from Val put me off. "I'm still taller than *you*," I grumbled to her, then turned my attention back to the guildmaster. "He's moving . . . He's going toward one of the smaller huts. Near to us, in fact. I think . . . I think that might be where he lives?"

"Yes," the blacksmith said, dropping me without a word of warning and causing me to crash to the floor. "This is where she is. I know."

I raised my eyebrows. "Alright, then. What's the—"

Val hopped the wall.

I made eye contact with the blacksmith.

"She not like plans?" he asked.

I shook my head. "No, she does not." With that, I took a few steps back, then charged at the wall, springing up it and grabbing the top. As I began to heave myself over, the blacksmith gave me a push—one that I wished I hadn't needed—and soon I tumbled into the bushes below. "Ow," I muttered.

"Yeah," Val agreed as the blacksmith plonked down on the other side of her. "Surprisingly spiky bushes, huh?"

"You could've warned me."

"And where'd be the fun in that?" she retorted, a twinkle in her eye.

"Come on," the blacksmith said. "Crystal is waiting. We save."

I nodded, pressing forward at a crouch, and keeping to the shadows of the building so that none of the musicians in the courtyard would see us. The great hulking orc blacksmith was not helping matters on that regard, so I chose to move quickly. "OK," I said. "We need to break into the guildmaster's quarters quickly. In my experience, there's likely to be a lock on the door, and now that I don't have my *Lockpicking* abilities any more . . ."

"It's OK," Val said. "If there's a lock, I got a plan for it."

"Care to share?"

"Not really."

I sighed, shaking my head, but pressed onward nonetheless; it wouldn't do for us to hang around much longer than we had to, and from what I'd learned of Val already, she wasn't going to change her mind any time soon.

Stealth: +40XP

We turned the corner in full view of the courtyard, standing at this point so as to hide in plain sight, and I tried the door. It didn't budge. "Locked. What's the plan?"

Val turned to the blacksmith. "Think you can smash it open?"

"Oh, good plan, Val. Not like that's gonna—"

The blacksmith stepped forward, raised one foot, and then kicked the door in. In front of us, a horrified guildmaster whipped his head around, and behind us, a dozen or more bards abruptly stopped playing their instruments.

"I think we better . . ." Val started.

"Yes," I agreed.

Val, the blacksmith, and I hurried inside the guildmaster's personal quarters, slamming the door closed behind us. While Val and I spilled further into the room, the blacksmith pressed his body against the door, reinforcing it.

A gentle pink glow appeared in the room, silhouetting the horrified guildmaster and his instrument, which was, surprise, surprise, a lyre. I scanned him with my *Basic Identification* ability.

> **Level 22 Lyreboaster**
> *Race: Tiefling*

Level 22? I wasn't going to be much help here, then—not without another inspired plan, like with the Worldbender.

"Yes, I am here, my love," the straining blacksmith said. "Yes, you look pretty today, too."

Val and I moved toward the source of the glow—Crystal—but were interrupted by our new friend.

"Don't let him play lyre!" the blacksmith cried as he struggled to hold the doors closed against the other bards, who were rapping on the wood and shouting for their leader.

I whipped my head back toward the guildmaster just as he strummed his instrument for the first time. With these initial notes, the lyre began to glow a soft yellow that overlapped with Crystal's pink. I didn't know quite what type of music was coming, but I sure as hells didn't want to find out.

I charged at the guildmaster, *slicing* forward with my blade. The man instinctively recoiled, shielding his body from the attack. But, of course, I wasn't aiming for his body—I already knew that I wasn't going to do much damage to *him*. Instead, my blade ripped through the lyre strings, eliciting flat twangs, and ruining both instrument and spell.

The bard's eyes widened with fury. "You . . . This was a gift! From a princess of the Goldmarch, no less! You would dare—"

"Oh yes," Val said, "we'd dare." She strode closer to their opponent with an arm held high, magicking plant roots that burst forth from amongst the floorboards, wrapping themselves around the guildmaster.

The man with the broken lyre kicked at the roots, wrestling with them as the tendrils twisted and turned, doing their best to avoid his blows—almost as if they were sentient.

I seized the opportunity; I might not be able to defeat a man of his level under normal circumstances, but right now, he was distracted. Maybe even a level 5 could overcome a level 22 in situations like this. Pressing forward once more, I held my cooking knife to the man's throat.

The guildmaster was distracted long enough for Val's summoned tendrils to get purchase, binding him to his current position.

At my rear, the blacksmith grunted; the pushing on the door was becoming too great for even him to bear. As the geode on the guildmaster's desk glowed brighter, the blacksmith turned his attention to it. "I am busy, my love," he said. "Please don't distract with talk of my bottom."

Val opened her mouth to speak, then apparently thought better about asking the obvious question there. "Any thoughts on . . ." She gestured to the doorway.

"Surrender," I replied.

"Surrender? I'm not bloody—"

"Not us! *Him!*" I locked eyes with the guildmaster. "You call your people off and I won't *slice* you." I could only hope he hadn't had a moment to *identify* me—that would affect how intimidating I came across . . .

"With that thing?" the guildmaster responded, his bright red eyes looking skeptically at the cooking knife. "I'm not sure a blade as blunt as that would even be able to slice through—"

"I assure you," I replied, "it'll kill you. It just might take longer in doing so."

The guildmaster looked back at me, gulped, and then slowly raised his hands in surrender.

Level 22 Lyreboaster defeated!

Knifework: +1,600XP
Knifework increased to Level 9!
Knifework increased to Level 10!
Base Points gained: +2 DEX, +2 STR, +4 Free Points (VIT/DEX/STR)

Not bad—1,600XP for just holding a knife to a man's throat. I supposed that the high-level differential had a lot to do with that, minus that Val had done most of the real work. I was about to chuck the free points into Strength—no time like the present, right?—when I noticed there were more notifications.

Ability Selection Unlocked . . .

Of course, I'd reached level 10 in the *Knifework* skill—I had a new ability choice. That would need some deliberation time, however, so I minimized the notifications until later.

"Tell them," the blacksmith said, straining, "tell them: leave us alone."

The guildmaster pursed his lips, but ultimately relented. "Bards . . . if you will please step away. I have this situation fully under control."

The bashing at the door stopped abruptly, and I heard murmuring from those outside as they discussed what to do. In the end, it seemed, they decided to follow orders.

"So . . . what can I do for you lovely ladies and gentleman?" the guildmaster asked. "I assume it is money you are after? I'm afraid I must inform you—the Bard's College revenue fund is unfortunately in a safe that requires two senior spell-casting members to open. You would need—"

"We here for her," the blacksmith said, pointing to the geode sitting atop the guildmaster's desk. She glowed more brightly when the orc's attention was fixed on her.

"Is that . . . all?" the guildmaster asked. "You mounted a rescue for . . . a rock?"

"*Geode*," the blacksmith grunted.

"My apologies, good sir—for a geode. If it was stolen from you, then of course you may regain possession of it, but—"

"Her," the blacksmith grumbled, "not *it*." Val gestured for him to keep quiet.

"But how do you intend to deal with the crowd amassed outside the door? And how might you explain this to the local guards? I know who *you* are, at least, Pieter."

The blacksmith—Pieter, apparently, considering we'd never bothered to ask his name; not that he had ours, either—shrugged. "One thing at one time," he said.

The guildmaster smiled, then gestured to the roots at his feet. "Perhaps, then, you will allow me to retain a semblance of respectability. And, in return, I ensure you leave these premises unharmed?"

Val narrowed her eyes. ". . . Sure? What did you have in mind?"

CHAPTER FIFTEEN

A Different Class

The guildmaster's lyre-spun spell sent me, Val, and the geode-clutching blacksmith flying from the man's personal quarters, tumbling across the tiled stone of the courtyard.

"Ow . . ." I grumbled—this both sincere and part of the plan.

"Do you see what happens when you mess with the Bard's College of the Eastern Tundras?" he bellowed, resulting in a round of applause from the other members of the college.

This was our cue to run away—before the other bards could realize that maybe they should restrain attempted burglars until the guards could arrive. Val led our motley trio—or quartet, when including Crystal—out of the compound, and we ran down the streets of Murderpost until satisfied that we'd escaped the college students.

"You're right," I said through gasps for breath. "Bards *do* suck."

"Pieter does not lie," the blacksmith said.

"Nobody should be *that* well-groomed," Val agreed.

Val and I saw the blacksmith and his igneous lover back to his store, and after the burly orc had lovingly placed Crystal on "her spot"—a task that involved a surprising amount of kissing—we finally pressed the matter of the deal.

"Out with it, Pieter," Val said. "Where's that customer of yours got to?"

The blacksmith sighed. "His name Lev. He my cousin's mother's aunt's roommate's soon-to-be-ex-fiance's godson. But we not that close."

"Where, Pieter? Where's he gone?"

"You find him in Carn. He has family there."

Finally, Val and I could relax. "Thank you, Pieter," I said. "I hope you and Crystal have many happy decades together."

"We will," Pieter replied, and then turned to Crystal as she glowed brighter. "Crystal say thank you as well. And also you have lovely bum. They her words, not mine."

"I . . ." I started, and a nudge from Val interrupted me from my instinctive response. "Thank you, Crystal."

We said our final goodbyes to our new friend and made our way back to the southern gate. From there, it was a good two or three days' travel until Carn, and neither of us wanted to wait around any longer—it wouldn't do to faff about and miss our chance at tracking this Player's assistant down.

So we headed out back into the countryside in good spirits, Val nattering on about a book she read a few years ago—something about Crystal reminded her of it—while I shifted my attention to the notifications from the guildmaster fight.

Ability Selection Unlocked
Select an ability from the list below:

Option 1: Slice II (Knifework)—*Upgrade to Slice.* Slice the enemy for physical damage +20 percent worth weapon's base damage and additional damage scaling on [STR].

Snore. Upgrades of abilities were never the most fun option, but I forced myself to consider it, nonetheless. After all, often upgrades to core abilities actually made them more viable long-term; that had been pivotal to my success in my past life. I wouldn't have made it as far as I had without a few such upgrades. Still, I could at least review the rest of my options first.

Option 2: Execution (Knifework)—Attack a target while undetected for +100 percent damage.

So I was still eligible to unlock *Execution*, but I wasn't so high a level yet that it skipped to the next upgrade. If I'd been able to jump straight to *Execution II*—whatever that might have entailed—I might have been more likely to go for it. As it stood, though, I ruled this one out.

Hidden condition met! Alternative ability choice unlocked.
Option 3: Closed Reach (Knifework) [Requires: Worldbender class defeated or Alteration studies]—Bend reality to narrow the gap between blade and target by up to 8 inches. Has mana cost.

My heat skipped a beat; that was a magick ability. Never had I thought that this might be an option, that *Knifework*, under the right conditions, might veer off into magick opportunities. Maybe that encounter with the Worldbender hadn't been such a pain after all, if it started to open a route into magick skills . . .

I turned to Val. "Can I ask you something?"

The sorcerer shrugged. "Sure."

"How do you unlock a magick skill?"

Val came to an abrupt halt, then turned and narrowed her eyes. "Did you unlock something, Styk?"

". . . Maybe."

The sorcerer raised her eyebrow expectantly.

"Defeating the cultist, back in The Hound and Hound, it's gotten me a hidden ability choice. And I was wondering—"

"If using that ability would unlock the associated magick type?"

"Exactly."

Val shrugged. "I guess." With that, she continued walking.

"You don't sound keen. Surely having some magick up my sleeve is better than if I just stick to the *Knifework*? Wasn't the whole benefit of this do-over to, you know, actually do things differently?"

"And *worldbending* is a perfectly acceptable type of magick. If you want it, get it."

"But you'd advise against it?"

Val shrugged. "I didn't say that."

I raised an eyebrow, but kept my mouth shut; something about this line of questioning was getting on Val's nerves. It wasn't like I knew the woman well, I supposed—perhaps she had a history with Worldbenders. Either way, I figured I liked the sound of having a magick skill.

Ability Unlocked: Closed Reach
Closed Reach (Knifework): Bend reality to narrow the gap between blade and target by up to 8 inches. Has mana cost.

Class evolved!
Level 5 Novice Bladespinner
Race: Human

There it was; not a magick ability in and of itself, but well on the way to unlocking me a magick skill tree. All I needed to do was find a suitable way to use it.

We continued our journey west in silence for a time, me not wanting to risk getting on my new acquaintance's nerves any more than I already had, and Val apparently not wanting to share exactly what it was that she didn't like about my new route of progression. After a time, she looked at me, the intensity in her gaze now faded some, compared to earlier.

"You took it, then?" she asked.

"How'd you know?"

"New class."

"Ah, right, yeah," I said. "Far better than *peasant*, isn't it?"

Val cracked a small smile. "It still has *novice* in it; I wouldn't get too excited."

I returned the smile, and we continued our long walk to Carn in silence once more. Val surprised me by saying nothing to ruin this moment of quiet—silence wasn't exactly a core tenet of her personality, it had seemed to me—and it was me, in the end, who shattered the silence.

"Val . . ." I started, already chickening out of this line of questioning.

". . . yeah?" she responded.

"You don't have a problem with me picking up *Worldbending* at some point, do you?"

Val sighed. "No, I suppose I don't. It's your progression, and you've got to make the choices that suit you best. And *Worldbending* combined with *Knifework*? I can see some interesting combinations there already. It's just . . . not all of us had the freedom to choose, like you."

"You wouldn't have chosen *Sorcery*? You were forced into it?"

To this, Val gave no reply, and I knew better than to push the matter further.

The sun set on our first day of travel, yet Val and I pushed on into the night; there was no knowing just how long our target was going to be in Carn. Any casual conversation had gradually faded away as we'd grown more and more tired, until—as was the case now—we trudged on in silence.

As we grew closer to the northern coast of the Iron Sea, the tree cover grew thinner and further between, and instead this fertile lowland was used for agricultural purposes. Hedgerows and low stone walls marked the edge of one farmer's land and the start of another, but certainly these weren't stopping anyone getting onto the land, considering I could just . . . step over them.

In my tiredness-induced haze, I found my footsteps growing hypnotizing. *Crunch, crunch, crunch, crunch.* Those were mine. *Tap, tap, tap.* Those were Val, spritely and small as she was. *Crunch, tap, crunch, tap, crunch, tap, thud, crunch—*

I stopped.

Thud, thud, thud-thud-thud.

Nope, I didn't know whose footsteps *those* were. I turned to the source of the noise, saw a man charging at me, yelped, and then stumbled backward over a low hedge.

It wasn't, perhaps, my finest moment.

But quickly I gathered myself, springing back to my feet just in time to see Val cast a spell that flicked loose gravel into the face of our would-be attacker.

The dual-knife-wielding man dropped one of his blades to paw at his eyes, doing his best to wipe the small stones from them and regain his vision.

I took advantage of the distraction to press forward, reaching my knife out and *slicing* forward with it, over the hedge, causing my stamina bar to drain ever so slightly. At my current distance, though, I missed. My initial instinct was to leap over the hedge, but I caught myself; what was this if not the perfect opportunity to try out my new *Closed Reach* ability?

I prepared myself to *slice* again, this time combining it with the activation of my *Closed Reach* skill. This time, as I struck, the world seemed to fold back on itself, bringing my target in range of the knife—or my knife in range of the target, perhaps? This time, it wasn't just my stamina bar that drained some, but my mana bar, too—the latter nearly depleting from just this one move. But that was just from not having invested in Intelligence, I supposed.

My wrist jolted as my knife made contact with the bandit's shoulder, and in my surprise that this had worked, I accidentally lost my grasp on it.

The bandit looked at me, then down to the knife wedged in his shoulder, then back at me again. ". . . Ow," he said, then he punched me in the nose.

I stumbled backward, forsaking the retrieval of my Basic Cooking Knife to clutch at my nose. A strange red liquid seemed to be flowing from my wound, and I couldn't seem to do much about it, considering that it was flowing between my fingers.

Ah yes. Blood. I remembered blood.

I grabbed a cloth from my backpack, clutching it to my nose, and then turned to charge at the bandit once more. While Val distracted the man with root-binding magicks—this, I was starting to understand, was a favored strategy of hers—I leaped over the hedgerow somehow even less gracefully than when I had fallen over it, then grabbed at the knife once more. No *Closed Reach* was required, this time—it had already found its target, now it just needed . . . some twisting.

The bandit roared with pain as the twisted knife ripped open the wound.

"Last chance to run," Val said, raising her hands in the beginnings of another spell.

She wasn't even done speaking when the bandit turned on the spot and bolted away.

"My knife!" I called after him.

In the distance, I saw the fleeing man rip the knife from his shoulder, throwing it to the ground.

"Nice," I said.

"Not a bad move," Val added, and I took this as her coming to terms with my new magick leanings. Speaking of—I had notifications to investigate.

> *Petty crook defeated!*

Wow—that was a terrible class. At least mine sounded cool. I brought up the rest of the notifications.

> **Knifework**: +800XP
> *Worldbending unlocked!*

"Got it," I said to myself. There it was; my first ever magick skill. Not level 1 yet, and therefore not even a basic ability attached to it, but . . . I had it. It was there. "I'm gonna need to start putting some points into Intelligence if I—"

Blood pouring from my nose muffled the latter half of my sentence.

"Ah right," I blubbered, turning to Val. "Forgot about that. Any chance you could heal this?"

Val stepped closer, gesturing for me to remove the cloth from my nose so she could take a better look. When I did so, she grimaced.

"That bad? I hope it hasn't ruined any of my good looks."

"That's a very vain thing to say."

"Yet I don't hear you arguing it."

Val leaned in closer to my nose. "Yeah, that's broken. A cut like before, sure— I could fix that. But I'm not advanced enough to fix a broken bone, like this."

I pouted. "What's the point in having *Healing* as a skill if you're not going to—"

"It's literally just for hangovers. We used to have a woman called Tokas, back in our old party. A very talented healer, among other things. She would've been able to sort it out, but . . ." Val trailed off.

"But?"

Val shrugged. "But the days of that party are behind me, I suppose. Look, I have some spare coin. We'll stop in at the next village, get their local healer to give fixing it a go."

"You think they'll have experience with broken noses?"

"Out here?" Val replied. "In the middle of nowhere? All there is to do is get into bar fights. I'm pretty sure a broken nose is the *only* thing they'll know how to fix."

With that, we continued onward, and even a broken nose couldn't ruin my good mood.

CHAPTER SIXTEEN

Waving Knives Around Menacingly

It was another two days before the gates of Carn rose before us—magnificent things made from the local ruby pines that these parts were so known for. At least, they were known for them before a wildfire had wiped most of them out nearly a decade ago. That didn't stop them from flying a red flag with a tree emblazoned upon it as their city's sigil, though.

Val and I passed through the gates between two guards who were very clearly hungover, judging by their pallid skin and droopy eyes, and I wondered if we might have time to head to a local inn before we tracked down our orc "friend." We wouldn't, of course—only the gods knew if he was even still here—but that didn't stop me licking my lips in anticipation of good ale.

"Thirsty?" Val asked me, eyebrow raised.

I shrugged. "If our man's not here, let's get us a drink, shall we?"

"You don't need to convince *me*."

We proceeded on down the narrow streets of this harbor town, the distinct smell of fish filling my nostrils, and—should my mouth open—making me taste it on my tongue, too. Not what you want, really. Trying not to think about the smell, I gestured toward the first tavern I saw. "Shall we ask around in there?"

Val, who I noticed was also wrinkling her nose, responded with a thumbs-up.

We stepped inside, finding it quite busy at this late hour, and we squeezed through the crowd for the bar.

"You start asking around, I'll get us a drink in?"

I nodded my agreement, and turned to the man next to me, figuring that was as good a place as any to start.

"Scuse me," I said, "sorry to interrupt. Was just wondering if you'd seen an orc named Lev pass through here? Big guy, got a battle-axe. Looks the sort to slaughter an entire town?"

The man gestured over his shoulder with his thumb, pointing at an orc just at the other end of the bar. "That him?"

I sighed; like it was gonna be that easy, like we were gonna find Lev in the very first place we—

My heart skipped a beat. Yep. That was him.

". . . Yes," I replied, and then instinctively ducked behind the counter.

"What are you *doing*?" Val hissed down at me. "I'm not gonna take you to places like these if you're going to act this way."

"He's here," I whispered.

"What?"

"He's *here*," I said again, nodding in the direction of the Player's orcish accomplice.

Val glanced at Lev, widened her eyes, and then ducked down with me. "You know," she said. "I'm not sure crouching down in the middle of a tavern is the best way to *avoid* notice."

"Good point," I said, and we both rose once more.

When our pints were in front of us, and the innkeeper paid, Val and I snuck off to some distant corner of the bar, from where we could watch Lev unnoticed.

"Quite good luck, getting an answer from the first person you meet. Is that something to do with your artifact?"

"Good luck?" I responded. "He almost saw us! And now we only get to have one pint. What sort of 'good luck' is that?"

Val shrugged, then gulped down some of her beer. "Fair point."

We fixed our attention back on the orc we were here to hunt down, and I *identified* him.

Identification: +500XP
Identification increased to Level 5!
Base Points Gained: +1 WIS, +1 INT, +1 Free Point (WIS/INT)

I quickly added the free point to Intelligence—on the basis that I was going down the magick route, and would need all the associated mana I could get—and minimized the notifications.

Level 27 Barbarian
Race: Orc

"How come I can see his class and not yours?" I asked. "You're the same level."

"Shh," Val said, and directed my attention back to Lev with a nod. "Look."

Nothing, to my eye, had changed. Lev was still there with his drinking companion, though they'd grown a little closer over the past few minutes.

"Yeah? What?"

"Look at them," she said. "He's not here with a mate, he's on a date."

"And so I repeat: yeah?"

Val rolled her eyes at me. "What happens after a date? If it goes well, you go back to their place. And you might . . ."

"Get a little bit distracted," I finished for her. "Right. Got it. So if they were leaving together right now, we should probably follow them, yeah?"

Val blinked, then registered the question and turned back to Lev's empty bar stool.

We loitered in the shadows across the street from Lev's date's place. It was a detached house with a rooftop balcony that surely looked over most of the town; Lev didn't have half-bad taste in men, apparently. Even better, it had a tavern across the road, from which Val had bought us a couple of top-up pints.

I tried a sip. "Elven pale ale?" I asked. "Really?"

Val shrugged. "Craft beer place. You know they love those elven hops."

I frowned, but sipped at the top of the flat beer, nonetheless.

"So, is there a plan?" Val asked between gulps of beer. I suspected she enjoyed EPA more than she was letting on.

"Why do I have to come up with the plan?"

"I got the beer; you do the planning. I thought that was . . . I thought that was what we decided, wasn't it?"

"*You* decided that maybe. And then didn't tell me that you had. But, as it happens, I reckon I do have a plan, yeah." I nodded to the rooftop balcony, on which Lev and his date were sipping at wine.

"Go on, then."

I pointed to the side of the house—a tall, flat wall, featureless but for a window on the first floor. "There," I said.

"Your plan is to scale an unclimbable wall?"

"No, my plan is to climb the vines on it."

Val raised an eyebrow, nodding to my beer. "Is that ale stronger than I thought? There aren't any vines on it."

"Well, I figured that was where you come in. You can summon them from the earth, right? You have the ability? How quickly could you do it?"

Val turned back to the house across the street and tilted her head from side to side. "Twenty seconds, maybe?"

I nodded. "Good. I reckon that'll be quick enough. Once we have the vines, we climb, then we have the element of surprise."

"And you think the 'element of surprise' will be enough, do you? Lev's a barbarian—they do serious damage. And it isn't like either of us are built to take a hit. What's your health bar cap out at, at the mo?"

"Don't ask questions you don't want to know the answer to," I replied. "Fine. If that plan isn't enough, then we wait, we hang from the balcony until the date progresses to a point where they're . . . distracted. And *then* we jump in, make them surrender before they even have a chance to deal any damage." I paused. "How's that?"

Val shrugged, gulped down nearly a full pint of ale, then rose. "Good enough for me," she said.

I had barely enough time to slurp down half the pint before Val arrived at the side of our target's building, beginning her—suspiciously unmarked by light— magicks and causing vines to shoot forth from the ground. I abandoned what was left of my beer to hurry across the street.

"Val," I said, "are you sure that—"

"It was your plan!" she whispered back.

I watched as the vines grew taller, licking at the white wall and winding their way ever closer to the top. They strengthened as they grew, turning from tiny sprouts to a plant that might have been there for years, all in a matter of seconds.

"Right," Val said, and stepped forward to test the vines with her hand. "Seems strong enough." She pushed me aside. "Ladies first."

We climbed slowly and deliberately, testing the rustle of the vines before shifting our weight from foothold to foothold and handhold to handhold. But in no time, we were at the top of the vines and shifting to hold on to the rim of the balcony instead.

"Is he distracted?" Val whispered.

I pulled myself up ever so slowly—this was far harder than it looked, though I supposed I was yet to invest all that much into Strength. Peeping over the rim of the balcony, I looked on at the orc as he held his date in his arms, their faces growing closer and closer together.

I sank back down. "They're making googly eyes. Is that good enough?"

"It's good enough for me."

"OK," I said. "On three. One . . ."

Val heaved herself over the edge of the balcony, and I was forced to follow suit. We charged across the broad rooftop balcony, me raising my knives, Val raising her hands, and the two men blinked at us.

"What in gods' names is . . ." Lev started, his eyes widening, and then he pushed his date away from him and to the floor, in an apparent attempt to save him. The date stumbled toward the floor, steadying himself against the side of the balcony, and began putting as much space between himself and the rest of us as possible.

While Val concentrated on Lev, brushing dust up into his eyes and beginning to bind him, I focused my attention on the other man. I held my knives high, ready to slash. It wasn't that I wanted to hurt him—as far as we knew, he was an innocent in all of this—so much as . . . well, I couldn't leave him hanging about here, could I? Not when we had some interrogating of Lev to do.

As I cornered the wide-eyed, cowering man, it occurred to me that there might be another way to handle this.

"Ahh!" I tried, raising my hands in the air, one of them wrapped around the cooking knife. "Scary!" OK, maybe not my best effort at being intimidating, but I was thinking on my feet.

The man screamed.

I started, not quite realizing that what I'd been up to had actually, you know, *worked*, but then pressed the matter further. "Gonna . . . gonna *slice* you!" I said. I waved the knife a bit for good measure.

Lev's date turned and fled, and with that, I was free to help Val deal with an orc many times my level.

I knew my *Stealth* was still a low level, but I was counting on Val occupying Lev's attention enough that it wouldn't matter as I crouched and began to sneak up on him. I hopped back over the balcony, hands on its rim, and slowly edged along it—all the while trying not to think about the long drop below me and the lack of vines, this side, to catch a hold on.

On the other side, Lev struggled against vines growing around his legs, but he seemed to be able to kick them away before they could get a proper purchase; he was strong enough that he could break them in their earlier stages.

And in that moment, as I edged around the balcony behind him, I prepared myself to strike.

CHAPTER SEVENTEEN

Running Away Menacingly

I heaved myself over the side of the balcony, leaping behind the enemy orc, then jumped once more to put my drawn blade in reach of Lev's neck. It worked, for a moment.

Distracted by Val, the orc hadn't noticed me get so close to him, and only really started paying attention to me once I had metal pressed to his flesh. Unfortunately, Lev reacted to this in a way that nobody before had reacted: he grabbed my knife arm, crouched, and wrenched me over the top of him.

I flew through the air and crashed into Val, who—judging by the noises she made as a result—was not impressed. As we pulled ourselves up off the floor, Lev growling at us, Val turned to me.

"Is that all you do? Put knives to people's necks?"

"And claim to be scary," I added.

"Yes, put knives to people's necks and claim to be scary," Val clarified. "Is that all you do?"

"I'm working on it, aren't I?"

Lev took a step forward; the fight was back on.

Val focused once more, beginning her winding roots again, but still the orc was too strong, able to break free of them before they could grow firm. While it slowed him down, it was only a matter of time before we were in arm's reach. I could only thank the gods that he didn't bring his battle-axe on dates—then we'd be in *real* trouble.

"Val?" I asked, starting to step backward. "You got any idea what—"

"You think you can occupy him for a minute? By yourself?"

I blinked. "What? No! I'm level five, Val, and he's level—"

Val answered by bolting for the balcony door, disappearing through it.

Both Lev and I looked to the door, and then back to one another.

". . . Hi?" I tried.

"You die now," came the response.

I nodded. "Right," I said, and then I, too, ran for the door.

I crashed through the wooden door, not bothering to twist the knob before I pushed it, causing it to crack from its frame before slamming into the wall beside it. Inside, I found myself in a bar area, complete with cocktail trolley, kitchen island, and a substantial collection of bottles.

A bar for the rooftop balcony? Fancy.

I charged onward, hearing the orc's heavy footsteps coming up rapidly behind me, and as I passed the cocktail trolley, I pushed it into Lev's way. From the sounds of the crash I heard a second after, he hadn't had too much of a problem brushing it out of the way.

So I tried next grabbing a couple of glass bottles from the counter as I charged past them, spinning on the spot to lob one, then the other, toward Lev's head. I stayed facing him just long enough to see that he easily deflected the first lobbed bottle, but—not expecting a second—the other one caught him in the face. It smashed, and a couple of large chunks were buried in his skin.

But it wasn't enough to stop him, only enough to make him hunt me more aggressively. I plowed on, toward the rear of the building, and spotted a stairwell. I leaped down it in one stride. "Ow! My ankles!" I said aloud, then immediately regretted saying this aloud.

I pulled myself up to my feet, doing my best to ignore the self-inflicted fall damage, and charged down the short landing I found myself in, for the next set of stairs. On my way, I grabbed a couple of picture frames from the wall—one of an elderly woman, maybe the owner's grandmother, and another of a man with the words *Rest In Peace* engraved at the bottom.

I threw them both at Lev.

Honestly, these picture frames—even with the glass panes—did about as much good as the bottles. Maybe less. There was a reason you threw bottles in bar fights, and not picture frames, I supposed. Something to do with the aerodynamics.

Reaching the next stairwell, very conscious that Lev had grown closer still, I hopped down it, this time taking the stairs three at a time and doing no damage to my ankles. As I plowed downward, I thought desperately about my—admittedly rather limited—list of abilities. Surely there was something, even at this low level, which could get me an advantage if used creatively? If not, then Val and I were going to have a big problem when it came to facing down the Player. If indeed I lived to get that far.

At the bottom of the staircase, now on the ground floor, I swung around the corner and . . . walked straight into the homeowner. Lev's date, now standing tall and confident, glared down at me.

"You're back, huh?" I asked. "What's changed?"

As Lev stormed down the stairs behind me, the date grabbed me by the throat and pressed me against the wall. I wrenched at his hand, trying to free myself, my legs dangling below me.

"You die now," the orc said again. Lev stepped closer, grabbing me by my knife arm, and nodding for his date to release me; he wanted to deal with me all by himself, it seemed.

"I'd really rather not!" I tried.

"No choice." Lev blinked at me. "Level *five*? You are this old and level five?" His eyes widened. "You are level five and think can defeat *me*?"

The orc's date ambled around behind him, and . . . I noticed something. The date was smirking. So quick a change in demeanor was it, and now he was smirking?

"Look, it wasn't my idea, alright?" I said. "The sorcerer I was with, it was her idea."

"You think steal from me?"

"No!"

The orc snarled. "So just kill me, then?"

"No!" I said again. "I mean . . ."

"So what want from me?"

I nodded to the orc's firm grasp around the wrist of my knife hand. "Maybe you can let me go, and then we'll talk about this?"

"No."

"At least loosen your grip? That hurts a little."

"No," the orc said again. "Tell me. What want from me?"

The smirking date stretched his neck by tilting his head side to side, and then he seemed to warm up his arms by rolling his shoulders and flexing his digits. Was this man about to kill me himself? Or . . .

And then I remembered something Val had told me a few days back. Something that she'd tried not to make a big deal of, and in doing so had made a very big deal of it indeed. She wasn't a human, or at least, wasn't *all* human.

She was part changeling.

The date's skin rippled as it changed, his body shrinking both in height and breadth. The rippling form was mirage-like; hard to look at, because whatever you thought was there, wasn't. Or at least, it wasn't for very long.

Sensing that something was wrong, Lev craned his head over his shoulder to follow my line of sight. In that moment, Val launched herself into a punch—not something I'd seen her do before. Her clenched fist caught Lev squarely in the temple, with enough force behind it that it would have knocked out any lower-leveled person.

It was just a shame that Lev *wasn't* low in level.

While the blow didn't knock him out, it did stagger him, and his grasp on my wrist loosened. I took advantage of the distraction to push against him, forcing the tip of my knife toward his throat. I made it close—oh so close—before the orc realized what I was doing.

"No, you don't," he said.

"Yes, I do," I corrected him, activating my *Closed Reach* ability.

The world bent, and the tip of my knife closed on his throat. I even overshot it a little, piercing the orc's flesh and causing a small trickle of blood to begin flowing down his neck. Val's vines—slow to form in an interior setting—wrapped themselves around the orc's legs, holding him firmly, and finally . . .

Lev raised his hands in surrender.

Level 27 Barbarian defeated!

Knifework: +2,500XP
Knifework increased to Level 11!
Knifework increased to Level 12!
Base Points gained: +2 DEX, +2 STR, +4 Free Points (VIT/DEX/STR)
Stealth: +100XP
Worldbending: +200XP
Worldbending increased to Level 1!
Base Points Gained: +2 INT, +2 Free Points (INT/WIS/CHA)
Ability Unlocked: Local Portal

"Knives on throats," I said to the orc in front of me. "It always works."

CHAPTER EIGHTEEN

There's Something about That Magical Artifact

"Alright, you be bad guard, I'll be good guard," Val whispered, now that Lev was safely bound by roots and vines in the other room, with no hope of escape.

"What if I don't wanna be bad guard?" I asked.

"Fine, you be good guard. I'm easy."

"Well, I didn't say—"

Val glared at me, and I stopped complaining. "You ready?"

I nodded and led us back into the room to begin the interrogation. "Alright," I said, taking first crack at the orc. "I think we can work all this out so that nobody needs to get hurt. But my friend, here, she's going to want some answers to some questions if she's—"

"You not want answers?" Lev asked me.

"Well, yes, I want them, too, but I'm not—"

"Then why try to say this her fault?"

"I—" I sighed, turning to Val. "You want to have a go at this?"

Val stormed up to Lev and slapped him across the face. Hard. "Alright, big guy. Time to start telling us what you know."

"Or what?" the orc spat.

"Or we find out just how far up your insides I can get my vines to grow."

Lev's eyes widened. ". . . OK. This good reason. What is it you want know?"

I pulled the Sisyphus Artifact from my jacket pocket, placing it upon a table in front of the orc. If his eyes were wide before, they were now bulging, and Val's were doing much the same.

"Styk, I didn't . . ." She trailed off, shaking her head.

"Why did your boss want this so badly?"

"You have . . ." Lev started. "You are . . . I *know* you. You are knife man. We . . . kill you. So, how is—"

Val held her index finger up to me. "Don't answer that." Then to Lev, she said, "We're the ones asking the questions here."

"It is you. *You* used this last charge. But . . . how? Is not possible."

"What did the Player want it for?" I asked, speaking over the orc.

"Is not obvious? Immortality! Do we not all want this?"

Val glanced to me.

"No," I said.

"No?" Val asked.

"No, there's got to be more to it than that. You killed dozens."

"Hundreds," Lev spat.

"You killed hundreds to get this artifact. There's got to be more to it than immortality. The Players are gods! What death do they have to fear?"

Lev shrugged as best he could within his tight bindings. "He not tell me this. But I have suspicions. The Ascended World not what it was once. The Ascended World . . . destroyed. I think Players have no home. I think heaven is gone."

Val shot me another glance, her brow furrowed surely as much as mine was; none of this made any sense, after all. We all knew the Players, the descendants of the great Architects themselves, only blessed us with their presence when they left their immortal plane. But this immortal plane . . . surely it was untouchable? Surely nothing could destroy the land of the gods.

I nodded toward the back room. "A moment," I said. When we were out of earshot, I semiwhispered to Val, "Are you buying any of this?"

"It'd be a bloody weird lie, wouldn't it?"

"It'd be a bloody weird truth too, though."

Val shrugged. "Fair point." She cast her head back into the other room to check on our prisoner. Apparently he was still bound, because she just waved smugly to him before shifting her attention back to me. "Let's follow the logic through; what do we know?"

"We know the Player wanted the Sisyphus Artifact."

"And we know it has the power to bring its owner back to life."

"And a boost to experience points, don't forget," I added.

"But only to those who die, right? And why would a Player need the boost? They're already stronger than most. So I think . . ."

I could see where she was going with this. "You don't think it's the experience point boost."

"I don't."

"But if it's the other thing—if it's the respawn that the Player wanted—then . . .

why? They're strong, sure, and I suppose they could die despite that, but could it really be that simple?"

Val weighed the thought, tilting her head side to side. She opened her mouth to speak, then seemed to think better of it.

"No," I encouraged her. "Go on. What are you thinking?"

"Maybe the gods are as mortal as the rest of us."

I raised an eyebrow. "You know to say such a thing is heresy, in pretty much every land in Alterra."

"The funny thing about ideas explicitly deemed heretical?" she responded. "They're quite often true."

I drew in a deep breath. "So . . . no grand plan, then? No monstrous plan on the part of the big bad? Just . . . a want to go on living?"

"Sometimes the simplest motivations are the best."

"The Player has gotta be paranoid if he's already thinking about his death."

Val shrugged. "Some people just don't deal well with their mortality."

"Alright," I said. "Fine. What's next, then? We gotta apply the screws to Lev, try and find out the Player's weaknesses, right?"

Val's face lit up, and she punched me playfully on the arm. "See, I knew you'd get it! You're taking to this like you were—"

A suspicious murmuring noise in the other room caused the sorcerer to come to an abrupt halt. We looked at one another, narrowed our eyes, and then poked our heads back into the other room.

Lev's date stood at his side, frozen to the spot as though not moving would stop us from seeing him, his hands around a knife.

"Hurry!" the orc cried, shaking against his bindings. "Cut now! Cut now!"

The date began cutting frantically, and Val and I both charged across the room.

"Arm!" Lev shouted, still struggling against the vines.

"No!" Val and I cried out simultaneously, reaching toward him.

But we were too late; the date sliced through the roots binding the orc's left hand, and Lev shoved his hand into his pocket, pulling forth a small purple gemstone. He reached out and smashed it against the wall behind him, and for a moment, the wall . . . disappeared. But it wasn't the exteriors of Carn looming behind him, so much as the grand, high-walled architecture of somewhere I'd never been before.

But Val had. "Auricia," she breathed.

Lev fell through the portal, still bound, and it closed behind him just in time to have Val collide with the wall.

"Hera's blade," Val spat, having bounced off the solid wall and fallen to the ground.

My head, and Val's, turned to the other man, who took a step backward and raised his hands in the air. "Now, wait a minute . . ." he said, and then before either of us could say a word to him, he turned and bolted away once more.

I held out a hand to help Val up from the floor. "Auricia?" I asked. "The capital of the Goldmarch?"

Val nodded. "It's where the Player is, I'd guess. Figure Lev's off reporting what just happened."

"That's . . . how can they be there already?"

The sorcerer screwed up her face. "I mean . . . even if you hadn't just witnessed portal magick, there are such things as boats, you know."

I shrugged; fair enough, it was a dumb question.

Val gestured to the artifact I'd left on the table. "Why do you still have this, anyway?"

"Kept me alive, didn't it? Thought it'd be a good keepsake."

The sorcerer sighed. "It makes you a target, Styk. You realize that, right? Whatever the deal is with that artifact, it's gonna come back to bite you. Or do you not think the Player is arming himself right now to come after you?"

"It's empty, though. He knows that. What could he—"

"Sure, it's empty. But now he knows *you* have the last charge in you. Didn't you get the impression that he'd wanna know how that happened?"

I gulped. "Well, we handled Lev once. I'm sure we can—"

"It won't just be Lev this time, Styk." Val's eyes were wide, fearful; it wasn't often I saw her like this, and it made me take notice. "He's gonna come back with the Player at his side. Maybe the tiefling, too. You and me . . . we can't handle that, even with me being as good as I am."

The house seemed suddenly eerily quiet.

"What'll we do?" I finally asked.

Val drew in a deep breath. "I hoped it wouldn't come to this, but . . . We're gonna need to put a team together. Specialists; people who've handled this type of thing before." She drew her hands down her face, pulling gently at her cheeks. "It's time we reunited the Hero Slayers."

Lev

Lev tumbled backward through the temporary portal, hitting the floor hard as his arms remained still loosely bound, and he was unable to reach them out and break his fall. It wasn't the soft dirt that he landed on, either, but the stones that acted as Auricia's paving.

The orc was aware of the people around him staring, but he ignored them, with the exception of a growl in their direction, which he allowed himself. The cut in the vines was enough for him, eventually, to wriggle free, and he instinctively reached for the battle-axe that he typically had strapped to his back.

But it wasn't there. He'd taken it off for his date, which meant it was . . . half a continent away.

"Hades's wrath," Lev spat. That axe had served him well, had split many skulls open in just one blow.

The orc looked around; at this distance, the portal had only been able to get him close to his destination, not perfectly on it. Such was the way of worldbending magicks—they were never perfect—especially when they'd been crammed into such a small gemstone. He knew where he was, at least, and he began his trek across one of the largest cities in all of Alterra.

Lev was pretty sure the manor Jacob had taken over had once been a brothel. There were too many cushions around for any normal household, and there was a mysterious mark on the wall of the bedroom he'd claimed as his own. The boss didn't seem to mind, though, and Lev hadn't wanted to be the person to suggest this to him; Jacob had a temper when he heard something that didn't suit him.

It was bustling with household staff when Lev arrived at the front gate. More household staff than the size of the building really warranted, if Lev was to make a guess—though it wasn't like he came from this sort of background. Cooks, maids, servants of all shapes and sizes hurried to see to Jacob and the party's every need, having been sent here by the queen. Whatever the arrangement was that Jacob had with the monarch seemed to have her greatly indebted to him. Lev would have asked but, again, he feared the pyroknight's temper.

Lev crossed the garden at the same pace at which he'd plowed through the city, never slowing. He stormed in the front door, slamming it aside, and causing a nervous young dwarven maid to drop a silver platter in shock. She looked up at him fearfully, with large brown eyes, and hurried about clearing up her mess. These servants knew fear.

As Lev crossed the atrium, a satyr chef with noticeably strong facial features approached him. This was about the only member of Jacob's new household staff who didn't fear the party—at least, not Lev or the tiefling. He held a cherry pie up in front of Lev's face.

"Lev!" he said. "You're here! And just in time to try out this new pie recipe I made." He pushed the tray in the orc's face as Lev tried to brush him aside. "Come on, Lev. I know how much you like 'em . . . Go on. Give it a go."

The satyr's incessant sales pitch finally became too much. If Lev hadn't had news for Jacob, he might have stopped to try some, but with this urgent task . . . He turned to the satyr. "No!" he shouted. "No time for delicious things now!"

The satyr cowered away, discouraged, and Lev continued up the staircase toward Jacob's bedroom. When he finally reached the door, all logic escaped him, and he slammed this door wide open, too.

Two young women gasped, pulling the bedsheets to cover their bare chests. Like Lev would be interested in something like that. Between them, Jacob—Lev's employer—scowled at him. The Player didn't seem to realize that any woman he'd "talked" into bed with him was an agent of the queen, here for purpose of espionage. But, again, Lev wasn't about to be the one to tell Jacob that—he'd seen what that pyrokinesis brand of sorcery could do.

"Didn't think I needed to tell *you* to knock, too," Jacob said. "I fired the last servant who did that, but—"

"I have news," Lev interrupted; it couldn't wait, and he trusted Jacob had the sense to understand that, rather than berating him for the interruption.

Jacob sighed. "Spit it out, then."

"Best we alone," Lev said, nodding to each of the two women, who were supposedly fearful of him, yet notably had made no attempt to leave.

Again, the Player sighed, and this time he rolled his eyes, for good measure. Lev had never expected such *human* emotions from a demigod such as this. "Fine," he said. "Ladies? Clear out. I'll finish with you later."

The two women paused, sharing a glance with one another, before eventually leaving. Lev waited for the door to shut firmly behind them before speaking.

"The Artifact came to find me," Lev said. "Along with its owner."

Jacob narrowed his eyes. "But it was expired? The last charge had been used?"

"Yes. Used on the man who hold it when we find it. The man we kill."

This revelation made the Player stand. He strode over to the window, caring not for his lack of clothing. Lev did his best to avert his eyes, but it wasn't every day you got to see a Player's—

"But that's not possible," Jacob said. "He doesn't have the bloodline."

"Respect, boss, but do we know this? Do we know he not . . ."

The Player shook his head. "He's not in the Council. If he was one of us . . ." Jacob trailed off thoughtfully, his gaze fixed on some spot outside, but not really looking at it. "No matter. What's done is done. He—"

"He come for revenge, boss."

"Who?"

"The man we kill. The man with *Legacy of Sisyphus*."

Jacob laughed out loud. He tended to do this; make something seem like some great joke. "The thief? He must be, what, level ten?"

"Five, boss." Lev paused as the Player laughed harder. "But you know what this effect does. He level five now, yes. But he won't be for long."

At this, the Player stopped laughing, his mouth warping from a smile to a snarl. "You make a fair point." He sighed. "I suppose it has been a few days since I got to kill anyone, and council work has been taking its toll . . . Maybe a quick execution will do me some good. Where was this man?"

"Carn, boss."

Jacob nodded. "Sharpen your axe. We set sail in the morning."

CHAPTER NINETEEN

The Lie of the Land

We booked rooms for the night in the tavern across the street—the one that served only craft ales, which Val *claimed* not to like, but the size of her bar tab begged to differ. Meanwhile, I'd nursed only a single stout, dwelling on the revelation that I now had a target on my head. And not just any old target—the target of a maniacal Player and his equally maniacal bodyguards.

"So," I asked a drowsy-looking Val, "these 'Hero Slayers.' Tell me about them."

She pulled her head up, furrowing her brow almost exaggeratedly. "I thought . . . You would've heard of us, no?"

". . . No."

"Are you sure?" she asked. "The Hero Slayers. We're literally famous."

"Oh, so you're famous now, are you?"

Val ignored the dig. "The Hero Slayers," she said again. "The legendary team, slayers of so-called 'heroes'—"

"Yes, I did get that bit."

"—able to stand up to any enemy that crosses their path? The powerful sorcerer, Val Vignor. Arzak Blorg, the mighty orcish warrior. The fearsome barbarian, Lore . . . I don't know his last name."

"How long were you on a team together for?"

"Shh." She continued, "The cunning ranger, Corminar—"

This name I knew. "Corminar? Not Corminar Cladenor. Hmm. Not really a *good* name, is it?"

Val's eyes popped. "What? You know *him*? Out of all of us . . . *him*? Great. I really need a PR consultant."

I shrugged. "We run in the same circles. He's not a slayer, though, or whatever you're calling yourselves."

"Not just *calling ourselves* . . ."

"He's a glorified middleman, really," I said. "Acts like a thief, but really he just uses his connections to subcontract to real—"

Val waved me down. "We can skip the boring business talk, Styk; nobody wants to hear that. Sounds like . . . you might have some idea where to find him?"

"What, did you not keep in touch after all your Player-slaying?"

"Styk . . ."

I sighed, but failed to suppress a mocking smile. "Fine. Last I heard, he was operating out of Fenrock. We get there, and I'm sure I can use my old Thieves Guild contacts to track him down."

Val slammed down the last of her pint and rose to get another.

"You sure that's a good idea?" I asked.

"Starting with him? It's as good as anyone."

"Drinking more," I clarified.

Val laughed. "I'm about to put my old team back together. Trust me, I *deserve* a drink or two."

"Ten."

"Don't drink-shame me." With that, Val staggered back over to the bar, and I turned my attention to the notifications I'd ignored earlier this evening.

From our battle with Lev, I'd racked up a decent amount of experience, even if Val had done most of the work. As a result, I'd gained another two levels in *Knifework*, put some more experience points into *Stealth*, and—best of all—leveled my *Worldbending* up to level 1. I quickly put my *Knifework* free points into Vitality—who wouldn't want more health?—then turned my attention to matters of magick.

With level 1 being the first "real" level of a skill, I'd unlocked my first *Worldbending* ability, and quite the ability it was.

> **Local Portal (Worldbending)**: Create a portal to another location within current range of sight. Uses mana/second.

My mind raced with possibilities. I could use it combined with *Stealth* to get the element of surprise on an enemy, or to bring myself closer to them with my knives. I could get us across town in a flash, or maybe even use it to steal some stuff. *Just why didn't I look into* Worldbending *in my last life?* I asked myself.

There was one major catch, however: that "Uses mana per second" part. My current mana was minimal, at 19 points. I largely had myself to blame for this one; only *Identification*, of all the skills I'd been leveling up, granted me any Intelligence, and this stat was the one directly linked to my mana reserves.

What's more . . . I hadn't exactly been speccing into it with my free points. I made a mental note to prioritize this stat in the near future, if I was going to get the most out of my new *Worldbending* skill. Speaking of . . .

Worldbending increased to Level 1!
Base Points Gained: +2 INT, +2 Free Points (INT/WIS/CHA)

I still had some free points to spend. Not second-guessing myself, I pushed those two points straight into Intelligence, bringing my mana bar up to 21 points. It was progress.

Level 5 Novice Bladespinner
Race: Human

Power Bars:
Health: 20 / 20
Mana: 21 / 21
Stamina: 22 / 22

Base Stats:
Vitality: 10
Intelligence: 11
Dexterity: 12
Strength: 21
Wisdom: 9
Charisma: 0

Looking at my stat screen, I could see I'd made huge progress during the week and a bit since I'd . . . well, died. Sure, I was still only level 5, and my Charisma was dreadful, but I had a "proper" class now, and I was growing fast. With the addition of *Worldbending*, the world was my oyster. And who needed Charisma anyway, without any social-class skills to play with?

Skills Menu:

Knifework—Level 12:
Slice
Stab
Closed Reach

Identification—Level 5:

Basic Identification

Stealth—Level 1:
Basic Stealth Attack

Worldbending—Level 1:
Local Portal

Yes, I thought to myself, *this was good*. This was progress. If I could do all that in a handful of days, then in months? In years? I could be one of the strongest men in Alterra.

I'd just need to survive that long.

There were only so many hours of travel I could manage without giving in to the urge to test my new ability.

As Val and I strolled down a particularly secluded part of the long, winding road from Carn to the Tundra capital of Fenrock, I found myself raising my hand, willing a portal to form ahead of me, and forcing every ounce of concentration into it.

Nothing happened.

". . . What're ya doing?" Val asked.

"Nothing," I replied.

"You're trying to do magick, aren't you? Trying to use that new ability of yours?"

"No. I was stretching."

Val ignored me. "You're doing it wrong."

"Yes, I got that. But unless you want to tell me how—"

The sorcerer shrugged. "Sure."

I stopped midstep. "Sure?" I asked.

"Sure. If you ask nicely."

"Val . . ."

The woman kept on moving. "Nicely," she called back over her shoulder.

I sighed. "Will you teach me how to use magick?"

"*Nicely*, I said!"

I screwed my mouth up, then stuck my tongue out at the woman's back. "Will you *please* teach me how to use magick, *please*, Miss Sorcerer Woman Ma'am. Please, please, please, pretty please with a nemberry on top."

When Val turned back to face me, her eyebrow raised, she saw that I was clasping my hands together in mock plea. "That'll do." She walked back over to where I'd stopped, and grabbed me gently by the wrist. "Alright. Technically, the hand movements aren't necessary; you can do magick without them. But most magick users find they help focus the spells, so do whatever feels instinctive with them. The bit you're missing is . . . you need to envision the spells happening. Picture it in your mind, like."

I couldn't resist raising an eyebrow. "What, it's that easy? I just picture a portal somewhere and point at it, and—" I flicked my hands toward a random point in a neighboring field, and a great purple light accompanied a portal glowing into life, just for a fraction of a second. In the distance, down the path, a matching portal opened—just where I'd imagined. A small chunk of my mana bar depleted with the use of the ability.

Worldbending: +10XP

"There you go," Val said, clapping me on the back. "So easy, an idiot could do it. Case in point, I suppose."

The purple glow of alteration magick faded in the seconds after the portal did. "You know, I been meaning to ask: how comes all your magicks don't have a glow? Every other time I've seen someone using magick, there's light coming off them. Worldbending purple, illusion red, and sorcery blue. So why aren't you lighting up with—"

"Do you want to interrogate me about the science of magick, or do you want to jump through a portal?" Val interrupted me.

"Good point."

I turned my attention back to the path ahead and focused this time on a point much closer to me. If, as the ability details explained, it cost me mana for every second I held the portal open, then I wanted to make sure I got through in time. I held this point in my mind, then I matched it with a spot on the path a good couple of dozen yards ahead. I drew in a deep breath, charged forward, and then opened the portal.

Worldbending: +40XP

I leaped through it, flying through the air, and a ripple of eerie, spine-chilling coolness washed over me.

And then I was further down the path—just like that.

I allowed the portal to close behind me and noticed that these couple of seconds alone had used up a good half of my mana reserves; holding portals open was damned *expensive*.

Turning back the way I'd come, I waved to Val. "I did it!" I cried out, forgetting myself in my excitement.

"Yes, now you're over there!" the sorcerer called back, matching my level of excitement, but hers meant sarcastically.

I resisted the urge to stick my tongue out again, then concentrated on portaling myself back to her side. This time, the *local portals* came more naturally to me, and I got them open within a couple of seconds. I took another deep breath, preparing myself for the spine-tingling coldness again, then, finally stepped through.

. . . Just as my mana reserves depleted.

Worldbending: +40XP

The portal closed behind me, very nearly catching me, and I wondered just what would have happened to me if I'd been crossing through. This question was swiftly answered when I looked down to my hand.

"Val . . ." I said, holding up my knife hand, and in it, a blade cut clean in two. "I think I'm gonna need a new weapon."

CHAPTER TWENTY

The Middleman

It was over a week later by the time we finally reached Fenrock. I'd spent a decent chunk of this time perfecting the use of my one magick ability, and I'd gotten the lead time on generating portals down to under a second—though I found that the greater the distance between the portals, the longer it took me to form them.

As enjoyable as having a magick ability was, it wasn't like it'd made the journey much quicker. Any portal-skimming—as I'd called it; Val wasn't a fan of this name—of the road was limited to my eyesight, and I'd only been able to open a couple of portals a day due to my current low Intelligence stat and associated mana reserves. As neither of us had any mana potions on us, I didn't recover my mana until I was sufficiently rested, which didn't happen until the evening. So . . . yeah. Fun to have, but not, so far, a game-changing ability.

Still, using the portals came with rewards of experience, and I'd managed to get not just my *Worldbending* skill up to level 3—and invested all possible points into Intelligence—but as a result, my overall level had increased to level 6. I was moving up in the world.

Already "moved up in the world," it had turned out, was Corminar Cladenor. My Thieves Guild contacts in Fenrock had very quickly pointed us in his direction, and they hadn't needed to talk around the point, either, because he'd gone legit.

Or, at least, Corminar had gained the *appearance* of going legit. He had an office in the commercial district at the very center of the city, in the first floor above a bakery that was selling loaves capable of making my mouth drool.

The sign on the door read: CLADENOR ACQUISITIONS. To the eyes of passersby, this wouldn't elicit even a raised eyebrow, but for those in the know, however . . .

At the doorstep, Val stopped, then sighed, seemingly bracing herself.

"Problem?" I asked.

The sorcerer tilted her head from side to side in some sort of calculation. "Me and Cor, we didn't exactly get on much."

"I thought you adventured together?"

"I adventured with the rest of them; he just happened to be there. Honestly, it would've been better if we'd found any of the other three first, but . . ."

"But we're here now," I finished for her. "Play nice."

"I will," Val said, "he won't."

I didn't believe her for a second.

With that, the sorcerer slammed the front door open, and we stormed up the stairs into Corminar's commercial premises.

A small, nervous goblin stood from the front desk, raising a bony finger in the air. "I'm afraid he's in with clients right now. Would you want to leave a—"

But Corminar's receptionist never got to finish that question, because Val slammed the door open, revealing a tall, good-looking elf sitting behind a grand desk on a grand armchair, with two older dwarves sitting facing him. The dwarves sat upon noticeably *less* grand chairs.

The elf turned to face Val—and by extension, me—and whatever words he'd warped his mouth to say never came out.

"Nice place," Val said, walking into the office and making herself immediately at home, perching herself on the end of the desk. "Can see why you traded in the slaying life."

The elf seethed silently, seeming to weigh the words on his tongue before responding. He held his index finger up to his dwarven clients and said, calmly, "One moment." When he turned to Val, he was less calm. "Vignor!" he shouted. "What in Elysian's Plains do you think you are doing here?"

Val shrugged. "Paying a visit to an old friend with a new friend."

I shouldn't have been happy to hear myself be described as a friend, but I was; it'd been a good while since I'd hung around someone long enough to earn the label.

"Old friend," Val said, gesturing to Corminar, "meet new friend." She gestured to me. "New friend, old friend." She gestured back to the elf.

"I think you're supposed to use names," I suggested, but it landed on deaf ears.

"I am with clients, Vignor," the elf said, nodding to the two dwarves who sat, silent and confused, in the only other two chairs in the room. "Could you not have—"

"Good point," Val said, then turned to the clients. "I'm sorry, he's double-booked." She gestured them up out of their chairs, and—albeit confused—they did as suggested.

"I am *not*—" Corminar started.

"His assistant will reach out to make a new appointment," Val continued, speaking over the elf. She hurried the dwarves to and out the door, waving before pressing it shut behind her.

Corminar stared at her, nostrils flaring. "Are you here for a reason, or just to lose me business? Because I—"

"There's another one," Val said.

Immediately, the fury on the elf's face faded, and he replaced it with an expression of . . . if I had to describe it, I'd say it was somewhere between terror and "I've just eaten a good meal but I'm starting to wonder if it's going to come back up again." "Who?" the elf asked. "Where?"

"Come," Val said, grabbing his coat and bow from the coatrack and tossing them to him. "Best we talk over a beer."

Corminar took us not to a tavern, but to an elven wine bar. This was the type of place where not only was there a written drinks menu, but it didn't include any prices. For both of those reasons, I—and Val, judging by her face—didn't feel like we fit in here. Corminar, on the other hand, most certainly did.

The bartender—also elven—waved knowingly to Corminar as we entered, to which Corminar replied with a point to the table in the corner. The owner winked, and with this apparent permission, Corminar sat us down by the front windows, a small pot of impossibly vibrant cut flowers placed in the middle. They didn't use a single word throughout this interaction, and I understood from this that Corminar was in here *a lot*.

"As you so rudely interrupted a perfectly legitimate business meeting, I would ask that you pay for our drinks," Corminar said to Val as we surveyed a menu which wasn't written in elvish, but might as well have been. "This is the only elven wine bar in Fenrock—can you believe it? You would have thought even Plainsmen would have taste enough to appreciate a fine drink when it is put in front of them."

"We do," I replied. "Usually it's brown."

Corminar pursed his lips, said nothing to me, and turned his attention back to Val. "And . . . this is . . . ?" he asked.

"Styk," Val and I responded at the same time.

The elf raised his eyebrow. "Interesting name."

"Likewise," I said.

"He's the one who found the Player."

Corminar's interrogating gaze seemed to soften upon hearing this piece of information. "And you survived? What level are—"

"Best not to ask," Val interrupted. "He's sensitive about that."

"No," I said.

The sorcerer smirked. "'No'? Yes you are. You—"

"I wasn't replying to you." I looked to Corminar. "No, I didn't survive. Hence the . . ."

"Level six," the elf finished. "How?"

"An artifact; one I was paid to steal. I was holding it when—"

Corminar Cladenor's eyes widened enough that I cut myself off. In the silence that followed, three vibrant red wines were placed on the table in front of us; Corminar apparently had a usual order, too. Finally, the elf spoke. "Not the *Sisyphus Artifact?*"

My stomach lurched, and in answer I pulled the metal octahedron from my pocket and placed it on the table.

". . . Oh," Corminar said.

"Explain yourself," Val demanded, leaning across the table so she didn't need to speak at more than a whisper. Despite the low volume, her tone was menacing.

"A few months ago, a man came to visit me," Corminar said. "He acquired my services to track this object down, and, of course, I accepted the job. But when it took longer than the timeframe I had provided, he took back his up-front payment and pursued it himself."

Pieces started sliding into place for me. "This man," I said. "What did he look like?"

"A handsome one. Beautiful blond hair, and muscles that had me reconsidering the nature of my usual client relationships, at least until that dreadful tantrum he had on our second meeting."

I turned to Val, making pointed eye contact.

"It's him?" she asked.

I nodded.

The sorcerer reached over the table and slapped Corminar. "You idiot! Did you not *identify* him at all? You should have known—"

The elf, who was cradling his cheek and pouting about the pain, cut in, "In my business, *Vignor*, the less we know about our clients the better. Of course I didn't *identify* him; that would fly in the face of—"

"Hold on," I said. "I was hired to retrieve that artifact, too. How can there be two separate . . ." I trailed off, and the answer occurred to me in the same moment as it occurred to Corminar.

"Petalia," we both spat.

Val looked from me to Corminar and back again. ". . . Who?"

"You really don't *ever* get your hands dirty, do you?" I asked.

"I don't see any reason that I should." Corminar didn't seem to think this a point of pride, apparently.

"Can someone fill me in here?" Val asked.

I pointed to the elf. "This guy, he subcontracts. Doesn't do any of the hard work—"

"Attracting clients *is* the hard work," Corminar said, and I waved the defense away irritably. "Perhaps if your *charisma* was beyond that of a newborn child's, you would understand that."

"And in this case, he subcontracted to a half dryad named Petalia."

"And how does this . . ." Val started, before the answer came to her. "Ah. She hired *you*."

"Yes," I replied.

"Now I understand why the job took so long," Corminar mumbled keeping it quiet because he surely knew it wasn't a good defense, really.

"Was this man *really* a fundamental part of your team?" I asked. I'd expected Val to not get on with him—I hadn't expected it to be even more true of myself.

Corminar held up a hand and counted on his fingers as he listed the vital attributes he brought to the table. "*Archery. Discussion. Herbalism.* Three areas that not a single other *Hero Slayer*"—he said the words under his breath, as though if anyone overheard them, it might cause trouble—"has even unlocked. And I assure you, having a ranger on the team is far better than . . ." He gestured to Val. "What was it you do? Cure hangovers?"

"That's only part of it," the sorcerer replied.

"Look," I said, slamming my hands down on the tabletop without really meaning to, splashing red liquid out from Val's still full glass. "Val, here, she said you could help. That if we put your old team together, we can kill him. But if you'd rather sit here bickering—"

"What level is he?" the elf asked.

"Forty-two."

Corminar raised his eyebrows. "Forty-two? And you think we'd stand a chance?"

"Val says that we can overcome any level difference with a good enough plan."

"Yes, Val says a lot of things," Corminar responded. "That does not mean they're always true."

Before Val could interject, I said, "She's been right so far. Me and her, we took down a level twenty-seven barbarian just last week."

"What was your contribution to this skirmish?"

"Some."

Corminar sighed and did not try to hide having done so. Perhaps he even exaggerated it. "So what's he done, then? What crime has he committed that it is worth putting our little family back together?"

"Did you hear about Plainside?" Val asked.

"Yes, I—"

"That."

". . . Oh," Corminar said. Silence fell over the table as Val and I allowed him to process this information. "In that case," the elf finally said. "I suppose I will join you."

"Just like that?" Val asked. "You used to know how to drive a bargain."

"Just 'like that,' as you would say. Or, rather, *nearly* 'just like that.' I do have *one* small favor to ask, first."

CHAPTER TWENTY-ONE

A Good Old-Fashioned Heist

Corminar's requested favor was not, in fact, small.

Over the course of a couple of glasses of wine each—enough that I was feeling it a little—Corminar told Val and me that he was in a bit over his head.

"Who is it, Corminar?" Val asked, in that exhausted tone of voice that might be used between siblings. "Who's put a bounty on your head?"

Corminar took another sip of wine—the last of his glass. Before he could raise his hand to order more, Val stopped him. "The Red Thorn," he finally said.

I sank down in my seat. "*Poseidon's depths* . . ." I muttered.

Val shot me a curious glance; she didn't know who they were.

"Exiled elves," I told her.

Corminar nodded. "Not exiled, but in practical terms . . . yes, exiled. Their crimes have made them pariahs in the homelands; they have no choice but to eke out an existence away from the Dawnwood."

"They're a dangerous lot," I continued. "I've not encountered much of them, but that's . . . that's because I've avoided them. I've—"

"Never thought to go into business with them?" Val snapped. I shrugged; I couldn't argue this point. The sorcerer glared at Corminar. "Seriously, Cor, what in the hells were you thinking?"

"I didn't ask—" the elf started.

"For my opinion? I don't care, I'm giving it to you."

"I didn't ask *who they were*. With the Cladenor name comes an assurance of anonymity, and—"

"Poseidon's *depths*, Cor," Val said, echoing my earlier curse.

The elf held up his hands, patting toward the floor—an attempt to calm us both down. "It is of no consequence; a matter easily fixed. All we must do is—"

"*We?*" Val asked.

"—collect that which all of my contractors have thus far failed to collect. Or . . . return from collecting. We retrieve the smuggled goods of a rival gang, deliver it to them, and my name shall be cleared." Silence fell over the table, and it fell to Corminar once more to shatter it. "I thought you were a thief, Styk? How did you put it . . . '*getting your hands dirty*'?"

"Cor . . ."

"Assist me with this, clear my bounty, and I will join you. That is the arrangement."

Val curled her lip, and I could tell she was fighting for her life against the instinct to say something surly. "Quid pro quo? You wouldn't help us with the Player just cos it's the right thing to do?"

"There are more important things in life than the 'right thing to do,' Val."

"Like what?"

"Like *money*."

As twilight fell, we put down our cups of tea—vital in sobering us up from the wine, for the task ahead—and Corminar showed us to a guard tower on the northern side of the city. The elf had instructed Val and I to hang back a moment while he spoke to the guard out front, saying he was going to charm her, and I immediately raised an eyebrow Val's way. But the elf strolled ahead and had the guard smiling in no time, and I again raised an eyebrow at Val.

The sorcerer shrugged. "He can turn it on when he wants to."

"So he just never wants to?"

"Not with me."

Once Corminar had charmed our way into the tower, we heaved ourselves up the seemingly infinite number of steps, and I was fit to throw up by the time we reached the top. Val and Corminar, notably, were barely out of breath. That was what being levels 27 and 25 did for your fitness, I supposed.

"You dying?" Val asked me.

I opened my mouth to respond, but couldn't get any words out. Instead, I only waved her down and joined her and Corminar at the western side of the watchtower.

"There," Corminar said, pointing to some spot in the distance.

"We can't see where you're pointing," Val responded.

"The larger building. You see the stone courtyard, and the four large buildings with wooden roofs, one on each side?"

Val nodded.

"That would be where our prize is located."

"So, walk in there, pick it up, and walk out? That simple?" Val asked.

"What? No. It—"

Val sighed; clearly she had been joking.

"—will be somewhat more difficult than that. The premises are owned and operated by a rival gang, who employ high-level warriors. There will be *at least* one of these so-called warriors at each doorway."

"So we . . ." I started, still recovering my breath. "Enter via the rooftops. They're . . . close enough to one another that we should be able to find a way across."

Corminar raised his eyebrows.

"Not as dumb as he looks, is he?" Val asked.

This time, I failed to resist the urge to stick my tongue out at her—an action that she returned in kind.

"Yes," Corminar said. "The rooftops are the route we'll need to take; I already have a route in mind, but there does remain one obstacle."

We fell silent, waiting for Corminar to explain to us what this obstacle was.

"Well?" Val asked. "Are you gonna tell us, or . . ."

The elf ranger looked surprised. "Oh! I thought you'd . . . I thought you would ask."

"Just tell us, Cor."

Corminar gestured to the right-hand side of the building. "Our route will take us into the warehouse on the northern side of the courtyard. They store our prize, however, on the southern side. Now, I do have a plan in mind for how we traverse the courtyard. On the second story of each adjoining warehouse, there is a balcony. I will use my *Archery* skill to shoot a rope across the courtyard, embedding it in the wooden beams supporting the building on the far side. Then, under the cover of darkness, we will slowly inch ourselves across the rope, one at a time, until—"

"Or I could just portal us across," I suggested.

"You . . ." Corminar asked as he and the other former Slayer turned to look at me.

"*Worldbending*," I clarified.

"That's alteration magick, Cor," Val said.

The ranger blinked. "Yes, I know what *Worldbending* is, Val. I'm just surprised that . . ." He gestured to me, as though that was enough information to fill in the gap.

"We killed a cultist," I said.

"Long story," Val added. "Don't ask."

"You flatter yourself that you think I would." Corminar turned his attention back to me. "Do you have the mana for it? Being that you are such a low level?"

I shrugged. "I can manage it for maybe four, five seconds. Enough to get us across."

"And, dare I ask, back?" the ranger asked.

". . . That might be a little trickier."

Corminar closed his eyes and breathed deeply, as though dealing with Val and I was some great hardship, then reached his hands into his pocket. He pulled out four small glass vials, filled with a viscous liquid that emitted a blue glow. "Mana potions," he said. "I always keep a few lesser-grade vials on me, as they often prove useful. They're not strong, but with—what I assume is—your very low mana cap, they should be more than enough to refill your reserves."

"You don't need to assume that," I said, resisting the urge to stick my tongue out at the ranger; doing it at Val was one thing, but I didn't want to make a habit out of it.

"Am I incorrect?"

"I didn't say that."

The ranger passed me the four vials. "Use them wisely. Get us in and get us out. That you can do, surely?"

"Your wish is my command."

With that, we turned our attention back to the rooftops below, the slate tiles lit slightly by the light of the crescent moon. In the distance, we could see trees outside the city's northern walls, swaying in the gentle breeze. Up here, away from the streets, Fenrock was almost . . . peaceful.

"So," Val asked, "when do we begin?"

I stepped forward, raising my hand to summon a portal down to the rooftops below. "Is there any time like the present?"

CHAPTER TWENTY-TWO

There's Something Alive in Here

Our footsteps tapped gently across the slate roof tiles as we traversed the city, keeping out of sight of anyone at street level. We leaped from building to building, and I thanked my lucky stars that Fenrock was a cramped and crowded city; while Val and Corminar might have been able to leap much further, I would have been in danger of going *splat* on the hard ground below.

We approached the building Corminar had pointed us at, the strange cross-shaped complex, doing so from the north side, just as the ranger had planned. There hadn't been time to question his plan of attack—I had a Player coming for me, after all—but I couldn't help but wonder if my brain for heists was better than Corminar's. It was too late now, anyway.

Corminar and Val leaped across to the roof of the warehouse on the northern side, landing hard on deteriorating tiles. The sorcerer caught a particularly disintegrated piece of slate, and when she released her foot from it, it began sliding down the sloped roof.

"Ah," Val said.

I reached out, instinctively beginning my *Local Portal* spell, not quite sure how I was going to stop the tile from smashing on the ground and alerting others to our presence—after all, it would need to land *somewhere*. I was beaten to it, though, by Corminar, who suddenly had his bow in his hand and released a couple of shots. The two arrows pierced the slates below the sliding tile, catching it before it could reach the edge of the roof.

"Val . . ." the ranger said, screwing up his mouth.

"What? Stealth isn't exactly my *thing*, you know?"

I leaped across the void, landing firmly on the warehouse roof, but Val reached out to grab my arm anyway. It was a nice—if very patronizing—gesture.

"Join my side," Corminar whispered, nodding to the edge of the roof at the other side, peering down over it. "It is just as planned: there is an open window." He turned to me. "This 'heist' business is hardly the most difficult of tasks, is it?"

Val and I made eye contact, communicating silently with each other just what we thought of this particular comment. Neither of us had a chance to say anything to Corminar before he crouched, grabbed the rim of the roof, and swung himself down and—presumably—through the open shutters.

The sorcerer shrugged, then followed suit, and suddenly it was my turn. This sort of acrobatics wasn't exactly in my wheelhouse right about now, but in absence of any other choice . . . I copied the two Slayers who'd gone before me, grabbing the rim of the roof tiles, and then threw myself over the edge.

Except . . . part of me hesitated in the final moment.

I stumbled, not swinging quite as much as I needed to, but the force still pulling me away from my grip on the tiles. As I began to fall, my heart skipped a beat. I reached out for the open window, and . . . Two arms reached out to yank me in.

"Told you he'd do that," Val said, her and the ranger standing over me where I'd fallen on the floor.

Corminar, visibly annoyed, passed the sorcerer a copper piece.

We passed through the upper rafters of the warehouse building silently, each of us making a concerted effort not to alert the workers we could hear milling around and shifting crates below us. I released a breath I didn't know I was holding when we reached the other end of the building—in a small room from which a balcony overlooked the central courtyard.

Stealth: +100XP
Stealth increased to Level 2!
Base Points Gained: +1 DEX, +1 WIS, +1 Free Point (DEX/WIS)

Finally, I thought; I'd forgotten how long it took to level up this skill. Still, at least it wasn't required for any of the basics. Even Val—who as far as I knew didn't have this skill at all—could stay out of sight and keep her footsteps quiet. Only when it came to stealth combat did this skill come in handy. So far, my only ability that scaled with either Dexterity or Wisdom was *Basic Identification,* which used Wisdom, so I put the extra point in that.

The three of us slowly peered over the edge of the balcony wall that looked out onto the courtyard. Across the way was another identical balcony, facing us. Through there, we'd find what Corminar was after.

"Alright," I whispered, preparing myself to create a portal. "Here we—"

Val snapped her hand up, grabbing me by the wrist. I shot her a question in the form of a furrowed brow, which she responded to with, "They'll see the glow. If not from your hands, from the portal."

Remaining still, I heard what she was worried about—two voices growing louder beneath us. Guards entering the courtyard.

". . . in the Reaches, yeah," one of the approaching voices said. "As far north as Garnokk."

"Garnokk?" the other replied. "You been on the doomsake again? Ain't no way the queen's been sending her troops up this way."

"That's what I heard, is all." The voice began to grow quiet again. "I ain't saying I seen it or nothing, but that's what others told me."

As we waited for them to pass, I took the opportunity to ask Val a question which had been weighing on my mind. "How come your spells don't create a glow, then?"

Val pulled something from her pocket, uncupping her hands from it just enough so I could see a gem inside, glowing green. "An *obscurem*. Hides the source of your magicks."

"Stupid name," I whispered. "Where do I get one?"

Val waved me down; this wasn't the time to have this discussion. Fair enough, really—I was just a bit excited to have some accomplices on this job. I never got to have accomplices.

Once we were satisfied that the courtyard was clear, we stood, and I held out my hand, imagining a portal both next to us and on the balcony opposite. "We ready?" I asked. "Cos we gotta move fast."

Taking a leaf out of Val's book, I didn't wait for a reply, and opened the portal. Corminar—surprisingly trusting in my ability—hopped through first, followed by Val, followed by me. All in all, we were through in under four seconds, my mana bar not yet half-drained, and—judging by the lack of shouting—thus far unseen.

A success, if I said so myself.

Worldbending: +50XP
Worldbending increased to Level 4!
Base Points Gained: +2 INT, +2 Free Points (INT/WIS/CHA)

I quickly dumped both free points into Intelligence—I needed the mana reserves, after all—and then nodded to the rest of the team. We turned our attention to the adjoining room, and something about it made my stomach twist uncomfortably.

In the center of the otherwise entirely empty room—not so much as a wall decoration in sight—was a single crate. Judging by Corminar immediately hurrying toward it, this was what we were after.

"Are we sure . . ." I started, not quite knowing what the rest of this sentence was going to be.

Val halted, her apprehensive body language suggesting that she, too, felt that something was off about this scene.

"Corminar," I said, forcing a serious tone. "There's something wrong here."

"Should I understand this to be your expert burglary knowledge emerging?" the ranger said, eyebrow raised to show that he thought little of it.

"No. Maybe. I don't . . ." I gulped. "Look at the room. There's nothing else here. The absence of anything else, in this room, is a *choice*."

"Perhaps they're decorating," Corminar suggested. "They could do with a feature wall in this room, perhaps a floral print wallpaper on the—"

"He's not joking, Cor," Val said. "Something's wrong here."

"Then I ask: does it matter? Our job—"

"*Your* job," Val corrected him.

"—is simply to collect the cargo by any means necessary. It is not up to us to wonder about the state of the room, nor the style of wallpaper best suited to its containing room. We do not ask questions, Val. Understand?" With that, Corminar continued on his approach and put his hands on the edge of the crate. He heaved it up off the floor, accompanied by a grunt that suggested it was as heavy as it looked—if not so heavy that one person couldn't carry it—and then . . .

Something growled.

Three pairs of eyes stared at the crate.

"Cor . . ." Val said. "Just what in the hells is *in* that thing?"

CHAPTER TWENTY-THREE

Now You're Stealing with Portals

"It is considered inappropriate to ask a client more details about the job than freely provided," Corminar said as the crate shook again.

"Ina . . ." I started. "Inappropriate? You get in bed with the Red Thorn, of all people, and you don't ask what you're stealing for them?"

The elf's lip curled.

"It could be *anything*. Who knows what power you could be giving them? Who knows what—"

"Be that as it may," Corminar interrupted, "it does not change the situation. We will continue as planned, and then—"

"And then we figure out what's in this thing before we hand it over," Val said, cutting him off. When the elf looked to be about to complain, she added, "And if we don't end up handing it over, you're just going to have to deal with looking over your shoulder until they forget about you."

"Should that be the case, the deal will be off."

"No, it won't, Cor. After this, you're coming with us either way."

The elf ranger huffed, but said no more on the matter; he wasn't so detached from reality to really think he was in the right, here.

"Alright," Val said, grabbing at the side of the box. "How heavy is this thing? How far can we . . ." She groaned as she picked it up off the ground, placing it back down a few moments later. Whatever was inside sounded like it didn't enjoy being moved.

Corminar nodded to me. "How much use will he be should this come to a fight?"

"I'm standing right here," I said, at the same moment as Val said, "Not much. He doesn't even have a knife."

The ranger raised his eyebrow.

"A portal chopped it in half," I clarified.

The eyebrow didn't lower any at this explanation, but the man reached into his belt, pulled out a long, thin knife, and threw it to me. I was lucky enough to catch it by the hilt and not the blade.

> **Item Equipped**: Ranger's Blade
> **Ranger's Blade**: +25 percent to Dexterity when using Ranger's Blade.

"Thanks," I said, not offering up that the Dexterity bonus was essentially useless to me with my current build; I was just happy to be armed.

"The Worldbender will escort the crate to the exit, using his alteration magicks to move it. Val—you and I will scout ahead, ensuring we keep out of sight."

"Fine," I said, raising my hands. "Shall we?"

"Wait," Val said, "what about . . ."

I opened a portal over on the opposite balcony—our route of entrance and exit—and another below the crate, and a great purple glow shone out from both, illuminating the otherwise dim courtyard as the box fell through. Outside, shouts erupted from the guards we'd passed by earlier; the glow hadn't gone unnoticed.

". . . that," Val finished.

Corminar held up an index finger in thought. "I have . . . a *second* plan," he said.

". . . Yes?"

"Run."

The three of us bolted for the balcony, hopping up onto its stone wall perimeter. I opened another portal ahead of us, bringing my mana reserves down already to about a third of maximum. As arrows flew over our heads, we passed through the purple spiraling clouds that formed the portal, and landed on the opposite balcony.

Of the three of us, only Corminar landed on his feet. Val slammed into the side of the box, her resulting grunt echoed by the creature or creatures inside, and I knocked my head on the top of the doorframe before falling to the floor.

"Perhaps I can offer training in elegance," Corminar said, before drawing his bow and firing a shot back at the guards who pursued us. From the cry of horror that followed, the arrow hit its mark.

I hopped back to my feet and led the charge into the hallway, meaning to get myself into a position to portal the crate along the length of it, back to the window from which we could reach the rooftop. Instead, however, I plowed straight into the broad chest of a guard clutching a sword that was possibly longer than my entire body.

"Oh," I said. "Hi . . ."

Two more guards stepped out of the shadows at his side.

The two groups of three stared one another down, just for a moment, before everyone jumped into action. Corminar fired a shot into the neck of one of the flanking guards, felling him, while Val whipped up a gust of dust that caught the other two—and me—in the eyes. Blinking, the largest of the remaining guards swung his longsword blindly in my direction, and I ducked just in time to avoid a rather extreme haircut.

Crouching, I flung one hand behind me toward the courtyard, and the other below the feet of myself and the guards. In the second before I opened another portal, I dived to one side, then the two guards fell through the portal and into the air above the courtyard.

Level 15 Mercenary defeated!

Worldbending: +400XP

One of the guards landed with a worrying *crunch* on the tiled ground, but the other one . . . didn't.

The broad guard instead reached his hands out and wrapped his thick fingers onto the side of the balcony, and with a heavy grunt pulled himself up. Corminar fired an arrow into the man's shoulder—and the guard didn't even seem to notice.

"Time to go, I think," Val said.

I reached one hand toward the crate on the balcony, the other to the other end of the long corridor, and—

The guard picked the crate up above his head—doing so with ease, I might add—and threw it at us. I thought fast, opening one portal down the end of the corridor, and another in the air between us and the guard. The crate sailed through the paired portals, and . . .

Hit the wall at the far end of the corridor with a crash.

The voices inside went deathly silent, and the guard's eyes widened. "Wait," he said. "That wasn't . . ."

If the sudden silence combined with the wide eyes wasn't enough to tell us to be scared, we were convinced when the otherwise fearless guard turned and leaped from the balcony.

Val, Corminar, and I turned slowly to face the crate at the end of the corridor. Even at this distance, I could see that it was no longer in perfect condition, one of the six sides knocked away by the collision with the wall.

A single three-inch creature crawled forth from the shadows, and my heart dropped, my skin began to crawl, and every instinct I had told me to expel the contents of my stomach. It was a being akin to an inkblot—deathly black in its appearance, a blob that protruded as many limbs as it needed at any particular moment. In this moment, two "arms" sprang forth to drag it along the floor toward us.

"I repeat, Corminar: just what in the hells is in that thing?"

It wasn't the ranger who replied, though. It was me; the man who'd seen them before. The man who'd lost nearly everything to them. "A mala," I said.

"A . . ." Val started, trailing off when she placed the name.

"And what would that be, pray tell?" Corminar asked.

"Oh, I'll tell you," I replied. "But first thing's first, we have to—"

"Get out of here?" Val suggested, already fleeing for the door.

"No." I shook my head, but it was the firm tone to my voice that caused Val to come to a halt.

"No?" she asked. "*No?* That's a mala, Styk. We stick around here, and we'll—"

"We have to kill it. We can't let it come loose. Not here. Not in a city. It'll . . ." I found myself unable to complete the thought. To think of what it would do, to this many people in such close proximity . . . I couldn't help but remember Ceah and what the mala had done to her. What it had made her do. What it had made *me* do, to put her out of that unimaginable misery.

(Sorry—I know this isn't exactly maintaining the light tone I've been trying to stick to as I recount my story, but it's the truth. And sometimes, amongst the fun and the escapades, there are moments like this: moments where the world's infinite ways to horrify are made all too clear, or where we're forced to relive echoes of tragedies past. I'll try to keep it light—I really will—but where the malae are involved . . . there really isn't any getting around that.)

I'd trailed off, but Val nodded; she understood where I was going with this. "Alright," she said. "Kill it. How?"

"Fire," I replied. "It's the only way. Don't suppose you have a fire spell in your repertoire?"

Val shook her head. "No fire. I can't conjure it, at least. But if I had a source, I do have some wind magicks . . ."

I nodded. "That'll do." With that, I stared down the mala approaching slowly, steadily, wetly, as it dragged itself down the corridor, and I downed one of Corminar's mana vials.

CHAPTER TWENTY-FOUR

Kill It with Fire

Shlop.

The mala dragged itself down the corridor, its form changing with every "step."

"Three things you have to remember with malae," I said. "One: don't let it touch you. If it touches you, you're as good as dead—not because it'll kill you, but because others will have to."

Shlop—another step with its wet, ink-like limbs.

"Second: when you're around them, you'll feel fear. Maybe fear unlike you've ever experienced before. You might even see things that aren't there. You'll have to ignore it."

Shlop. Shlop. Shlop. The mala began to speed up, the body seeming to lock in on me, even though it had no eyes that I could see.

"Third: the stronger you are, the more powerful they become. Which makes me uniquely placed to handle this one."

"Styk, what do you—" Val started.

"You two," I said, keeping my eyes fixed on the mala. "Find fire. I'll keep it occupied."

"Are you—"

"Fire. *Now*," I spat, though my spite wasn't directed at either of them. Well, maybe Corminar, a little bit.

The two of them scuttled away, though which way, I had no idea; I'd locked my eyes on the mala. Some made the mistake of thinking that the slow speed of the malae made them near-harmless, but that was far from the case. They never stopped moving once they made someone their target. They would find them, whether it took them an hour, a day, or a year. They were always coming.

As this mala neared, I reached forward, aiming to open a portal beneath the foul creature, and another above it. The goal was to trap it in an endless loop, one that would give us time enough to figure out a way to kill it. Or, at least, for as long as I could sustain it with my minuscule mana reserves and Corminar's potions.

The purple glow announced a portal opening beneath the creature, and soon it fell through, appearing at the ceiling, fell through again, appeared at the ceiling once more, and . . .

It changed form.

As I swigged from a glass vial containing a glowing blue liquid, the living inkblot grew wider—thinner, yes, but wider—and enlarged more and more with each appearance in the upper portal, until . . . It finally reached a size too large to fit through the portal. So quickly had it overcome this obstacle, as indeed, the malae did most obstacles. They always adapted. They always found a way.

I closed the portal; there was no point wasting my mana, especially when I only had two potions left. All I could do was back up slowly, around the corner, eyes fixed firmly on the creature that could consume everything that made me . . . me.

Finally, as I approached another corner, Val and Corminar returned, the latter holding a lit oil torch.

"Alright," I said, "Good. Now, whatever you do, don't . . ."

Corminar stepped forward, brandishing the flaming torch, and waved it in the mala's direction, as if to ward it off.

". . . do that."

The elf furrowed his brow. "Correct me if I'm wrong, but I thought you said fire killed it."

"It does, yeah."

"Then what in Alterra is the problem?"

"It also enrages it."

The mala came to a halt a dozen paces from us. It had no eyes to speak of, yet I could still feel its vision boring into me—as too could Val and Corminar, judging by their uneasy body language. A wave of dread washed over me; the creature was defending itself.

"Now you've done it."

"For your benefit, thief, one would normally provide someone with warning *before* they are in danger of making a mistake."

I rolled my eyes; if the other three members of the Hero Slayers were this much of a pain, then maybe I would just accept my fate and let the pyroknight kill me. Swallowing my irritation, I took a step back from the mala and held my hand out to encourage Val and Corminar to do the same.

"You might now start hearing things. Seeing things. Remember, it goes for the strongest first, so . . ."

Just at that moment, Corminar screamed, clutching his hands to his face and then lashing out blindly.

"What's his . . ." Val started, looking from him to me, and then her eyes widened. "Does that mean he's stronger than me, if it got him first?"

I shrugged.

"Well, that's deeply disappointing, isn't it?"

"Could just be that he was . . ." I trailed off when Corminar, previously just flailing at whatever he was seeing, now drew his bow. He pointed it at something that wasn't there, and Val and I just so happened to be standing *behind* the thing that wasn't there. "We should . . ."

"Yep," Val agreed, and we dived to the side just in time to avoid the first loosed arrow.

"Wonder what he's firing at," I said.

Corminar shouted the answer immediately. "*Bees!*"

"Bees?"

The sorcerer pulled a face. "Always had a bit of a thing about them."

"Bees, though? Usually malae reach deep into your soul, unpack your heart, tearing forth from it a fear that you didn't even really know you had. And he has . . . bees?"

Val nodded. "He *really* doesn't like them."

One of Corminar's loosed arrows hit the mala by chance, and *slooped* straight through it.

"OK," I said. "Bees. And his answer is to shoot at them?"

"My answer is to *hit* them," Corminar cried out. "Would it not behoove you to assist me?!"

"What did you say?" Val asked.

"I asked him if his answer was to—"

"No!" she cried out, clapping her hands around her ears.

"I was just . . ." I started, before realizing that she was no longer talking to me; the mala had her now. As expected, it was going to be up to me—the weakest here—to deal with this thing.

I nipped across the corridor between Corminar's ostensibly imaginary-bee-hitting shots and plucked the still-flaming torch from the floor where he'd dropped it.

"They'll see what I am!" Val roared. "They'll see it!"

I pressed on, ignoring the cries about true identities and swarming insects, and laid my eyes upon the mala once more.

"Styk?" a familiar voice cried out. Her voice was breathy, like a whisper, yet resonated off the walls around me. I spun around, looking for her, but saw nothing; unlike the others, I wasn't strong enough. The mala had less to work with—it couldn't form visual hallucinations for me, at least not so quickly.

"Don't leave me!" Val cried out, falling to the floor and clutching her knees to her chest. I could only assume she was talking to her hallucinations, rather than to me.

I took a step forward, toward the black ink-like shape that stood still, observing, preparing itself to strike when we were all distracted. I couldn't let that happen.

"Styk, are you there?" the voice cried out again. There was pain in her tone now. Just like the last time I'd seen her.

My arm shook as I raised the torch ahead of me, as though putting it between me and the mala would somehow break its spell over me. I stepped forward. Just the once; that was as much as I could manage.

"Wait . . ." the echo of the forgotten woman said. "Don't you want to see me? Don't you want to see me again?"

I steadied my hand. The last time I'd seen the owner of that voice, I . . . Suffice to say, whatever I saw wouldn't be real. *Couldn't* be real. Yet that didn't mean I wasn't yearning to see her with every fiber of my being.

I wrenched my attention away from the end of the corridor, where a shape was taking form, and turned back to the mala. All it would take was one short burst of inner strength—enough to overwhelm my desperate urge to see her again—and we'd be free of it. I'd never have to face up to what I'd done. I'd never have to see the knife in her heart.

As another of Corminar's arrows flew overhead, I steadied myself. Half thinking, half not, I launched myself into a freshly summoned portal, arriving in the air above the mala, and I swung the torch down upon it.

It squealed as it died.

Level ? Corruption defeated!

Worldbending: +300XP
Worldbending increased to Level 5!
Base Points Gained: +2 INT, +2 Free Points (INT/WIS/CHA)

Ability Selection Unlocked . . .

CHAPTER TWENTY-FIVE

Wanted

"What are you doing?" Val asked.

We were camped out in the living room of Corminar's Fenrock apartment, Val having claimed the armchair for herself, me having slept on blankets on the floor. As I blinked myself awake, apparently woken by the same noise as Val, I noticed a twinge in my back; I was too low a level to get away with sleeping in such discomfort.

Corminar didn't look over at us, and carried on rifling through his cupboards. "Where is it?" he muttered. "Where could it be?"

"Hey, Cor? Some of us are trying to sleep here, buddy."

The elf continued wrenching open cupboard doors and drawers, throwing their contents to the floor.

"Maybe if you told us what you were looking for?" I suggested. "Then we could help you find it, and then we could go back to sleep?"

A nod from Val told me she was grateful for that last part.

"A small . . ." Corminar started, then trailed off, as though lost in thought.

Val and I turned to one another. "Something small," I said.

"A . . . teaspoon?" Val guessed.

"A ring?" I threw into the mix.

"A list of all your good deeds?"

"A rabbit's foot?"

"Your p—" Val started, and was—fortunately, I suspected—cut off by Corminar.

The man stared into the latest of the now-open drawers. "Aha!" he said, and then pulled from it a small brass object, which—on closer inspection—turned out to be a pocket mirror.

"What . . . is that?" I asked.

"A mirror of truth," the elven ranger replied. "Ask it any question, and it will answer honestly, as per the limits of its knowledge. Invaluable, and—"

"Oi, mirror," I called out. "What are the chances of us killing this Player and surviving to tell the tale?"

"Much greater now that Corminar Cladenor joins with you," the mirror replied, using my voice.

"That's not really an answer, is it?"

"It is," the mirror said.

I narrowed my eyes, then flicked my gaze from the mirror to the man holding it. "Are you *sure* this is a mirror of truth?"

The ranger sighed. "Who is the most handsome person in this room?" he asked it.

"You are, sir," the mirror responded.

Corminar held up his hand as if to say "well, there you are." "Mirror of truth, as I say."

I shook my head, turning back to Val, who only shrugged—this wasn't something she cared enough about to interrogate. As I clearly wasn't getting any backup on this one, I turned my attention instead to the last of the notifications I'd gotten last night, after defeating the mala.

Worldbending increased to Level 5!
Base Points Gained: +2 INT, +2 Free Points (INT/WIS/CHA)

Ability Selection Unlocked
Select an ability from the list below:

Option 1: Skinsmith (Worldbending)—Toughen skin to act as natural armor. Strength of armor scales on [WIS]. Uses mana/second.

Option 2: Silence (Worldbending)—Create a bubble of five-foot radius in which sound is eradicated. Uses mana/second.

Option 3: Local Portal II (Worldbending)—*Upgrade to Local Portal.* Create a portal to another location within current range of sight or within a ten-yard radius. Uses mana/second.

Reading through, I was a little disappointed to see that I'd met no hidden criteria; the three options presented to me all seemed to be part of the default skill tree. That said, the novelty of being able to wield magick abilities was still alive and well in my heart—and this was the very first time I'd been able to *choose* my next ability; the first one I'd been given based on my part in killing the Ascendent Cultist.

Upgrading the *Local Portal* ability was very tempting, as the addition of a radius in which I didn't even need to *see* the destination had, surely, a good few use cases. On the other hand, the radius was only ten yards—it wouldn't exactly get me very far.

The *Skinsmith* ability was tempting, too. I'd never—either in this life or the one before—spent the time investing in an armor skill, for one simple reason: you didn't level up your armor class without getting hit. And I *didn't like* getting hit. So if I had a skill which would replace that . . . yeah, I could see that coming in handy.

And then there was *Silence*. What better a magick ability to complement my attempts to level back up my *Stealth* skill?

All three abilities, I noticed, required mana per second to operate them. Even though they didn't specify quite how *much* was required, I figured there was no harm putting my two free points into Intelligence again—this base stat now being my highest of the six, by far.

But this still left me with the choice of ability, and for the first time in a long time, I was struggling to decide. All of these had potential, definitely, but the *Local Portal* was already tried and tested. And I might get another shot at picking the others as I leveled up *Worldbending* further—they might even jump straight to stage 2, if I leveled the skill high enough. With that in mind, and a heavy heart, I selected option three.

Ability Upgraded: Local Portal II

Local Portal II (Worldbending): Create a portal to another location within current range of sight or within a ten-yard radius. Uses mana/second.

"I just got—" I started, but Corminar interrupted me.

"I believe I have everything of importance. Let us begin our journey."

"Cor, we just woke up," Val said, pulling herself upright on the sofa, clearly realizing that she wasn't getting any sleep tonight. "And the sun isn't even up. Why don't we—"

"The *Thorn* will be seeking revenge, Vignor. They know my place of business, and therefore it is only a matter of time before they locate my residence as well. It is best we depart with the dawn. Unless you know of any purveyors of exotic creatures from whom we might purchase a replacement—"

I sat up, staring the elf down. "We don't mess around. Not with malae. Not ever."

Corminar met my gaze for a moment, but it was he who broke it off first. He waved me away. "Nevertheless, malae or otherwise, I have failed to uphold my end of the contract with the Red Thorn; it is best I do not wait around for them to find me. Come—I will lead you to Lore, if indeed re-forming the Slayers remains your objective."

We scurried along the main road out of Fenrock as the first of the sun's rays washed over us. Moving so quickly at this hour was suspicious, but there were few people up and about to be suspicious *of* us, so we reached the gate without drawing too much attention. We could only hope that the few who did see us would not remember our faces; the Red Thorn could be persuasive in their methods of extracting information.

As we passed through the gate, grateful that the guards only worked day shifts in this city, it being as safe as it was, Corminar came to a sudden halt. Val and I kept going for a while before realizing the elvish Slayer wasn't following, and was instead staring at the city's message board.

"Catch sight of a mirror, buddy?" Val asked.

The elf didn't respond to this dig, instead continuing to stare on at the message board with a smirk on his face. "It looks as though I am not the only one highly sought after," Corminar said, pulling a scrap of paper from the message board and holding it up to his torchlight.

"What? What you got there, Cor?" Val asked as she and I joined the elf at his side, reading the notice over his shoulder.

The first thing that struck me was the crude depictions of two humans at the top of the page—the woman attractive, the man portrayed as having a boil on his nose and a hood not entirely unlike . . .

"Oh hey!" Val said. "It's us!"

"WANTED: By order of the Baron of Umlok," the notice read. "Sorcerer Val Vignor and peasant boyfriend 'Styk.'"

"Peasant?" I cried.

"Boyfriend?" Val protested.

"Wanted: dead or alive—for crimes of murder and jailbreak. Highly danger-ous. Reward: 20 gold coins."

"Twenty gold ain't bad, though, is it?" Val said.

I raised an eyebrow. "You don't seem too worried about this."

The sorcerer shrugged. "It's not the first time I've been wanted."

"It was thirty gold at one point, was it not?" Corminar asked.

"Thirty gold and the promise of a general's daughter's hand in marriage. I'm surprised *you* didn't hand me in."

"Me as well; perhaps the daughter was not as tempting as she might have been."

"Oh, she was—I think it would've been the prospect of General Kharniq as your father-in-law that would've put you off."

Corminar nodded. "Ah. Yes."

I glanced over the pair's shoulders to see two guards of Fenrock gently ambling toward the gate—the morning shift arriving for duty. "If you two are done reminiscing . . ."

Val and Corminar turned to see what I was looking at, then turned back to one another. "Could do a quick fight," the sorcerer said.

"We could. Two guards, three of us." Corminar glanced at me. "Two guards, two and a bit of us. I can't imagine it'd be our most difficult skirmish."

"Been a while since I whipped out my magicks," Val said.

I blinked, mouth hanging open. "It's been *six hours!*"

"Far too long," Val said.

Corminar nodded his agreement. "One must keep the body as limber as the mind."

I shook my head, fed up with the both of them, and began strolling out of town. "Lore's this way, yeah?"

CHAPTER TWENTY-SIX

Sweet Stuff

Tanar was about the most unremarkable town I'd ever set foot in. There were about thirty buildings, only one of which was an inn, and only one of which was a shop. The rest were houses, filled with happy, smiling families who waved to one another on the street, asking each other how their day was. The children played on the open road, shouting and laughing without a care in the world. Aromas of stewing broths and freshly baked pies wafted through the air, many of them coming from the local market, which—according to a particularly gregarious local—they put on every Apoday. Every face in this town was welcoming and smiling, and not a word the locals spoke suggested that this was anything but sincere.

All in all, I hated it.

Where was the drama? The fighting? The opportunities to pick the pockets of an irritating tourist? Not that I had the *Pickpocketing* skill anymore, of course. On the skill front, I'd spent the journey here *identifying* every person we passed, and I'd built up enough experience to level the skill to level 6.

Only a couple of weeks ago, the *Identification* skill had been game-changing for me, an easy source of experience that could get me leveling up fast. But, just as I'd realized as a child, it was a pretty useless skill, and boring, too.

(In fact, dear reader, as it's such a run-of-the-mill skill, I'm sure we can skip me reiterating any experience gains and level ups of this skill, can't we? Otherwise, there are going to be examples of +10XP here, and INT/WIS free point decisions there, and even if you wouldn't get bored reading it, I'd get bored telling you about it. So yeah—just assume I put that free point into Intelligence every time, because it's true about 90 percent of the time in the story still to come.)

As we walked into town, my eyes peeled for someone matching this Lore's description —"tall, muscular, and always smiling" was about all Val and Corminar could give me—a certain elf's eyes got drawn to the market stalls. More specifically, Corminar's eyes got drawn to a small stall manned by a young man, and I knew exactly what he had grown hungry for.

"I don't think now's the time to . . ." I started, but Corminar hurried off toward the stall, licking his lips. To save the elf from getting *too* sidetracked, I followed him. "I'm sorry for—" I began saying to the young market stall owner, but Corminar cut me off; he'd seen something he wanted, and he was going to get it whether I was there or not.

"Delicious," he said, causing me to raise an eyebrow at this opening gambit, but then I realized he'd been staring not at the local but at his goods. As in, you know, actual goods, rather than bodily ones. In front of the local man was a large and colorful array of . . . boiled sweets.

"Delicious," Corminar said again. "And how much, may I ask, are you charging?"

"One bag's two copper, sir."

Almost before the merchant had finished speaking, Corminar thumped two coins into his hand. He proceeded to fill the bag meticulously, scooping up four sweets of one type, and then two of another, one of another, four of another . . . Before long, the paper bag he'd been handed was not just full, but bursting at the seams and at severe risk of overflowing.

"Got enough there?" I asked.

"If the stall charges by the bag, then we would be fools not to maximize our return on investment." At that moment, he squeezed the bag just an ounce too tight, and a couple of the wrapped sweets fell to the floor.

I sighed, then bent over to snatch the sweets back up; if Corminar did it, it'd only result in him losing more of them.

An arrow whooshed over my head, and buried itself in the swinging, creaking wooden sign on the market stall that read Ted's Confectionary.

I stood back up, the confusion on my face matching the confusion on Corminar's, and the market stall owner's—Ted, presumably. Our three heads turned to face the direction from which the arrow had flown, and I saw a man a little older than myself nocking another arrow. He raised the bow back up at me, and Corminar, Ted, and I dove to the ground.

The elven ranger and I scuttled around the back of the market stall just as another arrow buried itself into the wood behind where I'd been only moments earlier.

"Red Thorn?" I asked Corminar as we cowered behind the stool at Ted's side.

"He was human," the elf responded. "And aiming at *you*. Though . . ." Corminar trailed off.

"Yes?"

"I'm sure I recognize him."

"A spurned former lover?" I asked. "Wait, does he think I'm your boyfriend?"

"Please," Corminar said.

"'Please, I wouldn't date him' or 'Please, I wouldn't date *you*'?" I asked.

"Come out, murderer," the mysterious archer shouted.

The local merchant looked from me, to Corminar, and back to me again. "Well, he could be talking to any one of us, I assume."

"Who did you . . ." I started, then shook my head, cutting myself off. "Forget it. That's not important."

We paused, before Corminar finally stuck his hand up in the air, into sight of the archer. He didn't leave it raised long enough to risk an arrow piercing it. "Excuse me?" the elf ranger called out. "Excuse me, which murderer?"

There was a pause before our aggressor spoke. "Which . . . what?"

"Which murderer," Ted clarified.

"Yes, I heard you; it wasn't that kind of 'what.' What do you mean, which murderer?"

"The confectionary industry is a cutthroat world, sir," Ted responded.

"Did you massacre hundreds at Plainside?"

Ah. It's me he's after, after all.

"No . . ." Ted replied.

"Then you can go."

"Are you sure? I don't want to stand up and get an arrow to the head."

The archer sighed. "Do you know the man they call 'Styk'?"

"That's not a very good name," Ted replied. I shot him a dirty look, and he shrugged. "Sorry."

"Step out from behind the stall, confectioner. On my honor as a guardsman, I assure you that you will come to no harm."

Nervously, Ted pushed his hands into the air, and then stepped out slowly from behind the stall. No arrow came; our attacker was a man of his word, at least. But who? A bounty hunter? No, he called himself a guard. But what guard would be so interested in the matter of Plainside that he pursued me halfway across a region?

Ted pointed to the pair of us still hiding behind the stall. "There's two of them," he said.

"Oh, thanks, Ted," I muttered, then fixed my attention on someone who deserved my irritation a tad more; the man who'd tried to kill me. "What do you want?"

"To capture you. Dead or alive. I assume the person with you is your sorcerer accomplice?"

I glanced over at Corminar, who seemed shocked to have been confused for a human woman, though his long hair and delicate features were perhaps partially to blame for this. "You're collecting the bounty?"

"I'm getting my fiancee back."

I screwed up my face. "Getting your fiancée back? What do I have to do with that? You sure you have the right guy?"

"You escaped from Umlok," the man called back. "Did you think this wouldn't have consequences? Your escapes lost me my job. And my employer, my future father-in-law, took Sae from me. Rescinded his blessing. My name is Captain Lambkin, and I will not rest until I have you in my custody. What is it to be, Styk—will I take you into my custody dead, or will I take you alive?"

"I would choose *alive*," Corminar suggested.

"Yes, thank you."

"Though perhaps there is a third option."

I raised my eyebrows. "You got any ideas?"

"Just one."

"Am I going to like it?"

"Do you have any choice?" the ranger replied.

I shrugged. "Suppose not. OK. Do it."

Corminar nodded glumly, then raised his hands to his face. Was this some hidden ability? Some trick of the elves of which I wasn't aware? Did Corminar have magicks within him, ones he played close to his chest? My questions were answered when he used his cupped hands to shout, "Val! *Val!* We need help!"

"That was your plan?" I asked.

"I did suspect you would not like it."

CHAPTER TWENTY-SEVEN

An Adventurer like You

"Yeah?" Val shouted back, across the small town. "What's going on?"

"What's the plan, Corminar?" I asked the elf at my side.

"When she presents herself, we flee. Opposite directions. Stay low, and stick to cover; I think I know where I recognize this man from."

"Yeah? And I'm guessing it's relevant?"

Corminar nodded. "I've met him at tournaments. I do enjoy the sport, and particularly the passionate fans. That is where I have heard this voice before; your Lambkin is the second highest leveled archer in the Tundras."

"How does that help us?"

The Slayer raised his bow. "Because I am the first highest."

"You can just say *highest*."

"Because I am the highest," Corminar said.

At that moment, Val appeared across the market, just in sight of Corminar and I without us having to stick our heads out from behind our cover. "What are you shouting about, Cor?"

"Now," Corminar said, and I didn't delay for even a second.

While my new ranger friend bolted out in Val's direction, I sprinted the other way, crouching as much as I could and diving between the milling locals, who seemed oblivious enough to the dangers of the wider world that they hadn't, you know, *run away at the first sign of trouble*. I dived behind a butcher's stand, a cloud of flies hovering above and suggesting to me that I wouldn't be buying meat from here anytime soon.

As I dove to the ground, I felt a sudden pain in my right leg. I looked down to my knee to discover it had a new, strange, arrow-shaped protrusion. "Ow," I said, more because I felt I should than because I actually felt any pain.

And then the pain hit me. "*Ow!*" I cried out, clutching at my knee. "Ow! Ow! Ow!"

"You're still alive over there, then, Styk?" Val responded, taking great delight in being sarcastic even about possibly mortal injuries.

"Ow!" I responded, tearing my eyes away from the arrow sticking out of me to see Val and Corminar crouching behind another stall—they hadn't managed to get far, then. I wondered for a moment what was the next stage in Corminar's plan, but then the truth hit me: there wasn't one. These Slayers definitely had a habit of making things up as they went along. If we'd stopped for a moment to think about it, I might have even thought to use *Local Portal* to get us out of trouble, but now here I was with an arrow sticking out of my knee.

Newly incensed, I grit my teeth and reached down to pull the arrow from my knee. Instead, I only managed to snap the arrow just below the head, but I decided that was good enough—especially considering my health bar was already about halfway drained, and I couldn't exactly risk doing further damage to myself. I was going to need Val and Corminar—with their surely much higher Vitality and health bars—to take more of the heat from here on out.

"There's three of us, Lambkin!" I shouted out, doing my best to hide the pain in my voice. "And only one of you. You'll get out of here if you know what's good for you."

"Oh yes?" came the reply. "Or what?"

"Or I'll take you down."

The ex-guardsman roared with laughter, so much so that it was obviously insincere; nobody found *anything* that funny, even something said by someone as utterly hilarious as myself.

I peered around the edge of the butcher's stall to get a look at the man. He'd lowered his bow, apparently already confident he was going to be the victor in this fight. In the distance, off to his right, Val and Corminar slowly rose to their feet.

"Take me down?" Lambkin said through fits of laughter. "Me? Please. You're level six, Styk. I don't know how that can be—especially considering what you did in Plainside—but that's what you are. What chance could you possibly stand against me?"

"It's not about the level," I started, then took a quick breather to get through a wave of pain, "it's about what you do with it. Besides, I managed to escape from you at level *three*, didn't I?"

Val and Corminar took rapid yet quiet steps toward the guard.

"That's because you had a friend with you," the captain retorted.

"Exactly," I said, and Val raised her hands.

The sorcerer pelted the man with rocks, using her magicks to whip them with a gust of wind, and the captain grunted with pain before diving to the ground.

At Val's side, Corminar raised his bow, arrow nocked, just as the cowering Lambkin did the same from his position on the floor. Each arrow released simultaneously, whooshing through the air at the ranger who had fired the other, and . . . the arrowheads smashed perfectly into one another. The two loosed arrows spun chaotically to the floor.

I wasn't in a position to waste the distraction, and so I'd already been preparing a move of my own, raising my hands to *portal* myself to the cover of another market stall. I released the portal on the ground beneath me, and I fell through it, my head spinning as the direction of gravity changed. As I tumbled to a fresh patch of ground, I glanced back to make sure nobody was following me through the portal—I didn't like the idea of closing it on them—before releasing the spell and preventing my mana from draining any further.

Glancing around the edge of this new market stall—fish, judging by the smell; if I'd known that, I might have picked a different one—I saw Lambkin spinning into a stand, releasing another arrow. But where the last had been aimed at Corminar, this one was aimed at Val.

Corminar's eyes widened, and he hurriedly released another shot, this one fired just in front of Val and again collided with Lambkin's arrow. Together they once more spun to the ground, but not without the tail end of one of the arrows scratching Val's cheek.

Corminar hesitated when he saw the blood flowing from his fellow Slayer, and this hesitation was enough for Lambkin to nock and release another shot. This time it was Val's turn to save Corminar, which she did by tackling him to the ground and removing his head from the path of the arrow. They scuttled to cover as Lambkin released another shot, but the damage was done; the captain had regained control of the fight.

With the arrowhead stuck in my knee, I wasn't going to be much help, at least not in the face-to-face sense—though I supposed that'd been true ever since I'd died, let's face it. But I still had a good three quarters of my mana left, and if I timed it right, my portals might just come in handy.

"Psst!" I half whispered, waving at Val and Corminar.

Corminar, with his improved elven hearing, snapped his head toward me. He raised a finely groomed eyebrow.

I pointed at my hand. "When you're ready," I whispered, "I'm going to . . ."

The elf narrowed his eyes; improved hearing or not, he couldn't tell what I was saying.

"Come out, come out, my dear friends," Lambkin said, stepping slowly toward Val and Corminar, bow drawn and at the ready. He hadn't yet seen me, at least.

I tried Corminar again, speaking slowly and mouthing the words exaggeratedly. "I . . . am . . . going . . . to . . . *portal* . . . you."

The elf's face didn't change, and that eyebrow remained arched. I resorted to gesturing instead. "I . . ." I pointed to myself, "portal . . ." I mimed activating a portal in front of me, and—

A portal opened.

Ah yes. It does that.

Lambkin's eyes shot to the glowing purple portal, as you might expect, and though I closed it almost immediately, it only resulted in the captain of the guard setting his eyes on me.

I moved fast.

As the once-captain swiveled his bow around to point it at me, I gestured for a portal to open once more. This time, I placed one of the portals between me and Lambkin, and the other in the air some way behind me—I didn't have a moment to look.

The released arrow shot through the portal, and I closed it immediately, saving the mana for later, because I was clearly going to need it. Behind me, I heard the arrow whoosh down out of the portal, followed by a grunt, followed by a cry of pain.

I cringed, looking back at the local merchant who'd been hit, and was about to mouth "Sorry!" when I noticed it was Ted. Suddenly I didn't feel quite so sorry about it, considering the way he'd sold us out earlier.

Ahead of me, Captain Lambkin drew another arrow, and if he kept it up like this, I wasn't going to have enough mana to portal all his ammunition out of harm's way. And if I stayed here . . . well, he'd circle around before long.

All I could do was portal myself out of here, perhaps create a distraction that would allow Val and Corminar a chance to—

From the crowd of onlookers—their expressions somewhere between terror and intrigue—stepped forth the tallest man I'd ever seen. Over his shoulder, he carried a young lamb, and in one of his hands he struggled to carry, fittingly, the largest sword I'd ever seen. A terrible scar ran down one of his cheeks, splitting his left eyebrow in two. He growled at Lambkin just loud enough to cause the man to turn around, and then before the captain could release his arrow, he bashed him in the brow with the butt of his heavy sword.

Captain Lambkin fell to the floor, unconscious.

Level 29 Ranger defeated!

Worldbending: +280XP

The towering, intimidating barbarian scowled down at the man he'd just knocked unconscious, then blinked, looked up at Val and Corminar, and broke into the widest smile I'd ever seen. "Val! Corminar!" he said, raising his arms in excitement and almost dropping the lamb from his shoulder as a result. "Are you two making enemies again?"

"Hi, Lore," Val replied.

CHAPTER TWENTY-EIGHT

The Good Shepherd

"Ow, ow, ow," I complained as Val pushed her low-level healing magicks into my knee. She'd removed the arrowhead . . . not *delicately*, per se, but with slightly more consideration than I'd maybe expected. Though her magicks weren't powerful enough to close the wound, Corminar had already bandaged it, and Val was at least able to numb the pain.

"What do we do with this guy?" the huge Lore said. Val and Corminar had told me he was tall, but *tall* was underselling it. Lore nudged the unconscious Lambkin with the tip of his foot.

"Kill him," Val suggested.

"I don't kill people for doing their jobs," the man holding a baby sheep over his shoulder said. "You said you have a bounty on you."

"One based on a lie."

"A big lie," I added, testing my knee. It wasn't comfortable, but it was going to have to do. Already my health bar was starting to very slowly recover.

"So what? He doesn't know that, does he?" Lore replied.

"If we do not eliminate the man, he will return," Corminar said. "There is too much at stake for us to allow such a man to go unchecked."

"I'm killing him," Lore said, nudging the man again. "If . . . he's not dead already. I don't hit *that* hard, do I?"

"You do," Val said.

Corminar nodded. "Very hard indeed."

"Oh," the man said. "Well, I'm still not killing him."

"Then what would you suggest?"

Lore stared down at the man, eyes seeming to be glazed over, before all of a sudden placing the sheep down on the floor at his side. He crouched down to look into the creature's eyes, held out his index finger, and commanded, "Stay."

"Baa," the sheep replied.

"Good." With that, Lore hurried off around the corner.

Val, Corminar, and I turned our attention to the lamb, who blinked back mutely.

"It's staying," Val said, surprised.

"Perhaps Lore hits his flock, too," Corminar suggested.

"You're saying you reckon he intimidates his sheep?" I asked.

"I do not believe they would be the most difficult animal to intimidate. If you think you would have trouble, then—"

"I didn't say that, I just meant—" I started, but Val cut me off.

"He's coming back," she said, nodding to the corner around which he'd disappeared.

Emerging down the road was a horse-drawn cart, an old farmer holding the reins, the massive Lore sitting by his side and causing the cart to tilt to one side. In the back, there was . . . a giant stack of manure.

"What you doing with the poo, big guy?" Val called out to him.

Lore clapped the cart driver around the shoulder, causing him to flinch. "My new friend, here, he's heading north. Up to the farms in the Reaches, up near Thistle."

We stared blankly on at him.

"I'm saying we dump him in the back."

"Ahh," I said, at the same moment that Val said, "Ohh," and Corminar muttered, "A surprising yet rather fitting solution to our problem."

The three Slayers—I didn't get involved due to my damaged knee—picked up the unconscious ex-captain and dumped him in the back, and the four of us watched him drift away into the distance.

"So," Lore said, "I'm guessing you wanna see the farm, yeah?"

Lore's farm was a good fifteen-minute walk out of town along a winding path—not quite a road—which went through a patch of lush woodland. On the other side, a small thatch-roofed hut stood in the center of the farm, with a patch of wheat on one side tended to by a young man, and a fenced-off area containing sheep in the other. It was in the latter that Lore placed down his carried lamb, though the lamb craned its head the other way, snapping its jaw toward the wheat, desperate for a bite. Lore and I introduced ourselves to each other properly, and then the shepherd gave us a guided tour of his plot of land. Val, Corminar, and I asked polite questions, but all three of us were clearly itching to get to the heart of the matter—why we were here.

It was Val who broke first. "There's another one, Lore."

Lore stopped midstep, and the smile—which had seemed to be endless up until this point—faded from his face. "You want me to come with you."

"Why else would we be here?" Corminar asked.

The shepherd's face warped into a frown, the sparkle disappearing from his eyes. "Thought you might be checking up on an old friend."

Val shot Corminar a dirty look. "We would, Lore, we would. I'd been meaning to for a while, I'd just been caught up in . . . Well, stuff. But it's happened, Lore."

"How many?" the shepherd asked, staring out onto his flock.

"How many? Just the one, but—"

"No," Lore interrupted. "How many have they killed?"

". . . Ah," Val said, then looked to me for an answer.

"Dozens. Hundreds, maybe," I said. "There wasn't a huge amount of them left, so I don't know for sure."

Lore sighed, his inner conflict clear on his face; this wasn't a man who worried about hiding his feelings. "Val, Cor, I . . . I got babies now. I can't just pack up and—"

"You have *babies*?" Val suddenly cried out excitedly. "Lore, why didn't you lead with that? Where are they? I have to see them; where are they?"

Lore turned and frowned at the sorcerer. "They're . . ." he started. "They're in front of you."

Val and Corminar looked around, scanning over the fields in front of them, before turning on the spot to look behind them.

"I don't . . ." Val started.

"You mean to say you adopted the young man?" Corminar asked.

It was Lore's turn to look puzzled. For old friends, they really were on completely different pages most of the time.

I leaned in between Val and Corminar. "He means the sheep," I whispered helpfully.

"No, he—" Val started, and then met the ranger's eyes. "Oh, gods, he *does*, doesn't he?"

The seven-foot-tall, scarred barbarian blinked down at them, glancing from their old friends to his woolly flock. "Yeah," he said, as though this should've been obvious. "They're my babies."

Corminar sighed. "Your reason not to join us on a quest of vengeance against the invaders from the ascended world is . . . sheep?"

"My babies," Lore corrected him.

"They're sheep, though," Val added.

"My babies are sheep, yeah."

"You know," I cut in, "I think we've kinda gotten to the heart of the matter here, guys. No need to hammer the point home any further."

"Can't . . ." Val started, turning toward the farmhand in the wheat field. "Can't he look after them?" Before Lore could answer, she put her hands to her mouth and shouted, "Oi, you! What's your name?"

The farmhand looked up at Val. "Seld!" he cried back.

"You reckon you can look after some sheep?"

"Yeah!"

Val turned back to Lore. "See? Seld's got it covered. We need you."

Lore sighed. "No, you don't. I ain't ever added much to the team, have I? What do I do that none of you do?"

"You have a massive sword," Val said.

Corminar raised his eyebrows suggestively, and Val pulled a face in response.

"Arzak has two!" the shepherd protested. "Not as big, but they do the same job. And she's smarter. And she hasn't got the . . . the . . ." He gestured to the scar on his face.

"Lore, she'd tell you herself she's not nearly as strong as you," Val said. "You're the muscle. The armor. The one who soaks up the damage. Without you, we don't stand a chance."

Lore looked from Val to me. "You were the one there?"

I nodded.

"Were they really that bad?"

"Pyroknight," I said. "Level forty-two. Burned a town alive."

Lore raised his eyebrows. "I'd need to get my armor enchanted."

"That can be arranged," Corminar said.

"Does that mean you're in?" Val asked, and I couldn't help but notice she seemed a lot more excited at this prospect than at the prospect of Corminar joining them.

Lore held up his index finger. "One Player," he said. Lore sighed once more, as though he resented having to make this decision. He heaved his giant, wide sword onto his shoulder, and turned to the field in which his flock was grazing. "First, I will do what has to be done."

Me and the two Slayers watched the man tread slowly but deliberately into the field, his weapon resting on his shoulder.

"Is he going to . . ." I began.

"I thought he described them as his 'babies,'" Corminar said.

"Guess he's gotta harvest the meat?" Val said as Lore raised the blade into the air.

"Mmm, lovely baby meat," I said.

"*Lamb* baby meat. It's weird when you don't say that bit."

Lore plunged the blade forward, hitting not animal but earth, thrusting the sword firmly into it until it stood on its own. "On my sword, I will return," the shepherd said solemnly to his flock, who sporadically looked up from munching on grass, with expressions of very little curiosity. "Seld will take care of you while I'm gone. Good care of you."

Lore knelt down in front of one of the lambs—the one he'd carried back from the town—and looked into its eyes. The lamb didn't seem to mind Lore's intimidating stature, the scar across his face, the deep booming to his voice.

He kissed the lamb on the forehead. "You'll be good for him, won't you?" Lore asked the sheep. "You'll behave yourselves?"

The lamb responded by chewing its mouthful of grass.

"And no more headbutting him, OK?"

"Baa," the sheep said, unconvincingly.

Lore kissed the lamb on the head once more. "There's a good girl."

The other three of us watched, each with at least one eyebrow raised, as the shepherd returned to us.

"What?" Lore said with a shrug. "I couldn't leave without saying goodbye to my—"

"Babies," Val and Corminar said in unison.

"Exactly."

I suppressed a smirk, but Val caught sight of it, and seeing it forced her to suppress one of her own.

"Alright," the sorcerer said. "Two recruits down, two to go. We go get Arzak and Tokas, then we go kill this Jake guy. Sound like a plan?"

Corminar nodded thoughtfully, while Lore pushed a smile to his face and gave the plan a big thumbs-up.

"How do you know he's called Jake?" I asked.

"Oh," Val said, waving the question down as though I should've known the answer. "They always are."

Corminar and Lore mumbled their agreement.

CHAPTER TWENTY-NINE

Wet Work

Progress had stalled.

While Corminar and Lore had been fairly straightforward to locate, the other two members of the Hero Slayers—Tokas and Arzak—had proven to be significantly more difficult. It had been a week and a half since we'd retrieved Lore, and only now did we finally have a line on one of them; one of Corminar's contacts placed Tokas in the large fishing town of Aptleed.

Aptleed was a town I knew well. I'd spent much coin as a teenager getting drunk in the taverns contained within the high stone walls leftover from an age long forgotten, and I hadn't much missed the intense stench of fish that plagued every corner of the town. I almost found myself excited to return, even if that might involve running into lovers past.

As we began our last day of travel toward Aptleed, I looked back on the progress I'd made leveling up my skills—particularly *Worldbending*, which I'd been focusing on. Messing about with portals over the past week and a half had gotten me up from level 5 to level 8. This was even despite the fact that "messing around" hardly yielded much in the way of experience points, though this was counteracted by the *Legacy of Sisyphus* effect massively up-weighting my XP gain.

> **Active Effect: Legacy of Sisyphus**
> Days remaining: 968 / 1,000
> *XP gain increased by +400 percent*

Already I'd made significant headway toward rebuilding myself up to a sufficient level—being up to level 7 now—and I was only a little over 3 percent through the effect's active period. I couldn't help but wonder just how strong I'd be by the end of it, assuming I lived that long and the Player didn't track me down and kill me long before then.

The thought sobered me, bringing me back to reality and the coastal road on the edge of the Iron Sea. The water lapped gently at the shore in the distance, a man on a small fishing vessel wrestling with a cumbersome net, though the sight of shapes emerging from the tree line ahead of us tore my eyes away.

At the front of our pack, Lore came to a sudden halt, his eyes on the men and women on the road ahead of us. My own eyes lingered on their long, thin blades, specifically.

There was a moment of pause before Lore roared, "Bandits!" and then all eight of us—bandits included—leaped into action.

If I'd managed to keep track of the fight last time around, it was because there had been only four of us: myself, Val, Corminar, and Lambkin. Now that the number of combatants had grown to eight, it was all I could do to focus on myself and not getting killed. Corminar and Lore seemed to focus on the two bandits on the right—though how they were handling them, I didn't know— and left the two on the left for Val and me.

Of course, Val knew that I wasn't quite up to handling myself just yet, and she cast a quick nervous glance in my direction. "Stay down," she said.

"I can handle my . . ." I started, before trailing off when I realized both that Val had already leaped away into battle and that I, in fact, could *not* handle myself. I stayed down, just as suggested, and watched as Val whipped up a storm of dust and vines—her go-to moves. For a moment, I thought I wouldn't even be needed, as Val seemed to be managing to hold off both of the bandits on the left, but then I heard a cry.

On the right, Corminar fell to the ground. Not bleeding, as I first thought, just unconscious. But this left our party down to two against four—a tough challenge even for high-level individuals, which they were not, particularly. I was going to need to get involved after all.

My initial instinct was to charge forward, knife drawn—still the Ranger's Blade, notably; I was not yet high enough in *Knifework* to get my old favorite out—and so that's exactly what I did. I was a man of instinct after all.

As I charged at the nearest bandit, growling, they turned toward me with wide eyes; apparently, they'd already *identified* my class and level, and thought me no threat. That I was now charging at them, then, was . . . astounding.

Level 18 Bandit
Race: Human

Maybe this wasn't such a good idea, I realized.

But it was too late; my blade had momentum, and I leaned into it, *stabbing* the bandit through his thick leather armor. The attack was well clear of any vital organs—unless we humans had a vital organ in our shoulder—yet it plunged deep enough to cause the man to grunt and stagger backward.

The bandit stared, eyes wide, at the knife sticking into his shoulder as I reached forward and wrenched it back out again. After all, it was the only decent knife I could actually equip; I wasn't keen to lose it so quickly.

"You get him?" Val called out to me, her voice slightly strained as she tried to deal with one of the other attackers.

"I . . . think so?" I replied, not quite believing it myself, just as the bandit pulled a hand to his wound and a gentle yellow-white light glowed into existence.

Uh oh. Healing magicks.

Being the strong and capable man I was, I turned and ran away. After all, what chance did I, a level 7, have against a level 18? It was a microcosm of a wider question: just what in the hells made me think I might be able to help take down a *Player*? But I put that other question aside for now and concentrated on my fleeing.

"Styk . . ." Val cried out irritably as I charged over uneven, mossy ground, toward the . . . sea.

I came to an abrupt halt at the water's edge; I hadn't quite considered what the plan of action was beyond running away. Behind me, loud—angry-sounding, if that was possible—footsteps grew nearer. I needed to think, and fast. By what means could someone of my level hope to come out of this alive?

The enemy grew closer and closer with every second that passed, and that did nothing for the growing panic taking root in my stomach. On a whim, almost, I reached inward for my *Local Portal* ability, meaning to buy myself some time, when an idea occurred to me that I could only label as . . . genius.

I turned my head for the sea. *Local Portal II* said "another location within current range of sight or within a ten-yard radius," and ten yards was not going to cut it. One hand stretched forward, reaching for the deepest, furthest part of the Iron Sea that was in sight, while the other reached for just in front of the approaching bandit. With clenched teeth and tight, apprehensive shoulders, I . . . opened the portal.

The contents of the Iron Sea plummeted out of the open portal into the bandit's face with an intensity I hadn't quite been prepared for. So shocked was I by the man flying through the air, propelled by a blast of water with enough volume to sate a whole town for a year, that I forgot for a moment to close the portal again. By the time I finally stopped using the power, my mana reserves were already approaching halfway empty, and that was with having invested a few more points in Intelligence over the past few days.

As a fresh water source washed over my shoes—these shoes were *not* waterproof, I realized—I looked at the bandit I'd aggressively bathed.

Level 18 Bandit defeated!

Worldbending: +1,000XP
Worldbending increased to level 9!
Base Points Gained: +2 INT, +2 Free Points (INT/WIS/CHA)

Defeated? Defeated was good, and far more than I'd hoped for. I passed the man on the rocky shore, glancing at his back for signs of life, and found myself strangely relieved when I noticed his shoulders moving up and down, ever so slightly. I shook my head; this was no time to be wrestling with questions of morality—Val and Lore were still fighting off the other three bandits, and they were going to need some help.

With renewed confidence, I charged back into the woods, making sure to keep the Iron Sea well within sight, and prepared myself to launch my newly invented water spell—well, kind of—at the bandits. But because I'd drained my mana reserves a good amount already, I realized I was going to need to wait; I only had one or two more shots at this.

Ahead of me, Lore roared with a rage I didn't know he was capable of as he swung his heavy, two-handed blade with ease enough to make it look as light as my Ranger's Blade. It was enough to repel two of the bandits' attacks, but he was doing little more than holding them off, and surely his stamina reserves would exhaust eventually . . .

On the other hand, Val was up to her usual tricks—a combination of her wind-based and vine-based spells. That she was in a woodland gave her an advantage of sorts, and it seemed it was only a matter of time before she triumphed against her foe.

So, I concentrated on Lore's two attackers.

"Lore!" I cried out.

The hulking barbarian class—I thought that class label was slightly unfair, knowing him somewhat now—didn't respond, all his attention fixed on fending off the attacks.

"I can see you're busy, Lore," I continued, "so don't worry about replying to me."

"He wasn't worried about that," Val called back to me.

"Thanks for the info. Lore? Could you . . . could you . . ." I searched for the word. "Duck?"

The sword-wielding shepherd, thrown by this request, faltered on his sword swing, and looked at me with both eyebrows raised. Fortunately, he shifted to the right just in time for one of the bandit's swords to pass safely by him; my request hadn't just cost him his life.

I seized the advantage, opening a portal just over my fellow party member and another in the depths of the Iron Sea. Again, water shot out of my portal at a rate of knots, sending the closer bandit flying across the woodlands, and pushing the other, staggering, to the floor. Having learned my lesson, I closed this portal quickly, leaving a quarter or so of my mana left.

Level 16 Bandit defeated!

Worldbending: +200XP

Lore looked at me with wide, excited eyes. "Woah! Where'd you learn *that?*" he said.

I responded by nodding toward the bandit who was still conscious.

"Oh, right, yeah," he replied, then hurried off to bash her in the head with the butt of his sword.

Level 18 Bandit defeated!

With only one bandit left, we had the advantage. And I, a Level 7 Bladespinner—well, *Novice* Bladespinner—had been the one to turn the tide. It was nice to feel useful. I raised my hands toward the sea and the bandit, readying myself to launch another wave over the last remaining enemy.

"Save your mana," Lore said. "We got this."

Val glimpsed the hulking barbarian coming out of the corner of her eye, and dove to the side to make the bandit turn, shielding Lore from his sight. As she pressed on with dust clouds and whipping vines, a great shadow grew over the enemy as Lore stood over them.

The bandit finally noticed his approach and turned to face him, gulping, raising his blade in shaking hands.

"Don't you even think about it, fella," Lore said, and didn't even need to swing his sword.

Level 19 Bandit defeated!

Worldbending: +400XP

CHAPTER THIRTY

Obstacles among Obstacles

We found the town of Aptleed under a self-imposed blockade. This, for people with rumbling stomachs—like me and Val—was bad news. I understood the reasoning; we'd witnessed firsthand just how out of control the bandit menace had grown in this part of the world. If they needed to shut the gates to protect their citizens, fair enough. I just wished it didn't come between me and a hearty bowl of stew.

The powers that be had barred shut the heavy wooden northern, western, and southern gates, and the only other obvious way in—through the port on the east—was being patrolled by perhaps two hundred of the town's guards. On the high stone walls, still more guards stared down upon the four of us, and I couldn't help but wonder just how much of the town's population had found employment as guards. It had to be at least three quarters of them, it felt like.

"Any bright ideas?" Val asked, hands on hips as she stared up at the looming stone wall.

"Perhaps we pursue Arzak first, and return to Aptleed on a more fortuitous day," Corminar suggested.

"Are you saying we've come all this way for nothing?"

The elven ranger shrugged.

"No, I'm not having that," Val continued. "We're all smart here"—she glanced to Lore, who didn't seem to notice—"between us, we can come up with a way to get in, surely."

"Can't you use your changeling abilities?" I suggested. "I feel like we don't talk about those enough."

"And do what?" the part-changeling herself responded.

"I dunno, pretend to be a guard? Walk us in as prisoners?"

"So I alone am supposed to have captured a massive barbarian, the first highest leveled archer in the Tundras, and you?"

"You can just say 'highest leveled,'" I replied, also picking up on the lack of complimentary description about myself. In the end, I settled for grumbling to myself about it.

"What about you? Can't you portal us in?" Val asked.

"I can, within ten feet or within line of sight. So best I could manage is top of the wall, for now, and right in sight of all those guards. I'm pretty sure I know how that one plays out."

"Yeah, alright, fair point," Val said. "Any other ideas?"

Lore opened his mouth, and drew in a breath like he was about to offer something, when a thought occurred to me.

"Wait," I said, "I know a way."

Three pairs of eyes looked at me.

"I grew up around here. Know the town pretty well. And if I'm not mistaken, there's a sewer outlet on the northeast side of town." I left out the part where I only knew about this entrance due to sketchy Thieves Guild activities.

"Alright, good," Val said, at just the same moment that Corminar said, "The *sewer*? You expect us to travel in through the *sewers*?"

"Got a problem with that, C?" Lore asked, a knowing smile on his face. He shared a look with Val.

"I am wearing suede shoes, for Hera's sake. *Suede!* Fine suede, in fact, and I should not want to—"

"And why in the hells would you buy suede shoes for adventuring, Cor?" Val asked.

"I would have you know they are very on trend in Fenrock. Besides, they were on sale."

I led our crew around to the northern side of town, back toward where we'd tried to enter originally, but this time took us off-road and into the woods that sprawled out this side of Aptleed. We pressed toward the wall, Corminar grumbling about his shoes most of the way, and eventually found—

"Styk, there's a whole load of soldiers guarding it," Val said.

Well, yes, we found *that*.

The four of us crouched down behind the cover of shrubbery—always good for cover, shrubbery was—and peered through. The soldiers in front of us were milling around casually within the shade of the trees, and it seemed like it was chance alone that they'd chosen this spot to rest at.

But this wasn't what other members of the team were focusing on.

"Interesting," Corminar mused.

I turned to him. "What is?"

"You don't recognize the emblem on their surcoats?" Val asked, and before I could answer, added, "They're Goldmarch soldiers."

Lore's mouth opened seemingly involuntarily at this revelation. "Goldmarch soldiers?" he asked. "What are they doing this far north?"

Val shrugged. "Why would I know? Do I look like Queen Amira to you?"

The barbarian looked to me, unsure how to answer.

"He doesn't know what Queen Amira looks like," I clarified for Val. "Neither do I, for that matter, so that was a bit of a hard—"

"I was asking rhetorically," the sorcerer cut in, apparently keen to put this conversation to a stop. Fair enough, really. "What do we do?"

"Perhaps it is best we wait until nighttime; they may adjourn."

"I'm hungry, though," I said, and for a moment felt ridiculous, until Val aggressively nodded her agreement.

"Why don't we—" Lore started.

"Changeling abilities?" I suggested.

"Why are you so keen on me shapeshifting?"

"I just think it's cool. Got a problem with that?" I replied.

Lore tried again. "We could just—"

"No, I haven't got a problem with that, but it's a bit weird, is all. I don't obsess over your . . . your . . ." She searched for something equivalent.

"Sad eyes?" Corminar suggested.

"Not quite what I was going for, Cor."

"Why don't we . . ." Lore said, then sighed and stood up from behind the bush. He waved to the twenty or so Goldmarch soldiers in front of us and cried out, "Hello!" with a large smile on his face.

Val and I looked to one another, horrified.

"Perhaps we put him on a leash?" Corminar suggested—the second unhelpful suggestion in as many minutes.

"Who goes there?" one soldier, an older man with a finer sword, replied.

"Just me!" Lore said, and stepped out from the bushes.

"At least he didn't—"

"And my three friends," the barbarian continued. "They're just hiding behind the bushes."

Corminar sighed, but ultimately was the first to stand and reveal himself. Val and I soon followed suit.

"Hi," I said, copying Lore's wave, though more timidly.

"Yeah, hi," Val added.

"We were just wondering," Lore pressed on. "What are you all doing here? Are you lost? Goldmarch is fifty miles south, I thought, though I'm bad at directions. I once got lost between my house and the pie shop, and I eat *a lot* of pie."

"That's no business of yours, citizen," the older soldier—the one in charge, it seemed—replied.

"Alright, yeah, fair point," Lore said. "Could I ask, though: do you see that sewer pipe behind you?"

The soldier turned, looked at the metal grate and then back to Lore. "I do."

"What, say, would you do if four people tried to get in it?"

"We are not here to interfere."

Lore narrowed his eyes. "Right, but . . ."

"He's saying we're going in there, and we don't want you to attack us," Val said.

"Yes, madam, I understood. I reiterate: we're not here to interfere. We're only on hand to help Duke Cambelny with his bandit problem, should he accept our aid."

"Duke not get on with Queenie?" Val asked.

"That's beyond my pay grade, I'm afraid," the soldier replied. "Though I don't think you should be calling her 'Queenie.'"

"Do you think she looks like her?" Lore asked.

The soldier blinked at him, the burly, towering man with the wide grin on his face. "Who? Looks like who?"

Lore pointed to Val. "Her. Do you think she looks like Queenie?"

"Queen Amira," the soldier corrected him.

"Do you think she looks like Queenie Amira?" Lore tried.

"I . . ." the soldier started, shaking his head. "I don't know. Sure. If you want."

"So you don't know what she looks like, either?"

"I know what she looks like, it's just—" The soldier caught himself, holding his hands in the air in defeat. "Look, if you want to sneak into Aptleed, then it's no skin off my teeth."

"I don't think teeth have skin," Lore said.

The soldier didn't bother hiding his sigh. He stepped aside and gestured toward the sewer pipe that was slowly oozing . . . *material* . . . into a small pond. "Please, be my guest," he said.

"Great!" Lore said, and turned back to the three of us still standing at the edge of the woods, before his face dropped.

"No time like the present," Val said, moving toward the sewers with a spring in her step that probably didn't befit the task before us.

"Guys . . ." Lore repeated.

"Does anyone have a change of footwear I could borrow?" Corminar asked the soldiers.

"*Guys!*" the barbarian tried once more.

"Yes, Lore, whatever is it?" Corminar replied, still eyeing up the soldiers' boots.

The barbarian gestured toward six bandits stepping out of the trees behind us. "Gods, not again," I mumbled.

At the same moment, Val turned to the soldiers and nodded toward the bandits. "Let me guess," she said. "You won't interfere?"

The captain nodded. "We will not interfere."

"Great," Val said, and Lore reached for his sword.

CHAPTER THIRTY-ONE

Fighting among Soldiers

As Val, Lore, and Corminar charged into the fight, both screaming and swinging, I eyed up my almost entirely depleted mana reserves. It wasn't fair that bandits would attack us twice in one day, really; I didn't have the coin to afford mana potions. The only thing that would recover my mana was a nice long sleep.

But I wouldn't be getting that anytime soon.

At the edge of the tree line, one of the bandits caught my eye, and I stumbled backward, straight into the admittedly very chiseled chest of the Goldmarch captain. I looked up at him as the bandit strode confidently toward me. ". . . Help?" I asked.

The veteran soldier shook his head. "Sorry. Orders."

"But they're gonna kill me."

The captain shrugged. "Not my problem."

"Well, thanks very much," I said, and focused my attention back at the approaching bandit.

Level 22 Bandit
Race: Human

Oh, yikes. This one was stronger than the ones I'd faced down previously, and I didn't have a handily placed source of water up my sleeve this time. And I didn't even have more than one decent portal left in me. All in all, this meant I was going to have to rely on the two bog-standard *Knifework* abilities I'd managed to get so far, with not so much as *Closed Reach* to lend a hand.

I held my Ranger's Blade in the air, forcing my hand to remain steady as the woman approached. *What are my choices here?* I asked myself. I could hope this borrowed knife had decent stats, and rely on *Slice*, or I could put my weight behind it and force the blade through the woman's leather armor—but the latter required more stamina, and I'd kinda been forsaking Dexterity lately in favor of Intelligence.

So, when the woman grew closer, I chose another option entirely: I ran away.

Now, normally I would have had some shame about doing this, but there were two factors at play here. First of all, the rest of the team seemed to be managing all right with their own attackers. Secondly—and this was more important to me—I really didn't want to die.

. . . Again.

So, yeah, I ran away, but it's not like I was bolting for the hills. No, instead I ran for the cover of the huddle of soldiers who apparently *really didn't want to be involved.* Well, they were involved now.

I pushed through the midst of them, barging them aside, pretty confident that their orders not to intervene also applied to not hurting Level 7 Novice Bladespinners who were being a bit of a pain. Sure enough, none of them moved to attack me, but most of them either grunted with annoyance or scoffed at the idea that I was really going to do this to them. I couldn't feel too guilty about it—what were soldiers for if not protecting me from bandits? Even if they were, technically, a few hundred miles north of their jurisdiction.

I heard more groans erupt behind me, and it didn't take the glance over my shoulder to know that the bandit was following me through the horde. As I reached the other side of the crowd, I realized—as I often do—that I didn't have a plan for the whole "what comes next" bit.

So I swung a hard left and ran around the outside of the group. As I reached the other side, back where I'd started, the bandit reached the outside, too, and craned her head over the crowd to get a look at me.

"I, err . . ." I started, trailing off when the bandit started running clockwise around the group to do the same. By the time she was where I'd been a few seconds ago, I was on the other side again.

"Stop!" the bandit cried out, like I was gonna do *that.*

As the running continued, I scoured my brain for the next stage of the plan. At some point, even running would drain my stamina reserves enough that the bandit would catch up with me. That is, unless her stamina reserves were lower than mine, which I doubted, considering mine went up to . . . 23.

All this running had only postponed the inevitable; I needed to figure out a good use of my *Knifework* skills if I was going to get out of this. As the bandit suddenly U-turned, now running around the circle of soldiers anticlockwise, I took another look at her before I did the same. She was carrying a long sword—one that she looked like she knew how to use, but long enough that she was going to need room to swing it.

And that's when I came up with a plan.

I pushed back into the group of bewildered soldiers, one of them crying out "Oh *really?*" and tried to lose myself amongst them.

The bandit continued running around the circle for a few moments longer before realizing what had happened. As she peered around the soldier's shoulders—try saying that after a few pints of wine—I crouched, trying to hide. After all, if I held out long enough for Val, Corminar, and Lore to finish up, I might not even *need* to try out my risky plan.

Of course, that was the moment the bandit saw me. We made eye contact for a moment, wherein both of us paused, and then I tried to slink away slowly behind the closest soldiers. You know, just in case.

As the bandit pushed between the mass of soldiers—who'd been pressed together by our running around them, herded together much like sheep—I readied myself to *slice.*

I slid between the legs of two neighboring soldiers, moving around while I was out of sight of the bandit. I watched as she reached the spot I'd been a moment earlier, drawing her blade. But as she tried to swing it, she realized what would happen if she hit anyone, and so the sword arced through the air in a rather slow, cramped manner. Of course, she realized I'd moved again long before the blade hit the ground, and once again her head spun around to search for me.

I considered bolting for the group, heading for the tree line, but my stamina was already running low, and there was a good chance the bandit would catch me. No; this was a microcosm of our inevitable fight against the Player. It was weak against strong, and the weak could only succeed if they stuck to their plan. So stick to the plan I did.

The bandit pressed amongst the soldiers, step by cautious step, her eyes scouring the crowd for signs of me. But I stayed deathly still, crouched behind a soldier not three feet away from her. My plan depended on remaining hidden, getting the element of surprise, and—

"Oh for Hera's sake, enough of this," the captain said, and pointed straight at me. "He's there."

I gulped, and the bandit charged.

Like a helpless deer before a train of charging horses, I froze, eyes wide.

The bandit swung her blade into the air.

I thought to move, but my body didn't cooperate.

The swinging sword caught one soldier by the knee.

In the last possible moment, I dove to the floor, the long blade crashing into the ground where I'd been standing only moments earlier.

As the bandit and I stared one another down, the hit soldier's knee began to bleed. Two dozen pairs of eyes looked from the flesh wound to the bandit, and in that moment, I realized I'd won.

The soldier's orders not to interfere seemed to disappear at the first sign of blood. As eight or so of them closed on the bandit, the captain and a few of his most loyal soldiers tried to stop them.

"Orders!" the captain bellowed furiously. "Orders!"

It was enough to stop all but a handful of them. The three remaining soldiers—the most bloodthirsty amongst them, it seemed—stepped up to the bandit, looming over her, glaring down at her.

But though they closed on her, none of them drew their weapons. I couldn't help but wonder if this wasn't just a show, an intimidation, an act to scare some sense into the bandit without actually breaking from their orders.

I clasped my blade, ready to strike; if they weren't going to handle this, then I sure as well was. I had just enough mana left for one *Closed Reach*. So . . . I did that.

The blade pushed through the soldier's chest without harming him, emerging eight inches away—which just so happened to be inside the bandit's chest.

Level 22 Bandit defeated!

Knifework: +1,200XP
Knifework increased to level 13!
Base Points Gained: +1 DEX, +1 STR, +2 Free Points (VIT/DEX/STR)

Result.

The soldier who'd been standing between us looked down at his chest, shocked, as the knife emerged from it via bended reality, and not via his vital organs.

I pulled the knife back before I could run out of mana—just in time—and managed to avoid incurring the wrath of a good couple of dozen highly trained Goldmarch soldiers.

"Right," I said, brushing myself down and quickly putting both free points into my overlooked Strength stat. "If you all will excuse me, I have some sewers to break into."

CHAPTER THIRTY-TWO

Parental Guidance

Corminar didn't like that I couldn't remember how to navigate Aptleed's sewer system. Not that the others took the news much better, though at least Lore seemed to keep his mouth shut about it—unlike the other two. I'd protested that it'd been the best part of a decade since I was last here, so how was I to retain all that? This explanation was met with deaf ears and grimacing mouths.

The liquid contents of the sewer system hadn't been the only issue, either, though Corminar was much more preoccupied with this—and its effect on his posh shoes—than the other, which had been *giant rats*. And not a *basic* variant, either. No, these were variant: poison.

Of course, the sewers contained giant rats, Val pointed out. After all, that was where giant rats go. It's a tradition, almost; you go into a sewer, you ruin your shoes, you fight a big rodent.

They were hardly the most difficult enemies, none of them past level 6, but it was enough to make an already slightly sour mood . . . well, very sour indeed. At least the team made me do most of the work, which netted me enough experience points to get *Knifework* up to level 14. This meant both that I could put more free points into Strength to boost my knife skills, and that I was only one level off another ability.

So when we finally found our way out of the sewers, through a gate into a stable yard, I was near enough smiling, while the rest of the team were grumbling about bathing. Not that I didn't fancy one of them myself; I might have been pleased about my rapid progression, but I still had a sense of smell.

I'd recommended a local tavern to the team, but was perturbed to find that it had changed owners in the years since I'd last been here—and it had lost all its character. Val, Corminar, and Lore didn't seem to notice or care, however; they were just happy to be getting cleaned up.

As I pulled on a fresh set of clothes, I stared out of the window at the town beyond. It wasn't just this tavern that had changed, I noticed; the whole of Aptleed had. If this was once a place I'd thought of as "home," then it wasn't anymore.

Behind me, I heard the thunderous snores of Lore, who I'd been assigned a room with on this particular evening. Only now did I understand why I'd been such a popular roommate amongst the other two; neither Val nor Corminar could handle such loud noises.

"It's not bedtime yet, Lore," I said, and the barbarian class suddenly sat bolt upright.

"Just resting my eyelids!" he replied, and then hopped back up as though he'd been awake for hours.

We waited patiently outside the room of the other two, before I gave in first and knocked loudly on the door.

"Just a minute!" Val replied.

"It's getting late . . ." I said.

The door swung open, and a huffy Val stood with a towel wrapped around her hair. "My hair is drying. It was *your* idea to go through some sewers, if you'll remember, so you're gonna have to forgive me if I take a little while to get ready."

"What about Corminar? Bet he's itching to get moving, too, isn't he?"

The elf appeared at the doorway, his hair also wrapped up in a towel. "I do not air dry," he said.

I pursed my lips. "How long are you gonna—" I started, and then realized I wasn't emotionally prepared for the answer. "Me and Lore will be downstairs. You drink, Lore?" I asked him.

"Often!" came the reply.

Even the beer served at this tavern had changed, it turned out. No longer was it the heavy, ruby-red ale that I'd been looking forward to since stepping foot back in Aptleed, but instead it was a light, yellow affair—barely worth the label of *ale*.

"Nice beer!" Lore said, and out of social obligation I felt forced to agree with him cheerily.

"Can I ask you something?" I said to Lore, with the tone of a question that its answerer would not like.

"Yeah, of course." One good eye and one blinded one looked back at me, though there was a smile in both.

"Do you know how intimidating you look?"

Lore smiled a big, goofy smile. "It throws people off, doesn't it?"

"It doesn't 'throw people off,' Lore, it makes them run and hide."

"Yeah!" Lore replied, clearly taking this as a massive compliment. "Better that than having to fight them. I don't like fighting people. Not really."

"The giant sword begs to differ."

"Ah, you mean this?" Lore asked, pulling his only sword over his shoulder.

"Yes . . . that's the one."

The barbarian shrugged. "It was my father's. The Bane Sword."

"What was he? A soldier? A mercenary?"

"A blacksmith. He made it. Never once used it, though, I don't think."

"What was it the bane of, then?"

"Vines, mostly," Lore said. "But it's a good sword. I always thought about maybe unlocking *Smithing* one day, but . . . I dunno, I guess the day hasn't yet come."

Before we'd finished our first pints, Val and Corminar came downstairs to join us. Judging by Val's still quite wet hair, she'd rushed the drying job in order to get involved with the beer, perhaps feeling like she was missing out. Corminar's hair, on the other hand, was its typical luscious, perfect self.

"Alright," I said after downing the last of my beer and rising from the table. "Shall we?"

"Oh," Val said, raising an index finger as though to make a point. "I thought we'd . . ." Her eyes lingered on the beer.

I sighed. "We'll get you one for the road."

Val's eyes lit up.

Alongside three new friends and one rapidly diminishing flagon of beer, I made my way through Aptleed's streets, taking us to the location that we'd been given for Tokas, the healer of the Slayers.

It was a small home on the edge of town, one that shared its space with a flower shop. When we asked the proprietor—an older orc gentleman wearing an apron with a surprisingly garish design—he pointed upward. "Live above," he said.

So we went through to the back of the shop, climbed the stairs, and spilled out into the apartment above. The tiefling—Tokas, presumably—sat facing a desk, surrounded by paperwork, trash, and children's toys littering the floor, her head in her hands.

"I told you, I don't have it," the tiefling said.

"Toke?" Val asked.

Suddenly, Tokas pulled her hands away from her face, and spun around to face the four of us—though I couldn't see much because Lore had made the decision to put his wide, bulky frame in front of both me and Corminar.

"Tokas!" the great barbarian said, and though I couldn't see his face, I could tell from his tone that he was smiling.

"You . . ." Tokas started, and then her pose softened. "Hi, everyone. Where's Arzak?"

"We haven't found her yet," Val said. "She's next on the list."

"So I'm assuming . . ." Tokas began, and then her eyes fell to me, trying to poke my head over Lore's shoulder and mostly failing. Upon seeing me, the tiefling's eyebrows raised slightly in likely surprise that the Slayers were traveling with someone new. If I wasn't mistaken, there was a brief flash of red light that accompanied her realizing it wasn't just old friends in her apartment. If it was me, that flash of illusion magick would have been to hide some of the mess, though admittedly there was quite a lot in this house to hide.

Two young half-tiefling, half-human children ran screaming through the middle of us, and both Lore and I jumped aside to allow them to pass. Corminar, on the other hand, made no such effort, and one of the two children ran straight into his leg. They stopped their joyful screaming for a moment, bounced to the floor, then picked themselves back up again and continued the whole screaming-running thing they'd been doing so effectively before.

"What's with the boots?" Val asked, staring where the children had disappeared off to. "They're magick."

Tokas paused before answering. "Boots of Slowing."

"They don't seem to be working," Corminar offered.

"They did. At first," Tokas replied. "It turns out that weighing your children's feet down is a great way to get them to farm Strength skills."

"You're saying they have superstrong legs now?" Val asked.

The tiefling mother nodded.

I couldn't help but notice Val trying to suppress a smirk. Fortunately, Tokas seemed distracted by the rest of us, and didn't notice.

I stepped forward, offering a hand in greeting. "Styk."

"Tokas," came the reply and the responding handshake. "Have we . . . met before? You seem familiar."

I shook my head. "I don't think so."

This seemed a relief to the tiefling; her memory wasn't failing her. "You're . . . a new member of the team?"

"He's assisting us," Val said. "For now."

It was a bit of a surprise to me that our time together was limited, but I supposed it was. Once we killed the Player—*if* we killed the Player—our job would be done. There would be no reason for me to hang around with these people. And them, me.

At this answer, Tokas nodded.

"Toke, there's a new—" Val started, her voice taking on that serious tone that seemed to come so unnaturally to her.

"I'm in," Tokas replied.

Val blinked. "Excuse me?"

"You're saying there's a new Player, right? I'm in."

"But—"

"Let me take the kids around to my father's, and then . . . I'm in."

Val blinked again, her mouth hanging open.

"The others took more convincing," I explained.

"The others aren't single mothers," Tokas snapped. After a breath, her snarl faded and her eyes widened, as if she realized she'd spoken a bit harshly. "I love my children. I do. But they can be a handful."

"Especially once they have superstrong legs, I imagine," Val added.

"Yes. I'm in. Just one quick quest: kill a Player. It'll be the break I need."

It was my turn to blink at the tiefling. "That's supposed to be a *quick* quest? Who *are* you people?"

CHAPTER THIRTY-THREE

Getting out of Tight Spots

(At some point over the next few days, I did some math.

I know, I wouldn't have expected it of me, either; it wasn't exactly in my wheelhouse. I'm going to cut a long story short: I used up a lot of paper and a lot of charcoal doing some sums, and from three of the five times I did them I got the same end result. That result? Based on the fact that I leveled up *Worldbending* to level 9 when I unleashed the Iron Sea on those bandits, combined with the amount of leftover experience, I wasn't that far off getting *Worldbending* to level 10. And of course, as we all know, level 10 is one of those levels where you get to pick a new ability.

I mention this now for one very important reason: the five of us were currently hanging upside down, trapped inside a magically reinforced net trap, and my skills were about to have a lot to do with how we got out of it.

Let me rewind a few days.

I suppose this all started when we were on the road to—

No, wait. Now that I'm thinking this through, I guess it started a little earlier. The five of us were in a traveler's inn, and Val had convinced Corminar to partake in a beer or two. This had the secondary effect of getting him drunk, which had the—what's the word?—*tertiary* effect of getting him to loosen his purse strings and buy us all a few more drinks.

Even Tokas, who'd been broody and quiet since we'd picked her up—Val assured me she wasn't normally like this—cheered up a little. In fact, the only one of the five of us who didn't seem very drunk was Lore, but I suppose even he with his large build was a bit merry.

As a result, we may have been a bit loud with our conversation. We didn't say anything about killing Players—even *drunk*, we weren't that stupid—but we did mouth off about looking for Arzak and still not having a clue where she'd gotten to since the team dispersed. What we'd find out later is that an associate of Captain Lambkin had overheard this conversation, and so began the makings of the trap we were soon caught in.

A good few days later—I can't say exactly how many—a messenger approached us on the road. Someone with a letter addressed to me, weirdly; I was not the sort of person who often received correspondence. Val obviously had figured that out for herself, because she furrowed her brow at this news, though maybe she was just jealous that someone else was currently more popular than her.

Any shrewd readers among you might have some idea what was in this letter, and indeed it was the supposed location of the final member of the Slayers, Arzak Blorg. If the letter was to be believed—and yeah, we did believe it—then Arzak was in a small town a few miles south of Thistle Fort. That made sense, we reckoned; Thistle was an orcish city, and Arzak, after all, was an orc. So that's why we didn't question the note, but I concede now that not having done so might have been a mistake.

As we grew near to the town in question, we found ourselves traveling through dense evergreen forest. The trees were tall, the branches many, and even on the narrow road we could not see a great distance ahead, behind, or to the side of us. This was where Lambkin sprung his trap, and so I'll jump back into the narrative at this point, though please be aware that it begins with the assorted noises of five people suddenly finding themselves hoisted upward by a net.)

"Aah!"

"Whaa—"

"Uh . . ."

(And so on. You get the idea.)

Of the five of us, only Corminar apparently had any suspicions that something like this was coming. He'd had his bow drawn for a good half hour, and as the net hoisted him up into the air, he released a nocked arrow at a man stepping out from between the trees.

"A-ha!" a smug Lambkin said, then followed it up with "Oh balls," as an arrow buried itself in his arm.

Fortunately for the ex-captain, there wasn't room inside the net for Corminar to draw another arrow, or he might next have received one to the head.

"Lambkin . . ." I muttered, my voice strained by both my hanging upside down and Val's knee's proximity to my groin.

"You really thought you could cart me off in a truckload of dung and I wouldn't come looking for you?" Lambkin asked. "I was looking for you anyway!

That was hardly gonna change things, was it? And now you've walked straight into my—"

"You're monologuing," Val pointed out.

"Yeah, only villains monologue," I added.

Lambkin furrowed his brow. "I'm not monologuing, I'm explaining. Do you never talk at length with each other at all?"

"No, we mostly interrupt each other," Tokas offered timidly.

"Well, I'm not monologuing, OK? I'm definitely explaining."

Corminar gave up trying to fire another arrow. "It shares much of its framework with monologuing."

The ex-captain ground his teeth together, snarling. "I'm not going to say it again: I'm not monologuing, and—" Lambkin looked down at his wound. "Wow, this is really bleeding. Did you use some kind of poison to make me bleed more?"

"Yes," Corminar replied. "A bleed poison."

"Oh. It's just called that, is it?"

"Alchemists are not an imaginative bunch," Corminar said.

"OK, look," Lambkin said. "I'm going to go and find someone to tend to this. So, I'm just going to leave you here. You have your archer to thank for that."

Lore piped up, "Are you not worried about us escaping?" Though the last word of that was slightly drowned out by the sounds of me and Val shushing him.

Lambkin smiled—or, at least, gave a rough approximation of it; the pain from Corminar's poison was clearly overwhelming him. "Please. For this trap I spared no expense. I hired the most creative trap-maker in the Tundras. I'll go, I'll get myself an antidote, and I'll be back before you know it. Maybe . . . tomorrow morning? That'll give you plenty of time to . . . hang out."

On that note, the captain turned away, clearly thinking he'd done some clever wordplay with that last sentence. The five of us watched him go, from various heights and angles, and only once Lambkin was out of sight did Val start giggling.

"And what are *you* laughing about?" I asked.

"Didn't you hear the wording? The 'most creative trap-maker.' Not 'the best.'"

"I really don't see how that's important."

Val smiled. "It's important because Steve got sued for false advertising. And 'most creative'? That's how he brands himself since it was proven in a court of law that he was *not* the best. And if it's a Steve trap, then . . ."

"There's gonna be a way to break out of it."

"Exactly," Val said.

Armed with this information, I found renewed vigor to figure out a way to escape. While Corminar and Lore wrestled with the Bane Sword, which was currently pressing against its owner's chiseled chest, Val and Tokas tried some sort of magick which seemed to require them to hold hands and chant. This left me not needed by anyone else, and at this point I circled back to the math I'd done over the last few days.

"Corminar, I need some—"

"I am rather busy at the moment, Styk."

I rolled my eyes and instead plunged my hand into the man's pocket, which was conveniently placed considering we were all hanging upside down in a tangle. I pulled from it a surprising number of potions—was this pocket enchanted to be larger on the inside?—and returned all but two glowing blue ones.

Mana potions.

I tried, first of all, opening a portal within the trap itself, but had no luck; there simply wasn't any room what with all of us in the way, and with a few limbs poking through the net at odd angles. So instead I returned to leveling the skill up, opening and closing portals in the surrounding area, and slowly accumulating more *Worldbending* experience.

Val was first to notice. "Oh look, Styk's gone completely insane."

I ignored her and carried on with my approach, until, finally . . .

Worldbending increased to level 10!
Base Points Gained: +2 INT, +2 Free Points (INT/WIS/CHA)

"Styk," Val said, "I really don't think now is the time for—"

"Shh," I replied, "I'm trying something."

Val stuck her tongue out at me and went back to her chanting, like that was such a better use of time.

Ability Selection Unlocked
Select an ability from the list below:

Option 1: Weaken Metal (Worldbending)—Your magicks find flaws within nonenchanted metalwork, and enhance them, leading to objects becoming immediately weaker.

I craned my head around Lore's arm to look up at the clasp that was holding us. It was definitely metal, but there were two potential obstacles. First of all, Steve's involvement meant that the clasp was almost certainly enchanted. And the other issue? Even if it wasn't, all that *weakening* it would do was send us crashing to the floor, still trapped within the net. And, based on where Lore's greatsword was pointing, I didn't think this would end well for at least one of us.

> **Option 2: Skinsmith II (Worldbending)**—Toughen skin to act as natural armor. Strength of armor scales on [WIS]. Uses less mana/second.

Well, that one was no help at all. I couldn't think of any application for this skill that would get me out of this particular mess. Not that I should really have been thinking so short-term, of course. I still had, at least, another option . . .

> *Hidden condition met! Alternative ability choice unlocked.*
> **Option 3: Portal Slice (Knifework)** [Requires: *Knifework* skill unlocked]— *Passive*. Portals can now be spawned within nonsentient objects. Doing so slices through all objects that are not reinforced by magick.

It was as though the Architects themselves were smiling down upon me; this was perfect. I supposed that *Worldbending* and *Knifework* skills had some good synergy between them, because this was the second time that having both skills had proven useful—after getting access to *Closed Reach* the first time around.

> **Ability Unlocked**: Portal Slice
> **Portal Slice (Knifework)**: *Passive*. Portals can now be spawned within nonsentient objects. Doing so slices through all objects that are not reinforced by magick.

Downing the second of Corminar's mana potions to replenish that particular power bar, I squeezed my hand upward, pointing at the spot just below the clasp that held the net trap together.

With the other hand, I pointed elsewhere—it didn't seem like it mattered where the other end of the portal was for this, only that it existed. And, within a second, the net came crashing down. I only thought at the last moment to kick the end of Lore's sword out from under his head.

The five of us spilled out onto the ground, the net trap unfolding around us, and I—admittedly—was the one who complained the most about the subsequent bruises.

"You know, Val," Lore said, after we'd all picked ourselves off the ground and dusted ourselves down, "I ain't think Styk's gone insane. I think he was actually being very clever."

Val opened her mouth to argue the point, and then walked off, grumbling.

"So," the barbarian continued, "Thistle Fort is out, is it?"

CHAPTER THIRTY-FOUR

Accepting Quests & Taking Names

We'd spent quite a few days looking for Arzak by the time we'd actually gotten a *real* lead on her whereabouts, and none of it had been particularly conducive to making full use of my *Legacy of Sisyphus* effect.

> **Active Effect: Legacy of Sisyphus**
> Days remaining: 956 / 1,000
> *XP gain increased by +400 percent*

Mostly we'd been wandering from town to town, looking for people who'd seen someone matching Arzak's description, and no part of this actually required a skill of any sort. I'd entertained myself by *portal slicing* through tree branches—at least as much as my mana reserves allowed—but I was getting to the point in *Worldbending* progression where these small amounts of experience didn't amount to much. In fact, I was still just where I'd been before: at *Worldbending* level 10.

So, as it was, I was itching for a fight.

Fortunately, that was just where our journey would lead us. The first tip we had on Arzak's whereabouts came from one of Corminar's "contacts"—this being the term Corminar consistently used for people who were, in fact, his lovers. The man in question, who I thought surprisingly short considering Corminar's usual taste, pointed us to the coastal town of Ironview, a good few days to our southeast. It took me two days of travel to realize that Ironview was in fact called Ironview because it looked out onto the Iron Sea. I made the mistake of realizing this aloud, and Val killed the next few hours mocking me for it.

Getting sick of Val and her incessant mocking of me—she didn't do that to anyone else!—I dropped back in our walking party and made an effort to strike up a conversation with Tokas. Tokas, I had come to realize, was *not* a reserved person; she was only reserved around me. I thought that maybe striking up some small talk might help tear those walls down.

She twitched her arm away from me as I got close. Not a great start, and very reminiscent of most times I'd approached women in taverns.

"Hey, Tokas," I tried. "We haven't gotten to speak much. Thought I could get to know you." And then, because that felt all incredibly artificial and forced, I added, "Tell me about your kids." As soon as the words left my mouth, I realized that wasn't any less forced-sounding.

"Why?" Tokas replied. "What do you intend to do with them?"

I blinked. "I . . . OK, sorry, I didn't mean anything by it. Was just getting to know you."

Tokas considered me for a moment. "With the greatest respect . . . is there any point?"

"What do you mean?"

"I mean: we do this . . . job. You get your revenge, or justice, or whatever you want to label it, and then you're done, right?"

We hadn't even finished forming the team and already people couldn't wait to get rid of me; it wasn't a great feeling, I won't lie. "Well, until then, I thought—"

"And that's if we *succeed*, of course. If this Player is as great and powerful as you've been telling everyone, there's a good chance we'll die in the process."

"Cheery thought."

"Either way, there's no need for us to build up some long-term friendship." Tokas paused, looking at me. "Do you agree?"

I pointed to the front of the group. "I'm going to talk to Val." Suddenly her insults didn't seem so bad; at least I wasn't necessarily sure if she *meant* them.

Val smiled at me for a moment when I approached, then blinked, confused, and wiped it from her face. "Miss me?" she asked.

"Tokas is a laugh, isn't she?" I replied, ignoring the question.

"She's just direct; you'll get used to it. What did she tell you? That your hair-style doesn't suit you? Because it doesn't. There, I can be direct, too."

"She told me we didn't need to be friends."

Val threw back her head and almost laughed it off. "Ha! Very on-brand for her. Both technically true and horrifically insulting. Love it. Real top-drawer stuff."

"I'm not—"

"Look," Val said, for a moment her tone switching to strangely serious. "She's a tiefling. You know what some people think about them. Can you blame her if she's learned to put up a rough exterior?"

I sighed, considering this fact. "I suppose I can't. But I don't *feel* like I'm gonna get used to it."

"You will, I promise. And if you don't, that'll be really funny for me. It's win-win."

"For you."

"And that's what counts!"

When we reached the Iron Sea, with the large, sprawling town of Ironview before us, I remembered why I'd never rushed to set foot in it before. Ironview was a questing town, the largest in this part of the world—at least this side of the Bladerocks—and my line of work . . . hadn't been the sort of work you put on the questing registers.

Working off-register meant that there was no guarantee anyone would pay up, of course. All the work that was registered in a questing hub like Ironview was recorded for the questing ledgers. Then, those who collated these records would make certain questers paid up to questees. Or was that the other way around? I was never clear on those labels.

That Val and Corminar had nodded to one another, sharing some unspoken understanding, upon learning of Arzak's whereabouts now made sense to me. They knew what she was up to: she was slaying. She just wasn't necessarily slaying Players.

Questing records were open, but only in the sense that *in theory* anyone could read them. In practice, there were ample layers of bureaucracy in the way, as we soon discovered.

"*Arzak,*" Val said again to the questing assistant, having just spent literal hours in the queue with me while Corminar, Lore, and Tokas got some downtime. To clarify, we hadn't volunteered, only drawn the short straws; both of us would have much rather been downing an ale.

"I've got an Alsack?" the questing assistant replied.

"You know we just went through exactly the same conversation with your colleague, right?"

"Subordinate," the assistant corrected her.

"Arzak Blorg," I tried, before the riled-up Val could say whatever insulting thing had come to mind. "An orc."

"Alsack is a goblin."

"That's because they're *an entirely different person!*" Val said, voice strained, literally pulling at her hair.

I tried to calm her by gesturing at her with my palm, though this seemed to only redirect her anger onto me. I hurriedly turned back to the questing assistant. "Would it help if I spelled it out for you?" Before the employee could say anything, I pulled out some scraps of paper which I quickly flipped over to hide my shoddy mathematical abilities from when I was working out my *Worldbending* progression.

"Oh, Arzak!" the office worker said. "Why didn't you just say that?"

"We *did* bloody well—" Val started, until I glared at her to make her stop.

Then, moments later, I realized she was absolutely right. "Wait, we *did* say that!"

The questing assistant only shrugged, murmuring something about human pronunciation—even though he himself was a human—and delved into the back.

Turning back, I saw a pair of elves in the queue behind us giving us the dirtiest expression I'd ever seen an elf give *anyone*, both of them tapping one foot irritably on the floor. I smiled politely at them. "We'll just be a moment."

"Blame the—" Val started, and then this time managed to stop herself. She looked up at me. "You know, slaying monsters, climbing mountains, hanging out with you lot . . . all that I can handle. The only thing I can't handle is—"

"Bureaucracy?"

"—jobsworths like these people seem to be." Fortunately, she kept her voice quiet for that bit. "I'm gonna need a drink after all this, I can tell you. Arzak—sorry, 'Alsack'—can wait."

"I'm feeling an amber."

"Ooh yeah," Val said, simply the thought of beer seeming to soothe her. "Or a ruby."

I shrugged. "Sure. Keep that image in your mind, and I'll handle this."

Val smiled, her eyes glazing over. My plan to calm her down had worked. And surely the task before me—overcoming bureaucracy—was far simpler than *that*.

I leaned over the counter, my eyes looking this way and that in the back room that was filled with tall bookcases. Satisfied that nobody was there, I . . . hopped it. I kept low in the back room, knowing full well that I absolutely was not supposed to be here—but then, I'd spent most of my life being places I wasn't supposed to be. I knew the drill, even if I didn't yet have the skill tree to back it up: tread lightly, keep to the shadows. Who needed passive bonuses anyway?

I glanced up at the bookcase next to me, a giant *G* emblazoned on a brass plate and mounted to its end. *Would Arzak Blorg be under* A *or* B? I wondered, and then set about hurrying down the *A* end of the room anyway, considering as she'd be up that end either way.

As I got to row *F* or so, footsteps echoed on the stone floor in front of me, and I dived down the row, keeping to the bookshelf to stay out of the way as a questing assistant—not the one who'd been "helping" us, I noticed—meandered past me, humming to herself and reading a book about caring for dustcats.

Clearly these people had no intention of actually doing any work, and my decision to get it done myself was definitely the correct one. Once the woman had long since passed, I pressed on, having to hurry between bookshelves when I suddenly noticed that another employee was in the *D* row.

I blinked, coming to an abrupt stop. That was our one! In row *D*! What was he doing *there*? These people really were useless.

When I got to *B*, I tried my luck there first—and it paid off. There, nestled between Blorfenley and Bloss, was a thick wad of papers labeled *Blorg, Arzak*. I thought about leafing through them and finding the latest quest, but considering there were footsteps quickly approaching—from the *D* row, if I wasn't mistaken—I chose instead to get out of there, looping back around on the other side of the bookcases to avoid our irritating questing assistant.

The pair of elves looked disapprovingly at me as I hopped the counter, caught the tip of my right foot on the side, and fell to the floor.

Stealth: +1,200XP
Stealth increased to Level 5!
Base Points Gained: +3 DEX, +3 WIS, +3 Free Points (DEX/WIS)

Ability Selection Unlocked
Select an ability from the list below . . .

Level up!
You increased to Level 8!

Hah, and even an ability. I hadn't expected *that* much success from my spur-of-the-moment vault over the counter. *Take that, bureaucracy!*

"What was that?" Val asked, souring the mood slightly with her raised eyebrow.

I shrugged. "It was taking too long. Besides, I needed some more *Stealth* XP."

"Did you get it?"

I thrusted the wad of papers up in the air. "Oh yes."

"Great. Let's drink four beers, and then let's go find Arzak."

I nodded, then looked at the documents once more. "You don't think they'll miss these, do you?"

Val shrugged. "Who cares? Beer, beer, beer, beer, Arzak—got it?"

CHAPTER THIRTY-FIVE

The Worryingly Abandoned Castle Carn

As Val and Corminar leafed through the stolen records, they were shocked to find out just how much mercenary work Arzak had been taking. Lore, Tokas, and I sat back, beers in hand, as the two of them pored over each and every job. I contented myself to look again at my choice of new abilities, as afforded me by my growing of *Stealth* to level 5.

As always, low levels meant that the ability selections weren't very exciting, especially without any hidden conditions met, which . . . spoiler alert: there weren't any. This meant that I only had two abilities to pick from, and one of them was even just an upgrade on my existing ability; I'd had far better selections in my old life.

Ability Selection Unlocked
Select an ability from the list below:

Option 1: Stealth Attack (Stealth)—*Passive.* 50 percent boost to damage when unnoticed by enemy.

There was the upgrade: a boost to the damage dealt if I hadn't been noticed by the enemy in question. It was a *good* increase, don't get me wrong—up from 10 percent to 50 percent—and I supposed it was just having been spoiled by all these *Worldbending* ability choices that had me reluctant to take it.

> **Option 2: Danger-Sense (Stealth)**—*Passive*. Your senses grow keener; you are 30 percent more likely to notice traps and ambushes.

This wouldn't have been a bad one to pick if I was still in my old line of work. In fact, I think I *had* owned this ability at one point, but it had evolved into *Identify Traps*, which was much more effective at locating them—as long as you actually activated the ability.

With my line of work apparently having changed from theft to slaying—at least for the foreseeable future—there was only one good option. Perhaps I'd get another shot at *Danger-Sense* at level 10, anyway.

> **Ability Unlocked**: Stealth Attack
> **Stealth Attack (Stealth)**: *Passive*. 50 percent boost to damage when unnoticed by enemy.

I nodded, forcing myself to be excited about this ability choice, and found myself coming up a little empty. *Oh well*, I told myself. *It's early days; if I keep leveling up as quickly as I am, I'll be selecting from ridiculous or overpowered abilities before I know it.*

I looked back up at the two members of the team standing over the table, parchment fanned out in front of them.

"I don't believe this," Val was saying. "She handled a rockrat infestation in Colrosz . . ."

"A pair of malae, by herself," Corminar called out, holding up a piece of paper.

". . . Not one, not two, but *three* ogres up in the Bladerocks . . ."

"Saved a cat from a tree," Corminar said. "Though perhaps that one is not quite so impressive."

"Look here," Val continued, "in this one, she's got a new team!"

"We do not know that she is still working with them, Val. Perhaps she—"

"It's marked four days ago," the sorcerer added.

Corminar considered this. "Then perhaps she *is* still working with them. It does not mean she has replaced us."

"And why wouldn't she? If you'll remember, she was the only one who wanted to continue. While the rest of us . . ." Val trailed off.

"Thought we knew what we wanted out of life?" Lore suggested. "Wanted to, like, grow as people? Or not, I dunno."

Val and Corminar each raised one eyebrow at the barbarian, who shrugged and went back to his beer.

"Where is it?" Tokas asked. "The latest quest. Nearby, I assume?"

"Some place called . . ." Val squinted at the paper, but not because she couldn't read it—I knew her eyesight wasn't bad. "Castle Carn? Anyone know it?"

Corminar and I shook our heads.

"Nuh-uh," said Lore.

"The seat of the once-queen of the Tundras, back when they were called the Kingdom of Avalon, fallen into disrepair since the kingdom fell, and host to many a disreputable faction over the decades since. Located a few miles to the north-northwest of Ironview, though on a clear day it is said you can see Ironview from its tallest tower," said Tokas.

Val, Corminar, Lore, and I all turned to look at Tokas, and this time eight eyebrows were raised.

"What?" Tokas asked. "Do none of you read the history books?"

"They turn that stuff into *books*?" Lore asked.

"They turn lots of subjects into books, dear," Corminar said. "Though I do share your tastes." The pair of them shared a look that I made a mental note to get to the bottom of at some point.

Now was not the time, however, because Val opened her mouth with a vital, and worrying, piece of information. "It says here . . . it says she never came back from it. Missing, presumed . . ." Val trailed off, and the rest of the group hurried away to pack up their belongings.

"Right," I said to nobody in particular. "I suppose we're off, then."

(You know those stories? The ones you tell kids . . . what are they called? Fairy tales. There's so often the gallant knight quested to retrieve an attractive member of a royal family from some evildoer's tower. Maybe there's a dragon guarding it, or an ogre on the bridge, or some other obvious manifestation of supposed evil. The tower itself is dark, crumbling, dead vines creeping up it, and more often than not there is a black cloud hovering over it, just in case you didn't get the message that this is a *bad place*. I suppose these authors have to be heavy-handed with the imagery; kids aren't usually the quickest to pick up on subtext.

Anyway, I bring this up because I want to paint you a picture of Castle Carn. Imagine that fairy tale tower, housing the attractive royal, and all of its obvious "evil" characteristics. And then make it ten times more foreboding.

There you go, you have it—a rough approximation of Castle Carn.)

The five of us stood atop a crest, looking at the immense fortress known as Castle Carn nestled against the foothills before us. It possessed not one of those evil fairy tale towers, but seven. The walls were cracked in places, crumbled in others, and pristine just about nowhere. The only signs of life therein were a couple of bats, each of which were roughly the size of a neereagle. And if you've never seen a neereagle before, imagine me stretching my hands out as wide as I can manage, and saying "They're this big."

"And we wanna go in *there*, do we?" I found myself saying, immediately outing myself as currently the most scared of the lot of us.

"We go in, we find Arzak, we get out," Val said, without tearing her eyes from the castle.

"And the other members of her team?" I asked.

"Not interested."

"Perhaps we might complete the quest?" Corminar suggested. "After all, there was *quite* the bounty on—"

"The quest?" Tokas asked. "What *was* the quest, anyway?"

"An elderbeest. In the dungeons."

Tokas held up a hand. "I vote just Arzak."

Lore hurriedly also raised his hand.

"What's a . . . what's an elderbeest?" I asked, apparently the only one of us in the dark about this particular creature.

"A bloody huge deer—" Val started.

"Oh, that's not so bad."

"—that is filled with the infinite nothingness of the time before Creation."

"Oh, that's quite bad."

Lore leaned forward to add helpfully, "Even one bite can tear you from reality."

"Oh, that's *very* bad." I thrust my hand into the air. "Another vote for just Arzak. That's three votes now, we win. Just Arzak. No elderbeest."

Val raised an eyebrow.

"What? I'm level 8!"

"No, it's not that, it's just that I don't think any of us were going to suggest we take on an *elderbeest*, Styk."

"Well, I . . ." Corminar started, and then looked around, reading the metaphorical room, ". . . wasn't. I wasn't going to suggest that."

With five deep breaths—three of them coming from me—we stepped forth and began our journey across a narrow plain and toward the looming Castle Carn. Even with the outer wall so crumbling in places, there was really only one way in—through the main gate which had survived all these years. At least, the archway that had held the gate had survived; there was only the barest hint of wooden planks scattered around the inside, as though something had once burst in. I didn't know my history well enough to decide if this detail was significant.

The grounds were eerily quiet as we pressed inside, and that we were apprehensive enough not to speak did little to shatter this silence. As the heavy wooden door squeaked closed behind us, a wave of terror washed over me and I grit my teeth, willing myself on. Tokas used her illusion magicks to create an orb of light that floated above us, illuminating the otherwise bone-chillingly dark castle interior. Here, in the center of the building, there were not even the small arrow slits by which to navigate, only the remnants of old, empty sconces.

In the middle of the castle's entrance chamber was a wide stone plinth—one which Tokas's ball of light hovered over, seemingly of its own will. As I stared upon it, a worrying realization dawned on me.

"Someone's been here," I said. "Recently. Look at the dust; someone's swept part of it."

"Arzak?" Lore asked, his eyes now darting around the shadows at the perimeter of the room.

"Could be," Val said.

"Could not be," Corminar added, ever the optimist.

Silence swept over us once more as each of us considered just which one of these options this might be. We moved further into the castle, through a central passageway at the center of this grand atrium.

"Arzak?" Lore called out. "It's—"

He didn't get the chance to finish that thought because Val put her hand over his mouth.

When Val had removed it, a confused-looking Lore asked, "What?"

"We're trying to find her," Val said. "If there's really anything else in here, we don't want *it* to find *us*."

Lore nodded. "Oh yeah. Good point."

The chamber we found ourselves in next had little to distinguish it from the previous, particularly in the low light of Tokas's illusion magicks. Tapestries that had perhaps once been grand hung from the ceiling, now faded. A fireplace—now blocked—had indents within it that suggested it had once held jewels, but that these had since been stolen.

"Should we split up?" Lore suggested.

"*Split up?*" both Val and I repeated back at him, aghast. "That's a sure way to get us all picked off," I added.

Val nodded. "Yeah. We stick together or we don't do this at—"

A noise from down one of the adjacent corridors cut Val off, and our heads all snapped to the source of it.

"Something's moving," Lore said.

"But friend or foe?" Tokas asked.

We remained still in the almost-darkness, listening for more sounds—but none came.

Corminar stepped toward where the noise had come from. "I suppose, as the adage goes, 'there is only one way to find out.'"

We followed Corminar deeper into the castle, and I couldn't help but think he probably considered himself the bravest of us, though in truth he was probably just the most arrogant about his own strength. As we got further down the corridor, the noises sounded out again, louder with every step.

It was people—that was a good sign—but the noises themselves seemed to be . . . chanting. "*Not* such a good sign," I muttered to myself, causing Tokas to flash me a look.

At the other end of the corridor, we pressed ourselves against the wall, keeping out of sight, and with a flick of her wrist, Tokas made the light disappear. After all, there was already the glimmering light of fire in the room beyond. The chanting was in a language I didn't understand, but—judging by the expressions of the rest of the party—it wasn't Arzak speaking.

Val crouched, poking her head around the corner, and then she scuttled into the room.

"Val!" I whispered. "What are you—"

Her head poked back around the corner. "I'm checking, alright? It might be they're friendly. They might know where—"

"They're *chanting*, Val. When have you ever known groups of chanting people to be anything but evil?"

"I was part of a meditation class that once . . ." Lore started, but Val spoke over him.

"I'm gonna look, and then I'll be back. Alright?"

"No, not alright," I said, reaching out to grab at Val's arm, but missing. I spilled into the room behind her.

"You don't have to worry about—"

"Who's there?" a new voice called out.

Val and I spun our heads to the woman who'd spoken.

". . . Arzak?" I tried.

The woman looked confused. As did her two friends, all of whom were wearing a robe with a familiar symbol emblazoned on the back—a golden sun with a line breaking through it. The symbol of the Cult of Ascendancy.

"Arzak's an orc, idiot," Val said, whacking me around the back of the head. "Whereas this lot are . . ."

Level 25 Ascendant Fire Cultist
Race: Elf

". . . evil," I finished, as the woman closest to us summoned a ball of fire.

"Don't gloat," Val said, and prepared herself to fight.

CHAPTER THIRTY-SIX

There Are Things That Lurk in the Darkest Corners of This World and Most of Them Will Eat You

"I'm not gloating, I'm just reiterating that I was right," I said.

"Styk?" Val said, her eyes on the three women with fireballs hovering over their upturned palms.

"Well, I was!"

"Styk!" she shouted.

"What?"

"Duck!"

She dove to the floor just as the first fireball came shooting our way, and I followed suit with just enough delay that the spell singed the ends of my locks. "You know, you really are a pain sometimes," Val muttered, scowling over at me from her position on the floor.

"OK," I replied as the other two fireballs soared overhead. "Any ideas how to deal with this?"

She shrugged. "One."

Val leaped to her feet once more just as the three Ascendant Fire Cultists were whipping up new fireballs, and with the twist of her right hand and lower arm, she summoned a billowing gust of wind that twirled around her wrist. "Honestly, I'm probably the worst person to throw fireballs at." With this, she released the wind, sending it billowing in the direction of the cultists, blowing the flames into their summoners' faces.

The cultists screamed with pain, clutching their cheeks where the conjured fire had burned them, and then—with clenched teeth—turned their attention back to Val. As the three of them switched strategies, this time conjuring a ring of fire around Val and I, Corminar stepped out from around the corner.

The elven ranger released an arrow that caught one cultist squarely in the neck, causing them to break from their magicks and instead clutch at their wound—one which was losing . . . quite a lot of blood. The circle of fire around me and Val became less intense, but still roared high enough that we stood little chance of getting out.

Lore stepped out next, but instead of coming out swinging, as I might have assumed he would, he came out with his hands raised. "Alright!" he bellowed. "Alright, enough! We don't need to fight each other."

"You dare interrupt our ritual?" the closest of the cultists shouted.

"Ritual?" Val asked. "We don't care about any bloody ritual. We're just looking for our friend."

"Yeah," I added, "what's this ritual for, anyhow?"

The same cultist responded. "Only by burning this world to ashes can we ascend to the heaven from which the Players have traveled!"

"Did you hear that, Val?" I said to her, doing my best to suppress a smirk, but failing miserably. "Not just evil—crazy, too!"

As it turned out, this was *not* the right thing to say, as it caused the cultist on the left to roar with anger and then loose another fireball at us. Val wasn't quick enough with her wind spell to catch it, but the cultist breaking from the circle of flames spell did mean that the fire was weak enough now to hop through— which Val and I both did.

Free of the circle, I readied myself to *portal*, thinking to use it to pull one of the cultists in reach of Lore, to be dealt with by means of massive sword. But, still new to the world of magicks as I was, I didn't move fast enough. Two of the cultists worked together to try a new tack: a wall of fire that came charging toward us.

As Val tried to whip up a gust to blow it back at them—something that even *I* could have told her would have been fruitless—the bulky Lore charged across the room and tackled the pair of us back to the ground.

"I only just got up!" I complained, and in answer Lore blinked at me, confused.

As flames caught an old, dusty curtain behind us, I couldn't help but, for a moment, flash back to Plainside, and the destruction courtesy of the pyroknight which had set me upon this quest to begin with.

"Anyone got an idea?" Lore asked as the flames continued to billow overhead.

"I already told Styk: just the one, and I already tried it." Val directed her attention at me. "Can't Mr. Portals figure something out?"

"My surname is—" I started to correct her, but Val reached out and patted me on the head.

"Very good, but maybe not the time."

I stuck my tongue out at her, even though she was right; my focus should probably have been on dealing with the three mad cultists rather than on bickering. As the three of us cowered behind a long table—one that was made of a famously flammable material: wood—I craned my neck up to look at the three cultists. Each of them seemed not at all worried about their mana reserves, because their stream of flames was constant, a wall of fire crackling above us.

"Well? Any ideas?" Val asked, echoing my earlier question.

"Three," I replied.

"Show-off."

With that, I pointed my hand toward where I wanted one of the portals to be, up above the fire cultists. I couldn't see that spot, of course—not from where we were cowering behind cover—but with enough concentration I was sure I could get the portal where I wanted it. After all, since the upgrade to *Local Portal II*, I should have been able to create a portal within a ten-foot radius, even without eyes on it.

As the familiar warmth of a brewing portal spread within me, I prepared the other "end" of the portal. And I did it within the waves of fire crackling overhead.

Screams erupted near instantly from the other end of the chamber, as the wall of fire entered my portal and came out billowing down onto its creators.

"For fire sorcerers," Lore said, "they ain't exactly specced much into fire resistance, have they?"

"OK, hotshot," Val said, "what now?"

I answered her question by moving the closest portal end from the air above us to the ground below us, and the three of us started tumbling toward our aggressors.

Lore was already prepared to strike, this time bringing his massive sword down and toward the closest of the cultists. Val wasn't prepared, but mostly because she seemed to prefer glaring at me, presumably for opening a portal underneath her without any warning. I *should* have been more prepared, but honestly I was approaching this fight one thing at a time.

As I fell, rolling across the hard floor into one of the cultist's legs, I pulled my Ranger's Blade free. Without too much thought applied, I struck it at the nearest body part, which happened to be the cultist's ankle. At least I buried it deep.

If the screaming had been fading since the cultists slowly extinguished the fire that encompassed them, it grew loud once more as my knife met flesh. And, more importantly, Lore's Bane Sword cleaved one of the cultists in two.

Level 20 Ascendant Fire Cultist defeated!

Worldbending: +1,000XP

Worldbending increased to Level 11!
Base Points Gained: +2 INT, +2 Free Points (INT/WIS/CHA)

That was a good sign; that I'd been given so much experience despite Lore delivering the final blow meant that returning the fire to the senders had dealt a lot of damage. This meant that the remaining two were surely weak. If also . . . red with anger.

I carried on slicing haphazardly at the nearest cultist's ankle until she glared down at me, snarling, and raised her hand in the air as though about to prepare another spell.

"Uh-oh," I said, and then *portaled* myself out of there and back behind cover. It really was a useful skill when I remembered to use it.

Just as I was about to let the portal close behind me, Val cried out, "St-yy-k . . ." I looked up and saw Val on the precipice at the other side, flailing her hands in the air to keep her balance.

I kept the portal open, my mana reserves draining considerably, and was almost immediately glad that I did, because Val lost her fight against gravity. I allowed the portal to close just as Val finished falling through it, and part of the reason I let the spell go was that she managed to land *on me*.

"You need to warn us when you—" Val started, then a wall of fire erupting overhead interrupted her.

"Lore?" I called out.

"Busy!"

"Corminar?" I tried instead.

But it was Tokas, not the ranger, who suddenly came bolting out of the corridor. I'd been starting to wonder where she'd gotten to—if she was even interested in helping us at all—and so the sight of the newest member of the team was welcome, even if she didn't seem to like me all that much.

As she stepped into the room, she flicked her hands out at her sides. Despite there being no telltale red-tinged glow of illusion magicks—presumably Val had set her on to obscurems—within the blink of an eye there was not one Tokas but two. She flicked her hands again, and then there were four. And then eight.

The cultist that Lore wasn't currently tussling with staggered backward, eyes wide, breaking the spell for a moment as she didn't quite know where to direct it.

Amongst the flames, a new face stepped into the skirmish. The Player's. The pyroknight's, his tiefling bodyguard at his side.

I froze.

My heart seemed to beat louder than ever.

I—

"Styk?" Val said, clutching me by the shoulders. "Styk? Are you OK?"

"I . . ." I started, blinking her into focus. "The Player. He's . . ." I pointed to where the pyroknight had just entered the room, but standing there, in his place, was Corminar.

Val, hunched over me, looked over at Corminar, then blinked back at me. "You're seeing things."

"I'm not seeing things; he was there!" I shouted.

Val glanced around at Corminar, Tokas, and Lore, who were turning the tide on the remaining two cultists. Satisfied that we were winning, she turned back to me. "If he was there, one of us would have seen him. It's the fire, Styk. It's reminding you of Plainside, and what you . . . what you saw there. You're traumati—"

"I'm *not* bloody traumatized!" I said. I wasn't. I really wasn't. "I saw him. Him and the tiefling. They were here. They were . . ." The logical part of my mind caught up with me; Val was right. If they'd been here, someone else would have seen them.

Val didn't say anything more on the subject, but looked on at me for a few moments. "Come on," she said, pulling me back to my feet. "Let's finish this."

I nodded.

Saving the rest of my mana reserves, I opted instead to accompany Val in leaping the table and running—on my own two legs!—toward the enemy. While Corminar and Val focused on helping out Lore, I fixed my attention on the cultist who was dealing with the great many Tokases.

It wasn't hard, finishing this fight. I wish I could now say that it was my trademark quick thinking and problem-solving that allowed me to bury my knife in the woman's neck, but it wasn't. No, the answer here was simple: having a team was valuable.

While the real Tokas stepped suddenly out of the swirling copycat crowd and punched the cultist in the nose, I simply walked up behind her and activated my *Stab* ability. Both of the remaining enemies went down at almost the same moment.

Level 21 Ascendant Fire Cultist defeated!
Level 25 Ascendant Fire Cultist defeated!

Worldbending: +1,500XP
Worldbending increased to Level 12!
Base Points Gained: +2 INT, +2 Free Points (INT/WIS/CHA)

Knifework: +700XP

The five of us collapsed in relief that the battle was done, hands being placed on knees, arses being placed on disintegrating old chairs. When one such chair collapsed under Corminar's weight, none of us had the energy to mock him for it. We rested in this way until we finally all regained our breath, and then Lore was the first person to speak.

"Anyone hungry?" he asked.

Val made an exaggerated retching sound.

"Lore, are you serious?" Tokas asked.

The barbarian held up his hands in the air. "What? It was hard work!"

"Nobody's saying it—" I started, but then approaching footsteps made a chill crawl down my spine.

Our heads snapped to the source of the noise—a figure cloaked in darkness, growing slowly closer, and with each step revealing themselves to be taller and taller, until they were near looming over us.

"Just wondering . . . how are we all doing for mana and stamina?" I asked.

CHAPTER THIRTY-SEVEN

Running with Elderbeests

The great hulking creature—one with a figure that put even Lore's to shame—remained oddly still at the edge of the darkness; only their silhouette and golden eyes were illuminated by the low light of the remnant fires.

"Of all nasty creatures in nasty places . . ." the figure said, "I do not expect find *you* here."

The creature stepped into the light, revealing themselves as a tall, ageing orc with a wide smile on her face, just below a pair of very thick spectacles.

"Arzak!" Lore cried out, immediately dropping his sword to the floor with an almighty clatter and running to embrace the woman we'd been searching for.

Arzak returned the hug with slightly less enthusiasm, but also with a good-natured smile nonetheless. "It is good see you too, old friend." Her accent was notably orcish, but clearly tempered somewhat by spending lots of time amongst elves and humans. She wore on her back not one but two swords, each long and thin, and—to my naked eye—seemingly sharp enough to cut through solid wood with ease.

"What all doing here?" she asked. "Take mercenary work without me?"

"Looking for you!" Lore said, having released Arzak from his hug but clearly wishing he hadn't.

"And why is this?" Arzak asked, and then her face mellowed some as she came to the obvious conclusion. "Do not tell me . . ."

Val nodded. "Another one."

"Where?"

"Plainside," I said, and the orc looked at me for the first time, considering me.

"That was Player?"

I nodded.

Val pointed to me. "He was there. He saw it firsthand."

The orc raised an eyebrow, pausing for a moment, clearly to *identify* me. "And how is this? Must be only one who escape."

"I—" I started, but Tokas interrupted.

"Perhaps a story for later? We are, after all, in the middle of a dungeon, and there is an elderbeest hanging about."

Arzak furrowed her brow. "Yes," she said. "More than one. They said baby beest. We told that it easy job and—"

"'We'?" Corminar repeated.

"They all dead," Arzak replied. "I almost dead, too. I lucky, like new friend here." She nodded to me. "But . . ." She pulled the swords from her back, and one of them was notably shorter than the other. It took me a moment in the low light to realize that the shorter one had been snapped in half.

No, I realized after another moment. It wasn't snapped in half; those were teeth marks at the end.

"I stop bite with sword. Half of sword bitten from reality."

"Right. And the reason we haven't gotten out of here yet is . . . ?"

"I take quest? I *finish* quest."

Val stepped forward to Arzak. "If you think we're helping you, you got another thing coming. We're not here to get killed. Or . . . erased, or whatever those things do to you. Leave the elderbeests here—they'll only be feeding on the bad types who still use this place—and come join us. There's bigger fish to fry."

Lore's stomach rumbled at the mention of frying fish.

Arzak looked nervously behind her. "Hmm. I did wonder how one woman kill four elderbeests."

"Four?" both Val and I immediately repeated.

"At least," came Arzak's reply. "I think—"

The noises that erupted down the tunnel behind Arzak were monstrous, loud, and clearly came from a creature that had never once worried about being stealthy.

"Hm. There is one," Arzak said, then turned her back to us.

Tokas moved first, bolting back the way we'd came with me hot on her heels. I didn't hang around to see if the other four were hurrying this way, too, but from the sounds of footsteps at my rear, it seemed like at least *some* of them were.

A few moments later, this very question was answered by Lore calling out, "Arzak! Corminar! You ain't gonna handle it by yourself!"

The pairs of footsteps fading behind me caused me to turn, and I could see Val and Lore looking on, horrified, as Corminar and Arzak stood their ground against the creature.

After a second more, the giant deerlike creature charged into the chamber, slowing only slightly at the sight of the fire remaining from the earlier fight. It was a monstrous being, but not because it possessed long claws or sharp teeth, or any of the usual sorts of things that said "avoid me if you want to live." No, there was a far more bone-chillingly terrifying vibe to it. Its eyes seemed hollow, the blackest of blacks with a small dot of bright light in the centers. As it roared, I saw behind its jaw, and saw the great nothingness that lay within it. Not black, not empty—simply . . . nothing.

"Arzak!" Lore cried out. "Cor!"

But the pair of them didn't pay him any heed, instead running and launching themselves toward the creature.

I thought quickly once again, which isn't to say I thought *well*, but in this case it was about as good as I could do. Flinging one hand forward and one hand back down the corridor behind me, I cast a *Local Portal* that Arzak and Corminar couldn't help but tumble through, bringing them far away from the creature and causing Tokas to hop around them as she fled.

Val made an approving shape with her mouth, and on her signal, the three of us began to charge from the elderbeest once more.

Up ahead, down the dingy corridor, we could see two figures that definitely *weren't* fleeing.

"Run, you idiots!" Val cried at Arzak and Corminar, and for a moment I took comfort in the fact that Val was calling someone else an idiot for once.

"We can slay this foul creature if we—" Corminar started, but Val interrupted as we charged past them, the elderbeest worryingly close behind us.

"It can slay you, maybe. Don't make me make him *portal* you again!"

"I'm not a dog; you can't just order me to . . ." I protested, but trailed off when I realized I absolutely was going to have to *portal* them again. With the same outstretched arms as before, I opened another portal below Arzak and Corminar, and another one in the chamber ahead of us. They fell through it just before the elderbeest could snap its jaws around Arzak.

"Any reason you're not using the portals for us?" Val asked.

"Yes. Panic," I replied, then was about to create another pair of portals for Val, Lore, and I, when I caught sight of my mana reserves. "Also, I'm nearly out of mana. You want me using it all up?"

"No," Val grumbled, and the three of us pressed through a slightly-too-small doorframe into the next chamber, all of us stumbling on one another and then toppling to the ground.

As we picked ourselves up off the floor, Arzak muttered loudly ahead of us, "Close one," and then grabbed at Corminar as he tried to charge back into the fight. "Maybe fight is too much. We leave now, handsome one."

Corminar tripped over his tongue in apparent indecision between complaining about having to leave and gloating about being called handsome, and instead settled for trying to pull himself loose of Arzak's strong grip. In this, he was unsuccessful.

Now that we were all running in the *correct* direction, I was a little less worried about my dwindling mana reserves—now about a quarter remaining—and so when the elderbeest came upon Val, Lore, and me, I was already ready with the portal. We tumbled through, Val somehow landing in Arzak's available arm while Lore and I fell to the floor once more.

This time, the pair of us were quick to pull ourselves back up to our feet, and it was a good thing, too, because the elderbeest was continuing to accelerate, moving faster than I would have thought possible of a creature that size. "It's gonna catch us!" I cried.

Everyone continued to run, but Corminar shot an arrow from his position under Arzak's right arm—one that seemed not to irritate the elderbeest even a smidgen, judging by the lack of complaint. Under the orc's other arm, Val brushed her hands to one side to build up a gust of wind that would catch the ample amount of dust and temporarily blind the elderbeest.

I didn't turn to look at its reaction, but from the sounds of the loud thunk that followed us passing out through the main entrance, it was blinded enough to hit its head on the doorframe.

But that only delayed the inevitable; it wouldn't stop it.

The six of us charged out into the open, with Tokas way ahead, passing through the gate.

"Don't suppose elderbeests don't like sunlight?" I called out.

"No luck such as this," Arzak growled in response. "Ideas, now."

Nobody could give Arzak the answer she was looking for, and each of us remained quiet but for our increasingly loud breaths.

"Through gate," the orc bellowed. "There we fight."

"Fight?" Val protested. "I thought you'd come around to—"

"It is fight or it catch us. What choice?"

Val again had no answer, and we pressed on. Lore and I, at the back of the group, kept our eyes fixed firmly on the gate ahead of us, and not the strange high-pitched whining sound that seemed to emanate from the monstrous beast at our rear—a sound that grew louder with every moment that passed.

As we passed through the archway, it was time. Time for one of those trademark Styk quick-thinking strategies. Maybe, I realized, we wouldn't have to fight after all.

The moment I was clear of the archway, I jumped to the floor, facing upward, rushing my hands into the air. Each hand I pointed at a different corner of the archway, and in the blink of an eye, I poured all of my remaining mana into a *Portal Slice.*

At first, the stone archway only cracked, both in its top-left and its top-right corners, and I thought I'd royally screwed up with the whole "throwing myself to the floor" bit. But Lore—not someone who I was coming to think of as a quick thinker—saw what I was doing, and he responded in kind.

The great barbarian took his sword by the hilt, and as throwing a javelin, launched it into the stone at the top of the archway.

As it hit, the stones began to crumble, and the top of the arch—and the remnants of wall atop it—came tumbling down just in front of the charging elderbeest. It roared with frustration, and both me and the five Slayers waited with bated breath for any sign that the elderbeest had given up the attack.

Due to the resulting notifications, myself, Corminar, and Arzak—those who had attacked the beast in some way—breathed a sigh of relief.

Level 28 Elderbeest defeated!

Worldbending: +2,800XP
Worldbending increased to Level 14!
Base Points Gained: +4 INT, +4 Free Points (INT/WIS/CHA)

That was a *lot* of experience considering we didn't even slay the beast, only instead narrowly avoiding getting eaten by it. I quickly placed all my free points into Intelligence—as was tradition these days—hoping it would replace my mana bar somewhat, and then moved to stand up, thrusting my hands into the air. "We did it!" I cried out, exhilaration washing over me.

Then the world grew faint and suddenly I was falling, exhausted, to the ground.

Ernas

Ernas knocked on the door at the back of the shop where his daughter lived.

"Punnas? Lopas?" he cried out as he entered, not wanting to scare his grandsons by entering unannounced. There came no answer, only the distant pitter-patter of footsteps. "It's your grandad! Tokas . . . Your mother sent me to look after you!"

One head, then two, popped out from around a doorframe. There they were: Ernas's only two grandsons, handsome young chaps despite the human blood they got from their good-for-nothing absent father.

"Erny?" the two kids said at once, and then stormed out to meet him. Ernas was forced to label it as *storming out* because their feet hitting the ground seemed to make the very building shake.

Ernas crouched down to hug his two grandchildren, taking one in each arm and holding them close. "There's my boys!" He pulled his head away from the hug. "Let me take a good look at you; you look like you've grown all big and strong since I last saw you!"

"Very strong," Punnas—always the more talkative of the two—said.

"Mmmmm," echoed Lopas, talking around a chubby thumb in the corner of his mouth, "strong."

Ernas *identified* Lopas first, part of him expecting to find this twin progressing less quickly than the other. He internally berated himself for that assumption.

Level 2 Dreadstomper
Race: Tiefling/Human

". . . What?" Ernas said aloud, and his two grandsons turned to look at him.

"Where's mama?" Lopas said, already losing interest in his grandfather's sudden outburst.

The old tiefling ignored the question and turned to *identify* Punnas instead.

Level 2 Doomstomper
Race: Tiefling/Human

"Where's mama?" Lopas said again.

"She's . . ." Ernas started, unable to take his eyes away from the words hovering in front of him, "she's away for work again."

"What do?" Lopas asked.

"What does she do? She . . . she helps catch bad men."

"Mmm . . . boudy hunner," Punnas added.

"I—" Ernas started, but couldn't help but switch back to an earlier track. He pushed a smile onto his face. "You're level two, now! That's so, so impressive for young men your age. Tell me, though . . . do you know what a 'doomstomper' is? Or a . . . 'dreadstomper'?"

"Mama says boots make go strong."

"Your mama says *what?*" Ernas repeated.

"Boots. Strong," Lopas echoed his doomstomper brother. "We got *kickboxing* skill!"

"What boots, sonny?"

Punnas blinked up at him, then suddenly turned on the spot and staggered into the main room, the floor shaking with every step.

Lopas stared on at Ernas, still not fully released from the hug, and asked, "Mama is bouny hunner. What are you?"

"What am I? Do you mean what do I do, as a job?"

Lopas nodded.

Ernas grew worried about the continued stomping in the other room, and picked Lopas up to take him through with him. "I was a fletcher, my boy."

"Fletch?"

"I made arrows, for bows. But I don't do that anymore. Nowadays, I spend most of my time hiking. The great outdoors, you know? Fresh air, beautiful landscapes."

Lopas blinked back absently.

"Yeah, you know what I'm talking about."

"Here boots!" Punnas suddenly cried, rushing—stomping—into the center of the room and holding a pair of small leather workman's boots in the air, a proud smile on his face.

If Ernas still had questions, they were answered when he *identified* the shoes.

> **Boots of Minor Slowing**: +40 percent resistance to walking. Negatively scales with [STR].

"Ah, I guess that explains that one, then," Ernas mumbled. He'd never been the best parent to Tokas—the gods knew that was true—but he wasn't sure he was entirely on board with his daughter's own parenting style. But then, after what she'd been through with her partner disappearing on her . . . Ernas had never been through anything like that, so who was he to judge? The worst thing that ever happened to him was . . .

He stopped to think, then realized nothing bad *had* ever happened to him. What a great life he'd lived.

"Alright, boys?" Ernas said, putting his hands on his knees so that he could get down to his grandsons' eye level. "While your mum's away, I'm going to introduce you to the best thing this world has to offer, OK?"

"OK!" Lopas mumbled.

"We already know about *chocolate*," replied Punnas.

"I'm not talking about chocolate, I'm talking about—"

"Toys?" Punnas tried.

"No, not toys, either. This is far more majestic than—"

"Cots?" Lopas guessed.

Ernas blinked. "Cots? What are cots?"

"They fluffy and go *brrrrrr.*"

The old tiefling narrowed his eyes, trying to get his head in the same space as a two-year-old's. "Do you mean . . . cats?"

Lopas smiled. "Yes! Cots!"

"It's . . . it's not *cots*, either, but we might see some on the way?"

"Yes!" Lopas cried, throwing his hands in the air and then falling over as a result. He looked down at the floor, eyes wide, seemed to consider crying, and then cheered once more. "Cots!"

"Alright, get your shoes on!" Ernas said. "If we get out now, we can make it up the Turnip Mound in time for sunset. And sunset is a . . ." He turned to see the two boys sat on the edge of the sofa, their legs dangling off, Lopas's shoes on the floor beneath him and Punnas's placed loosely on his feet. "What are you doing?"

"We need you do laces," Punnas said.

"Did Tokas never teach you?"

"Too hard," Lopas said.

"Strong *legs*, not *fingers* . . ." Punnas added, and then—as if to demonstrate—kicked his left leg once. The shoe shot across the room, smashed through the window, and fell out into the street. "Oopsie."

Ernas gulped. "You'll keep your legs still for me, won't you? If I tie your laces?"

"We will!" Lopas said, immediately wiggling his legs around.

"Mama makes us promise this, too. Says we give black eyes."

Ernas gulped, looking from the shoes, to the feet, and then back to the shoes again. Did he really want to crouch down in the firing line of those things? "On second thought," he said. "Let's stay in. I'll get you some chocolate."

"Hooray!" both kids cheered, and in the process Punnas shot his legs forward so hard that the remaining loose shoe flew into the air with such force that it broke Ernas's nose.

"*Hooray . . .*" Ernas echoed, with far less enthusiasm. He could only hope that Tokas wouldn't be away for work *quite* so long this time.

CHAPTER THIRTY-EIGHT

Why Did We Ever Break Up the Team?

I woke up on a bed with a crick in my neck that spoke to the poor quality of the mattress. Blinking the world back into life, I pulled myself semiupright, resting on my elbows to get a look around.

"Oh, you're awake," Corminar said from a seat in the corner of the room.

"And you're watching me sleep."

The elf ranger shrugged. "One of us needed to make sure you recovered. Fully draining a power bar can be . . . a rather dangerous affair."

"Got us away from the elderbeest, though, didn't it?" I replied, then reconsidered my question. "How comes it's *you* watching me sleep?"

"A poor roll of the dice," he replied. "But as you're awake now, we should go; the rest of the team are waiting downstairs."

"Drinking?"

"Naturally."

I nodded, began to move, and then looked down at myself, under the bedsheets. "Err . . ."

"Yes?" Corminar replied.

"I'm naked. I kinda need you to leave before I can get out of bed."

The elf raised an eyebrow. "Believe me, Styk, I have already seen everything."

"How! How could you have— Oh, you were the one who stripped me, weren't you?"

"I thought it better for your recovery that you sleep well."

I pressed my lips together. "Very kind of you."

Corminar held his hand out toward the door as if to say "shall we?" and I sighed, heaved myself out of bed, and pulled my clothes back on.

"Did you wash these?" I asked.

"Yes. In my lavender soak."

I pushed my lips together approvingly. "Nice. Very nice." I paused for a moment. "Don't tell Val I said that."

"I am going to."

"OK."

Downstairs in the inn, we found the other four members of the Slayers. While I'd expected to find them smiling, sipping beers, and perhaps trading stories of times past, I instead found them standing and shouting at each other.

"No," Arzak was saying. "You all abandon me. I remember this. Start own business, tend to sheep, run off with man . . ." the orc trailed off when she turned her attention to Val. "I still not know why *you* leave."

"Just stuff," the sorcerer replied.

I sat at the end of the table and helped myself to a still untouched—at least, hopefully untouched—ale.

"'Stuff'?" Arzak repeated. "OK, not tell me. This is point: you all leave, you all do own thing, and now all decide to go back to way things were? No. This not OK with me."

"Why?" Val asked. "Cos you think you're so high and mighty? We need you, yes, but we need every person here. And everyone else? They've rejoined the team without too much convincing."

Corminar put a finger in the air to raise a point of contention. "I was forced to by other circumstances. The Red Thorn—"

"Red Thorn?" Arzak repeated. "There is *Red Thorn* involved in this?"

"Yeah, that's actually news to me, too," Tokas said, and Lore nodded his agreement.

"That's not the point and you know it," Val responded. "Red Thorn? Yeah, we can deal with that later."

"What *is* point, then?"

"The point is that there's a Player running around killing whoever the hells he likes, and we're about the only team in the world who know it!" Val didn't stop for breath. "Anyone else out there? They see a Player killing people, they assume they've got problems with their eyes. Only us . . . only *we* know better. Without you, we stand less chance of killing him and surviving to tell the tale. But you better believe we'll give it a go anyway."

Tokas tilted her head from side to side as though she wasn't sure about this particular point.

"I know this," Arzak replied.

"Then why won't you join us?"

"Because is too hard!"

"Hard? Of course it's hard, it's killing Players! None of us signed up to this task in the knowledge it was going to be—"

"No," Arzak interrupted, then sighed and sat down on the opposite side of the long bench to Val, making the table shake. Lore grabbed his beers—yes, two—to stop them from spilling. "Not this. Is hard . . . to lead."

Apparently this was new information to Val, because she didn't immediately have something to say on the matter; it was hard to render that woman speechless, even for a moment. Without replying, she sat back down, it seeming like the situation was calming down some, and the few other patrons of the inn turned their attentions back to their own conversations.

"When I lead, I worry about all you. I make sure you don't do dumb things."

"We do not do—" Corminar started, but a pointed cough from Lore made him trail off.

"It is constant . . . headache. It is constant stress. I am too old for this now." Arzak sighed, her shoulders slouching.

"Don't, then," Val said. "Nobody ever asked you to be in charge."

As Arzak's shoulders raised once more, taking Val's words as having rude intention, Val quickly rushed to clarify.

"I mean, you fell into that role cos you were good at it. But we've all grown since back then. Maybe we don't need a leader anymore. Maybe we can just . . . be a team."

Arzak considered this for a moment. Well, more than a moment, really—a few minutes. In the meantime, I, Lore, and Tokas sipped on our drinks, while Val and Corminar—typically the biggest drinkers among us—sat waiting for Arzak's answer.

"OK. I join, but I not lead. We have . . . equal footing. If screw up . . ."

". . . then it's on us to fix it," Val finished.

"Yes."

"OK."

"Good," Lore added.

As silence washed over this typically lively group, we sipped at our beers once more, and then Arzak—now truly engaging with the task ahead of us—asked a simple question. "What we have?"

"Pyroknight," Val answered. "Level 42."

"Two accomplices," Corminar added. "An orc and a tiefling."

Arzak nodded. "We dealt with frostknight already. This must be similar. What else?"

"They were hunting something. Burned a whole town to the ground to get at it," Val said, then looked to me to follow up.

I pushed my hand into my pocket, wrapping my fingers around the artifact. I paused before revealing it, asking Val a silent question with my eyes. She nodded in answer, and I pulled the octahedron out for Arzak to see. Both the orc and Tokas leaned forward to get a closer look.

"This is . . . *Sisyphus Artifact*?" Arzak asked. "What it do?"

"Brings you back to life," I said, staring at it. Then I tossed it casually in the air, catching it again. Tokas almost seemed to flinch. "Or, at least, it used to. I used the last charge."

"Ah, that how you escape Plainside?"

I nodded. "But not without losing every skill I'd ever earned. At least it gives me a pretty significant XP boon to help get me back on my feet again."

"Can I . . ." Tokas started, reaching forward for the artifact, but Arzak's domineering presence overwhelmed her question.

"Do we know why they want this?"

"Re-spec?" Lore suggested.

"Or maybe they knew about the experience boost but not about the 'having to die first' bit?" Val said.

Arzak nodded. "We should find out. Val, Styk, Lore—you three go find more about this artifact. Learn why Player might want it. Me, Tokas, Corminar— we go learn more about Player." She trailed off, and the table went silent. "I mean . . . if this what everyone else want to do? I not in charge."

A moment later, Val broke into a smile. "It has my vote."

Lore nodded. "Mine, too."

"How did you decide on these teams?" Tokas asked.

Corminar stood from the table, apparently under the impression that we were going to set about this work right now. "I, too, agree with this course of action. We have not yet learned about his weaknesses—information that has served us well when dealing with previous wayward Players."

"Sit down, Cor," Val said. "We're not going yet."

"No?"

"No," Lore said. "I could do with some lunch first. And the stew here looked pretty good."

"I rather think we can do better than *stew*," Corminar protested.

"Sit down, Corminar," Arzak said, and the ranger immediately did as suggested.

"Six stews, is it?" Lore said, beginning to stand, but in this case for the bar rather than to leave.

"You've been buying pretty much every meal between her and Carn, Lore," Val said.

Lore shrugged. "My wool is popular. It pays well."

"Still, let someone else get it." Val's eyes drifted over the crowd and landed on the tiefling. "Tokas? What about you, this time?"

Tokas looked uneasily over at the barmaid, who was drying up a glass while intently returning the stare. Come to think of it, I realize the barmaid might well have been staring at Tokas this whole time.

"Oh, err . . ." Tokas said. "I'll give you the coin, but maybe . . . someone else could go and order it?"

"Why?" Lore asked, his tone curious rather than aggressive.

"I just . . ." Tokas gestured to her horns. "I don't think—"

"I get," Arzak said, standing upright and storming over to the barmaid without giving anyone a moment to argue it.

As the conversation around the table continued, I kept my gaze on the orc. She was leaning in close to the barmaid's ear, whispering something that was taking far longer than placing an order for six stews. Whatever Arzak said, it had the barmaid suddenly hurry away, and she didn't once look over at Tokas again.

We ate our stews—as delicious as Lore had suggested they would be—polished off another ale each, and then said our goodbyes. For the next week or so, it would be just Lore, Val, and me. At the time, I hoped that we wouldn't run into any trouble without the rest of the Slayers. Having an illusionist, a ranger, and another huge warrior on our side could be the difference between life and death in some cases.

This hope, it would soon turn out, would be in vain.

CHAPTER THIRTY-NINE

Talking Shop

With the Slayers having split up, the atmosphere was much quieter. Almost too quiet, in fact, even with Val's incessant commentary about absolute rubbish. I was happy that Val and I had been joined by Lore—he was the member of the Slayers who I'd meshed with the best over these past couple of weeks, though I suspected he got on with absolutely everyone.

We were heading for the town of Birrow, along the northern coast of the Iron Sea, based on a tip that Arzak had given us. There—if our orc friend was to be believed—was an expert in magical artifacts, who could take one look at the metal octahedron that had brought me back to life and give us a full account of its history. Again, I stress, that's only what we'd been told; I was of the opinion that I'd believe that when I heard it.

We traveled at a reasonable pace, as we needed to meet back with the rest of the team at the inn we'd been staying at in a little over a week, and it would take most of that time to get to Birrow and back again.

As we walked, we made idle conversation, and it wasn't long until the giant, intimidating barbarian was being very complimentary about my newly acquired abilities.

"So cool," Lore said. "I love those portals so much. And proper powerful, if you use them in the right way, I reckon."

"Are you saying he hasn't been using them in the right way?" Val asked, gently teasing, but this teasing element going completely over Lore's head.

"No, no!" Lore hurriedly added. "I loved that stuff with the water. That was a lot of fun."

I let the barbarian off the hook by changing the subject. "You've never told me what *your* abilities are. I mean, I've seen you slash at stuff, but what's the mechanic behind all that?"

"Mechanic? You mean how does it all work?"

I nodded. "Yeah."

"Oh right, well . . ." Lore shrugged, his cheeks reddening some. He was almost bashful about this topic of conversation. "Well, they ain't as exciting as you two's abilities. None of them magick or anything. I get Strength bonuses on my attacks—stabbing, slicing, and the like . . ."

"Ah yeah, I got similar ones for my knife." I pulled my Ranger's Blade out to reinforce the point, and then immediately thought that maybe this came across like comparing sizes—a competition that I would *definitely* lose. I hurriedly put the knife away again, not completely able to ignore the resulting smirk from Val.

Lore nodded encouragingly. "Yeah, there's a lot of overlap. But you get more Dexterity bonuses than I do. For me, it's all Strength. And then I got some other stuff—*Heavy Armor*, which means I don't tire as much, and I can keep it quiet. But I want to get some *Smithing*, too."

"*Smithing?*" I repeated.

The barbarian shrugged. "I wanted to get into it as a teenager. Thought I was gonna be a blacksmith when I grew up. But then . . . stuff happened. Guess fate had different plans for me."

"It has its way with all of us, Lore," Val said.

Lore looked thoughtful for a moment, before eventually nodding his agreement. "Yeah, I s'pose it does."

"You ever thought about pursuing the *Smithing* skill now?" I asked.

"Yeah. Yeah, I'd like to. I thought about getting a setup back on the farm, but I never got around to it. Maybe once this Player is killed, though . . ." Lore smiled at the thought. "I could make armor for my sheep!"

Val clapped her friend encouragingly on the back. "You think there's a broad market for that, do you?"

"Probably!" From the light in Lore's eyes, the sarcasm was lost on him.

Once again, I found myself saving Lore from his own kindness. "What about you, Val? Feels like you're always pulling out new tricks. You got anything you've not told me about?"

"Nope!" she said hurriedly.

"What, just controlling the wind? Controlling nature?"

"Just roots and branches," she corrected me. "Though I suppose I've got that summoning spell."

"Summoning spell?" I asked.

Val kept her gaze fixed in the direction of travel. "Don't worry about it; I never use it."

"She's a good healer, too!" Lore added helpfully.

"I can cure a hangover. If that's your definition of *good*, then—"

"It is," I said, and Lore nodded his agreement.

"—I guess I am, but nothing like Tokas, of course. How's that knee injury I fixed?"

I glanced down at it—the spot where Lambkin had gotten me with one of his arrows. "It clicks when I walk."

"Exactly—maybe not a *good* healer."

On the road up ahead, I spotted a group of people dressed in black. I put my hand instinctively to my knife, since based on my experience of late, I'd come to expect trouble on the roads. As the strangers approached, though, they passed without any trouble, and based on their teary expressions I realized that the black outfits were due to mourning.

"You got your changeling abilities as well, at least," I said. "Not that you seem to use them, ever."

"There's a hard limit on them; I'm only a quarter changeling, aren't I? Got to use it sparingly."

A thought occurred to me. "Hey, speaking of magicks, do you think this magick expert could get me one of those gems you have?"

"Gems?"

"The thing that stops people seeing the glow of your magicks."

"It's an *obscurem*, Styk, not a *gem*."

I stuck my tongue out at her and then caught myself. Was this really who I was these days? Someone who stuck their tongue out at people? Val really was a bad influence. "Looks like a gem to me."

Val removed the gem from her pocket. It was just plain black for now, not glowing with the green hue of Val's magicks, as she wasn't currently using any abilities. "You act like these things are so rare."

"Well, I've never seen anyone else who has one."

"Magick users don't tend to rub them in others' faces; the whole point is to hide the magick. If you know someone has one, then you're automatically suspicious of them."

"You have no idea how rare they are, do you?" I asked.

Val sighed. "Literally Tokas has one. The only other magick user in our party. Look, we'll get you one, but maybe let's focus on killing this Player—"

"Can I have yours, then?"

Val stared at me with hooded, unimpressed, eyes. "No."

"But you said they're common!"

"I didn't say I didn't need it, though, did I?"

I resisted the urge to stick my tongue out at her, this time. Instead, I looked back at Lore, who was taking in this conversation with his eyebrows raised.

The conversation moved on, into the mundane and—at times—the obscene, though Lore was largely responsible for the former and Val the latter. It was nice to be traveling with other people, not just because the roads had grown so dangerous these days, but because . . . I was learning to enjoy the conversation. And yes, I was even including Val's irritating digs at me in this.

Eventually, the conversation drifted around to something I'd been meaning to ask for some time now: how they'd come to realize that the Players weren't all they were cracked up to be.

Val was reiterating the story like it was one she'd told a hundred times. "There was this Player, back home in the Goldmarch, who'd been given this quest that everyone had been talking about for weeks. Huge payout. Came from a relative of the queen herself. But the mission? To hunt a changeling.

"Now, I know what you're thinking: I didn't stick myself in the middle of it, some noble pursuit to save one of my grandfather's kind. No, the changeling in question was a no-good murderous vermin; she deserved to die."

"Who are you to—" I started to ask.

"Oh shh, Styk," Val said. "Anyway, this Player, she didn't track down the changeling in question. No. Instead, she tracked down *me*. It didn't matter to her that I wasn't the one the hunt was for; she just wanted her payout. So she tracked me down, forced me into the wilderness, and she hunted me like a wild animal. But she didn't know that the wilderness is where I'm strongest."

"So you killed her? By yourself? Just you against a Player?"

"What did I say about shushing? No, I didn't kill her. I was lucky to escape alive, in fact. Remember that summoning spell I mentioned earlier? The one I don't use?"

Val paused, and I kept quiet, having taken on board the instruction to "shh,"

"You can answer the question," the sorcerer clarified.

"Yes, I remember. I could've just nodded. You know, with all this shushing it really seems like you just like me doing whatever you—"

"So I used that spell," Val continued. "It was the last time that I did, in fact. Reason is, I can summon the bogspawn perfectly fine, but I can't . . . control it. Whether it attacked me or attacked the Player was just the roll of a dice, and I . . . was lucky. Nothing more. The Player survived, as far as I know, but must have thought me too much trouble, because she didn't come after me again. Maybe she thought I *did* control the bogspawn. Who knows?"

"I don't," Lore pitched in, and Val notably did not shush him.

"But my whole worldview was upended. I'd believed in the Players, just like anyone else. I'd been that naive young woman myself. So I dedicated my life to telling others what the Players are capable of. Few listened, though, in the end. Just a select few . . ." She gestured to Lore, and by extension the whole of the Slayers.

"Can I speak now?" I asked.

"Speak, applaud, whatever you like," Val replied.

"I choose 'speak.' What happened to that Player? If you didn't kill her, is she still alive?"

"I don't think so. I never saw the body, but I heard she was eaten by an elder-beest. That's why we don't screw around with them."

"We managed alright with ours, I thought."

"Ours was a weak one," Val said.

Lore nodded his agreement.

"What about you, big guy?" I asked, turning my attention to the barbarian. The smile instantly faded from his face. "I had a family. I don't anymore."

I nodded, and a pang of guilt erupted in the pit of my stomach. Val glared at me, and behind Lore's back I mouthed 'What? You didn't say!' in response.

The journey was quieter after that, with Lore retreating into himself for the next day or two, and he only perked up once more when he smelled the fragrant aromas of delicious food coming from the many stalls of a market town—one strategically positioned to be on the route of anyone traveling around the edge of the Iron Sea. While Lore hurried off in search of food, shouting excitedly, I cast my gaze over the rest of the market.

"Oh no," someone nearby said. "Oh *no*. Not *you*."

(Remember that trouble I mentioned earlier? Here's where it started.)

CHAPTER FORTY

Water under the Bridge

I turned around to see a face that took me a moment to place. When I did, it wasn't so much the man's appearance that tipped me off, but the stall he was standing next to—one marked Ted's Confectionary.

"You're the people who got me shot!"

Val, who hadn't placed the face quite as quickly as I had, furrowed her brow. "What? When?"

"When that captain was after you. That . . . that . . ." Ted searched for the name. "Lambkin!"

Val's eyes widened with realization. "Ah, you!"

"You with your funny portal things and that elf with his luscious hair, and you with your . . ." Ted trailed off, looking at Val. "I don't really remember what your deal was."

". . . Sorcery?"

"Right, sure. Whatever. Point is, you got me shot. And look at my stall!" Ted pointed at three holes in the wood on the side. "Turned it into a porcupine, you did!"

"Technically, it was the guy who was after us that—" Val started, but I cut her off. I didn't think Ted had much up his sleeve, but at the moment I was keen to avoid trouble as much as possible.

"Our fault for hiding behind it," I said. "But what would you have us do? We had to hide somewhere—that we chose your stall was nothing personal. And besides, you did try to sell us out a bit, didn't you?"

Ted glanced down at his feet. "Suppose I did a little. But that doesn't make up for—"

"How's this? We buy some of your sweets, and we call it even? Put this behind us?"

The confectioner looked back at me, not blankly, but as though he was deep in consideration. Only when Val got impatient enough that she was about to interrupt him did Ted finally speak.

"Alright," he said, pulling some blue sweets not from the top of the stall but from the compartment at the back. "You're buying these, though. They're the ones with my highest profit margin."

Val raised her eyebrow, but ultimately slammed coins down onto the stall. "That cover it?"

Ted swept the whole lot into his pocket. "Ought to, yeah."

"Great," I said, taking the sweets. "So now we—"

"No change, then?" Val asked.

"Nope," Ted said. "Enjoy your sweets."

Fortunately for him, another customer turned up just as Val was about to launch into one of her trademark irritable tirades. I took the opportunity to lead her away.

"It's done. No point picking a fight."

"You're paying me back," she said.

As we walked away from the stall, we heard a pointed cough behind us. "Hope we never meet again!" Ted called out, waving with a wide, insincere smile on his face.

We left the small market town with full stomachs, and Lore had clearly eaten a lot when he'd been off on his own, because he was rubbing his belly in a very self-satisfied manner. Maybe it was for this reason that Lore turned down my offer of some of Ted's blue sweets, which had turned out to be actually rather delicious. They were blueberry flavored, but had an undercurrent of creaminess to them. As a result, Val and I absolutely demolished them, and the fight over the last one nearly came to blows.

The road at this point swung away from the coast by necessity of the geology. There were tall hills—not anything to rival the Bladerocks, of course—but with harsh enough cliffs that the road had to weave between them. The path veered from the rocky beaches and passed through a narrow valley with high cliffs towering over us on each side, making the road dark and foreboding. The thick brush of evergreen trees only made it darker still.

So *of course* this was where the trouble began.

It started with a growl, but not one of beast or monster. No, it started with a growl coming from my stomach, one that was so loud it seemed to scare the birds from a nearby tree.

Val opened her mouth to laugh, but found that, instead, a burp came out.

This, of course, was incredibly hilarious to the grinning Lore, but Val and I could no longer find anything funny because we were both diverting all our energies to trying not to vomit.

Lore realized we were in trouble when both of us keeled over, clutching our stomachs, our faces pale. Knowing him, it probably took all three signs for him to have any idea that something was going down.

"What the . . ." I gasped, simply speaking those two words almost enough to tip me over the edge from not vomiting into vomiting.

"*Ted* . . ." Val groaned. "*Poison* . . ."

"Uh-oh," Lore said, watching as the pair of us staggered to hold ourselves up against a nearby tree.

The path began to spin, the dirt in front of me one second, the high cliffs and canopy in front of me the next.

"That cheeky . . . little . . ." Val retched, and the sound of her doing so echoed around the narrow valley, making more birds flee than I had done. At first, my sorcerer friend "brought up" the usual stuff—mostly the food we'd purchased at the market town—but after a moment it changed. She wasn't vomiting food anymore, but . . . water.

I blinked, not quite taking in what was going on, and then a moment later the poisoned sweets caught up with me, too. Water projected forcefully from my mouth.

"What do I do? What do I do?" Lore cried, his eyes wide, part of him wanting to rush to my aid, part of him wanting to rush to Val's. "Poison? Do you need an antidote? Do I—"

"Not . . . poison," Val said, this change in circumstance apparently having informed her some. "Summoning . . . charm. Summons . . . water."

That seemed to be about the extent of it; the volume of water erupting from my stomach was surely more than my body could naturally hold. "Will it"—I paused to retch—"kill us?"

"Only if we don't . . . get it out."

At the echoes of our retching, most of the wildlife in the valley and the surrounding area fled, presumably thinking that Val and I were some monstrous creatures, screeching and growling. The average bird probably couldn't comprehend the idea of "spurned confectionary vendor getting revenge on people who'd put him in the middle of a fight by giving them charmed sweets that would summon water into their stomachs." And that was fair enough, really; I was much smarter than a bird and *I* could barely comprehend it.

For a moment, I considered trying to put a portal inside my own stomach to get all the water out, but immediately stopped myself. If I let it close on my flesh, there was no knowing what internal damage I'd do to myself. Besides, I'd never tried opening a portal *inside* someone before—surely that wasn't possible, was it?

There wasn't the opportunity to continue this line of thought because more water came pouring out of my mouth. "Is it ever going to—"

"Is it ever going to what?" asked Lore.

". . . stop?" I finished.

Lore looked to Val for an answer.

"It . . . will. Cheap charm. Won't . . . last long."

"Is it long enough to fight off some wolves?" Lore asked.

Val furrowed her brow even more than she was doing already. "Weird . . . example. Why?"

"Cos there are five wolves walking down the path," the barbarian answered. "Came to check out the noise, I reckon."

"Ah," Val said, followed by, "*Aaaaah*," as a load more water came out.

"Lead them away!" I managed to gasp.

Lore looked at me, nodded his understanding, and then pulled his sword free. He mumbled something about "revenge for what you lot did to my sheep" and then charged, screaming, toward the approaching beasts.

I tried to watch him go, but the water had weakened me, and instead I tumbled to the ground. I faced upward, at an old rope bridge hanging across the top of the chasm, and quickly I found myself drowning on the water erupting from my stomach. With a stifled groan, I pushed myself over, and the water washed over the surrounding ground, lapping at Val's shoes. At least she was too distracted to care.

In the distance, I heard shouting—from Lore—and growling—not from Lore. Was he really taking on five wolves at once? Even at a low level, it would be hard to occupy that many enemies in one go.

With all my might, I heaved myself back to my knees, and turned my attention to Lore and the wolves.

The answer to my earlier question? No.

No, Lore was not handling five wolves at once. He was handling three.

And the other two were approaching fast.

"Val . . ." I said.

"I see them."

"Any . . . ideas?" I gasped.

Val replied with a retch, and I turned to fix my attention back on the closest wolf, *identifying* it.

Level 14 Wolf
Variant: Storm
Identification: +100XP

With this, I leveled up my *Identification* to level 8, but I dismissed those notifications immediately. After all, I had a wolf to fight.

Scratch that: a *storm* wolf to fight.

I pulled my knife from my belt, vomited more water, and scoured my brain desperately for a plan.

CHAPTER FORTY-ONE

Dances with Storm Variants

At my side, Val staggered to her feet, readying herself for the battle ahead. On any normal day, a Level 14 Wolf—no matter the variant—would cause her no trouble. On a day where we had water being summoned into our stomachs . . . the stakes were a tad higher.

Of the two wolves approaching us, one cast its attention onto me, the other onto Val. It would be two one-on-one fights, then—excluding Lore's three-on-one down the road. The wolves' eyes glowed a gentle cyan color, and as they snarled at us, lightning crackled around their bared fangs.

"Right," I mumbled between waves of water, "storm variant."

The wolves came to a stop not ten paces from us, growling, their rear legs coiled and ready to spring forth. Val and I tried to steady ourselves, preparing for the fight ahead.

I flexed my fingers around the knife in my hand, and prepared my other hand to release a portal—though where, I did not yet know.

The wolf closest to me leaped, soaring toward me, and a split second later, its fellow beast did the same toward Val.

I twisted, bending out of the way just as the wolf jumped past me, aiming to *slice* at it with my knife, but interrupted by more of the water erupting up my throat. In the end, distracted by Ted's poisoning, I missed the creature's side entirely, and it turned to face me once more as it landed.

Alright, concentrate, I told myself, ignoring Val's tussle with the other beast and focusing on the one that had set its sights on me. *You can do this.*

As the wolf prepared to pounce once more, I snapped one hand toward the ground and one to the fraying rope bridge hanging overhead, at the top of the cliffs. As it jumped, I opened a portal, immediately falling through it and allowing the wolf to pass overhead. I landed heavily on the rope bridge, water pouring from my mouth, and it creaked as it swung from side to side. I focused my gaze on the fraying rope. "Don't you dare," I told it, as though my instruction might stop it from snapping.

This was good, I reckoned; I'd put some distance between myself and the wolf. That bought me some time to think. Ample time, even, to work out just what I was going to—

A scream erupted down below; one interrupted by gargling.

I leaned over the edge of the bridge and focused on the source of the noise: Val, ambushed by the wolf whose attention I'd successfully lost.

Oops. My bad. Maybe I didn't have *quite* so much time as I'd thought.

With that, I opened another pair of portals, draining my mana reserves to almost halfway. But whereas last time I'd gently placed myself onto the bridge, this time I opened the exit portal some way above one of the wolves. I leaped through it, arcing my knife through the air, and successfully buried it in the wolf's shoulder as I landed upon its back.

It howled with pain, and I instinctively gripped on tightly as a fresh batch of water began flooding from my mouth, coating the wolf's fur.

"Aaa-aah," I groaned as the wolf began to run about, doing its best to shake me off its back. If it wasn't for how deeply I'd buried the blade, it would have managed it with ease, but as it was, I had a solid handhold.

At least, I did until this latest batch of vomited water seemed to show no sign of ending. This wasn't enough by itself to trouble my grip, but the fact that it was quickly covering the beast's fur meant that it was increasingly . . . slippery.

The wolf made a sudden turn, flinging its back legs in the air, and at that moment I lost my grip. My knife, however, didn't.

I crashed into a tree then staggered back to my feet, focusing on the growling creature, my blade still stuck in its right shoulder.

Alright, Knifework is out. What else do I have?

There wasn't time to think, as the beast launched itself at me before I had a chance to move, distracted by the incredibly irritating ongoing vomiting. The wolf buried its front teeth in my shoulder, pinning me against the tree, and I couldn't help but roar with pain.

And if I thought the bite was bad enough, it was *nothing* compared to the bite once the beast had activated its storm variant powers. Lightning shot between its teeth and into my flesh, burning it. I tried to ignore the smell of cooking meat, particularly because *I* was the meat.

I screamed through the pain, desperately stretching my arm out to pull the knife from the wolf's shoulder. I nipped at it with my fingertips, just barely skimming the hilt, almost there, almost there, almost—

I vomited once more, a huge burst of water covering the wolf's head and bared fangs, drenching it.

And the water, combined with the more typical stomach contents, conducted the lightning.

The wolf, too, roared with pain, releasing my shoulder. Due to the water coating the beast's snout, the storm powers no longer fried at my flesh, but now blitzed the creature's own face.

I took this moment of relief to fall to the floor, clutching my shoulder. From there, I could just make out Val through my blurry vision, on the back foot against her own ambushing beast.

"Vomit on it!" I shouted. "On its mouth!"

Val risked a turn to me, presumably pulling a face like I'd just given her a terrible idea. "*What?*"

"Vomit on—" I was cut off by my body deciding to demonstrate my instruction at that very moment. I shook my head, spraying water everywhere, then charged toward the wolf and the knife that was still protruding from its shoulder.

It saw me coming and spun its body around to face me.

With so much momentum on my side, however, I couldn't stop, and committed myself to leaping over the beast, reaching out for the knife as I went. Sadly, I didn't so much as touch the knife hilt, and the wolf spun around and knocked me to the ground. All in all, it wasn't my best move. Not like that *portal slice* that collapsed the arch on that elderbeest.

As I tried to stand back up, the wolf pounced on top of me, baring its fangs, and it was all I could do to grab at its neck and chin to keep those teeth away from me. "Where's this water when you *need* it?" I spat through clenched teeth.

I willed myself to bring up more of the liquid, but nothing was forthcoming—the sweets were finally finished—which meant that I wasn't able to use the wolf's storm powers against it. I was back to relying on my own skill set; one that had grown significantly, but still was—at least *mathematically*—inferior to a level 14.

I released my right hand from the wolf's neck, relying on my left hand under its chin to keep those fangs the hells away from me, and it pushed in closer. The wolf's putrid breath washed over me, making my eyes sting, and I forced myself not to think about it. All that mattered in this moment was getting my right hand around that knife.

Again, I could only barely graze it with my fingertips. I reached further, harder, trying everything I could to get my hands about that knife.

Reach. The word echoed around my head, reminding me of a vital ability. What if . . .

> **Closed Reach (Knifework):** Bend reality to narrow the gap between blade and target by up to 8 inches. Has mana cost.

Yes! There was nothing in there about having to actually *hold* the knife in question. I focused on the blade buried in the wolf's shoulder and activated my *Closed Reach* skill, draining a good amount of my remaining mana in the process.

Reality itself folded around the wolf, pushing the blade deeper into its flesh, and the wolf howled once more. Immediately the pressure on me released, and the creature staggered backward, thick red liquid pouring down its left side.

I pressed the advantage, reaching out for the blade this time not with spells but with my hand, and I twisted it—hard.

It howled one last fading howl, and for a moment I felt sorry for the creature. After all, it was only doing what it was built to do: hunt prey, find sustenance. Ultimately, though, if it was me or it, then the choice was easy. I'd twist that blade again without hesitation.

As it fell to the floor, new notifications popped up in front of me—and very exciting ones indeed.

Level 14 Wolf defeated!

Worldbending: +800XP
Worldbending increased to Level 15!
Base Points Gained: +2 INT, +2 Free Points (INT/WIS/CHA)

Ability Selection Unlocked
Select an ability from the list below . . .

Knifework: +800XP
Knifework increased to Level 15!
Base Points Gained: +1 DEX, +1 STR, +2 Free Points (VIT/DEX/STR)

Ability Selection Unlocked
Select an ability from the list below . . .

(And yes, dear reader, you *are* reading that right. Not one but two abilities, both happening at the same time, if only due to random coincidence.)

I fought the instinct to bring the lists of choices up immediately and instead settled for helping Val finish off her wolf.

Then, it would be up-skilling time.

CHAPTER FORTY-TWO

Inside Sheep

Lore cleaved the last of the wolves in two with one final great swing of the Bane Sword, and all three of us finally relaxed.

"That fight make you hungry, too, Lore?" I asked.

"I don't get hungry after fighting animals. Too sad."

"Unlike when you kill . . . people?" Val pointed out.

The shepherd only shrugged in response; clearly he too could see the hypocrisy in this. We paused for a moment to regather our breaths before Val very correctly pointed out, "Maybe we should get going? You know, in case there's more of them?"

Once we were farther down the road, and out from between the high cliffs, I brought up my ability selection notifications once more, starting with *Knifework*.

Ability Selection Unlocked
Select an ability from the list below:

Option 1: Stab II (Knifework)—*Upgrade to Stab.* Put your weight behind your wielded blade and force the tip through tougher hides and armor. Damage scales on [STR]. Damage increased by an additional [+20 percent].

It was a decent opener; an upgrade to a core ability that I'd relied on to get me out of trouble a few times already. And an additional 20 percent damage? That didn't sound like much, but it quickly added up, especially if I got new equipment . . . or leveled it up enough that I could use my old Blade of Samal that I'd been lugging around with me all this time.

I went back into the selection screen.

Option 2: Deft Hands (Knifework)—*Passive.* Your handling of blades borders on the magical, and you are able to draw your blade faster than most.

I'd had this ability choice last time around, and I'd forsaken it for the seemingly much more exciting *Execution. Execution* had proven handy on occasion, sure, but then just how often would I have saved myself a scar or two if I'd been just a tad quicker on the draw?

Still contemplating my *Knifework* ability choices—just the two this time!—I minimized this screen for now and brought up *Worldbending* instead. *Maybe there would be some way of combining the two*, I thought.

Ability Selection Unlocked
Select an ability from the list below:

Option 1: Revert Self (Worldbending)—Immediately remove all active effects from yourself.

Nope.

No, no, no, I absolutely did *not* want that. The reason I was progressing as fast as I was—outside of the Slayers getting me into awkward situations—was because of the *Legacy of Sisyphus*. And do you know what that was? That's right, an active effect; I immediately ruled out this ability choice. Obviously.

Hidden condition met! Alternative ability choice unlocked.
Option 2: Far Hands (Worldbending)—[Requires: At least 1 Portal ability unlocked]—While active, your Bareknuckle attacks have a 20-foot range, extended through portals.

OK, now we were talking—this was an ability that didn't essentially condemn me to death, so that was pretty great. Already I could think of plenty of applications for it—who wouldn't want to attack someone from twenty feet away? And maybe I could use it for snatching some spare coin here and there . . .

Option 3: Ash Husk (Worldbending)—Convert your flesh to ash, strengthening it against flame for ten minutes. Gain 50 percent resistance to fire attacks.

Option 4: Frost Husk (Worldbending)—Convert your flesh to frost, strengthening it against ice for ten minutes. Gain 50 percent resistance to ice attacks.

Well, the application for at least *one* of these was obvious, considering our target was a pyroknight. But they weren't the broadest of abilities, either, were they? They only offered temporary resistance, though at least it was at a pretty high level; 50 percent was definitely nothing to sniff at.

"What you doing, Styk?" Val interrupted me, and I could see from her face that she knew full well what I was doing.

"Ooh!" Lore said, his eyes lighting up when he realized what was going on. "You get yourself a new ability?"

"Two."

"Two?!" Lore seemed barely able to contain himself, and it wasn't even one of *his* abilities.

"Oh yeah?" Val asked. "Why haven't you been telling us about all these skill upgrades, then?"

"I *was* asking you! And you've not been at all helpful!"

"Well, I told you to focus your free points on just some of the base stats, didn't I?" Val said. "I assume you're doing that? I don't see you getting any more charismatic as the days go by."

I stuck my tongue out at her—why did I keep doing that?—and replied, "We both know that's not how stats work. I don't see you getting more intelligent, do I? And I assume you build up your mana at every opportunity?"

Val returned the sticking-out-tongue gesture.

"So, yeah, *of course* I've been doing that. I've been putting them into Intelligence—"

"For the mana reserves, yeah, like we said."

"—and I've been putting them into Strength, because that's what my *Knifework* abilities scale up on. I'm doing all that. But I could do with more help from you guys."

Val shrugged. "If you got more questions, ask them."

"Well, you're a magick user, right? What should I be picking in my *Worldbending* ability selections?"

"I don't know *Worldbending*," Val replied. "I'm a sorcerer. I know *Sorcery*."

I tossed my head back in exasperation. "Then what help are you?!"

"Hey, I might not know *all Worldbending* abilities off by heart—who does?— but I can still be useful. Give me some specifics."

"How am I supposed to plan my build if I don't know what's coming?"

Val screwed up her face. "When you said you wanted to learn from your past life, I thought you meant, like, focusing your free points, making sure to upgrade your abilities rather than going wide with them, training up a handful of core skills rather than spreading yourself too thin. Didn't we talk about this already?"

"Well, yeah. I'm doing all those things. *Obviously*, I'm doing all those things. I just thought—"

"What, that there'd be some, like, encyclopedia of all possible ability choices? That doesn't exist, Styk."

Lore nodded his head in agreement.

"Sure, everyone gets a few core choices, but we both know that the abilities get more and more varied as you get stronger. Look—you did *Knifework* last time around, and you've learned from that, right?"

"Yeah . . ."

"Then what more do you want? What you want me to give you isn't how life works, Styk."

I held my hands up in the air in surrender. "Alright, alright. Help me with the specifics, then. A *Stab* upgrade or *Deft Hands* for *Knifework*?"

"What did you pick for *Worldbending*?"

"Well, nothing yet, but I was thinking *Far Hands*. One thing I didn't do last time around—last *life*—was synergize. I want to do that this time. Or, rather, I want to *keep* doing that this time."

"You're going to have to tell us what that does, Styk," Val said.

I told her, and then, for simplicity's sake, explained the other choices, too. (To save you all the trouble of going through all that again, dear reader, I have spared you this part of the conversation.)

"Alright," Val said, "*Far Hands*. Yeah. That sounds good."

"Particularly good for stealing things, I thought," I said without thinking, before quickly adding, "Not that I do that anymore."

Lore skimmed over this point, apparently not being too worried about stealing. "It said '*Barehanded* attacks,'" he pointed out. "I dunno if you can use that for stealing."

"My hands would be bare, wouldn't they?"

"And would they be attacking?" Lore asked.

"Fair point. So you're saying if I took that, I'd have to start leveling up *Barehanded*, too. I can do that."

"No," Val interrupted.

"No?" I prompted. "People usually say 'no' and then follow it up with an explanation."

"To level up a skill, you need to use it, right? For crafting skills, you craft. For magick skills, you cast. For combat skills . . . you fight, killing or otherwise ending combat. If you want to level up *Barehanded*, you're gonna be losing out on *Knifework* experience, when that could serve the same purpose."

"But I'd level up faster!" I protested.

"So what? That's a vanity thing, Styk. Trust me, I've met so many guys out there who have been level thirty or more and who I could beat in a fight with my eyes closed. Pretty sure Tokas's kids could beat them in a fight, even. No, you gotta focus your efforts, particularly where there's an opportunity cost like that.

If you wanna spend your downtime, I dunno, sewing, then sure, get yourself a *Needlework* skill. But combat skills? They should serve a purpose that your existing ones don't, otherwise you're just wasting valuable experience."

I looked to Lore for confirmation. He nodded. "Why d'you think I just have *Two-Handed*?"

"Fine. Alright. So, not that ability, then," I replied. "So I guess it's . . ."

Val shrugged. "I wouldn't normally recommend an ability as specific as *Ash Husk*, but considering where our journey is heading, and who is most likely to, you know, kill you . . ."

"Maybe fifty percent fire resistance wouldn't be so bad. And it's not like I have much health, as I'm not speccing much into Vitality."

Lore nodded encouragingly. "Plenty of fire specialists out there. I reckon people like the drama of it, don't they? You know, 'ooh, fire!'"

"The cultists," Val and I said at the same time.

Lore pointed to us as though he'd been thinking the exact same thing.

Ability Unlocked: Ash Husk

Ash Husk (Worldbending): Convert your flesh to ash, strengthening it against flame for ten minutes. Gain 50 percent resistance to fire attacks.

"What about *Knifework*, then?"

Val shrugged. "I could go either way on this. Lore? You probably know better than me."

"Take the upgrade," he said very quickly. "Always take the upgrade."

"But *Deft Hands* could be good?"

"The upgrade. Always," Lore said. "As long as it's for an ability you actually use. This scar?" he pointed to his face. "That's what happens when you don't take the upgrade." When Val raised an eyebrow, Lore added, "I'll tell you another time."

I sighed. "Alright, then . . ."

Ability Upgraded: Stab II

Stab II (Knifework): Put your weight behind your wielded blade and force the tip through tougher hides and armor. Damage scales on [STR]. Damage increased by an additional [+20 percent].

"Got it," I said.

"Nice!" Lore echoed, and then clapped me on the back and began walking once more. "We'll make a *Slayer* out of you yet, yeah?"

"Maybe if he works out how to use his portals properly," Val added.

"What? What do you mean?"

"I mean half the time you waste the mana, don't you? Don't think I didn't see you pop up to the bridge and down again, back there."

"That's only because you were in trouble! I was trying to save *you!*"

"Ooh, so noble," Val said. "I would've been fine."

"Well, what would you rather I do, then?"

"Could try closing it on someone," Lore suggested, shrugging. "Might be bloody, but . . . you know, whatever floats your boat."

"It closes on inanimate objects, yeah," Val responded. "Spells, though, they have a habit of working differently for things that are alive."

I blinked at her. "You couldn't have told me this sooner?" I turned to Lore. "And you couldn't have *suggested* this sooner?"

"I assumed you knew! Look, I'm not saying that the portal would *definitely* not close on a living thing, but the wording of this whole *Portal Slice* ability you have seems to suggest it."

"OK, but how can I—" I started.

At the same moment, Lore's eyes lit up as he set them upon four-legged creatures in a neighboring field. "Sheep!" he cried out excitedly.

Val and I looked to one another, and the sorcerer nodded.

"What?" Lore asked. "What are you thinking?" He looked from us, to the sheep, and then his mind caught up. "You're not going to—"

"Try it, Styk," Val said.

"You ain't gonna . . ." Lore said, color fading from his face.

"I try it on an animal, or I try it on a human," I replied. "Sorry, Lore, but there's only one way to find out what happens."

I reached out one hand toward the sheep, prepared myself for the seemingly inevitable bloodshed, and then willed a portal into existence.

Nothing happened.

"OK, right, yeah. Can't open it through a living creature. Suppose that would be world-shatteringly overpowered, wouldn't it?"

"Told you the *Portal Slice* description implied that."

I ignored Val and instead opted for hopping the fence then ambling up to the nearest sheep. It bleated at me, but wasn't bothered enough to move. "Alright, I'm just gonna . . ."

I opened a portal at the sheep's side, and then I gently nudged the creature toward it. It didn't budge.

"Go on," I said, "go into the magical floating purple light."

Still, nothing.

"Kick it," Val suggested.

"I'm not gonna kick an animal."

"What, kicking it isn't on, but cutting it in half is perfectly fine?"

"That's different!" I protested.

"How?"

"That's . . . that's science."

I put my shoulder into the nudging this time, and on this occasion the sheep was bothered enough to step away from me, putting its back legs through the portal.

As soon as it was through, I released the spell, and the portal snapped shut.

Only . . . it didn't. Not quite. I wasn't bleeding mana, but part of the portal remained around where the sheep was standing, fitting its form perfectly.

"How are you doing that?" I asked the sheep, and the resulting bleat suggested that it wasn't doing anything.

"It's not working!" Lore cried out, thrusting his hands in the air in celebration. "It's alive!"

"Is it . . . stuck?" Val said.

I nudged it once more, harder still this time. The sheep staggered backward into where the remnants of the portal were, and disappeared out the other side—where the other end had been moments earlier.

I waved my hand into the space where the portal had been, and found . . . nothing. The portal had snapped closed behind it.

"It didn't work," I said, turning back to the other two.

"We saw!" Lore said excitedly, arms still raised in celebration.

"Could still always use your portals to drop it from a great height, though, couldn't you?" Val suggested.

Lore pressed his lips together. "Don't you dare."

I didn't dare; I didn't want to upset Lore more than I had already. But now I had an idea for the next bandit we came across . . .

CHAPTER FORTY-THREE

Late Fees

"And you think I give out information for free, do you?"

We'd finally reached Birrow and asked around for directions to the supposed magical artifact expert, only to get raised eyebrows from everyone we asked. The problem wasn't that nobody knew him so much as they knew *too much* of him. Apparently, he was a bit of a scourge on the town, between summoning monsters and accidentally exploding buildings—all things that had been caused, it was said, by the artifacts he was inspecting.

As such, a certain member of our group—no, actually, I'll name him; it was Lore—was a bit apprehensive when we entered the artifact expert's small rickety house, and even went so far as to jump when the bells above the door chimed. Val, not at all apprehensive, had told the old man we'd found inside what we were after, and that was what had resulted in the aforementioned response.

"We have coin," Val said.

"Not huge amounts of it, though," I added. It wasn't strictly true, but I already had the impression that the man in front of us would state extortionate rates if he knew we'd pay them.

"I do not deal in *coin* . . ." the old man said, sat behind a grand old wooden desk, paying most of his attention to a huge book he gripped in leather hands. He was surrounded by yet more books—quite a collection, in fact—though these were outnumbered by what I could only describe as "trinkets," including a little brass model of a sheep. Lore had his eye on that one.

"Right. OK. So what do you deal in, then? Silver? Antique plates?"

"Favors," the man said.

"What?"

Val looked to me. "If you're after sexual fav—"

"Stop telling people I deal in sexual favors!" I interrupted.

The sorcerer shrugged. "Sorry," she told the old man. "Can't help you." After a moment of pause, she turned to Lore. "Unless . . . ?"

Lore held her gaze, and slowly shook his head.

"Nope, you're out of luck."

"I ask not for favors of sordid kinds," the artifact expert said. "But I *will* require of you a great debt. A quest, in fact. One so demanding that I do not expect all three of you to return to me—at least not . . . alive. Should such a payment be too much of you, I understand, but know this: never will you receive the information you—"

"Alright, cut to the chase, Grandpa," Val interrupted. "What's this quest? What do you want us to do?"

"I wish for you to . . ." The old man paused for effect, then suddenly picked up a stack of books from behind him, plonking them onto the desk. ". . . return these library books."

"Return . . . library books?" Val asked.

Sharing the sorcerer's confusion, I picked up the stack of books and leafed through them, reading aloud their titles. "*Magicks Through the Ages, Ten Ways to Defeat a Wounded Murlock, Miss Feather's Great Delights . . .*"

The old man hurriedly took that book out of the pile. "Oh, not that one; that one's mine."

"I don't get it," I said, putting the books down where they were.

"No, me neither," Val added. "What's the catch?"

"If you think this quest too great an ask, then . . ." the artifact expert trailed off forebodingly.

"No, we're not saying that, we're saying . . ." Val sighed. "OK, you win. We'll complete this great quest for you. Where's the library?"

"The other side of town."

Our "great quest" took us on a journey that lasted all of, maybe, five minutes—and that was including waiting for Val to finish looking in a shop window at a dress that she described as having "almost enough pockets." As far as quests go, I hadn't been on one that required so little travel time since my father sent me on a "quest" to steal the neighbor's jewelry.

The library itself was a surprisingly grand old building, and I had to guess—from the comparative age of the architecture—that the rest of the town was built around it. We entered through large double doors, into an atrium that itself was larger than most inns and contained bookshelves fully stocked, each about three Arzaks tall. Dwelling amongst the stacks were zero patrons and a small handful of librarians. At least I thought they were librarians, having never stepped foot in a library before, I was only basing this assessment on a stereotype—they were all old, wearing dusty clothes, and looked ready to throttle anyone who dared speak.

"Looking to return some books!" Val dared to say, loudly and without a care in the world.

Surprisingly, nobody immediately sought to kill her, though the glares that each of the librarians gave her came close to doing the trick. Of the three librarians, only one of them seemed willing to follow up on Val's request.

A woman in black robes—to the others' gray—sighed, placed down a stack of books she was apparently sorting, and then walked over to the front desk where we were standing. She held out her hand expectantly. "Well?"

Val raised her eyebrows and made a face that I recognized as one of "trying not to stick her tongue out at someone," then handed the books over to the librarian.

The woman placed them down on the table and turned to their inside covers. There, in a language I did not understand, was what looked like a list.

"Hmm . . ." she said.

On the next book, she did exactly the same thing.

". . . just as I thought . . ."

We waited patiently—well, semipatiently; Val was tapping her foot—for the librarian to finish, and when she did so it was with the thud of covers being closed.

"You do know that these books are two centuries overdue?" the librarian asked.

"Nope," I said.

"Do I look that old to you?" Val added.

"The other guy didn't, either, to be fair," Lore added. At a disapproving look from Val, he added, ". . . but still much older than you?"

"There is a penalty for such a delay in returning these books," the librarian said, taking a step back from the front desk. "You have incurred the ultimate late fee, in fact: death."

Me and the two Slayers blinked at her, trying to work out if this was some strange librarian form of humor. There was no sign of a smile.

"Death?" Lore asked. "What kinda library is this?"

"Is that a pun? Like on 'late'?" I put in, feeling that this was the most pressing concern in this moment.

"Yeah, that feels like a stretch," Val added. "Late? Late fees? I just don't see it."

"This is a weird way to run a library," Lore continued, apparently mulling over their business practices.

"Agatha!" the librarian in black shouted, and one of her colleagues poked her head around a bookshelf.

"Yes?"

"We have a two-century return," the woman apparently in charge said. "*Many* two-century returns, in fact."

The other librarian nodded, then ran off amongst the bookshelves once more.

"You do know that I'm not the one who borrowed these, right?" Val asked. "You don't *seriously* believe I'm over two hundred years old."

"Why would I not? I'm four hundred," the librarian replied.

Val hesitated, looking the woman up and down. "You *have* to give me your skincare routine."

"I must give you nothing, except death."

"Very dramatic," Val replied. "Are we really gonna keep pretending you're gonna kill me for returning some late library books? Ones that I didn't even borrow?"

"Val . . ." Lore said nervously.

"They're not gonna kill us, Lore," Val said to him, and then turned back to the librarian. "Look. We picked these up from—"

A ball of ice shot across the library, passing the head librarian by a hairsbreadth, and missing the three of us only because we dived out of the way just in time. Across the library, Agatha was grasping an old book in her hands, both her pages and her eyes glowing.

"OK," Val admitted. "Maybe they *are* gonna kill us. Styk? Lore?"

"On it," Lore replied.

CHAPTER FORTY-FOUR

Too Much Reading, Not Enough Punching

"On it," Lore replied, and then he turned and started running away.

The library doors snapped closed, seemingly of their own accord, and a glowing rope bound them together, locking them. A glowing line erupted around the perimeter of the building. Even *I* knew enough about magick to know that this was a ward; neither flesh nor spell was getting through that.

"Lore, I meant *fight!*" Val shouted.

"Oh? I thought we could just run away." Another bolt of ice soared through the air, and Lore joined us in cowering behind the library's front desk. The spell just about caught his hair, freezing it. He shivered. "Alright, I guess we should fight."

"You think?" Val cried out as another ice ball smashed into the other side of the desk.

"Strategy, quick," I interjected; there was one librarian firing spells at us, another one who surely soon would be, and a third out there somewhere—we didn't have time to mess about.

Val looked to me. "If we kill them, the magick lock fades. It's the only way we get out."

"Alright. Looks like they're reading their spells from that book." I risked a glance over the desk and almost got hit in the face by a ball of ice. While I was peeking over, I saw that the chief librarian—did librarians have chiefs? Probably not—was moving to the bookcases, possibly to pick up a spell book of her own. "Val, I'll *portal* us to the ice one. Get ready."

The sorcerer nodded.

"And me?" Lore asked.

"Stop the other one from reading."

"Got it."

I flung my hand over the top of the table, aiming a portal in the rough direction of the air above the casting librarian, and opened its partner beneath us. Val, Lore, and I tumbled through, but the barbarian got caught on the edge of the portal. I lost sight of him as Val and I fell through the portal and it snapped closed behind us.

Val was quick to move, conjuring up a gust of wind that pelted the librarian's book and ripped it from her hands.

The aggressor stopped for a moment, eyes widening, and then dived to the floor to grab the fallen book.

"Don't let her—" Val started.

But I was already moving—no *Worldbending* or *Knifework* required for this one—sprinting across the floor and kicking the book out of the librarian's hands. She screamed with frustration, apparently unable to cast without a book to guide her, and that was the moment the third librarian reappeared.

A ball of darkness floated across the room, bending the light around it and pulling loose objects—books and reading spectacles, mostly—toward its surface. This attack from the third librarian didn't move as fast as the fireball, but I knew from prior experience that any shadow attacks like this had the potential to do serious damage.

"Val!" I shouted, pointing at the new attacker.

"Yes, I'm trying!" she cried back as she summoned a blast of wind that billowed toward the third librarian. But just before the blast hit the enemy, the man read from his book and a shining light in the shape of a shield glowed to life before him, protecting him from Val's attack.

"Styk, he's got a—"

"Yes, I have eyes!" I replied.

"You literally *just* did the same thing to me."

I ignored Val's response and realized I was now forced to split my energies between two librarians—the other one still being occupied by Lore. To my left, one librarian hurriedly crawled between the aisles of large shelving units toward the fallen book, which was about three feet away from her outstretched hands. And to my right, at the end of this particular bookcase-lined corridor, the latest addition to the fight began speaking aloud from the heavy tome he held.

It was quick-thinking time.

I drained some of my mana reserves by opening a portal beneath the fallen book and dropping it onto the head of the third librarian. While he remained unhurt, he was at least distracted enough from his spell-reading to go "Ouch! What was . . ." and look behind him. Only once he spotted the book on the ground did he return to his reading, and before I knew it, there was another shadow ball hurtling toward me.

I dived to the floor, narrowly missing the projectile flying overhead, and had another bright idea—I was full of them today. I opened a portal beneath the fallen book once more, and this time portaled it into the air above me, snatching it for myself as it dropped. I leafed it open to a random page and . . .

Realized it wasn't in the common tongue.

I couldn't read it; this was useless to me. Perhaps not such a bright idea after all, though at least it kept it out of the hands of—

"Styk, watch out!" Val shouted.

I looked up, saw a shadow-form charging at me, and panicked. Not yet was having portal magicks so second nature to me that I instinctively used them to get out of trouble, and instead I dived behind the cover of a bookcase, dropping the again fallen book in the process.

"No!" one of the librarians roared as the shadow ball crashed into the bookcase I was cowering behind, tearing up some of the shelves' contents as it collided.

I poked my head out of cover to see the male librarian, ward still up, resisting Val's windswept attacks with ease, the dust pouring around the ward but not hitting him. As I watched, the man began the process of conjuring up more shadow magicks.

"Val!" I shouted.

"What!"

"At me! Aim it at me!"

"Why?" the sorcerer cried back.

"Just do it, will you?"

Val sighed, then flung a hand at me, summoning a great dust of wind that collected the ample dust that lined the floors and bookshelves. In the moments before this great cloud of dirt hit me, I opened another portal, pairing it with one behind the librarian's ward.

The man stopped midspell, staggered backward, and clawed at his dust-filled eyes.

We wasted no time in charging at the librarian before he could recover, and I raised my knife to *stab*. I leaped through the air, putting extra weight into my attack, and swung my blade down into—

A ball of ice smacked the side of my hand, knocking my arcing knife wide but not quite pushing it from my grip. I spun, eyes wide, to see the other librarian had collected the fallen book once more and was in the process of launching another ball of ice.

It was time to fulfil an earlier promise. Next time we encountered a human attacker, I'd promised myself I would try dropping them from a great height.

I opened a portal under the feet of the ice-conjuring librarian and she yelped as she fell through it, finding herself dropping from the other end of the portal . . . which I'd put on the ceiling.

But if I'd expected this to dispatch our enemy completely, I was wrong. The librarian shouted words from her book and the air turned to patches of ice under her feet. She rode these frozen platforms to the floor, hopping from patch to patch before they had even finished forming.

"Aw, hells," I muttered as shouting from behind told me that the other librarian had recovered.

"The books!" Lore shouted from the other side of the great atrium.

"What?"

"They don't want us to hurt the books!" the barbarian clarified, which explained the librarian's distress earlier when one of their spells had caught the bookshelf.

Val launched a gust of wind at another shadow ball, sending it ricocheting toward the ice librarian.

"Lore!" I shouted. "I got an idea, but I need you."

"Is it gonna hurt?"

"A bit."

"And you don't got any better ideas?"

"No."

There was a pause, during which time I heard Lore grunt as he fended off one of the chief librarian's attacks. "Aite, do it!"

The moment I received permission from my friend, I opened a portal beneath him, and another on the ceiling.

"Styk!" he cried as he fell.

But I closed the portals as soon as he was through and opened another one beneath him. This one launched him into the side of one of the bookcases—the one at the end that the chief librarian was standing next to.

Lore collided with the bookcase with a grunt, and the unit came crashing down, showering the chief librarian with books and then near flattening them under the weight of the thick wood. From the resulting notifications, I realized I'd incapacitated her.

Level 23 Ancient Librarian defeated!

Worldbending: +1,000XP

"Oh alright, I see," Lore said, nursing his arm.

"You will *leave* those books alone," spat the shadow magick librarian through gritted teeth.

"Oh, so I shouldn't . . ." Lore said, pulling a book from a nearby shelf and tearing it in half, ". . . do this?"

I pulled another book from a shelf near me and positioned my hands on the hard cover to do the same, only I couldn't do it. "Think I picked up a particularly strong one," I explained, and then settled for ripping pages out of it instead.

"You will stop!" the librarians echoed almost at once, flinging a spell each at Lore and me. While Lore avoided the shadow spell, a frost ball caught my shoulder, and I winced at the pain.

"Oh, will we?" Val replied. "Lore, push another one over."

The barbarian did as instructed, slamming himself into the side of the nearest shelving unit, and with a strained heave, slowly toppled it over, sending books spilling across the floor.

Under the streams of light pouring in through the great window at the back of the library, the frost librarian screamed with fury, and at that moment I had yet another—possibly—great idea.

"Lore!" I cried out. "Push them inward! Push them inward!"

"The librarians?"

"The bookcases!"

Lore nodded, heaving himself against the bookcase at the end of the column, grunting as he put all his might into it—but it wasn't enough.

I began running, dodging projectiles while opening a portal in front of me that I hopped through to join Lore at his side. With one eye on my dwindling mana reserves—I'd gotten careless about how long I left portals open for—I realized that we needed this to work. Otherwise, I was soon going to be useless.

I bashed my shoulder into the side of the bookcase, straining against it, and with my additional strength—not that it was much, compared to Lore's—the unit budged. The librarians, seeing what we were doing, began to concentrate their spells upon us, but Val used her wind magicks to skew them off just enough to avoid hitting us.

And then, the bookcase tumbled.

Unlike the others, which had been aimed outward at the librarians, this one tumbled toward another bookcase, knocking it over, which hit another, and another . . .

Lore's eyes lit up. "Dominoes," he said.

"And not just that," I replied, running up the slanted bookcase and on to the next. Lore joined me, and I used the last of my magicks to portal-drop Val to our side.

The three of us ran across falling bookcases, following the path of destruction just a few steps behind. Shadow and ice projectiles flew overhead, but we were charging too fast to be hit.

The last of the bookcases crashed through the window at the far end of the atrium just as we were reaching it, sending shards of glowing glass glistening through the air, pane and ward shattering as one.

We leaped through it, limbs scratching against jagged shards, and landed on the ground outside. As we gasped for breath, I received notifications of experience points for ending our combat.

> **Worldbending**: +800XP
> *Worldbending increased to Level 16!*
> **Base Points Gained**: +2 INT, +2 Free Points (INT/WIS/CHA)

"This?" Val said as we hurried away from the library before its remaining workers could circle around and find us. "This is why I don't like libraries."

CHAPTER FORTY-FIVE

Creation Myths

"Reveal your artifact to me once more, and I will inspect it," the expert said.

"Couldn't you have done that while we were busy almost dying for you and your bloody overdue library books?" Val asked.

The expert ignored her, his eyes fixed on mine. Within them, there was almost a hunger to get his hands on the Sisyphus Artifact, and part of me resisted the idea of handing it over—even temporarily.

Lore watched me carefully as I removed the artifact from my pocket and placed it gently on the desk in front of us. If I wasn't mistaken, he moved his hand ever so slightly closer to his sword—had he noticed the same hunger within the old man?

The expert picked up the Sisyphus Artifact delicately, almost as though he was afraid to touch it. "Hmm . . ." he said. "Hmm . . . Is it? It is, isn't it?" He coughed, placing the object back down on the table and taking a half step away. "It's real."

"I could've told you that," I replied.

"Do people often come to you with questions about fake magical artifacts?" Val asked.

"Not all of my customers know they hold fakes. When you said that it was this . . . well, I thought it couldn't be the real thing."

I took a seat on the one chair facing the artifact expert's desk. Val and Lore were going to have to stay standing. "Go on."

"There is little information about this artifact, for it has been lost to the years."

"It's old, then?"

The old man laughed, a raucous guffaw loud enough to shake the knick-knacks on his desk. "Old? Yes, you could say that. This object was made with Alterra itself, back when the Architects created our world. That even *some* information has survived all this time is a miracle."

I felt a chill wash over me. That I'd been carrying around something so old, something presumably crafted by an Architect . . . I shivered at the thought.

"I'm afraid all I can tell you is . . . the legends say that this artifact is inextricably linked to the lives of the gods. In what way, I could not guess, but my feeling is that the only way to find out would be to . . ." The old man licked his lips, apprehensive about his own forthcoming words. "Would be to take the life of a Player."

Val and I made eye contact, both of us making apparent painstaking efforts to keep our expressions neutral.

"We—" Lore started, not quite on the same page as the rest of us, interrupted by Val flicking her hand to him, signaling for him to stop.

The old man considered us carefully.

"You're saying that this Player," I said, "this *god who made the artifact*, he feared his own mortality?"

"I should think not," the expert said. "Alterra is just one of hundreds—if not thousands—of worlds that the Players rule over. That they might die in one of them would extinguish their touch upon it forever, true . . . But they have countless more lives on which to fall back. Their death in one? Surely nothing to them. Unless they have already been slain in all the others."

"What, then?" Val asked. "Why might a Player want such a device?"

"Perhaps they think it their birthright. Beyond this . . . I would not want to guess."

Val moved to complain, but the man was shrewd enough to see it coming.

"If you want more information, you might try Lillya, up north in Thistle Fort. She has access to the old orc tomes. Rumors say they hold information about the creation of this world that human eyes have never seen . . ."

We didn't have time to head north to Thistle Fort, of course; this would add weeks to our journey, and the rest of the party would have been waiting back southeast in only a few days. As a result, we parked this information—or at least I did; Val and Lore didn't seem so interested—and journeyed back to the tavern, where we discovered we were the first group to return.

So we did what any good team does while waiting for their other half: we drank. Val's seemingly endless supply of coin bought us pint after pint—after a while I was starting to suspect there was something magick going on in that pocket she kept pulling coins from—and I was a little woozy by the time someone suggested playing some cards.

It must have been either Val or me, because Lore quickly made his excuses, saying something along the lines of "I don't like 'em much" before disappearing up to our shared room and leaving me and Val to it.

Val taught me a game I'd not encountered before, called Toads. This game seemed to be a fairly basic trick-taking game with various drinking game rules layered on top, which pretty much made it the best game I'd ever played. Val got increasingly both furious and drunk as I kept winning, and both these factors seemed to improve her ability to bluff, until I was in much the same state as her.

"Where'd you learn cards, anyway?" Val asked.

I shrugged. "From my dad, before he passed. Always loved a game or two. Or, well, no. He loved *betting* on a game or two."

"Did he win much?"

"No."

"And does this explain . . ." Val started, drunk but not so drunk that she didn't know when to trail off.

"Why he died surrounded by people stabbing him?" I replied. "Yeah. Yeah, I suppose it does. And that's why I don't gamble."

Val raised an eyebrow. "You? Not gamble? I've seen you take plenty of risks when we're fighting."

"Mostly to save your arse."

The sorcerer blinked. "I've never been in a situation I wouldn't have been able to get out of. Don't credit yourself too much, portal boy."

I raised my eyebrows and exaggeratedly rolled my eyes to let Val know what I thought of *that* response, but I let the subject lie. "Point is, I don't tend to gamble money. I don't like the idea that my dad's passed it on to me. His habits, I mean. He might not have done, but . . ."

"You don't want to open that door to find out?"

"Exactly."

I must have passed out somewhere into the twelfth round, because at that point I felt a bucket of cold water wash over my head. I blinked myself back to reality accompanied by a pounding headache.

Tokas stood over me, empty bucket in hand, and over on the other side of the bar table, Arzak stood with another empty bucket over a gasping Val. "You . . . you . . ." she spluttered, eyes wide. "You drowned my cards!" She pulled her hand from the wet table and two playing cards came with it.

"I buy new pack," Arzak responded.

"You are still drinking on the job, then?" Tokas asked. "And I see you're influencing this one much the same."

"This one?" I repeated.

Val shrugged, then clutched at her head, hand glowing with the pale yellow-white light of healing magicks. "He's already a bad influence."

"Oi!" I said, nodding at her hand. "You got me drunk; you can sort out *my* hangover first."

Val pointed at Tokas, who sighed. "She can do it."

"You *both* can do it," I corrected her. "It's a bad one."

"That's not how healing magicks work," Tokas replied as she reluctantly placed her hands very gently on my head.

"You can only be healed from one source at a time," Val confirmed. "If I started healing you, then Tokas tried, you'd just get my magicks. And you want hers anyway. They're better."

Tokas smiled politely, grateful for the compliment.

Already the pounding headache was starting to fade, and before long I could think straight once more.

"Not too much," Arzak said. "Deserve some pain."

As Tokas pulled her hands away, I protested, "I thought you said you weren't gonna be the boss anymore!"

"I no boss Slayers around. They just know good advice when hear it."

I resisted the urge to stick my tongue out at Arzak; something told me she wouldn't take it in quite the same spirits as Val did.

Tokas shrugged. "The boss says you deserve a hangover."

"She's not the boss," Val mumbled, at the same moment that Arzak said, "I'm not boss."

The tiefling shrugged again. "Same end result."

"We should try hair of the—" Val said.

"No," the orc cut in. "No more drink. Serious business now." She glanced to Tokas. "Get Lore. We talk now."

"What's going on?" Val asked. "Did you find something out?"

"Yes," Arzak replied. "We find our strategy."

CHAPTER FORTY-SIX

Flaming Headaches

"Where's Cor?" Val asked, nursing a freshly brewed—and strong, if it was anything like mine—tea.

"Lore said he was just coming," Tokas said, having reappeared from the stairs to the room upstairs.

"What he doing?" Arzak asked.

"Putting on clothes. I walked in on him naked."

Arzak smirked—an expression I hadn't realized she was capable of. "A feast for eyes."

Lore trudged down the stairs a few moments later, the floorboards creaking with each step. I couldn't help but notice just how red his cheeks were.

"Where is Corminar?" Val repeated.

"Did something happen to him?" I added.

Arzak shook her head. "No. He get supplies. I explain soon." She turned to the still blushing barbarian. "Sit. Talking time."

Lore silently did as suggested by the orc who had *definitely* sworn off all thoughts of leadership.

Val held her hands out, palms up, as if to say "Go ahead," though I was more interested in getting some food in me first.

"I'm just gonna . . ." I started, pointing to the bar.

Arzak pulled a half loaf of bread out of her bag and plonked it down on the table in front of me. "Eat."

I shrugged, and then I, too, silently did as the orc suggested.

"We travel to Longreach," Arzak explained. "Big orc population there. I sent bird ahead to ask for records."

Tokas raised her eyebrows. "And records they delivered. Hundreds of them. Far too many for any reasonable person to—"

"Records?" Val asked. "What records? Arzak, this is why Lore and I usually do the anecdotes; you lot leave out important details."

"Records on fire."

"The records were *on fire?*" Lore repeated, eyes wide.

"On fire *magicks*," Arzak clarified. "On pyroknights, as this Player is. Not . . . not on fire."

"It might have made for better anecdotal value if they were," I put in, and Val nodded her agreement.

"Records were not on fire," Arzak repeated.

"Can we get back to the point now?" Tokas asked, her black eyes scouring the group and then landing on me. "I thought *you* of all people might want to know what we've found. Or do you have another resurrection artifact on you, for after Jake kills you?"

The smile drained from my face. "How do you know they're called Jake?"

"They're always called Jake."

For the second time on this journey, the Slayers all muttered knowingly about this subject.

"We get records. Records of fire magick. Of killing people with fire magicks. In this we look for answers to Player problem."

"We got ourselves *too* many records," Tokas added. "As it turns out, there's been no small number of pyroknights throughout history. There's something about the fire that attracts people to it, I suspect."

"It's pretty," Lore said, and Tokas nodded.

"So we ask members of my clan to help. We not tell them we looking to kill Player; even orcish not understand truth of Players. Together, there is eighteen of us—I count—and only two days before we due back here."

"I didn't care much for the other orcs," Tokas said, nodding to Arzak. "They weren't like you."

"I . . ." Arzak narrowed her eyes, assessing whether the tiefling intended this as a compliment to her, or an insult to her people. "Thank you?"

Tokas smiled; it was the former, then. I moved to give Val a knowing look, but she had her eyes fixed on Arzak.

"So we look," the orc said, getting back to the matter at hand. "All of us, we look and pull out all records where pyroknight killed. We look for similarity. For . . . what is word?"

"Themes?" Tokas suggested.

"For themes. And when pyroknight die, it turns out there often very similar cause: they run out of mana."

Val blinked. "That's it?"

"For this Player to have gotten as strong as he is, at the level that he's at, he must have invested heavily into *Sorcery*," Tokas said. "His *One-Handed*, while present, has been overlooked—as is often the case for pyroknights, due to the allure of new *Sorcery* abilities. This man relies heavily on his fire magicks, and not so much—as far as we can tell—on anything else."

"OK," Val said. "So we just drain his mana, and that's that? It's done?"

Before either Arzak or Tokas could respond, Val continued.

"Cos I can tell you now, it won't be that simple. If he's specced solely into *Sorcery*—and believe me, I understand that temptation perfectly well—he'll also have specced into Intelligence. His mana reserves will be through the roof. And at that level? I can't even comprehend how high that'd be."

"Yes, we'd need to avoid the attacks," Tokas replied.

"Err . . ." Lore put in. "You lot might be agile and stuff, but I've never really been much for moving fast. I'm a heavy build, guys. I take the damage rather than avoid it. But if this Player's attacks are as strong as we've been saying, then I won't . . . I ain't gonna survive this."

"You ask where Corminar is," Arzak said. "This is why he not here."

The orc trailed off, causing me, Val, and Lore to impatiently await the next part of that thought.

"You're going to need to explain that one a bit further, Arzak."

"He is a—"

"Ranger," Lore said knowingly.

Arzak shot him a funny look. "Yes, ranger. Also alchemist. Make potions. So he go buy ingredients for potion. Fire resistance."

"It should allow us to survive longer," Tokas added.

"Longer, yes," Val replied. "But long enough? Come on, Tokas; you're a magick user, you should know better. A lifetime of investing points into Intelligence would create quite the mana reserve. Do we really think a few potions are going to make a difference here?"

Lore raised his index finger. "Especially if I get hit every time he attacks."

"Especially if Lore gets hit every time the Player attacks!" Val added. I didn't know if she even realized she was repeating Lore.

"Surely you found something else?" I asked, suddenly growing worried that this really was all we had to play with. If it was, then I might as well have signed my own death warrant in that moment, for all the difference it made.

"Only the obvious," Tokas said. "Water. It puts pyroknights at a natural disadvantage if we can douse any flames quickly."

"How often?" Val asked.

"How often what?"

"How often did water help, in those records you found?"

Tokas's gaze flicked to Arzak, and the moment of silence that passed between them didn't do much to reassure me.

"In cases where not exhaust mana . . . Access to water help in around fifteen percent of cases."

"Fifteen per—" I repeated under my breath.

"We've done more with less," Tokas said. "Remember the last Player we took down? We had to act fast to stop them killing more innocents. We didn't have the time on our hands like we do with this one. So we moved in quick, with little prep work, and—"

"This one's stronger. You must know that this one is stronger." Val rose from her seat and paced the length of the room, hand on chin. "Styk, perhaps if you kept dousing us with water, that's some extra resistance."

"Portals?"

"Yeah, portals."

"We'd need to be by a river. Or the Iron Sea would be better." I paused, then added, "And I'd need as many mana potions as I can carry; this Player may have had a lifetime to build up his Intelligence, but I haven't. There are only so many portals I can summon."

"That's OK," Val said, "it's only one tactic."

"What are the others, then?"

"Well, I dunno! Maybe *you* could come up with something?"

I raised my eyebrows. "I was gonna suggest the water thing; you just beat me to it!"

"We shouldn't go up against him if we don't think we can win," Tokas said. "There's too much to lose."

"We're not there yet," Val said. "We're not getting defeatist yet."

"Could drench *him*," Arzak suggested.

"Do we think that'd work?"

The orc shrugged. "No records. Nobody tried this."

"More like nobody who tried it lived to tell the tale. You never heard of survivorship bias? Just how much is this all skewed by who came out of it alive? For every one person who beat a pyroknight by draining their mana, there could be a hundred who drained their mana and then *still* didn't win. You think of that?" Val realized she'd snapped a little too hard, then shook her head and flashed Arzak a smile of apology.

"No way of know." Arzak sighed. "This best chance. We get potion satchels each, carry as many potions as possible. Beyond this—"

The tavern door slammed open, revealing the last member of our party.

If the dramatic flourish with which Corminar opened the door wasn't clue enough—after all, he was prone to drama—the pallid tone of his face told me something was wrong.

"News," he said, forsaking full sentences for about the first time since I'd met him. It wasn't just the apparent anxiety that had him acting this way, I noticed; he was out of breath, too, like he'd run here. "The Player is in the Tundras. Not a day's travel from here. He's coming."

Corminar's eyes shifted to me.

"For you."

Gwyneth, Chief Librarian of the Ancient Estat Order

The other two librarians pulled Gwyneth from beneath the toppled bookcase and fallen books, yanking on one arm each—a method that Gwyneth didn't much approve of.

She brushed herself off, decades of accumulated dust having now coated her robe. "We must never speak of this," she told her two employees, without daring to meet either's eye. "If anyone were to discover what occurred here . . ."

"The order would be a laughingstock," Ruben replied.

Gwyneth nodded, though she couldn't help but notice that tone of wry amusement that was so typical of Ruben. Could she trust him not to tell that other man down at the local tavern? If news reached as far as the town, there would be no hope of controlling it.

"Clean it," Gwyneth snapped, pointing at the falling books. She strolled with purpose toward the basement steps.

"Oh? And what will you be doing?" Ruben asked, as though it was *her* fault that these three adventurers had destroyed the interior of the library. In Gwyneth's eyes, it was just as much Ruben's doing—as well as those terribly slow shadow magicks he *insisted* upon using.

"Order business," Gwyneth replied, and hurried down into the thankfully untouched basement. Here was where the truly powerful books were kept, where Ruben had borrowed his spell book from, and wherein a very specific book was stored for safekeeping. Gwyneth scoured the *Worldbending* shelves, finding the book in question covered in a thick layer of dust that spoke to the years since its last usage. This particular book contained spells that didn't bend the landscape, but people. Rather, it bent *memory*.

If Gwyneth was to survive this humiliating incident with no word getting back to the order, it was her employees' memories that she would need to fiddle with. This wasn't the first time—that rather embarrassing incident last century involving a discarded banana peel had been the first—and Gwyneth was sure it wouldn't be the last.

She skimmed to the page in question, marked by a folded corner. This was a habit she allowed herself only for the most vital of information; normally she would not dare mar a book in this way. She reached within herself, grasping her not inconsiderable mana reserves, and focused her attention on the two fellow librarians upstairs. As she started whispering the spell, their forms glowed within Gwyneth's vision, and as she concentrated on the events of the last few hours, she saw these glowing forms reenact those humiliating moments.

In an instant, the memories were gone. The fellow librarians would not be able to speak of Gwyneth's failings, for they would have no idea that which had occurred here.

Gwyneth drew in a deep breath, preparing herself for a stream of questions that would surely be forthcoming when she appeared once more.

But when she returned upstairs, she found that she had more visitors, and her two colleagues were staring blankly at them.

"I'm sorry," she said to the rather surly-looking human and orc. "We've had enough visitors for one . . ."

Gwyneth trailed off when she noticed the body the human had dropped in front of him—that of the old man on the other side of the village. The one who had considered himself an expert in . . . At that moment, Gwyneth couldn't quite remember.

"I asked you where he went," the man repeated, turning his hand upside down and summoning a ball of fire within it.

"I'm sorry, sir, I don't know who you—"

Gwyneth's colleague didn't have a chance to finish that sentence. The apparent sorcerer pointed his fireball-wielding hand toward her, and within a moment, Gwyneth only had *one* colleague.

"You next," the human sorcerer said, turning his attention to Ruben. "Where is he?"

"Where is who?" Ruben asked, his eyes on his colleague's fallen, charred body. "I don't know any 'Styk.'"

"Really?" the sorcerer replied. "I thought watching your friend die would have done the trick. We know he came here; the old guy told us. So start talking, or . . ."

Ruben began to speak the words from his spell book, but he was not quick enough; at the click of the sorcerer's fingers, the book went up in flames. He had no shadow magicks left at his disposal.

"Where is he?"

"Where is *who*?" Ruben repeated. Poor man, it wasn't his fault.

The man very slowly drew his hand, fingers splayed, and pointed it in Ruben's direction. "Last chance."

"I don't know who—"

A stream of fire erupted from the man's hand and enveloped Ruben. He only screamed for a second.

Gwyneth found she couldn't move, but it wasn't the result of any kind of magicks. It was fear.

The man fixed his eyes upon her. "I'll only ask this—"

"They didn't remember!" Gwyneth suddenly blurted. "I erased their memories!"

"Ah, so *you* still remember, at least?"

"I . . . I . . . I . . ."

"Spit out," the orc growled.

Gwyneth gulped; there was a question she had to ask first. "What assurances do I have that you will leave me alive if I tell you?"

The sorcerer responded by waving his hand toward the bookcases and releasing fire upon them. Their contents—the protection of which was Gwyneth's solemn duty and life's work—began to burn. "You don't have any. But do you think buying time is helping your case?"

"West!" Gwyneth squealed. "I saw them running west! I know no more than that, I swear. I swear!"

The human looked to his orc accomplice and nodded. Just as they were turning to leave, Gwyneth risked another question. She had to, for the sake of the books.

"Please, will you . . . will you extinguish the fire?" she asked.

The human looked at Gwyneth, tilting his head as though considering her. There was a moment, while the fire crackled and spread, that the librarian thought he might do as she asked.

"No," the sorcerer said, and turned for the door, slamming it shut behind him.

Gwyneth couldn't afford to waste any time. She rushed for the exit the moment it swung shut. If she didn't, she would fall victim to the smoke before much longer.

As she reached it, it too erupted in flames.

CHAPTER FORTY-SEVEN

Prey

"The Player is in the Tundras," the elf said. "Not a day's travel from here. He's coming. For you."

I gulped; I allowed myself that, just this once.

"How do you know this?" Tokas asked him, her eyes about as wide as mine surely were.

"There was a merchant, in the store. News of Players travels quickly in these parts. They spoke of a pyroknight's attempt to save librarians from a horrific fire."

"Librarians?" I repeated, meeting Val's gaze.

"Horrific fire?" Lore repeated. "You don't think . . . You don't think *he* started that?"

"Yes, Lore," Val said, then immediately shook her head, not bothering to follow that up with some supposedly good-natured insult. "We're not ready. Do you have the potions?"

"I have as many relevant ingredients as were on offer in this backwater town," Corminar replied. "I will craft as we walk."

"It enough?" Arzak asked.

"Walk where?" Lore asked. Lore won simply because he was louder.

"The sea," Corminar answered, his gaze shifting to Arzak. "You told them about the water, yes?"

"We figured that bit out all by ourselves."

"It enough?" Arzak repeated.

Corminar's lack of answer was deafening.

"Gods . . ."

"Strip your armor," Corminar suggested.

"Cor, this is not the time to be hitting on us," Val replied, and then after a moment added, ". . . again."

"We will move faster without armor. To be stripped to our loincloths would give us greater agility, and a far greater chance of avoiding his attacks."

"And a far greater chance of dying if he *does* hit us."

"Our options are speed or defense," the elf replied. "Certainly not both."

"I choose armor," Lore answered instantly, tightening the straps on his own.

"There time yet to decide," Arzak said. "We go now. We talk. We think. We plan."

I began to rush up to my room to gather my things before immediately remembering that I, you know, didn't *have* any things. In fact, the only "things" I had were the five Slayers trying to save me—and they were all here risking their lives to kill this Player before he killed me.

Arzak stood with her hands on her hips, shaking her head from side to side as she watched Lore, Corminar, and Val—no surprise on that last one—bickering about the correct strategy, while Tokas stared at the top of the table, head in her hands.

Maybe this wasn't the team I would have *chosen* to defend me, but it was all I had, and I would have been lying if I said in that moment I wasn't grateful to each and every one of them.

I wasn't going to tell them that, though. "Alright, chop chop!" I said, clapping my hands loudly to get their attention. "Let's go, people. Unless you wanna face down a pyroknight on dry land?"

"No," Arzak backed me up. "We not want this."

"Well, then . . ." I gestured for the door.

The Slayers were oddly quiet as we traveled, the thought of the fight ahead likely weighing on their shoulders as much as mine. We all knew that our fleeing to the coast of the Iron Sea was only delaying the inevitable; we would clash with the pyroknight before long.

I took some solace in that this team had fought Players before, and presumably—I hadn't heard of any dead friends—all survived to tell the tale. But, I supposed, it didn't do any harm to be quiet, to prepare ourselves for the fight ahead. Surely that was what all my new acquaintances were doing.

"How far are we from the coast?" I asked, breaking the heavy silence. "Two days? Three?"

"Two, assuming we continue at this pace."

"And . . . will he catch us? In that time?"

Corminar swallowed his initial response. "Perhaps. Will he move at a faster pace than us? Yes. But perhaps those we pass will not be as forthcoming or as accurate in their directions. We can only hope."

I nodded; this wasn't the answer I wanted to hear, but it was, at least, an honest one. "I'm not ready," I whispered. "Thought I'd have more time. Thought I'd have more abilities."

Corminar considered me carefully, having been the only one with hearing good enough to hear my despair. "It is of no consequence," he replied, speaking lightly so that only I would hear. "This is what we do. This is what the team is for."

"Then why are you so nervous?"

"Going into battle against a Player is no everyday occurrence. It is better that we are cautious than cavalier."

The logic was sound, but did little to soften the upset in my stomach.

We traveled onward, heading south toward the relatively calm Iron Sea, where we could stand our ground with the greatest advantage. We passed through towns and villages that were situated on the main traveler's road, stopping only for food, and wasting not a moment otherwise. In the back of my mind—and surely the rest of the team's—we felt the pressure of the Player, catching us up with every second that passed.

Corminar handed out a small red vial every few minutes, these being the fire resistance vials that would give us a small extra advantage against the man who hunted us. As he handed me my first, I *identified* it.

Greater Potion of Fire Resistance
Effect: +50 percent resistance to fire sorcery

Fifty percent.

It didn't feel like enough, not with the battle being so close now. This would halve the amount of damage that the Player could deal to us, but half of a huge amount was still . . . a pretty huge amount. With no specialist armor on, and such a low investment into my Vitality skill, even one solid hit could kill me. This fact hadn't escaped me, though I was doing my very best not to think about it.

We passed through another village, not stopping for food, and for the second time Lore didn't even *suggest* stopping for food. Merchants tried to flag us down, offering fresh blades and—according to my *Identification*—pretty terrible potions, apparently correctly assessing that we were a gang of adventurers heading for battle. We ignored them all, only Arzak of the group responding to them in any kind. "No. We no need."

When the village was some way behind us, Tokas piped up with, "They might have had better fire resistance potions. We should have checked."

"They did not," Corminar replied.

"How do you know?"

"I know."

There wasn't the mood among us to continue the verbal spat, and so the elf and the tiefling let the matter drop.

And then screams erupted in the village behind us.

All six of us halted instantly, slowly turning to the source of the uproar.

"Two days, you said," I told Corminar. "We were supposed to be at the sea!"

"I *hoped* it would be two days. I assured you of nothing," the elf corrected me.

"It could not be him?" Lore suggested, his tone hopeful.

In the distance, flames engulfed one of the buildings.

"OK, it's him," Lore continued, no longer hopeful.

"What are the options?" I asked.

"Same as they always are: run, or fight."

Tokas roared, clutching at her head, the building stress apparently becoming too much for her. She grabbed Lore by the shoulders—no small feat considering their comparative size. "Please, everyone . . . Run! Run like your lives depend on it, because they bloody well *do*!"

"We don't—" Corminar started, but Tokas was far from finished.

"These Players, these Players that come into our world nowadays, they're not like they once were. They have no world to return to—the Ascended Realm is dead. They'll do anything to survive these days. Anything! They're desperate. They'll kill you. Please, just . . . just run!"

"How you know all this?" Arzak asked.

"Yeah, and why in the hells did you not say anything sooner?" Val added.

"Please," Tokas said, tears beginning to form in her eyes. "Please, run! This one, he won't be like the ones we've faced down before. He . . . he . . ."

"And what about *him*?" Val asked, pointing to me. It was the very question I had on the tip of my tongue. "This Player isn't going to—"

"He's already dead," Tokas said.

I pulled a face. "Well, thank you for the vote of—"

"But the rest of you, you still might live. He doesn't know who you are. He won't track you down. He won't—"

"No," Val interrupted. "No, I won't abandon him."

To my own surprise, I smiled.

"Me neither," Lore added.

Arzak stepped up to Tokas, grabbing her gently by the arm. "We Slayers. We not run."

"Nor do we give up the opportunity for such a challenge," Corminar said, pulling his bow from his shoulder.

The screaming grew closer, villagers from the nearby town running for their lives. The flames grew higher, great plumes of smoke now billowing into the heavens.

"You go if want," Arzak said to Tokas. There was no malice in her tone, and only kindness in her eyes. "We no judge you."

But Tokas shook her head, wiping away the tears from her cheeks. "No," she said in a croaky voice. "No, it's best for me if . . . It's best for . . . for everyone if I help you."

Arzak nodded. "Then we fight Player once more. Get ready."

CHAPTER FORTY-EIGHT

Bringing the Fire

I pulled the cork free from the vial Corminar had handed me, and the resulting pop was echoed by the five other pops of the Slayers doing the same. I gulped the liquid down without letting it touch the sides of my mouth—I knew from experience that potions rarely tasted good—and forced myself to ignore the heat that erupted in my throat.

> **Active Effect: +50 percent Resistance to Fire Sorcery**
> Minutes remaining: 59 / 60

When I finished, I tossed the vial aside—right then was not the time to worry about littering—and looked to the rest of the team, signaling that I was ready with a nod.

"Here?" Tokas asked, gesturing to the dirt road. "Is this really the best we can do?"

The twist of Val's hand—with no magical glow due to her obscurem—told me she was doing some sort of magick.

"Have better suggestion?" Arzak asked. "If no sea, then—"

"Northwest," Val suddenly interrupted.

"What?"

"Northwest," the sorcerer said again, nodding to the edge of the tree line at the side of the road. "There's a pond there."

"How could you possibly . . ." I started, but the rustling of bushes just where Val had been nodding went some way to answering that question. If I wasn't yet going completely insane, I was sure I had seen a hare staring at us.

"Trust me," Val said. "It's not the Iron Sea, sure, but . . . maybe it'll be enough."

We ran into the cover of the tree line, taking little care to hide our tracks—there wasn't time, not when the Player was this close.

"This way!" Val shouted, pointing to a clearing ahead, the light of the afternoon sun illuminating our destination.

We burst out into the open, Lore stumbling at the edge of the small, green pond—one healthy and jam-packed with local wildlife. Val hadn't been lying when she described it as a "pond"; there really wasn't a huge amount of water to play with here. I kept my doubts to myself.

"Positions," Arzak said, and her and Lore turned back to face the way we had come, each of them planting their feet firmly into the dry mud.

Val and Tokas took positions on opposite sides of the pond, a good few yards behind the two brawniest members of the team.

This left Corminar, who took my arm and led me—thankfully—to the far side of the pond. "Prepare your portals," he said, pulling his bow from his shoulder. He pulled a vial from his jacket that contained a vivid green liquid and dipped all his arrows into it one by one. The elf flashed me a knowing look.

My head snapped forward as Arzak and Lore adjusted their grip on their swords, and soon I too could hear the rustling rapidly approaching through the trees. I held my hands up in front of me, one pointing toward the pond, the other toward the edge of the clearing. Corminar nocked an arrow in his bow.

Two figures stepped out from amongst the trees. One human. One orc.

The Player and Lev stopped at the edge of the clearing when they saw us, and their two pairs of eyes scanned across each one of us. Their gaze lingered on Tokas for a moment before settling, finally, on me.

"How?" the Player asked, matching my gaze. "How did you use it? How did you *survive*?"

I didn't answer, my every ounce of concentration fixed on the rest of my team, preparing myself to move as soon as they did.

"No, you know what? Never mind. I don't care." The pyroknight held out his hand. "Just give it back."

This time, I answered. "It's spent. You know that. It's useless."

A wide smile crossed the Player's face. "Ah! Yes. I thought so, too. But then *you*, of all people, led me to an expert in Birrow. An old man who gave me some answers. Some answers that I only now realize that he didn't give to you. I suppose that's the difference between having a friendly conversation and . . . well, torture."

Lev nodded solemnly.

I gulped, my eyes flicking to Val, to Arzak, to Lore, willing them to move. I wasn't sure how much more of this I could take; the pressure was getting too much. "What?" I finally asked. "What did he tell you?"

The pyroknight shook his head. "No . . . no, you can get your own information. Well, you *could* if you were walking away from here. In fact . . ." The Player looked at each of the Slayers in turn. "All the rest of you can still walk away from this, if you so choose. Any one of you." The man's eyes lingered on Tokas once again, who admittedly looked closest to accepting this offer, being that her arms were shaking.

Nobody spoke, and six pairs of eyes stared down two.

"No?" the Player prompted us. "Are you—"

Lore snapped first.

The barbarian charged forward, swinging his Bane Sword overhead as he roared.

The pyroknight reacted near instantly, summoning a wall of fire in front of himself, and with the flick of a wrist, sent it billowing toward Lore.

I hissed through my teeth with fear just as Lore jumped to one side, narrowly avoiding the flames. *Ah, not so much*, I quickly corrected myself, seeing the skin of his left arm singe.

I hopped to it, sticking to the plan and concentrating on the pond—and trying to ignore the fact that the wall of fire had caught one of the nearby trees. Swinging my other hand toward the Player, I opened a portal, emptying the bulk of the pond's contents—both water and wildlife—onto the enemy, drenching him.

The pyroknight roared with frustration, immediately forgetting about Lore and setting his eyes upon me.

"Uh oh," I said. The drenching had been part of the plan, but drawing his attention . . . hadn't.

Meanwhile, Arzak had been charging forward at the left-hand side of the pond—or, damp hole, as it was now—and she swung her dual blades forth in a complex attack. Lev ran between her and the Player, blocking the two swords with a new axe of his own, then used his free hand to grab Arzak by the throat.

Corminar released arrow after arrow after arrow, each of them finding their target—the Player's chest. But the pyroknight, for his part, simply didn't seem to care; it was just like my ricocheting knives at Plainside all over again. That almost seemed like a lifetime ago by this point.

"I thought they were poisoned!" I shouted, while Val ran forward to summon roots around Lev's limbs, preventing him from strangling Arzak, but not getting enough purchase to fully restrain him.

"They most certainly are!" the elf ranger replied.

Oh. That's really not good, then.

Tokas sent healing magicks Lore's way, accompanied by a brilliant yellow-white light, as her obscurem was apparently set up to hide her illusion magicks only. The burnt skin of Lore's left arm healed back to its former self within an instant—but there was a limit to how much Tokas could heal, both in terms of time and mana reserves.

Healed, Lore pressed forth once more, swinging his sword in another long arc—an arc long enough that it gave the Player a moment to react. Again, the pyroknight sent fire magicks the way of our barbarian, and again he narrowly *almost* avoided getting hit. This time, though, the layer of water I'd poured over the enemy dampened the spells. The pyroknight was still using as much mana, but his attacks were doing less damage.

Tokas had to heal Lore once more, but this wasn't the end of the world. We needed the Player to use up all his mana after all, and if Lore could learn to start doing that *without* getting burned in the process, we might stand a chance. Already the emptied pond was starting to help.

Val managed to get some purchase with one of her summoned roots, what with Lev being distracted by Arzak's incessant attacks. She yanked his axe arm backward with these tendrils, giving Arzak an opening. She pressed the attack with her blades, cutting through the other orc's thick armor and drawing the tiniest amount of blood. But it wasn't long until Val's roots snapped, and the enemy orc had his guard up once more.

The Player fought his way past Lore, using his weakened fire magicks to repel my brawny friend. The pyroknight's eyes never left mine, and I reached for the Ranger's Blade—a weapon that wouldn't kill the Player unless the rest of the team had done a *lot* of damage to him already.

"Drop him!" Val shouted. "Styk, drop him!"

"On it!"

I reached one hand to the heavens, opening a portal as high as I could manage, and then, still staring the Player down, dropped him.

He fell instantly, and in the split second I thought I'd bested him, I noticed one hand gripping the side of the portal.

No. Of *course* it wouldn't be that simple.

CHAPTER FORTY-NINE

Bad Timing

The Player's other hand snapped to the edge of the portal.

Looking up in the air above me, I could see the pyroknight hanging there, hundreds of yards above the ground. But he wasn't going to fall, at least . . . not without some encouragement.

"Lore!" I shouted. "Push him through!"

As Lore charged to the lower end of the portal, I closed it in order to save the last little-over-a-half of my mana reserves. From our testing with the sheep, I knew this would do no good beyond that; portals were only good for slicing through nonliving matter.

The Player heaved himself upward before Lore arrived, getting a good look at the barbarian charging toward him. This only seemed to motivate the pyroknight further, and he gritted his teeth, roaring as he pulled himself back through the closing portal onto solid ground. The Player flung one hand through the air to point it at Lore, and the resulting fireball caught Lore squarely in his chest, sending him soaring across the clearing.

It was a good job that the Player was still wet from the pond, otherwise that alone might have done more damage than Tokas could have healed. The tiefling hurried to Lore's side, healing him, but this left me and Corminar alone to deal with the Player.

The flaming tree crackled as the Player hopped back onto his feet and made for me once more.

"Corminar?" I prompted my elven accomplice, and he released another arrow, this one burying itself in the side of the Player's neck.

The pyroknight didn't slow for a second, reaching across to snap the arrow at the head without even grimacing. It was a shame; if he'd tried to pull the arrow out entirely, the resulting blood loss might have helped turn the tide of this fight.

Lore rolled across the ground, patting at his chest to extinguish the flames, his sword buried at an awkward angle in the mud at his side.

"Cor!" Val shouted across the pond, her and Arzak having drawn Lev away from the rest of the fight, his rear vulnerable to us.

The ranger, betraying little of the surely huge amount of fear he possessed, flashed his eyes from the Player to Lev, loosing a quick shot into the enemy orc's exposed back.

"Thanks!" Val cried back, and their tussle continued.

The Player was closing on me quickly, and I found myself stumbling backward, wracking my brain desperately for the next step. I could open a portal above him, leap on top of him, *stab* him. But that would give me only one chance to kill him—otherwise fire magicks would surely be heading my way pretty swiftly.

Or I could try the portal-drop strategy again, though now that I'd lost the element of surprise, it was sure to go even worse than the last time, and I'd waste precious mana.

The first branch from the blazing trees cracked and dropped to the ground just where Lore had been moments earlier.

My other option was to try a *Closed Reach*. My blade could get pretty deep within someone's flesh, if I could just get close enough without being burned to a crisp.

Whatever I was going to do, I was going to need to do it fast, because I could see the whites in the Player's eyes.

The pyroknight pushed both hands forward, fingers splayed, pointing right at me. Instinctively I dove to the right as a ball of fire rocketed overhead, and I decided it was *definitely* time to activate my new ability: *Ash Husk*.

My skin rippled, the change starting at my fingertips and moving like a wave up my arms. The flesh turned from light brown—and surprisingly soft—to a hardened charcoal-like texture, rough and coarse and, more importantly, 50 percent resistant to fire attacks. The only downside was that it had drained my mana reserves a great deal more than I'd expected. If I'd not been panicking as we'd fled the tavern, I might have tested it sooner, but then again, we wouldn't have had time to rest—and our bars replenish anyway.

Corminar was about to loose another arrow when he caught sight of me, in my new demon-like form, and the shock of it was enough to distract him. The released arrow flew over the enemy's shoulder.

"Concentrate!" Tokas shouted at him—an instruction that had the Player turning to the tiefling, eyebrow raised.

It was enough of a distraction for me to run for the cover of a large elm tree at the edge of the clearing. I didn't look back at the Player, but I knew he'd seen me, because a fireball hit the other side of the tree just as I reached it. Its flames lapped around the trunk and forced me to crouch, cowering, to the floor.

"He's coming, Styk!" Lore shouted as he ran into the fight once more.

I heard a battle cry from Lore, followed by the crackling of another fireball, followed ultimately by Lore flying across the clearing and hitting a tree not so far from mine with a grunt. His tree, however, was already aflame.

"Lore, watch out!" I shouted to the dazed barbarian as one of the branches over his head cracked, its breaking caused by the bulky man colliding with the trunk.

He wasn't going to move fast enough—that much was clear—so I used yet more of my mana to open a portal between the branch and Lore, catching it as it fell and launching it into where the pond had been. The flaming branch landed with a hiss. It was a wasted opportunity; if I'd had another half second to think about it, I would have launched it at the Player. But I still had mana left, for now—there was time yet.

I stepped out from behind the tree. "Alright, come get me, you . . . you . . ." An apt insult escaped me, so I settled on "Come get me, *you!*"

The pyroknight wasted no time, storming toward me with a hand raised.

The moment I saw the glow of magicks forming, I opened a portal between us—one which captured the fireball and sent it flying back to its caster. Again there was a hissing sound, and the Player's clothes caught on fire. Judging by the resulting roar, this attack *had* dealt some decent damage to the man. I guess that's because it had been created by someone of his level—*him.*

Spitting blood, the Player tried another fireball. This one I caught with a portal but he shifted out of its path once it came out the other side. The pyroknight roared again, and this time pushed the butts of his hands together to summon a fire wall.

My portals weren't enough to catch the wall of fire in its entirety—which was presumably why he'd switched up the spells—and instead simply created a circle in its center. The flames caught the Player, but the edges of the fire wall also caught me. I'd dived to one side to avoid it, but I'd been too slow, and the flames had tickled at my arm.

The *Ash Husk,* as well as the dampening effect from the pond, limited the amount of damage I took, but even then . . . I was horrified to see my health bar decrease by almost half. I could feel it, too—that attack *hurt,* and my right hand wouldn't be the same without some very skilled healing.

As I heard the hiss of fire on damp clothes once more, my stomach lurched. That hissing meant that the fireballs were evaporating the layer of pond that I'd portaled onto our enemy. And that evaporation meant . . .

The Player stopped, eyes wide, looking down at himself as he realized the exact same thing.

"Lore!" I cried to the barbarian. "Stop him from—"

The pyroknight flung a hand to each side, his eyes on me, his mouth warped into a snarl. An instant later, flames erupted on the earth around him, creating a shield of fire that even had Lore reconsidering his attack.

I could see the steam as the flames evaporated the pond water from his skin, and the despicable man's snarl grew into a somehow even more unsettling grin.

Our advantage was gone.

"Now!" I shouted. "We have to act now!"

I didn't wait for a response from Corminar, or Lore, or Tokas, and I charged toward the pyroknight. As I ran, time seemed to slow down, and the only thing that ran through my mind was:

And what in the hells *are you thinking?*

But Lore, Corminar, and even Val were charging toward the Player, Arzak apparently currently able to deal with Lev by herself. Val reached forward, summoning a gust of wind that blew a gap in an arc of the flaming circle. Lore swung his Bane Sword high, and for what it's worth, I was preparing to *close my reach.*

The Player swept his still outstretched arms forward, and the flames suddenly shot toward each of us. I had a chance of not getting hit, and summoned a portal in front of me that returned me to the edge of the clearing.

Lore and Val, however, were burned. Horrifically.

Tokas ran to heal them, only able to do so one at a time, which left Val rolling across the dirt, screaming.

At the sight ahead of me, and the sound of screaming, images of Plainside ran through my mind once more. I found myself scrambling backward across the dry dirt, not a thought for the flaming trees encompassing us, just desperate—so, so, desperate—to flee.

I scrambled into a pair of feet.

Slowly, I craned my neck to see how this could be. A new figure stood next to me at the edge of the clearing, bow in hand, eyes wide, apparently not quite knowing who to fight.

Lambkin. He'd found us once more.

"Stop!" the once-captain roared.

Nothing changed, of course.

"Stop, in the order of the Baron of Umlok. Stop your fighting at once!"

The Player, mildly irritated by this interruption, flung his hand over his shoulder, throwing a fireball in Lambkin's general direction. It caught the ranger in the shoulder, sending the ex-captain spinning to the ground at my feet.

He roared with pain, but roaring through it, he brought himself back up to his feet and raised his bow once more. Lambkin pointed the arrow at the pyroknight, but instead of shooting, his eyes widened again.

He'd *identified* the pyroknight. He knew they were a Player.

It was a small thing, but in this desperate moment, I'd take any good news I could. In this case? Lambkin now knew. He knew I was right.

CHAPTER FIFTY

Aflame

"What in all the hells of the underworlds below is—" Lambkin started, and as the pyroknight started flinging another fireball in the man's direction, I reached up and yanked him to the ground.

It is funny how things go. I was never *massively* keen on killing another person, but after all the stuff that Lambkin had put us through over the past few weeks, if someone *had* to die, then . . . Well, suffice to say, it was better off being him than me. But now, things had changed in an instant. Lambkin now saw the truth for himself—that a Player really was behind the devastation of Plainside—and that meant one very specific thing in my eyes: he could be an ally.

"It's him!" I shouted as I pulled Lambkin for the cover of the trees. "You see now, right? You see? He's the one who did that at Plainside. Him!"

Lambkin, dazed, took a moment to nod his acknowledgement.

"We need to kill him, alright?" I shouted over the crash of another fireball on the other side of the tree we were cowering behind.

"Kill a . . . Player?" Lambkin repeated.

"Kill a *monster*," I replied.

This sobered Lambkin some, and after a gulp, some color returned to his otherwise pallid face. He drew his bow once more, stepped out into the space between the trees, and was immediately caught in the chest by a flaming ball. It knocked him back across the woodlands, landing with a crash.

I poked my head around the tree, risking a fireball to the face, to get the lay of the land. Tokas pulled a screaming Val—gods, that sound hurt me—up to her feet, one hand emitting glowing yellow-white light as it closed up her burns. Lore stood once more—could nothing stop this man?—despite the clearly horrific wounds he'd suffered in the same strike that had set Val screaming.

While the pyroknight was distracted by the charging Lore, Lambkin pushed himself up to his feet. The ex-captain had clearly invested in Vitality considering he was able to do so after a direct hit from fire magicks—and without a fire resistance potion in him at that. He joined Corminar in firing a torrent of arrows at the target, most of them hitting flesh, but still doing little more than irritating the man. Surely the damage dealt would add up at *some* point, though.

The Player instinctively moved to attack me once more—I was his target after all—before hesitating. He turned on the spot, now facing toward where Tokas was rapidly healing the injured Val.

I saw immediately what he was thinking.

This battle had become a stalemate; the ever-impressive Arzak was a match for Lev, and the rest of us seemed like *almost* a match for the Player. At least, it was close enough for the pyroknight to be uncomfortable about it. If the battle was to turn in the enemies' favor, they'd need to start eliminating us. And who better to start with than the woman screaming in pain?

"Lore!" I screamed.

The barbarian's eyes snapped to me for just a second.

"He's going for Val! He's starting to pick us off!"

Lore's eyes widened further, and with a possibly unintentional roar, he rushed the Player once more. Doing the same thing over and over and expecting a different result was madness, so it was said. But Lore's abilities were geared toward only one type of attack: up close and personal.

The pyroknight put up a wall of fire in Lore's direction as the barbarian grew nearer, and I flung my hand forward to open up a portal between them for just a second. I closed it around the fire wall, ridding it from Lore's path and giving the barbarian an opening.

This was the first time I saw the Player panic, doing a double take at the charging Lore but not reacting fast enough to block the man's sword. Lore swept his Bane Sword in a wide arc, powerful enough to cleave through the Player's leather armor and bury itself in his side.

The pyroknight roared.

All around the clearing, the rapidly growing flames froze for a moment, and then darted toward each of their commander's enemies. A tendril flicked at Val, causing the screaming to evolve into crying. One smacked Lore's side, causing him to lose his grip on his family's sword. More still hit the two archers, and though I couldn't see them through the raging flames, I could tell it had done them decent damage because the torrent of arrows stopped.

As for me, I saw the tendril of flame coming, and I resorted to my most robust ability, opening a portal in front of me just in time for the flames to move through it. Their other end licked at the Player's face, but didn't deal any decent damage to him, as far as I could see. I couldn't have everything.

All this *had* to have drained the Player's mana a good amount; it was the first time I'd seen him use this ability, and there was only one decent reason not to use an ability as powerful as this—it cost too much mana. We were getting there. We were draining him.

Still the Slayers pushed on, Lore gritting his teeth through the pain and charging for his disarmed sword. The arrows resumed their arcs through the air, though more and more missed their target as the two archers struggled with their injuries.

"We're not gonna . . ." Val gasped through the screams. "We're not gonna make it!"

Lore dove at the sword just as the Player shot a fireball in the discarded weapon's direction, sending the Bane Sword skittering across the hot earth.

Tokas, still healing Val, eyed the sword, which had come to a halt not seven feet away from where she was crouched.

"Styk!" Corminar cried out, his eyes on the Player advancing on our screaming friend. "A portal. In front of his face."

The pyroknight couldn't hear the elf's instructions over the sound of the crackling fire—now near enough encompassing the clearing—because he didn't react. This gave me sufficient time to do as Corminar instructed, opening a portal just in front of him . . .

The elf raised his bow, aiming for the portal.

. . . And another portal right in front of the advancing Player's face.

Corminar shot.

The arrow flashed through the air, slipping through the portal that was closing even as it passed through it, and hit the Player's face.

No, I realized when the Player roared once more. Not his face. His *eye*.

This was enough to distract the roaring Player from Val, making him turn to the archer. He flung his arm up and sent flames flying toward Corminar before he could do much to move out of the way. The ranger took flames to one side and rolled on the hot earth to extinguish them.

Through the flames, I stared at the pyroknight as he clutched the area around his eye, as though massaging it. Despite the fact that it had been hit by an arrow, it still seemed to be in fairly good condition, little more than bruised. The Player's Vitality was through the roof if he could make it through a hit to such a vulnerable place with this level of damage.

But he *was* taking damage, I noticed.

Whereas before he'd been ignoring the arrows that had hit him—he looked almost like a porcupine at this point—now our attacks were truly hurting him.

The wound in his side, too, had enraged and slowed him, though it was looking not as bad—or good, from my perspective—as I had initially thought.

Behind the pyroknight, Tokas stood from the no-longer-screaming Val, her eyes still on Lore's fallen Bane Sword.

I made myself not look—the Player had his eyes on me, and I didn't want to give him any signal of what was coming.

Tokas stepped toward the sword, not moving quite as fast as I would have liked, her hands shaking.

As the Player began to cast his eyes over his shoulder, Lore charged forth once more, this time unarmed. It was enough, at least, to stop the pyroknight in his turn, distracted by thoughts of sending fireballs Lore's way—which he did, blasting Lore to the ground.

Tokas pulled the Bane Sword from the dirt, dragging it with an unease that suggested she didn't have the skill or experience to use it properly, and she grimaced as she reached the Player's rear.

It wasn't enough, I realized. It wasn't enough, but I had an ability that might just turn the tide.

I used almost the last of my dwindling mana reserves to fall through a portal on the ground, reappearing just above where Tokas was holding the blade. As I fell toward the hilt, I prepared myself to activate *Closed Reach*; neither I nor Tokas had the *One-Handed* ability, so our damage dealt would be minimal. That was unless the tip of the blade was suddenly folded into the enemy's flesh.

The world seemed to slow as I fell that last two feet.

The Player turned to look where I'd gotten to. Tokas's eyes widened. The pyroknight growled, preparing to strike. I reached forward for the sword in Tokas's hands and . . .

She dropped it.

"No!" I screamed.

Tokas stumbled backward, suddenly flinging her hands out at her sides. "Lore," she said. "Carry me."

The moment those words left her mouth, obscurem-hidden illusion magicks shot from her hands, forming shapes all throughout the clearing before Tokas fell, drained, to the ground. They were familiar shapes, I realized. *Our* shapes. A hundred or more Slayers appeared amongst the flames, no substance to any but the real ones, but enough of a distraction to . . .

"Retreat!" Lore shouted, picking up Tokas from the ground and cradling her in his arms. "Retreat!"

In the confusion that followed, the six of us withdrew from a battle we seemed now destined to lose, leaving the Player to roar furiously as he threw fire at the illusions of us.

Trees, aflame, fell behind us as we ran.

CHAPTER FIFTY-ONE

Disillusions

The cave was silent.

Arzak, Val, Lore, Tokas, and I had made it out together, fleeing through the burning forest until we outran the Player and his flames, the illusions of us keeping our enemy occupied.

All of us were hurt to some degree, from Tokas and I who'd escaped most hits, to Arzak who had significant gashes and other sword wounds in her flesh, to Val and Lore, who had received the worst of the fire damage. It was these last two that Tokas silently tended to, though she couldn't heal them entirely; she'd had only two mana potions on her person, and Corminar had disappeared with the rest of them.

"Do you think he's alive?" I asked, shattering the silence.

"He alive," Arzak replied instantly. From her snappy tone, there was no room for argument in this matter.

Movement outside the cave, in the depths of the forest, made me and Val flinch. A moment later we saw its source—a deer. A simple, plain old deer.

"He'll find us," Val said, her voice breathy as she tried to talk through the pain. "He's a good tracker. The best of us."

"Better than the Player?" I asked.

"Don't do this now," Tokas said, concentrating on her healing, presumably making it as efficient as possible.

"Well of course *you* would say that," I replied. "You don't wanna talk about it? I bet."

"What this mean?" Arzak asked.

"She had the opening! *We* had the opening! We could have finished this!" After a moment, I realized that not only was I shouting, but tears of anger were dotted on my face.

Tokas remained quiet, apparently focused on the task at hand. But even Val's expression suggested that the rest of the team, too, wanted answers.

"There was no guarantee," Tokas said. "Think what he'd have done if he survived."

"Surely nothing worse than he was bloody *doing already*! Did you not see the attacks Lore took? Do you not see the burned flesh you're working on right this bloody moment?"

Tokas didn't reply. Infuriated, I brought myself to my feet. Before I realized it, I was advancing on her with my knife drawn.

Arzak's hand snapped out to stop me. "No. We not do this."

"He's a Player," Lore said glumly, still cradling his arm. After this, I suspected, there would be more than just the one scar on his face, especially if Tokas wasn't able to heal it anytime soon. "We never know if we're gonna beat them. And we didn't exactly have much time to plan. Normally we have a trap, we have more advantages."

"This time we were on the run," Val added.

Lore nodded. "And for both of the others, we—"

My heart skipped a beat when I realized what I'd just heard. "'Both'?" I repeated. "What in the hells do you mean 'both'?"

Lore's face paled. "Did we not tell—"

"Just how many Players have you killed?" I demanded.

Nobody responded.

"How many? How *bloody* many?"

"Two," Arzak finally answered.

I opened my mouth, but for a moment no words came out. ". . . Two? *Two*? All this time I've been following you, I've been thinking that you're all some kind of experts in taking these people down. But you've only killed . . . You've only killed *two*?"

"They're powerful!" Val replied. "And we've killed a good few other people who needed to go, too. Just not always . . . Players . . ."

I shook my head erratically, blinking, hoping this was some kind of joke. "So?! How can you call yourselves The Hero Slayers when . . ." I trailed off for a moment, my mouth moving but again no sounds coming out. "*Two*?"

"That's more than anyone else on this gods-forsaken world has killed!"

Still, the head-shaking continued. "I'm screwed. I'm totally and utterly screwed. This Player, he's not gonna stop coming for me, you know. He's not gonna stop until I'm dead."

"He won't stop until all us dead now," Arzak said.

I closed my mouth, thinking this piece of information through. "Then . . . why? Why do all this? Why get in the middle of it?"

A moment of silence followed, and I didn't recognize it as being one of confusion until Val finally gave me my answer.

"Because it was . . . Cos it's the right thing to do," she said.

I awoke with the morning light, alerted by footsteps approaching the mouth of the cave. My instinct was to reach for my blade, to do something, to do *anything* to protect us from what was surely the Player, here to finish what he started.

But it was a very welcome face that stepped out of the trees instead.

"Cor!" Val shouted, then immediately regretted making so much noise, putting a hand to her mouth.

"Is everyone . . ." the ranger said. "Did everyone make it?"

"You were the last," Val said, and threw her injured arms around our elf friend.

Corminar's eyes bulged at the sight of her injuries. "You're still hurt. Didn't Tokas . . ."

Val shook her head. "Out of mana. We need your potions."

When Corminar entered the cover of the cave, the rest of the Slayers stirred, and each were equally happy to see that they hadn't lost a member of their party over the course of the evening.

"Lambkin escaped, too," Corminar said once all the hugging was over. "I saw his tracks while I was tracking you."

"And the Player's?" I asked.

The ranger shook his head. "I didn't see them. But I would advise against staying here much longer; the more distance we put between us and him . . ."

". . . The more chance of survival?" I finished.

Corminar nodded.

"We need plan," Arzak said. "We should heal first. Then we must find way of overcoming Player."

"Then we need a few days," Tokas added. "I'll heal what I can, but these wounds run deep. We need rest. We'll need to buy ourselves some time."

"OK. What we have? What we use to buy time?"

"I would be able to disguise our tracks," Corminar said. "It would not fool a more advanced tracker, but I do not believe either of them to be so adept."

"OK," Arzak said. "Good. What else?"

"We could plant some lies in villages?" Lore suggested. "Talk about people who look like us heading in other directions."

"And how might we do that if we are the ones planting such rumors?" Corminar asked.

"Someone here can hide their face, though, can't they?" Lore said, nodding to Val. "She can . . ."

But I didn't hear the rest of this conversation.

Lore's words about hiding faces triggered a sudden and horrifying chain of thoughts, each more terrifying than the last. Hiding faces. Yes. But it wasn't just one of us who could do that. It wasn't just Val's changeling ancestry. Tokas had illusion magicks, too, didn't she?

This seed of thought planted itself in my brain, and though I searched for evidence that it couldn't possibly be true, everything I unearthed seemed to be evidence in the thought's favor.

The very first thing I'd seen when I'd walked into Tokas's apartment above that shop was a flash of red light. A flash of illusion magicks. Of course, she hadn't had her obscurem equipped in the comfort of her own home, so I *would* have seen that spell's glow. Ever since then, though, Tokas had an obscurem on her person. Something about my presence had given Tokas a need to cast an illusion spell.

But how could that have been if she didn't know me?

A memory flashed in my head. The very first thing Tokas had said directly to me.

"Have we met before? You seem familiar."

I'd thought at the time that was just an idle question, a kind of introductory small talk. But I'd learned since then that Tokas wasn't exactly the sort of person to put much stock in such things. So was that question rather . . . a test? A test to see if I recognized her?

More thoughts came pouring in, each worse than the last, sending a chill down my spine.

She hadn't killed the Player. She'd had an opportunity to kill him, and she hadn't. She'd justified it as fear, but . . . what if that wasn't true?

And how had she known so much about them? Just before the attack, she'd told us that the Players didn't have a world to return to, that the Ascended World was dead. Putting aside the questions of how that could be possible, how could Tokas . . . *know* that? How could she know that without spending time with Players?

Castle Carn.

The visions of the scene played before me once more. Amongst the flames, I saw the Player. I thought I did, at least. And I thought I saw the Player's tiefling accomplice. Val had told me I was traumatized, but . . . what if I really hadn't been? What if I'd just glimpsed the truth?

I pulled my knife from my belt, and I stuck it under Tokas's chin.

"Woah!" Lore cried out.

"What's—"

"Show me your obscurem," I demanded of her, the tip of the knife causing a little blood to trickle down the tiefling's throat.

The Players all looked at me like I was insane.

"Give it," I said, my knife hand shaking not with fear but with anger. "Give it now."

"Styk, what are you—" Val started.

"You say these obscurem things are common? We'll replace it. I'll pay, even." I turned back to Tokas. "But you're giving it to me. Now."

"Styk, whatever this is . . ."

"Let him have it," Lore said.

"Lore, not *you*—"

Lore shook his head, that simple act interrupting Val, then said, "Styk has a point more than you lot think. If he wants this, and all it'll cost us is an obscurem, then, you know, let's just hand it over. Let's keep everyone happy and minimize any bloodshed."

"Give it," I snapped again, eyes fixed on Tokas.

Arzak moved her hands slowly toward her swords.

"Don't," Lore said, his eyes on Arzak, his hand moving to his own weapon. "Don't. We don't need to do any more damage here."

"Tokas, I think you better hand it over," Val said, her eyes suggesting she still didn't understand what this was all about.

The tiefling, finally, reached a trembling hand into her pocket, and pulled from it a gem. A gem that was glowing red even in this moment. She had an illusion spell active.

At that moment, I knew I was right.

I reached forward, snatched the obscurem from Tokas's hands, and threw it to the ground. "Lore, destroy it."

The barbarian swung his sword high then crashed it down onto the obscurem. As the gem shattered, the glow faded, and the spell attached to it dispelled.

With the illusion gone, I saw Tokas's real face.

I saw the tiefling from Plainside.

CHAPTER FIFTY-TWO

Among Us

"It's her!" I screamed, instinctively stumbling backward rather than driving my knife point into the woman's throat. "It's her!"

Both Lore and Arzak, a moment earlier both with hands on weapons, looked both alarmed and confused at one another.

"It's who?" Val asked. "That's Tokas. What are you—"

"She . . . No . . . She . . ." I spluttered. "She'd cast an illusion spell on me. She'd had me seeing another face."

Tokas inched slowly toward the entrance of the cave.

I shook my head, my tongue stumbling over the words I wanted to shout. "She's the tiefling from Plainside!"

If I'd expected the rest of the Slayers to immediately attack her, I would have been sorely disappointed. They all stood very still, and very confused.

"Styk, what are you *talking* about?" Val asked.

"Don't you see? That's why she wouldn't kill the Player! She's . . . she's . . . working with him!"

"I'm not working with him," Tokas said, voice shaking, already halfway out of the cave. "He's mad. You're not going to believe this guy, are you?

"Why are you walking away?" Val asked.

"In case you *do* believe him."

"We're not gonna . . ." Val shook her head, turning back to me. "What do you mean she's the tiefling from Plainside? How in the hells could that possibly even be?"

"I'm telling you, she was there! The face I'm seeing now, in front of me, she was there, by his side!"

"This can't—" Arzak started.

"Why would I lie? What could I possibly gain from this?"

"She's a Slayer!" Val said. "I've seen her help us kill Players with my own eyes. She'd never join up with—"

"Well, she did!" I cried. "I couldn't tell you why; ask *her* that! Val, you remember back in Castle Carn? I told you I thought I saw the Player and the tiefling."

"You were traumatized. It was being surrounded by fire that—"

"No! No, it wasn't the bloody fire. It was *her!*" I pointed at Tokas. "I saw her face. I saw her real face through the flames. She must have let the spell slip, or—"

Tokas took another step toward the mouth of the cave.

Corminar raised his bow. "Halt," he told her. "Until this is resolved."

"Why do you think she's running?" I asked. "It's cos she knows I'm right, and sooner or later I'm going to convince you of that. She's evil, I'm telling you!"

Tokas's eye twitched. "I'm not . . . That's not . . ."

"If you let her go, who knows what evil she'll unleash? Maybe she'll go find the Player. Maybe she'll tell him where we are. Maybe she'll—"

"But, Styk?" Lore weighed in. "She was helping us, in the fight. If she was on his side, then . . ."

"I don't have all the answers, I'm just telling you: she's evil!"

"I'm *not* evil!" Tokas cried. "Stop saying that! I'm not evil, I'm not. I'm not. I'm not. I'm just—"

"Tell them!" I shouted over her. "Tell them what you are! Tell them what you *did!* There were children there, Tokas. Children. And you—"

"You don't know what it's like to be a tiefling out here! Everywhere you go, you're greeted by stares at best and the wrong end of swords at worst. You people—humans, orcs, elves—you all get a chance at thriving. But us tieflings? We don't get that chance. There's no thriving for us, not in this world. We just have to play the cards we're dealt."

"We've always treated you with kindness, Tokas," Lore said.

"You? Yes. Yes, you have. All of you are kind. That's why I tried to save you. That's why—" Tokas caught herself when she realized what she'd said.

"Tried to save us? What you mean?" Arzak asked.

Tokas took another step backward. Corminar fired an arrow above her shoulder, its head digging into the rock behind her. A warning shot.

"Why do you flee, Tokas?" Corminar asked.

"Because you mistrust me. Because of . . . You are kind, all of you. But the kindness of some doesn't make up for the mistrust of a not inconsiderable minority. There are people out there who . . . And when you have children to look after—"

"Don't pretend you did this for the kids," I spat. "I told you. There were children at Plainside. You helped him slaughter innocents."

Tokas broke. "I didn't know! I didn't know. I didn't . . ."

Corminar's face paled. Arzak staggered backward at this all-but-admission.

Val and Lore, on the other hand, turned to her with a fury on their faces that I didn't think either of them capable of. "You *what?*" Val screamed. "You *didn't know?* You helped him, but you're saying you *didn't know,* like that would make it right?"

"I didn't . . ." Tokas said, stumbling back. "I didn't . . ."

"I saw those graves," Val said. "I saw how many there were. I saw what you did."

"I didn't hurt anyone! I was there, but I didn't hurt anyone. My job . . . my job was to—"

"You were complicit," Val said, grabbing one of Arzak's swords from the orc's frozen hands. "He wouldn't have brought you if he didn't need you. He wouldn't have done what he did if you hadn't gone with him."

"How could you, Tokas?" Lore asked. "How could you join up with a Player, after all we've seen them do?"

"I'm telling you," the tiefling replied through streams of tears. "I didn't have a choice. I had to—"

"There is always a choice," Corminar said, finally finding his voice. "You are just as bad as them now."

"We should kill you," Val spat.

"No!" Tokas screamed, then flung her hands forward and filled the cave with replicas of herself. Some of them looked to charge us, and the Slayers reacted in kind.

We drew weapons—bows, knives, swords—and sliced at the copies of Tokas that launched themselves at us. The *slices* of my knife didn't hit flesh, and as the blade tip passed through the apparitions, they faded away. Lore, Corminar, Arzak—each of them faced the same, defeating the visions of Tokas with just one swipe.

Until there was just one of them left.

In the confusion, the real Tokas had approached Val, wrapped her hands around her neck and pressed her into the wall. "I'm not evil!" she was shouting, desperately. "I'm not evil! You've got to believe that! You know me. I'm not!"

Corminar raised his bow. "Release her, Tokas. Release her now."

"You won't fire. You won't. It's me. You won't hurt me. I saw you deal with those illusions—you barely would've sliced my skin. You won't hurt me. You won't." From the fact that Tokas had asserted this so many times, I could only imagine that she was trying to convince herself, rather than Corminar.

"Please do not force us to find out," the ranger replied.

At this, Tokas released her grasp on Val's throat, stumbling backward once more. "Please," she tried one last time. "Please believe me. You know me. You know I'd never do anything like this."

"We know nothing," Arzak said.

Tokas turned her head to the orc, and something in her eyes changed. If Arzak, too, was against her, she didn't stand a chance of convincing the Slayers—that's what she seemed to think.

"What do we do with her?" Styk asked.

"This not about you," Arzak replied, her eyes glued to the tiefling.

"Don't blame him for it. We wouldn't have known if not for him." Val's voice was quiet. I'd never heard it like this before.

"You need a healer," Tokas tried. "You need me to . . ."

Arzak began to shake her head, and the tiefling trailed off.

The rest of the Slayers stared the tiefling down, not sure what was to happen next, none of them apparently keen to make the first move. After all, whoever moved first would be the one to decide how all this played out. And none of them wanted this blood—the blood of a friend—on their hands.

It was Tokas, finally, who moved.

She turned and ran, out of the cave and toward the forest.

For their part, the Slayers watched the woman flee, all of them frozen by this horrific revelation. Only Corminar—at times, the strongest of us—moved, raising a bow and pointing an arrow in the direction of the fleeing tiefling.

"Cor . . ." Val breathed, the tone of defeat thick in her voice. "You should—"

The elf released the arrow. It soared through the air, across the not inconsiderable distance between him and the woman who had once been his friend. It was some distance, yes, but one over which I knew he could shoot the wings off a fly.

He missed. The arrow soared a foot or more over Tokas's head.

"You missed," Lore said. "You never miss."

"I know," Corminar agreed.

CHAPTER FIFTY-THREE

We Didn't Start the Fire

Almost a week had passed since our disastrous encounter with the Player.

I, along with what remained of the Slayers, had been keeping to the shadows, spending much of our time in the dense evergreen forests that bordered the northern coast of the Iron Sea. Here, we could stay out of sight not just of the Player and Lev, but of any locals who might jump to offer this information to our enemy.

Val, making use of her changeling abilities, had been the one to amble into a village—never the same one twice—and either purchase us some more food or steal it. We had one eye on our dwindling coin reserves after all. But Val's changeling abilities were limited due to her only having a small amount of changeling blood. This meant that she couldn't take on another person's face all that often, and sometimes it was up to the rest of us to sneak into a town under the cover of darkness, and . . .

Well, there's no glamorous way of saying this, so I'll put it frankly: we'd go into towns at night, and we'd look through bins. It was quite a fall from grace for this thief extraordinaire, I'll tell you that.

Val and I hadn't been wasting the last few days, however. While we'd been hiding, recovering from the deep scars that the butcher of Plainside had inflicted upon us, we'd been training. For my part, I'd been working on my *Knifework* and my *Worldbending* skills, training the former up against any local wildlife—much to Lore's chagrin, though he knew not to say anything—and the latter simply by casting portals. I'd kept these portals down low to avoid the glow attracting any attention.

Now that we'd suffered such a great defeat, I'd realized that maybe I could have been less lax about my progression. Sure, I only had so much mana to cast portals, and needed to manage my reserves well, but I certainly hadn't used all of it every day. And, as it turned out, Corminar could craft some weak mana potions from a lot of the more common plants in this area, which he'd been doing for me when we stumbled across any.

Since our defeat, I'd leveled up both of my key skills a couple of levels, putting *Knifework* at level 17, and *Worldbending* at 18. I'd naturally not unlocked any new abilities during this time, but those additions to my base stats were valuable. I'd even put a few into Vitality this time around, as I'd perhaps been a bit lucky to avoid significant damage in our battle with the Player.

I'd even considered picking up a crafting skill, but I had no tools or, frankly, any imagination at this particular moment.

Val, on the other hand, had been trying to level up a skill she'd forsaken over the years, happy to use it exclusively to cure hangovers. Now that Tokas had left the party, we were relying on Val to heal any wounds—a fact that none of us had needed to tell her; she set about trying to progress almost immediately.

Her progression was limited, however, by the fact that we soon had few wounds to mend. Without a target, Val couldn't cast her magicks, and therefore couldn't generate experience. She'd settled for a very low-level healing spell on the deep wounds that she and Lore had suffered at the hands of the pyroknight, though this kept her progression to a minimum. It definitely wouldn't be enough to turn the tide on the Player—or even so much as catch up with Tokas—when he eventually tracked us down.

It was my turn to rummage through bins for food this night, and I'd done well to avoid it so far. I tried to think of it as an opportunity to level up my overlooked *Stealth* skill, and less as something vermin would do. I left the burnt, abandoned farmhouse we'd been sheltering in—I think we all appreciated the irony of this—as clouds smothered the full moon, casting true darkness upon this area of the Tundras.

The nearby village was small enough that it didn't appear on any maps. There were only seven buildings, none of them a tavern—perhaps why Val hadn't changelinged up this evening—and the only place of business a small shop that seemed to double as a stable. I figured this was my best bet for edible food; the owner wouldn't be able to sell food that was at the end of its life, but it would probably still be edible.

I crept around the back of the shop, keeping low. I couldn't see anyone around, but there was no sense risking it. Just as I was opening the bin at the rear, my eyes landing on some promising-looking potatoes, when I heard voices approaching.

"... came through here earlier. Weird chap."

I looked around, desperately searching for somewhere to hide, and ended up jumping into the bin just in time.

Stealth: +200XP
Stealth increased to Level 6!
Base Points Gained: +1 DEX, +1 WIS, +1 Free Point (DEX/WIS)

I remained deathly still while the two pairs of footsteps grew closer. It wasn't that I was worried about these people attacking me, of course. But if they saw me, that was two pairs of eyes who might report me back to—

"Stranger than Eric?"

"Nobody's as strange as Eric, you know that. Eric doesn't walk around in burnt clothes, though, at least."

Burnt clothes? This wasn't promising. Had the pyroknight come through here already? Was he pursuing us with so much haste that he hadn't even bothered to change his clothes after the fight?

"Well, what'd he want?" one of the locals asked.

"Looking for people, he was. A couple of humans, an elf, an orc—"

"What's such a ragtag group doing 'round these parts, then?"

"Well, I ain't saying they *were* 'round these parts, am I? Just that this bloke was looking for them."

The less edible items in the bin, I noticed, were letting off a pretty unpleasant smell. I resisted the urge to gag.

"Blimey, criminals around here? That's the most exciting thing that's happened 'round these parts all year."

"What, more exciting than that time you found that potato that looked like a rockrat?"

"Well, no, but that was mostly because I sold it for so much, didn't I? Paid for my . . ."

The voices trailed away, just out of earshot. I remained still for a while longer nonetheless, trying my very best to ignore the stench of the bin rising through my nostrils.

Finally, when I could bear it no more, I leaped from my hiding place and dived to the ground. I remained incredibly still, just in case either of the two men were still around, but I heard nothing. Only when I thought it was safe to do so did I rise to a crouch and begin running back to the abandoned farmhouse, completely forgetting the potatoes.

I ran across the road, keeping low, rising only when I was confident the dense trees concealed me. From there, I ran as fast as I could, the sprinting draining my stamina—a power bar that I didn't usually have to worry about—and I burst back into the farmhouse, sparing little concern for making too much noise.

"Where's the grub?" Val asked, looking at my empty hands and not my pale face.

"Someone in town was looking for us," I said, ignoring the sorcerer.

Corminar rose to his feet, his bow suddenly in his hands. "At this very moment?"

"No. Earlier. But that doesn't mean we've escaped him, does it? Means that he could be in the woods, closing on us right now. We should go, we should get moving, we can skip dinner this once. We can—"

Our heads turned as a branch snapped outside. We remained still, quiet, barely a breath heard in the silence. Corminar slowly and steadily nocked an arrow and prepared to fire.

Another footstep. Closer now.

Corminar held his bow with perfect focus, his eyes on the doorway. "Were you followed?" he hissed.

A figure stepped into it, silhouetted by the moonlight.

"No," I breathed, preparing myself for the inevitable flames, for the pain, for the torment.

But then the man stepped forward into the light cast by the dim fire. A bow over one shoulder, a satchel over the other, Lambkin looked at each of us in turn. His clothes were torn and burnt, and it was only at this point that I realized it hadn't been the *Player* asking for us in town.

"You!" Corminar shouted—louder than was wise, considering the circumstances. "We've had quite *enough* of you."

Lambkin thrusted his hands into the air in surrender, seemingly just in time to avoid taking an arrow to the head. "I'm not here to fight!"

"Then why here?" Arzak demanded. These were some of the first words she'd said since Tokas's betrayal.

Lambkin paused to consider his words, the silence stretching seemingly into infinity. And then, finally, he said, "I've seen buildings burned to the ground. I've seen Goldmarch soldiers in the Tundras. And, worst of all, I have seen Players doing evil. All with you lot at the center of it. I suppose I'm here to learn just what in the hells is going on."

Lambkin came bearing food, and for that reason alone, I think, Corminar allowed the man to join us at the fireside. As we ate, taking care to nibble only a little at a time on the provided bread rolls, we told Lambkin the truth of what had happened over the past month and a half. Where before, the ex-captain of Umlok wouldn't have trusted in our story, he now listened carefully, asking clarifying questions here and there, but seemingly taking our word as fact.

When we finally finished, Lambkin spent some time staring silently into the dwindling fire, and the Slayers and I joined him in this moment of reflection.

The flames grew dimmer, and for a moment I considered waving my hands through them, testing the limit of *Ash Husk* while I was at it.

"I have something," Lambkin finally said, pulling forward his bag and flipping it open. "A gift. For all of you. Think of it as an apology."

We watched as the man pulled out a number of items: a blade that I could not yet effectively wield; a collection of small potion vials, of varying colors; and an array of unmounted arrowheads.

"I borrowed some supplies from the Barony of Umlok," he explained.

"When you say 'the barony,' do you mean the castle or the lands at large?" Val asked.

"Yes," the ex-captain replied, before picking up two of the vials that glowed the brightest. "These are the strongest healing potions you'll ever set your eyes on. They're the baron's, really, to be used in case of a dire emergency, and of a quality that only the richest and most powerful could ever afford."

Corminar took the vials in his hands, inspecting them against the light of the fire. He nodded his approval.

"They good?" Arzak asked.

"I admit that they are of a higher quality than I myself could craft."

"They'll automatically heal whoever drinks them, and they'll do it very quickly," Lambkin said. "If for a fairly limited time. But I only have two. If you are to use them against this Player, then—"

"Who says we fight Player?" Arzak interrupted.

Lambkin blinked at the orc, confused. "Is that not the only way that this ends? Or do you intend to run forever? Surely you must realize that either he dies . . . or you do?"

Arzak said nothing.

"We will fight the Player," Corminar confirmed, handing the two vials to Lore. "In our own time. Lore?"

"Yes?"

"Give one of the vials to Arzak. If we are to fight again, it is the pair of you that will be receiving the most damage."

I nodded my approval; I would've suggested the same.

Lambkin began to hand the knife over to me, but I held out my hand in a halting gesture.

"I can't use it. Not yet," I said. "Not for a long time yet."

"Hold it until you do?" the captain suggested.

I shook my head. "I don't want to weigh myself down more than I have to. Think we're gonna need to move fast, when the time comes."

Lambkin nodded. "Alright. It's here when you need it. Consider it my atonement." He handed over the arrow tips to Corminar. "And these, I should've equipped back when I came across you. But how was I to know that . . ."

"I know what to do," Corminar said, more snatching than taking the arrowheads.

Lambkin didn't say anything about the snatching, but considered Corminar—and the group at large—carefully. "I wanted justice. Not for those who died, but for myself, and for what I lost. I wanted the right thing but for the wrong reasons, and that I took for granted that it was you responsible for the crimes instead of a Player . . . I am sorry. But, perhaps, if I might make a suggestion? Hate me for it later. For the time being, we could fight alongside one another."

Tokas

Four months earlier

"Punnas? Lopas?" Tokas said, rubbing the sides of her temple in an attempt to soothe the seemingly ever-present headache. "Why don't we sit down for a bit, hmm? Maybe sit and play with our toys? And *sit*?"

More and more, Tokas felt the temptation to get the local enchantress to have a look at casting *slowing* on the children's boots. Maybe she'd get some peace and quiet, and just *maybe* she would be able to keep the apartment clean. Either that, or Zarin was going to have to quit one of his jobs and help her out with the twins.

How they would then pay their rent would be a matter for another day.

"OK, Mummy," Punnas said. "We sit." He plonked himself down on the floor immediately, right in the middle of the kitchen.

"Why don't we go sit in the bedroom? You too, Lopas," Tokas said, encouraging them with gentle gestures of her hands. "Please?"

Solemnly—perhaps understanding that Tokas was struggling—Punnas took his brother by the hand and led him off into the other room.

Tokas breathed a sigh of relief. She put the kettle on the magma stone and scooped out a small handful of tea leaves into her cup. Tea would make it all better. It had to. At least, it wouldn't make it *worse*.

A knock at the door made Tokas realize she had closed her eyes. She had to have fallen asleep for a moment, because the kettle was already warm, if not quite boiling.

"Yes?" Tokas called out.

She waited for a response, but none came.

"Yes? What do you want?"

Still there was no response, so Tokas stormed over to the front door and swung it open, revealing a handsome young human with some strange quality behind his eyes.

"Tokas, I take it?" the human said.

"I . . ." Tokas started, but was forced to trail off when the human pushed into her apartment. It was at this moment that she started to realize just how much trouble she was in. "My husband will be home any minute," she said.

"Oh yeah?" the man replied, making himself comfortable on Tokas's sofa. "Tiefling like you, is he?"

"Human," Tokas said.

The man nodded, patting the back of the sofa absentmindedly as he looked around the room.

"What do you—"

"I'm told you specialize in illusion magicks."

"I do."

Again, the man nodded his head. "Good. You're coming with me."

"I'm not going anywhere," Tokas replied, taking an unconscious step backward.

The man sighed. "I'm going to make this simple. You're coming with me, or you're not going anywhere ever again."

Tokas stared back at the man, considering her abilities, preparing herself to use the apparently much-in-demand illusion magicks to escape. She caught herself; there were the twins in the other room—it wasn't that simple. Tokas prayed they would remain this uncharacteristically quiet.

"Have you *identified* me yet?" the man finally asked.

Tokas didn't reply, but did exactly as suggested. After all, what was the harm?

When she saw the result, a lump lodged within her throat. Others would not know the danger that a Player posed, but she? She knew very well. Tokas could only hope that this particular Player—a pyroknight—would think her not clued in to the truth of their kind.

"Oh, I . . ." she started. "I'm sorry, sir, I didn't realize I was dealing with a—"

"Yes, yes, alright," the pyroknight said, waving her down. "I get plenty of that. And, frankly, I'm sick of it. But the boss says it's important we preserve our image and all that, so I gotta stop killing people."

Tokas blinked; she hadn't expected the conversation to go this way.

"But, you know what? I don't *want* to stop. I'm a pyroknight; I burn people. That's what I do. If I can't do that, I'm powerless. So I figured . . . what's the next best thing? Either I don't leave anyone alive to tell the tale—something easier said than done—or I work some illusion magicks to give people the wrong idea. That's where you come in."

"I won't help you murder anyone," Tokas said. She couldn't help herself. She couldn't even so much as speak that lie.

The Player smiled. "You will. You—" the man stopped suddenly, his attention fixed on some spot behind Tokas. The hallway.

Tokas knew what she'd see before she turned.

Lopas stood in the hallway, holding one of his toys, his wide eyes staring up at the intruder.

"Go back in the other room, sweetheart," Tokas said, forcing her voice not to strain. "Go back in with Punnas." She immediately caught herself. She shouldn't have said that. She shouldn't have said she had another.

The Player watched Tokas's child slink back off into his room once more, and a wide, toothy smile crossed his face. "Oh, I see! Maybe convincing you is going to be easier than I thought."

The room fell silent as the pyroknight left the rest of that thought dangling there, unspoken but present.

"I won't hurt anyone. I won't *help* you hurt any—"

"We both know you will. A year of your service, that's all I require. After that, the Council's plans should be fully in motion, and it won't matter if the world hates us. Then you can go back to your family. And you'll still *have one*."

It took until now for Tokas to realize she was crying. "I won't . . . I won't . . . I'm supposed to *stop* your kind, not—"

But she was interrupted by the front door opening once more. Zarin stood in the doorway, eyes upon Tokas and full of love. Brilliant, handsome, fatherly Zarin. A human that she'd never expected to love.

When he saw the pyroknight, his expression morphed from one of love to one of confusion.

Two months later, Tokas was in Plainside.

In the weeks since that fateful encounter, she and Jacob had picked up another member of their party, an orc called Lev. Lev was a mercenary, not a true believer, and just as ruthless as Tokas had come to expect of one of his kind. The orc closed a vital gap in Jacob's metaphorical armor; though the Player was a pyroknight, his weapon-based abilities suffered from a lack of investment in stamina. This meant that Jacob was strong on the magicks, but could only use his sword—one summoned from fire—sparingly.

Fire was raging around the trio, and Jacob had—this time, at least—spared some of his fire resistance magicks to protect Tokas and Lev as they walked through the burning ruins of the Collector's manor.

Tokas didn't know what Jacob's orders were—only that he had some—and

yet she was under explicit instructions not to mention this little detour to anyone. The rest of the Players, somewhere out there, they did not know about this.

But Tokas knew better than to ask; she still sported the burns from last time
she'd questioned him. Burns that even healing magicks couldn't immediately fix.

As they progressed through the burning building, three knives suddenly shot
out from around a corner, burying themselves in Jacob's chest. Every part of
Tokas wanted to grab hold of those knives and twist them, subjecting Jacob to
the same kind of pain she'd seen him inflict countless times over the last few
weeks. But she didn't.

In fact, as the Player reached down to pluck his prize—a metal octahedron—
from a dead thief's body, Tokas closed her eyes.

She thought of Punnas and Lopas, being cared for by her father.

At least they would live.

CHAPTER FIFTY-FOUR

Rekindling

"Perhaps it has escaped your notice, but we lost our healer," Corminar said. "What chance could we have?"

It had been another day of hiding in the forests north of the Iron Sea since Lambkin had joined us. The ex-captain had been surprisingly capable at foraging, and what with the nuts and berries he had provided, along with the food stolen from local inns, I was feeling full for the first time in a few days. For a moment, I could almost forget about my inevitable destiny: a scorching, painful death.

"Val can heal," Lore pointed out, gesturing to the woman in question.

"Yeah, a headache, maybe," I said. At Val's irritable expression, I added, "What? It's true."

"We rely on the Lamb Kin's potions," Arzak said.

"*Lambkin.*" The ex-captain tried to correct her for the third time. It didn't take.

"It's not enough," Val said with a sigh.

"It'll have to be," I replied. "We all know where this is headed. Unless you want to spend the rest of your lives running from this man, hiding in forests . . . We have to face him at some point."

"*You* have to face him," Val said. "He told the rest of us we could go."

"I'm pretty sure that was before you all tried to kill him."

The sorcerer pulled a face. "Might be a risk worth taking. Figure that's better odds than if we were to face him again."

"Then let us change odds," Arzak said. "We not prepared, last time. We panic. With preparation, we do better."

"I don't know what kind of preparation will let us defeat *that*," Val said. "You saw what he did to us? What he did to me? What he did to Lore? The only way we survived that is because we had Tok—" She caught herself at having spoken the tiefling's name. "Because we had a healer on hand."

"Then move faster," Arzak suggested. "Me and Lore take potion. Take hits."

"It's not an . . . *insurmountable* problem," Corminar agreed. "If we were to stick to ranged attacks, at least. There is no reason for any of us—with the exception of Arzak and Lore—to be fighting at close range."

"You're talking like you're actually considering this," the sorcerer said.

"Val," I started, "if I remember correctly, *you* were the one who kicked this whole thing off. Killing this Player was your idea. It's too—"

"That was before he burned half my stomach off. I can't . . . I don't want that to happen again."

"We won't let it, Val."

"You can't guarantee that."

I shrugged. "This fight will happen eventually anyway. This Player's just going to keep following us. What did you think he'd do when he finds us? It's going to involve fire."

Val said nothing; clearly she could see that I was right, but the idea of facing the pyroknight down again—very understandably—was one that she struggled with.

"You don't have to come," I finally said.

At this, the sorcerer balked. "What, and let the rest of you do it without me? You lot wouldn't stand a chance." She allowed herself a reluctant smile—one that I returned in kind.

"We didn't have time to prepare properly last time," I said, hoping to reassure her. "We do this time. This time, we can bait him into a trap."

"Bait?" Arzak asked. "What bait?"

I shrugged again. "The same thing he's wanted all along. Me. We drop some carefully placed rumors along the way, and the Player will come running, I reckon."

The orc considered this and then nodded. She looked to Val, prompting her with raised eyebrows.

". . . Alright," Val said with a sigh. "Say we do this, we're gonna need to give ourselves all the advantages we can. What do we have?"

"The potions," Lore suggested.

"Yes, I was taking that one for granted. What else?"

"Well, speaking of things I brought with me," Lambkin said. "There are the arrowheads." He turned to Corminar. "Perhaps we could split them? Between my arrows and your poison, that's some pretty decent damage we could be dealing."

"Why?" Arzak asked. "What so special about arrowheads?"

"They offer a boost to poison effectiveness," Corminar answered. "I concede that they are valuable, though I do not see this as being the difference between victory and ending up a pile of ashes."

Val winced at this thought, but went on nonetheless. "That's OK. We're not looking for a complete game-changer, we're just looking for lots of little advantages. Maybe none of them alone would help us win, but maybe all of them put together . . . Maybe that's enough."

The group went silent, and for a moment I thought that might be the extent of our advantages. In order to keep the ideas coming, I offered, "If I open a portal beneath him, maybe one of you—Arzak or Lore—could push him through?"

"You don't think he'd survive falling to the ground?" Val asked. "We've seen how much health he has. It's off the charts. Honestly, I don't know how he's managed to spec so much into both Intelligence and Vitality—the math just doesn't add up."

"He might survive, yeah, but we're just talking about things that might help, right?"

Lore nodded. "Give me a signal, and I'll push him through."

"Sure. What kind of signal?"

"Oh, err . . ." The barbarian scratched at the back of his head. "A bird call?"

"I can't do bird calls."

Val rolled her eyes. "How's this? The signal can be you shouting 'Lore, push him through the portal, you big bloody idiot!'"

Lore didn't seem very impressed by this, but he let it slide. We were letting a lot of stuff slide, as of late.

"And if we keep moving south, we can fight him on the coast," I said. "That was always the plan, wasn't it? Open the Iron Sea on him. We saw how much even that small pond dampened his powers—even *I* survived a glancing blow, though maybe my *Ash Husk* had a lot to do with that—so just think what'd happen if we dumped the whole bloody sea on him."

Val stood up, and—judging by her body language—was clearly energized by this brainstorming session. "Slow down there, portal boy. You can only dump so much water on him; your mana will run out before long. And we don't want you fainting on us, do we?"

"Again," Corminar added, but there wasn't any malice to it.

"I was being hyperbolic," I replied.

"Big word for a portal boy."

"Please stop calling me 'portal boy.'"

"OK, knife boy," Val replied.

I tossed my head back in irritation.

"There one other thing," Arzak said. "This other orc. He strong. I not able to fight him alone."

"I will assist you," Lambkin offered, but Arzak shook her head.

"This not what I get at. What if we not *have* to fight Lev?"

Val leaned in. "I'm listening."

"What if we get him first?" the orc posed. "Would need separate him from Player. I don't know how—"

"I do," I said. I turned to Val. "Remember back in Carn? Lev had a—"

"His boyfriend," the sorcerer said. "I was thinking the same."

"We'd still need to draw him away from the Player. Maybe at night, when he sleeps?" I hesitated for a moment. "Players . . . they *do* sleep, don't they?"

"Val should impersonate him," Lore suggested. "Draw Lev away. And when he's far enough from the Player, we jump him."

"Do we not believe that such commotion would stir the Player from his slumber?" Corminar asked. "How far do you reasonably expect to draw him?"

Val shook her head. "No idea. I've got no clue what the man is even like; I could say the wrong thing at any moment, and my cover would be blown. It's not like it's the first time I've adopted that disguise after all."

"Then I'll portal you," I said. "We'll find cover down the road, in amongst the trees. I can open a portal as far as I can see, so as long as you draw him into the open . . ."

The sorcerer nodded, and then a small smile started to cross her face. "Are we . . . are we doing this? This feels like it could work. Are we doing this?"

"I believe we are," Corminar confirmed.

Arzak stood up suddenly. "Any reason we not start now?"

"Better now than later," Val added.

With that, we stood from the dwindling campfire, and we stepped toward the door. We would need to track down the Player before he could track us down, but how hard could that have been? You couldn't shut people up about the news that a Player—a spawn of the Architects!—had passed through their town.

"Hey, guys?" Lore said.

We—the whole group but the barbarian—turned back to see him still standing by the fire.

"There is *one* other thing that might be useful." He stuck out his hand. Whatever he was holding, we couldn't see it from this distance.

The five of us stepped forward to get a better look at the small blue object in his hand.

"Huh," I said, once I realized what it was. "That could work."

CHAPTER FIFTY-FIVE

Break a Lev

"He's in there," Val said.

Over the past few days, we'd made our way south toward the coast of the Iron Sea, and were careful to be seen *just enough* that the locals would point the Player our way. If we were too obvious about it, the Player might have known that something was up, that we were leading him into a trap, but us running away as soon as we were spotted surely put that idea to bed.

Now we were at a small fishing village—one small enough that it didn't feature on the map I had, but large enough at least to have an inn where the Player and his assistant could stay. It was the perfect place to execute stage one of our plan, yet every member of the Slayers—plus me and Lambkin—were nervous enough that our faces were pale. If this went wrong, this meant that the Player would be upon us once more, and we really, *really* wanted to eliminate Lev before that could happen.

"Is the Player with him?" I asked hopefully.

"What do you think?" the sorcerer replied. "Yeah, he's there. The innkeeper was making a big deal out of it and all."

"It still Plan A, then," Arzak said, nodding as though mostly to gather the strength to proceed.

"You're all clear on what you're gonna say?" I asked Val.

The woman shrugged as she changed her form, her flesh changing shape in a not dissimilar way to how my *Ash Husk* ability worked. Soon it wasn't my friend Val but Lev's boyfriend who stood before me. Or who seemed to, at least. "Like Cor says, I'm not gonna say much. I'm gonna let my eyes do the talking."

Corminar nodded knowingly.

"Do you really get people into bed with just your eyes?" I asked.

The elf ranger replied, "I am yet to attempt it without looking at them," which wasn't really a good enough answer in my book, but now wasn't the time for follow-up questions.

"Alright," Val said with a sigh and an unfamiliar voice. "I guess I'll . . ." She started for the tavern, leaving the rest of us under the cover of both the moonless night and the canopy of the trees.

"Val?" I said.

The sorcerer stopped and looked back at me with strange eyes, yet I could read them just as well as I could the real ones.

"Good luck," I added.

Val nodded, and then turned to walk into town, her attention fixed on the tavern.

The moment Val stepped into the tavern and out of sight, I raised my hands in preparation; there was no knowing how quickly she'd retrieve Lev. Behind me, there was a clearing into which we would drop Lev, and potentially Val, too—depending on how physically close they were leaving the tavern, and whether Val needed to push him through.

The five of us stood deathly still, eerily silent, ten eyes on the door of the tavern. Minutes passed, and still there was no sign of Val. As I continued holding my arms up and ready to go, they began to ache.

"You don't think she . . ." I started, leaving the rest of the question to hang in the air.

"I reckon we'd see if the Player had attacked her, wouldn't we?" Lore asked. "All he has are fire attacks, and that building's made of wood."

I tilted my head in acknowledgement, but it didn't do much to calm the anxiety in my stomach.

When the door to the tavern opened a few minutes later, I released a breath I didn't quite realize I'd been holding. Val—in her current form—stepped out first, leading the burly orc by the hand. Lev followed with a furrowed brow, as though he didn't quite understand what was going on.

And that was fair enough, really. If he hadn't been so groggy he might have started asking questions we didn't want him to ask. Questions like "Why are you here?" and "How did you know where I was?"

I prepared myself to open a portal, but while the pair were this close to the tavern, it was a little tricky to aim. I waited as Val led the orc forward, until . . . he came to an abrupt halt. Val turned back to face him.

I couldn't hear the words coming out of the orc's mouth, but if I was going to put money on it, I would have guessed he was asking either or both of the previously mentioned questions. The questions we didn't want him asking.

Val faced the orc, feigning a casual stroll to one side, turning Lev so that he was facing away from us. She held a hand behind her, flicking it desperately, and it took a moment for me to realize that it was a signal.

"Oh, err . . ." I said, and opened a portal on the ground just behind Lev.

Val immediately launched herself at the orc, and—as he had his guard down—she had no trouble in pushing the pair of them through, bringing them falling into the clearing behind me.

As they tumbled across the ground, Lev looked around with wide eyes, and Val scrambled to her feet, immediately shaking off the other form and allowing herself to gag. "Gross, gross, gross . . ."

The rest of the team hurried into action.

Corminar and Lambkin fired the moment Lev was through the portal, though they used their standard arrows—we had planned to save the fancy arrowheads for the Player.

"The Traveling Stones!" Val shouted in her normal voice, reminding us. "The Traveling Stones!"

Arzak charged, dual swords in hand, but Lev reacted by pulling his axe up—a real shame he hadn't left it in his bedroom—to block one then the other. When Lore also joined the skirmish with his one greatsword, Lev swung up a foot to catch him in the chest, knocking him backward.

Arrows caught him in the shoulder, but his leather armor was thick enough that the damage was minimal enough to ignore. Either that, or he had incredibly high Vitality like his current employer—he could take some decent hits without having to worry about his health bar.

With Arzak and Lore on the attack, and Corminar and Lambkin firing arrows, it was up to me and Val to get the Traveling Stones that we knew he possessed. After all, he'd already escaped from us once this way, and if he was from such a rich and fancy place as Auricia, he probably had the funds for more.

I hopped over to him through use of a portal. Was it lazy to use a portal to close twenty feet? Not if I was in a hurry, I decided; that was just good sense.

Arriving at Lev's side just as he was swinging his axe to block Arzak's latest attack, I crouched to avoid the arcing weapon, and then thrust two hands into two pockets.

The orc paused, blinked at me, and mumbled, "Excuse me?"

I threw the contents of his pockets away, noting as they soared through the air that absolutely none of the objects were the gemstones I'd expected, instead consisting of a few coins, a scrap of paper, and a ring of keys. But I was acting too dependently on impulse to not follow through with the move, and I opened a portal just below where I'd thrown the orc's belongings, the other side tossing them into the ocean. It almost seemed rude, though I did suppose we were also about to kill him. The phrase "adding insult to injury" came to mind.

"Pockets empty!" I shouted, then portaled myself out of the orc's reach once more just as he swung the butt of his axe handle to hit me while parrying Lore's attack.

"Alright, press!" Val shouted. Now that there was no chance of Lev escaping, the plan was to eliminate him as quickly as possible—any noise had a chance of attracting attention, and any attention had a chance of waking the Player and having him join the fray. We didn't want this. Not yet.

"Hmm," Lev said, backing up slowly as he saw yet more people moving to attack him. "This not good." He suddenly turned and dived backward, over a fallen, rotting tree, dropping his axe in the process.

It occurred to me and Val what was happening before it did everyone else, because we'd seen it the first time around. There was only one reason this orc would drop his axe: he was fleeing.

Lev grabbed his shirt and ripped it open, revealing a chiseled green chest beneath that Corminar might have commented on in better circumstances.

"Lovely," the elf said.

OK, maybe in these circumstances, too.

In the middle of that chest that Corminar was admiring while raising a bow at it was a necklace, and on that necklace was a familiar gemstone. This was why Lev's pockets didn't contain any Traveling Stones, then—because it was around his neck.

Lev snatched the gem from his chest at the same moment that Corminar fired, an arrow piercing his hand but doing little to stop the burly orc from yanking the gem free.

I charged toward the enemy orc, opening a portal in front of me to help close the distance. Val, starting to understand how I operated these magicks, anticipated this move, and she jumped through the portal alongside me.

We spilled out at Lev's side just as he threw the stone to the ground, opening a portal through which I could see the towering, glamorous buildings of Auricia. Only this time around did I notice the purple hue at the edge of this portal; the enchanter responsible for these stones had to be a fellow Worldbender. It crossed my mind that I, someday, might be able to create the same—but now wasn't the time to think about that.

Val reached forward for Lev as he tumbled through, stepping across continents in the blink of an eye, and instinctively I reached out to grab her, yanking her backward and to the floor.

"No!" she roared. "No!"

"You can't go through!" I told her. "You can't! We need you here!"

"He's guilty!" she screamed. "He needs to pay. He needs to pay for what he did!"

She scrambled forward, ripping herself from my grasp, forcing me to open another portal in front of her to stop her in her tracks.

"We have to kill him!" she roared, and I reached out to put a hand over her mouth, muffling her next few shouts.

"Shh!" I said as Lev's portal to Auricia closed before us. "He'll hear us!"

Worldbending: +400XP

Val screamed into my hand once more, but I couldn't make out the words.

"Quiet!" I said again. "It's done, Val. It's done."

Finally, upon realizing that I was right, the sorcerer stopped struggling against me. "Can I take my hand off your mouth now?"

"M-mm mm-mmm," Val replied.

"What?" I repeated, releasing her.

"I said 'yes you bloody well can,'" she clarified. Val stared on at where Lev's portal had been only moments earlier.

"Expensive way to get around, I reckon," Lore said, strolling slowly up to us.

"Perhaps that is some small consolation," Corminar mused. "Not justice for all that he has done, but I do enjoy knowing that we have cost him a small fortune."

Val continued to glare at the spot where Lev had been standing moments earlier. "He needs to pay."

"We'll get him, Val," I said. "But later. You gotta remember: this is a victory for us. Auricia is half a world away. The Player is alone now. We've given ourselves a chance."

CHAPTER FIFTY-SIX

Wet Work: Redux

It was morning.

We'd slept as best we could, considering each of us knew what tomorrow would hold. To maximize our chances of killing the Player, we had to strike before he picked up any new allies. Before he replaced Lev, really. This meant that the attack would begin the moment the pyroknight stepped out of the tavern. All of us knew this, but some of us—Arzak and Corminar—were dealing with it better than others. I'd tossed and turned all night, getting some sleep, but only fleetingly. The little sleep I'd had was plagued by dreams of Val and Lore getting burned, or—worse—*me* getting burned.

We ate breakfast—a selection of increasingly stale breads, and the last of Lambkin's stores—in near silence, sitting around a small clearing in the forest while one member of our team kept an eye on the tavern. It was early still, as we hadn't wanted to risk missing the Player. It turned out there was no danger of that; the pyroknight was a late riser.

With the last of the bread making its way into my stomach, I fiddled with the vial that Corminar had given me. It was a strong mana potion—at least for my level of Intelligence—and would keep me opening portals far into the battle. I didn't know if the battle lasting a while would be a good thing. Would that mean we were chipping away at the Player's mana, or that we weren't finishing it quickly enough?

I stilled this line of thought when Lore poked his head through the trees. "He's out," the barbarian said glumly.

Arzak and I nodded, and Val sighed loudly.

"You alright changing twice in two days?" I asked again.

She shrugged. "It's not . . . ideal. Costs a lot of mana after the first time. But I guess that's what the potions are for." She held up a glass vial which was glowing, notably, a hell of a lot more than mine.

I pulled myself to my feet, a hand drifting to my belt, checking that my Ranger's Blade was still there. I knew it would be; this was just a nervous habit.

"Ready?" Arzak asked, making a pointed effort to look at each of us in turn, even Lambkin. One by one, we nodded. "Then we go kill Player."

With another sigh, Val closed her eyes and willed her skin to change. Her flesh rippled, bulged, and green-ed as she took on the form of the orc who had fled. It would allow her to get close, and it might just allow her to use Lore's secret weapon.

"OK, I'm—" she started, spluttering. "These tusks are h-hard to talk around, aren't they?"

Arzak nodded. "They mouthful. So orcish not use many words. This efficient and good grammar, in orc language. But means when speak common, people think we dumb. Unfair stereotype."

"We know you're not dumb, Arzak," Lore offered with a reluctant smile. The reluctance was probably more about the task ahead of us than anything else.

Arzak nodded her reply, then turned back to Val. "Remember: not talk much. Few words. OK?"

"OK. I won't t—" Val spluttered again. "Not talk much."

"Good."

Val, in her new form, picked up Lev's axe from where he'd dropped it, and heaved it over her shoulder with a grunt. "Heavy," she said.

"That is idea," Arzak replied.

We looked out of the cover of the trees at the Player, staring around town with a furrowed brow and a hand shielding his eyes from the sun.

"Alright," Val said.

"This is it, then," I added.

"Do or die," Corminar said, this being about the coolest thing he'd ever said.

Val took one last deep breath, then stepped from the cover of the tree line. She waited a good while before calling out for the Player, so as not to draw his attention to us in our hiding place.

The five of us watched her go, hands on weapons, ready to strike at the first sign of trouble.

"Any reason we didn't try and attack him while he was sleeping?" I asked.

"Would you like be stuck in wooden building when fighting pyroknight?" Arzak replied.

"Fair point."

We remained quiet as the pyroknight set his eyes on Val—thinking her Lev—and then asked, very loudly, "And where the hell have you been?"

"Lev" shrugged, and then held out a hand, a small blue object held within. "Shopping," she said. "Want sweet?"

"There is *one* other thing which might be useful," Lore said, holding out something in his hand.

The five of us stepped closer, and of the lot of us, only Val and I recognized what he was holding—a small blue sweet, courtesy of that utter pain in the arse merchant Ted. "Huh," I said. "That could work."

"Will it still be enchanted?" Lore asked, his eyes on Val.

"No reason it wouldn't be. This kinda thing . . . it's there until it's activated. In this case, it activates when you eat it."

"What is it?" Lambkin asked. "What's going on?"

"Cursed sweet," I said. "Summons water into your stomach."

The ex-captain raised his eyebrows. "OK. Of course it is."

"How do you even have it?" Val asked Lore.

The barbarian shrugged. "When you bought them, I was full. But I didn't want to miss out. So I snuck one out of the bag while you and Styk were bickering. You two bicker a lot, you know that?"

Val pulled a face that suggested she didn't think that was true, while Corminar and Arzak nodded knowingly.

"She bickers a lot with *everyone*," I said.

"Forgot I even had it until a couple of days ago," Lore said. "The sweet, I mean. And then I thought . . . maybe it'd come in handy?"

"Oh yes, Lore," Val said. "I think it just might."

"A . . . sweet?" the Player asked. "You left me unprotected while I slept so that you could . . . buy sweets? What has gotten into you, Lev?"

Val shrugged. "They good sweets." She stepped forward, unwrapping it and pushing it toward the Player's mouth.

"I don't want you . . ." The pyroknight staggered backward, shaking his head in disbelief at the orc's actions.

"Eat sweet," the fake orc said again. "Trust me. Is good."

The pyroknight stared at Val for a moment. "Maybe . . . later?"

"No, now."

"I'm not—" the Player started, but was interrupted by Val trying to push the sweet into his mouth once more. "Gods damn it, Lev, stop this!" He grabbed Val by the wrist, preventing her from pushing the sweet any closer to his mouth.

"No!" Val said through gritted teeth, her arm pushing against the Player's. "Eat!"

The pyroknight blinked at Lev's arm. "Why are you so weak this morning?"

"Uh-oh," Lore said at my side.

"It's not gonna work, is it?" I asked.

"It's not."

Alright, new plan. I stepped out of the cover of the forest, thrust both hands forward, and I created a pair of portals. I placed them carefully—one of them was just under where Val was gripping the sweet, and the other . . . was just in front of the Player's agape mouth.

Val, more familiar with my portals, reacted first. She dropped the sweet into the portal, and it fell straight into the Player's mouth.

The pyroknight released Val, staggering backward to grab at his throat, the sweet clearly already partway down it.

"Make him swallow!" I shouted, charging forth from the trees. "Make him swallow!"

The wide-eyed Val looked from me to the Player, and then flung herself forward, slamming the butt of her hand into the man's throat.

He gulped.

"What in the . . ." he started, turning to face me. "Blueberry?" His eyes settled on me, widened some, then flicked behind me, and widened some more. Just from this expression, I knew that the rest of the team were charging from cover behind me.

Two arrows shot over my head, narrowly missing my ears—I didn't like to think about what sort of damage they'd have done to me if they'd *hit* me—and buried themselves in the Player's chest.

Val cricked her neck and her disguise rippled away.

"Where is he?" the Player spat. "Where's Lev?"

"Ran off crying," Val said. It was only *mostly* a lie. Then she whipped her hands to the ground and summoned roots which climbed the Player's legs.

The pyroknight had little trouble freeing himself from them, but they slowed him down, and Val was relentless in her summonings.

"Styk! The sea! The sea!" she shouted, like that wasn't exactly where I was headed and like that wasn't going to give the game away to the enemy.

The pyroknight spun to launch a ball of fire my way, so I summoned a portal in front of me, landing me on top of the thatched roof of the tavern. From here, I had a key advantage: a vantage point from where I could see both the Player and the edge of the great Iron Sea.

As I saw Lore and Arzak grow close to the enemy, I summoned a portal behind him, the other high above the sea. "Now!" I shouted.

Of the close quarters–attackers, only Arzak wielded her weapon, which was perhaps the Player's first clue. He sent retaliatory fireballs at Arzak, seeing her as the greater threat because of the pair of swords she grasped, and worried less about Lore.

But when Lore grew close enough, he pounced, leaping at the Player and pushing him toward the open portal behind him.

Instead of responding with an attack, the pyroknight snapped his hands out at his sides, grabbing the sides of the portal just as Lore reached him.

Lore bounced off the enemy, but pushed against him once more, trying with all his might to just . . . push . . . him . . . through.

In one of the Player's outstretched hands, a flame flickered, one unlike the rest. It wasn't a fireball, or a wall of flame, or anything we'd seen before. This fire slowly took shape. Before our eyes, it took the shape of a sword.

I closed the portal just as the Player moved to strike Lore with his flaming weapon, saving Lore from the worst of the burns. Instead, I turned the strategy on its head, opening a portal above the pair of them and another in the shallows of the Iron Sea itself. There was a crash as water poured through the portal and collided with the ground and man below. The pyroknight's flaming sword hissed, struggling to retain its intensity against the contents of the Iron Sea.

The Player turned his attention to me, correctly identifying me as the source of this water, and charged free of the portal's torrent. He dived to dry ground, rolled, and when he was upright again, he sent a fireball hurtling toward me.

No, not me, I realized as I moved to shield myself. The pyroknight wasn't looking to burn me. He was looking to burn the building.

The thatched roof, untouched by my torrent of water, caught fire instantly. I stumbled backward, trying to avoid the flames while keeping my footing on the slanted surface.

"There's people in there!" Val shouted.

"On it!" I shouted. I let the original pair of portals close and I opened a new pair, the resulting spray of sea battling the rapidly growing blaze. Below, people screamed as they fled from the building, and I took some solace in that this surely meant people weren't in danger of sleeping through it. Some people I knew— Lore, really—I absolutely could envision sleeping through an act of arson.

Out of the corner of my eye, I saw Arzak and Lore charge once more, this time both of them holding their weapons. The Player reacted by flinging his hands to his sides and conjuring a protective ring of fire around himself—a strategy that I was expected to counter with my water-assisted portals.

"Styk!" Val shouted.

"I can save these people, or I can do that," I cried back at her, voice strained. "Which is it gonna be?"

"No, it's not that, it's . . ."

I risked another glance away from my portal-based firefighting to look at the Player. He was choking on something. Or, rather, he looked like he was going to be sick.

I knew that look. I'd suffered this once before.

Ted's cursed sweet was kicking in.

CHAPTER FIFTY-SEVEN

Everything We Have

"Come on! *Come on!*" I shouted to nobody in particular as I rapidly closed and opened portals, dumping the contents of the Iron Sea on the parts of the tavern still aflame.

Through the now-patchy thatched roof, I saw a young tiefling woman holding a child, and for a moment I thought I glimpsed Tokas again. I shook my head, ridding myself of the image. It wouldn't be right for me to start thinking all tieflings were guilty; that's exactly what Tokas had said her experience of life as a tiefling had been. It maybe didn't help her case that she, specifically, *was* guilty.

Shouts from behind me told me that the fight against the Player was still raging, but I didn't have time to glance over. Below me, the woman and child cowered from rapidly spreading flames, and I thrust a hand forward to open a portal in the room and drench it with water.

The woman screamed, and then—once I'd closed the portal—she looked up at me, dripping wet, like I'd done something *wrong*. She clutched her baby close to her chest while she continued staring daggers at me.

"Sor—" I started to apologize, then caught myself. No, I wasn't going to apologize for saving someone's life. "Get everyone out!" I shouted at her instead.

"Why?" came the reply.

"Are you serious?"

"Looks like the fire is out."

I blinked. "For now, sure. But I've only got so much mana, and that guy isn't gonna stop summoning fireballs anytime soon. Alright?"

The woman stared blankly back, and then at last nodded.

I sighed, turning away to face the battle once more, and hoping that the tiefling really was going to carry out my suggestion. The Player stood with flaming sword in hand, Lore at the floor beside him, and Arzak rushing in for another attack.

Another pair of arrows shot across the town as Corminar and Lambkin fired their poison-tipped ammunitions toward the Player, one missing, one hitting. If I had to guess, it was likely Lambkin who had missed. He was the *second* highest-leveled archer in the Tundras, after all—a fact that Corminar had murmured in his sleep last night as though to remind all of us. These arrows didn't seem to weaken the Player like we'd anticipated; green marks appeared on the pyroknight's skin as the poison spread, but it didn't seem to grow much further. If I wasn't mistaken, these marks were also quickly fading.

The water, at least, was working. Both the Iron Sea and the summoned stomach-water had dampened the Player's fire attacks, as evidenced by the fact that Arzak and Lore weren't yet burned to Tartarus. Though the high-level healing potions in their systems might also have explained that. I could only hope they hadn't exhausted much of their healing powers, because it seemed this fight had a long way to go yet.

I jumped from the rooftop into a summoned portal, emerging at Val's side some way from the fight. I couldn't help but notice that she had her eyes closed; something that didn't seem massively like it was going to benefit her in the middle of a fight. "Err . . . what are you doing?"

"Shh."

"You know someone's trying to kill us, right?"

"Something new," Val explained. "Roots aren't working. Go fight."

I did as Val suggested, charging toward the Player, Arzak, and Lore, using just my own two feet this time so as to preserve my already dwindling mana reserves. I realized that maybe now was a good time to use the mana potion that Corminar had crafted for me—I might not have any time later. As I ran, I pulled the cork stopper free and downed the glowing blue liquid, watching as my mana bar replenished itself.

Ahead of me, Arzak and Lore clashed blades with the Player, the enemy parrying their attacks with apparent ease. Arzak swung one blade first, bouncing off the flaming sword, and then another. The Player pushed her backward with the second strike.

Lore, attacking perhaps half a second later, swung his heavy blade toward the pyroknight's torso, but was blocked at the last moment by the flaming sword. The barbarian pushed himself into the attack, not allowing himself to be bounced away like Arzak, and he gritted his teeth, trembling, as he tried to hold against the Player's pushback. His sword—the great Bane Sword—glowed orange, then red, as the heat from the pyroknight's flaming blade bled into the metal. Lore, seeing where this was headed, pulled back from the attack before his blade could weaken any further.

But he didn't stop. He and Arzak pushed once more, not giving the Player a moment of peace, as we'd planned. They both moved in to strike at once, before another burst of water erupted up the Player's throat. The burst blinded Lore for a second, and the pyroknight quickly turned his attention to the orc to parry her latest attacks.

At this moment, I realized that our poisoning of the enemy hadn't just weakened him; it had also given him a new attack—something that the pyroknight seemed to just now be coming to understand.

"Hit him harder!" I shouted to the pair of close quarters–attackers.

"Already everything we have!" Arzak cried back with a strained voice. "It not enough!"

"Not *yet*, it's not," Val replied, suddenly raising her hands to the heavens and opening her eyes. For a second she remained like that, posed like a statue worshipping the gods, before dropping, exhausted, to a knee. I glimpsed her pulling her vial—stronger than mine—from her pocket before my attention was torn away by a howling of a wolf.

No, *wolves*.

"Val, what have—" I started.

"Attack him!" she replied. "Attack him now!"

I charged into the fight, risking a portal behind the pyroknight to *stab* him quickly in the back. With my *Knifework* level and equipment level, it wasn't like it was going to do too much damage—but it was at least enough to enrage the man.

The pyroknight roared with frustration before turning to swipe at me, but I was quicker, closing the portal just before I could meet my inevitable end at the tip of a flaming blade. The portal closed on the very end of the man's fire sword, slicing it off. In any other fight this might have been game-changing, but I had a sneaking suspicion that the pyroknight could just . . . summon more sword.

Making use of my distraction, Arzak landed a couple of strikes, slicing through the enemy's armor and drawing blood. This—combined with an arrow that landed in the man's neck, releasing its poison in a green weblike shape—enraged him further, and he summoned a ring of fire around himself.

As Lore, Arzak, and I stepped backward, avoiding the flames, a commotion in the forest announced new guests. A swarm of wolves—ten, maybe twelve—leaped out of the cover of the trees and charged past the startled Corminar and Lambkin, then past Val. They kept their many eyes fixed squarely on the Player.

So that's what she's been up to. Val stared the pyroknight down as though issuing a challenge, but the Player didn't stare back. Instead, he parried a strike from Lore and snarled at the approaching beasts.

With the raise of a hand, the Player whipped his ring of fire into a spinning vortex, the flames licking the air around it and causing us to retreat further. When the pyroknight whipped his hand forward, the fire tornado blitzed toward the wolves, heading not in a straight line but zigzagging from beast to beast, eliminating them one by one.

Lore and Arzak—less hypnotized than me—ignored the wolves and pressed the advantage once more, charging for the now-unprotected Player. They attacked simultaneously, three blades against the enemy's one. The pyroknight ducked under Lore's relatively slow attack, parried one of Arzak's swords, and then . . . found the other wedged into the side of his neck.

(Now, I know what you're thinking, reader. You're thinking: oh, that's it, that's done. Sadly, no. It wasn't.)

The Player gripped the blade, not caring about slicing his hand in the process, and he wrenched it from his body. He didn't release it despite the blood trickling from his palm, instead summoning fire within that grasp. The blade grew orange, then red, and then finally, with one twist of the pyroknight's hand, snapped in two.

Lore ran in for another attack, which the Player dodged by stepping quickly to one side, one hand now clutching the bloody wound in his neck. With another almost monstrous roar, he dropped his flaming sword, flung this hand forward, and sent a six-foot-wide fireball soaring toward Arzak. The orc dived out of the way just in time, only suffering a mild burn that the potion should have quickly seen to.

This didn't help Lambkin and Corminar, however. The fireball continued soaring through the air, flying quicker than any before it, and Lambkin and Corminar had only enough time to lower their bows, eyes wide, before the fireball was upon them. Lambkin threw himself in front of Corminar at the last moment, apparently meaning to take most of the damage, but he was too slow— the spell hit both of them. The two rangers fell to the floor, clutching at their wounds.

Neither of them had the powerful healing potions. Neither of them had fire resistance potions.

Neither of them were still in the fight.

CHAPTER FIFTY-EIGHT

As It Started

"Cor!" Val shouted, hand reaching toward the fallen elf.

"Concentrate," Arzak replied, voice strained. She couldn't have known that Corminar was still alive, just downed, but I supposed the instruction applied either way—we needed to finish this if we were to survive.

However, Val ignored the orc's suggestion, and instead of focusing on attacking the Player, she rushed across the road to Corminar's side, beginning to use her rather pitiful healing magicks to keep him on this side of the mortal fold. Getting him back on his feet was beyond her, but keeping him alive? That might just have been achievable.

With the lack of poison arrows, and the impact of the cursed sweet beginning to fade, the Player was growing stronger once more. But Arzak and Lore kept up their attacks—they knew as well as I did that right *now* was the weakest that the Player was going to get. Swords clashed against flaming blades, Arzak and Lore doing their best to use their superior number of weapons to their advantage, and now and then they landed a glancing hit.

But Lore, too, took damage. The enemy was a master with his flame-summoned sword—I was beginning to think there was nothing he couldn't do, though perhaps that was just the level differential at play—and even outnumbered, he occasionally maneuvered himself past Lore's parries. From Lore's closing wounds, I knew the potion supplied by Lambkin was hard at work, and there was only a matter of time before it would run out of power. We needed to end this *now*.

"Lore!" I shouted. "I'm going to drop you!"

"Do it!" came the reply, the barbarian having been the quickest to trust me and my portal magicks.

Wasting not a moment, I opened a portal directly behind Lore's feet, and another on the other side of the Player. Lore parried one of the pyroknight's attacks and then allowed himself to fall backward through the portal. He rotated as he fell, bringing his blade around preemptively in an attack on our enemy. The Bane Sword caught the Player in the back before he could do much to respond—a deep slash that ripped blood from flesh, an amount that looked substantial even from my obscured point of view.

"Another!" Lore cried.

I whipped hands forward to do the same again, opening a portal behind Lore's feet and back on the other side of the Player. But where this had worked before, we had no such luck on the second time around; the enemy was a quick learner. Even before Lore had fallen backward into the portal, the pyroknight had thrust a hand out to send a fireball soaring at the other side of the portal.

Fire magicks met the barbarian's flesh with a hiss, and Lore roared with pain. But he was not the sort of man to let pain stop him. Lore continued on with the attack, slicing the weapon toward the pyroknight's chest, but the enemy blocked him once more.

We needed to try something new.

I looked at the Player, at the rapidly fading green patches where the poison arrows had hit, at the wounds which seemed fewer and farther between than I had expected, and at the tired way in which he swung his flaming weapon.

Maybe we didn't need to try something new, I realized. Maybe the situation had changed. Maybe an old tactic might come good this time around.

"Lore?" I said.

"Yes?" came the response from the barbarian, his voice trembling.

"Push!"

I snapped one hand back to the sky far above, and the other to the space behind the Player.

Lore dropped his sword, it clattering to the floor, and he put his entire weight into tackling the enemy.

The pyroknight instinctively snapped his hands out to the side of the portal, finding some purchase on that strange otherworldly glowing ring, but . . . it wasn't purchase enough. The full weight of the burly Lore—no longer burdened by the giant sword—was substantial. So substantial that the Player's hands slipped away from the portal ring, and instead . . . snatched at Lore.

They fell through together.

I snapped my head up to the other end of the portal, where two figures fell toward the ground, and time seemed to slow.

If we could get the Player to hit the ground from that height, then we'd surely deal a huge amount of damage to him, though there was no guarantee he'd be eliminated. There was *never* that guarantee with him, it seemed. But if Lore hit the ground from that height, he'd definitely die. That was no question. And that, obviously, needed to be avoided at any cost.

My hand, still outstretched to the heavens, prepared to summon a portal that would save Lore from the fall, but they tumbled together, the Player keeping a firm grip on the barbarian as they plummeted toward the ground. There was no way of getting between them. No way of saving one without the other.

For a moment, I'm very sorry to say, I entertained the idea of letting them both fall, but then my good senses got the better of me. How could I live with one of the Slayers dying to save me? I knew the answer: I couldn't.

So, with a pit in my stomach, I opened a portal beneath the falling pair, and another on the ground facing upward. When the two plummeted through it, the direction of gravity suddenly changed on them, and their climb into the air slowed, before they began to fall back toward the portal once more.

But I'd moved the other side—a handy trick that I really needed to make more use of—and this led to the pair of them tumbling out of the portal into the Iron Sea.

The pyroknight's summoned sword hissed as the sea finally extinguished it—an act that caused its wielder to snarl at me. Both he and Lore swam for the shallows while Arzak and I charged to meet them at the coast.

The Player threw fireballs at Lore as they swam, the latter doing his best to avoid them by taking dips underwater, but still getting singed on the top of his head.

When Arzak reached the water, she came to an abrupt halt.

"Problem?" I asked, standing next to her in the shallows.

"Hard to swing sword in sea," she said.

Another fireball hit Lore as he stumbled out of the water, catching him squarely in the back. His drenched clothes did a lot to limit the damage, but it was enough to stumble him.

No, I quickly realized, it did more than that. This hit—the most recent of many—did damage that didn't quickly fade. It didn't fix itself. The potion was exhausted.

"Arzak . . ." I started.

"What?"

"Lore's out of healing."

The orc grimaced, raised her two swords in preparation to strike, and nodded.

"Lore!" I shouted. "Get—" And then I realized that I could do better than warning him. I opened up a portal beneath him, pulling him from the water to dump him on the beach near his discarded sword. Further from his attacker, he was safer. He'd need to stay out of trouble, now.

"Why'd you—" he started, and then blinked. "I'm not healing."

"No."

"I see." Lore turned and ran for the Bane Sword, plucking it from the ground like it was a tiny thing rather than something I struggled to lift at the best of times. I'd tried while he was sleeping.

The pyroknight didn't summon a new flaming sword, instead opting to switch back to more traditional fire magicks. I could only assume his stamina reserves were not anywhere near as large as his mana; he had one weakness after all. As soon as the Player was in shallow enough water to stand, he launched one fireball, then another, at Arzak.

The orc parried one away before getting struck in the shoulder by the other, though still she plowed onward toward the enemy.

As the Player prepared another spell, I readied myself to create a portal, and caught one of the next attacks, sending the fireball soaring back at its caster.

Arzak continued wading on, and the Player did the same, apparently not at all perturbed by the sight of the orc rapidly advancing upon him. His hands flicked with more speed than ever before, producing more balls of fire—some of which I portaled away, some of which Arzak parried—and then a flaming wall before him. This spell moved as he did, pushing forward at the same pace, and forcing Arzak to stumble backward.

I opened a portal in the depth of the sea as far as I could manage, opening the other end above the flaming wall to extinguish it.

But I was too slow. Arzak couldn't run when she was thigh high in water, and so the attack had caught up with her fast. The flames engulfed her before I could put them out, and I looked for signs that the healing potion had given up. The burns healed fast, and for a moment I thought we'd lucked out. The orc shattered my hope when she shouted, "Active effect gone!"

Any more hits on any of us could be the difference between life and death.

Arzak continued staggering backward toward Lore and I on the beach, regrouping.

"Any thoughts?" I asked.

"Nothing we not do already. Styk? Portal us."

I stared at the approaching enemy. "Are you sure?"

Footsteps behind us announced Val rejoining the battle, apparently—or *hopefully*—having kept Corminar from death.

"The potions being out changes nothing," Lore said. "We still have to hit him hard and fast."

The enemy stepped onto the sand.

"Alright," I said. "If you're sure . . ." I opened one portal above the pyroknight, the other end at our sides, and Lore and Arzak leaped through. As they tumbled toward the enemy, they struck down with their blades, meaning to slice.

But the Player was getting wise to my tricks. With the flick of his fingers, he created another wall of fire, this one above him. Arzak and Lore passed through it as they attacked, the flames engulfing them. Though all three of their swords struck true, sending the Player stumbling backward and grabbing at his open wounds, they took untold damage in the process.

I quickly flicked open a portal under them, sending the pair into the shallows to extinguish the flames. Of the two of them, only Arzak pulled herself to her feet. She grabbed Lore by the collar, wrenching him from the water. His body was limp.

"Not dead," she explained. "Just—"

But she didn't get to finish that sentence, because a ball of fire caught her in the head. Arzak gritted her teeth together, growled an unconvincing growl, and then tried to raise her swords.

"Arzak, no!" Val cried out. "No, no, no . . ."

The orc's two blades fell into the sand, one landing point first. The orc, trembling, looked at her fallen weapons, and then she joined them.

I looked to the Player, who fixed his gaze on me.

"It's up to the two of us, then," I said to the sorcerer as she arrived at my side.

Val glanced back at me, her deep brown eyes wide with fear, and then she gulped. "Just like this whole thing started," she replied.

There was no point saving mana now; if we didn't end this in the next minute or two, we'd be dead. I drained a good part of my mana reserves activating *Ash Husk*, my skin rippling as it changed, and I searched my mind desperately for an idea.

Nothing came.

"We're dead, aren't we?" Val asked.

"Looks like it."

"Great."

CHAPTER FIFTY-NINE

Falling

The Player stepped toward us slowly and steadily, a smile on his face that said he didn't think there was any point hurrying. And why would he? Most of our strongest had already fallen. Was he really going to care about one sorcerer and a Level 9 *Novice Bladespinner*?

"We could run?" Val suggested, still standing at my side.

"I think we both know you're not gonna leave your friends to die."

"No, I suppose not."

The Player drew closer, pace by pace, and I found myself taking a subconscious step backward. Val, seeing me do so, followed suit.

"Any chances you have any more bright ideas?" I asked. "Cos I think I'm . . . yeah, I'm out."

Val didn't immediately say anything, and as always, when the chatter-mouth was silent, it worried me.

"Val, what are you—"

"There is *one* spell I could try," she said. "Remember what I told you? About the first time I got cornered by a Player? I summoned a bogspawn to get out of it."

"You said you couldn't control it," I replied. "You said it was dumb luck that it attacked the Player and not you."

The sorcerer nodded. We were both stepping backward much more quickly by this point.

"You still can't control it, can you?"

"Nope."

"What are the chances it attacks him instead of us?" I asked.

"One in three, I'd guess. And that doesn't account for the possibility that it just goes to finish off one of the others."

"I don't think I like those odds. I don't—"

"What other choice is there, Styk?" the sorcerer interrupted me. "Die? He's just so strong. Every hit he takes barely seems to stagger him. He got hit in the *neck* earlier, and that's usually enough to bring *anyone* down."

Val was right. He'd been hit in the neck; Arzak had wedged one of her swords in deeply. So deeply. And yet, now . . . the Player didn't so much as sport a scratch. Then, the truth dawned on me at last.

"Oh, Val . . ." I said. "We've been so stupid."

"Speak for your—"

"We know he's got off-the-charts Intelligence, that's how he's got so much mana. But we wondered how he had so much health, too, right? Surely he hadn't invested in both Intelligence *and* Vitality to this degree?"

"Well, yeah, I—"

"He hasn't, Val. He hasn't invested in Vitality much at all. Think, Val, think!" We were stepping backward at this point as fast as we realistically could without tripping. The Player, still, was closing on us. "We've been thinking that he wanted Tokas for her healing, but what if that wasn't true? What if it's her illusion magicks that he was after? Why would that be, Val? Why would that be, unless . . ."

In my peripheral vision, I saw Val's eyes widen. "He's not strong; he's a healer."

"Yes."

"But how does that help—"

The Player flicked up a hand, apparently sick of waiting—or perhaps worried about where our conversation was going—and flung a fireball at the pair of us. Val and I dived separate ways, the attack passing between us and barely catching my ash-armored arm.

The sorcerer touched her hands to the ground, her eyes suddenly growing black, and I realized what she was doing. She was resorting to the bogspawn.

"Val, no!" I shouted. "There's another way!"

"Tell me," came her reply, and her voice emerged distorted, warbling and deep.

"Heal him! Heal *him*!"

"What? What good will that—"

I whipped up a portal to protect myself from the Player's latest attack. "Remember my hangover?" I replied, not wanting to spell it out in front of the pyroknight in case he saw where I was going with this. "I asked both you and Tokas to heal it. Remember what you said?"

Val's eyes returned to their normal color and grew wide. She whipped her hands forward. "One source," she said. Yellow-white light, not hidden by the enchantment of her obscurem, poured from her hands and trickled at the tiniest possible pace into the enemy.

The Player couldn't heal, not anymore. All it would take was some decent damage from me, and I might just be able to take him down. I searched myself for the answer to this problem. How best would I be able to deal damage without him killing me first? Because that was still an issue. I needed to—

The pyroknight pushed a hand out at his side, and I was too slow to react.

As a giant fireball shot toward Val, I reached out to open a portal between them, but I was too late; the spell passed the point of the portal before I could get it open.

Val took the hit squarely to the chest, and she screamed.

As the sorcerer collapsed to the floor, trying to exhaust the flames that engulfed her, the Player turned on me. And he sighed.

"It's over. It's all over. You're mine now."

Val began to cough up blood. Just like that, my new plan was ruined. It was hopeless.

"Finally," the Player continued, "we can put all this behind us. Tana doesn't have to know what I tried to do to her. All evidence will be . . ." He held up a hand, summoning a small ball of fire to hover just above his palm. ". . . ash."

"Tana?" I asked, eyes sweeping the landscape, looking for an advantage. Anything.

"Did you think your antics only attracted my attention? No. The Council knows all. Sees all. Has its fingers in everything across all the western continents."

I looked from Val to Corminar and Lambkin, passed out at the edge of town, and then to Arzak and Lore, who'd pushed themselves to the limit to take this man down. All of them were on the verge of death. All of them, the Player would kill as soon as he was done with me. The only thing keeping them alive was . . . me.

They were screwed.

Against my better instincts, I closed my eyes. I figured that if I was going out, then I might as well not see it coming. Maybe that would spare me just an ounce of pain.

I breathed deeply, hearing the Player step closer to me, taking his time about the kill. Salivating at it.

And then a familiar voice roared.

I opened my eyes, and both my head and the Player's whipped to where the noise had come from—the road into town. If I'd expected salvation—and frankly, I hadn't—I definitely hadn't expected it to come in this form.

Tokas continued to roar as she charged.

I seized the advantage of the distraction to retreat behind the cover of an upturned water trough as the Player turned to loose a fireball at the woman he once traveled with.

Before the Player released his spell, Tokas launched one of her own, splitting herself into three, and then nine, and then more and more copies of herself. All of them roared in an eerie chorus as they launched themselves toward him.

The pyroknight released his spell at one Tokas, chosen by instinct, and the illusion faded away as the fire engulfed it.

"I'll be Val!" the many copies of Tokas shouted.

"What?" I replied.

"Your plan—I heard it. We do it. We do it now!" Tokas and the illusions scattered around the Player, each of them loosing a tiny trickle of healing magicks into the enemy, all of them fake but one. The Player, judging by his frantic turning, had just as much idea which was the real one as I did, it seemed.

I snapped back to reality, grasping my knife once more.

I realized I had just one shot at this. As soon as I did damage to the Player, he would eliminate me. I eyed up my power bars—mana was dwindling, but I still had plenty of stamina.

There was *one* way. One way where I could deal incredible damage. A way that I'd tried before to great success. I opened a portal in the sky high above the Player, and another at my feet.

I fell through it.

I knew, of course, that I was falling to my death. Outside of the warped reality the Ascendent Cultist had created in that tavern, all those weeks ago, fall damage would most certainly apply. I was falling to my death.

And yet, it didn't seem to matter.

I took solace in the fact that I would take the Player with me. Everyone else—all of those idiots I'd come to call friends—would get a chance to survive. That was enough for me.

As I fell, I turned myself toward the ground, seeing it hurtling up at me. I pulled out my knife, pointing it squarely downward, directing it toward the center of the Player's skull. I activated my *Stab* skill, putting all of my weight and the force of the fall behind it, and I resisted the urge to close my eyes.

This death I could face; it was at my own hand. It was of my own making.

With every second that passed, my speed increased. Below me, the still healing Tokas moved her illusions to preoccupy the Player, keeping him turning on the spot and firing spells at the tieflings around him.

He didn't look up until the last moment, and by then it was too late.

As I *stabbed*, the Ranger's Blade pierced his skull with ease, burying itself deep in the Player's brain, and I had just enough time to relish the kill before I, too, crashed into the ground.

Level 42 Pyroknight defeated!

> **Worldbending**: +10,300XP
> *Worldbending increased to Level 23!*
> **Base Points Gained**: +10 INT, +10 Free Points (INT/WIS/CHA)

> **Ability Selection Unlocked**
> *Select an ability from the list below . . .*

> **Knifework**: +8,900XP
> *Knifework increased to Level 21!*
> **Base Points Gained**: +4 DEX, +4 STR, +8 Free Points (VIT/DEX/STR)

> **Ability Selection Unlocked**
> *Select an ability from the list below . . .*

> *Level up!*
> *You increased to Level 10*

> *Class evolved!*
> **Level 10 Bladespinner**
> *Race: Human*

The pain was too much even to scream.

It was simply . . . overwhelming.

I was paralyzed, legs crumpled beneath me, blood spilling out like nothing I'd ever seen before.

Though Tokas hurried to my side, healing magicks at full power, I already knew it was too late. My eyelids grew heavy.

"Heal . . ." I whispered, ". . . them."

My health bar drained. Drained. Drained.

To nothing.

My ultimate plan had gone just like I expected: I died at the end of it.

. . .

. . .

. . .

. . .

. . .

Descendant of the Architects defeated!
Sisyphus Artifact: Charge replenished!

CHAPTER SIXTY

From the Ashes

Everything was dark.

Or, rather, it wasn't so much dark as it was that there was nothing. It was as though I didn't exist but for the notifications before me. I was in a limbo state of sorts, somewhere between life and death, floating in the aether.

> *Sisyphus Artifact: Leveled up!*
> **Artifact Upgrade Unlocked**
> *Select [2] upgrades from the list below . . .*
> **1. Increase Charges VI** [7 > 8]
> **2. Extend Active Period II** [1,000 > 1,500]
> **3. Increase Effect I** [+400 percent > +900 percent]
> **4. Add Experience Preservation Charge IV** [+1]

I was there, it seemed, because the *Sisyphus Artifact* was waiting to revive me. I could only assume it couldn't resolve the effect until the upgrade was unlocked.

I was going to live.

The revelation hit me like a hex spell, metaphorically knocking me from feet that I wasn't quite sure I possessed in this form.

> *Warning: Please resolve upgrades in the next [59] seconds, or user will be lost.*

This message focused me for obvious reasons, and I read through the four upgrade choices once more. I already had a charge replenished—presumably now one of seven charges remaining—so I immediately passed over the first option. Hopefully I wouldn't be dying a *third* time anytime soon, and therefore wouldn't need that.

I eyed up the timer on the message. Forty-two seconds remained.

The next two options were both ways of ensuring I got more out of the lifespan of the artifact, but I was too rushed to do the math on which one was better. I almost picked the both of them—I had two selections, after all—before I realized what the last option implied.

If I didn't pick that, it seemed, I would be reset back to level 0 once more, and I didn't much fancy that. No way. I picked that one without giving it another thought; I wasn't going through all that again.

> *Warning: Please resolve upgrades in the next [11] seconds, or user will be lost.*

There was no time. I picked one of the two middle options at random—getting it wrong was better than being dead.

> *Artifact upgrade confirmed!*
> *HP Depleted*
> **Sisyphus Artifact Activated**
> Charges Remaining: (0 / 8)
> *Preservation Charged Used: Respawning at Level 10 . . .*
> **Active Effect: Legacy of Sisyphus**
> Days remaining: 999 / 1,000
> *XP gain increased by +900 percent*

I gasped as I awoke, sitting bolt upright and eliciting a scream from Val, who had apparently been perched at my side. As the sorcerer watched, I felt my bones pop back into their joints as the breaks mended and as the open wounds fizzed shut.

"You're . . ." Val mumbled. "You're . . ."

"My head hurts," I said.

"Your *head?*" the sorcerer repeated. "After all that, your *head* hurts? How are you still alive? How are—"

I pulled the metal octahedron from my pocket, placing it against Val's hand. It was still hot to the touch. "Killing the Player," I said. "It gave the artifact a new charge."

"You knew that? All this time, you knew that would happen, and you didn't think to tell us?"

I considered Val for a moment before shaking my head. "I didn't know. I didn't know anything. Just what that old guy told us."

"You—"

"I thought I'd die," I said, putting it simply.

Val stared on at me, meeting my gaze more than was typical of her; usually she'd look away within a second or two. She touched my still healing right hand, and she squeezed it gently. "Thanks, Styk."

"No problem," I replied, concentrating all my efforts on keeping a straight face, and not letting Val know how much her squeezing my hand hurt. Suddenly, memories of earlier in the fight flooded my brain, and I realized where I was. I looked around for signs of other survivors.

Lore sat propped up against a tree, still clearly very injured, but breathing, and awake. Tokas crouched over Arzak, closing her wounds. The orc's gaze was fixed on the tiefling, her hand tight around her sword, as though she might still need to use it. Of the other two, there was no sign.

"Corminar?" I asked, and then after a moment of realization, added, "Lambkin?"

"Alive," Val said. "Tokas healed them; their wounds weren't as bad as Lore's and Arzak's. They're searching for ingredients—Corminar said he was going to whip up some health potions to fix whatever Tokas isn't able to."

My eyes drifted back to the tiefling. "She saved us, you know."

"I know. Doesn't change what she did, though."

"No," I said, watching as Tokas healed up the worst of Arzak's wounds. "I suppose it doesn't."

The Slayers, Tokas, Lambkin, and I took refuge in the half-burnt, half-drenched, recently abandoned tavern, taking it upon ourselves to pour an ale each, though none of us—even Val—did much in the way of drinking. We sat around a booth in silence, inspecting the last of our wounds, sipping the tiniest amounts of beer, or—in Lore's case—getting a moment of shut-eye. I couldn't blame him; after what we'd just been through, I was exhausted, too.

There was another outstanding matter to attend to, though.

As beer grew flat in front of us, and blood soaked into the—admittedly already plenty damaged—seating, Tokas prepared herself to speak. When the inevitable question finally came, she kept it simple.

"What will you do with me?"

Nobody moved, nobody spoke, and suddenly everyone found their beers incredibly interesting. Tokas didn't push the matter, just letting the topic fester, and when the silence finally became too much, both Val and Corminar looked to Arzak to respond. The orc wasn't their leader anymore, but old habits died hard.

"You are not in team now," Arzak said. "Beyond this, I not know."

Tokas nodded, taking this news with composure other than a large gulp, and then turned to Val. Her eyes asked if the sorcerer agreed.

"We should kill you, really," Val replied, meeting the tiefling's gaze.

Tokas choked back tears, but didn't say anything, only nodding once.

"Val . . ." Corminar started, but the sorcerer held up a hand to beg for his patience.

"But you've got two young kids, and your good-for-nothing partner has—"

"He's not good-for-nothing," Tokas interrupted, meeting Val's gaze with a sudden intensity in her eyes. "He was taken from me."

Silence fell across the table once more, thick in its essence.

"I'm . . . sorry," Val said. "I didn't realize."

Tokas nodded, accepting this apology. She would, of course; it was nothing compared to what *she* was guilty of.

"We won't take a mother away from two young children," Val continued after another moment of pause. She glanced around the table, to make sure nobody was disagreeing with her. "But Arzak's right; you can't travel with us anymore. Not after what you did. And if you step out of line again, if there's even a *sense* that you might be up to something . . ."

"I won't," the tiefling replied. "I promise."

"You'll forgive us if your word is not enough," Corminar said.

In the booth's corner, Lambkin—who had until this moment seemed uncomfortable to be involved in such a discussion—leaned forward. "I will check in on her occasionally, make sure she's sticking to her promise. If not me personally, then, well, I still know some guardsmen around the continent who owe me a favor or two."

Corminar looked to Arzak, who nodded after a moment of thought about this arrangement. When silence fell once more, faces turned slowly to Tokas.

"You should go," the orc said.

With no words, and a glum expression, Tokas nodded, then slid from the booth and ambled out the tavern without so much as a glance back.

"Did we do the right thing?" Lore asked, his eyes lingering on where Tokas had disappeared moments earlier.

"Could you have trusted her?" I replied.

Lore said nothing, and that was an answer in and of itself.

Lambkin sighed, groaned, and then stood up from the table. "Suppose I should be going, too, now that this is done."

"What'll you do?" I asked him. "Don't suppose clearing my name is in the cards at all?"

The ex-captain smiled an apology. "I'd try if I thought it was possible. But this . . . nobody would believe this. Not about a Player. No, what I'm going to do instead is make a quiet life for myself. I'll pay a visit back to Umlok, marry Sae—whether her father approves or not—and we'll find somewhere we can call home, out there in the Tundras. If all goes according to plan, you'll never hear from me again. No ambushes, no traps . . . nothing."

Corminar raised his still-full glass in salute, and upon this signal, the other four of us did the same.

"Good luck, lamb friend," Arzak said.

And then we were down to five.

"It's done," I found myself saying. "We did it. We won."

Val smiled at me, though I didn't find myself enjoying this victory as much as I might have expected to. The lack of a rapidly approaching death was nice, yes, but it left me with a feeling of emptiness; I didn't quite know where to go once this beer was drunk.

"I missed the challenge, I must admit," the ranger said, finally taking his first sips of beer and then recoiling at the taste. "Perhaps I shall put the procurement business on hold, and return to the Slaying. That is . . . if the rest of you might join me?"

"Well, *I'm* in," Val said immediately.

She looked to Arzak, who met her gaze for a moment, then nodded. "Yes. Important work."

Lore didn't say anything. At least, not until Val prompted him in the form of an elbow to the side. He winced at the touch. "I have sheep to return to," he said.

"Your babies," Val and I said in unison.

"My babies," Lore agreed. "I've already been gone too long. But, on the other hand . . . if we're not gonna stop these Players getting away with everything they do, nobody else is gonna, are they?"

Val smiled.

"You're in?"

Lore nodded. "I need to check in at the farm, first. And I'm gonna want some downtime there between kills. But, yeah . . . I'm in."

And then, to my surprise, four faces turned to me.

"And what about you, portal boy?" Val asked.

"Me?" I repeated, pointing to myself as though the question might be too vague. "Yeah, *you*."

"You prove handy," Arzak said. "I like portals."

"And I think, perhaps, our team has a vacancy these days," Corminar said.

"You'd trust me with that?"

Lore laughed. "What, you think any of the rest of us have *died* for the team? Think I trust you more than any of 'em."

"Come on, Styk, what do you think?" Val asked, taking my hand again, but more gently this time. "If this Council is what we all think, there's going to be a lot more of this kind of work coming our way soon. And I'd feel much happier about it if you joined us."

I paused, as if to appear to be giving the question some thought, even though I already knew the answer. "Alright," I finally said, then punctuated my reply with a sip of beer. "I'm in."

"Welcome to Slayers," Arzak said.

CHAPTER SIXTY-ONE

A Matter of Blood

In the days that followed, the Slayers—including its newest member, me—all made our way back to Lore's farm, where his "babies" were very happy to see him. His farmhand, Seld, had been happiest of all that Lore had returned, and had desperately tried to explain that the sheep had started playing a game where they could see who could headbutt him the most. Lore seemed to have been caught between believing his assistant and his sheep, and by the time I left a few days after that, he still didn't seem to have made up his mind.

Arzak and I had left Lore, Corminar, and Val at the farm while the barbarian had been trying to convince the ranger to help him shovel sheep waste—something I suspected he wouldn't be successful in.

The reason I'd left them was a temporary one: since the battle with the pyroknight and everything that happened afterward, I wanted to learn more about the artifact I had in my possession. No longer was it just a "spent" object, one that I carried around simply for reasons of sentimentality. No, now I realized there was more to it than that, that I might unlock power beyond my imagination if I just focused on getting the most out of it.

The last supposed "expert" we'd spoken to—the old man with the overdue library books, now dead, if the Player was to be believed—had given me the name of someone else who might be able to help me. Lillya, up in Thistle Fort, might be able to tell me more about the metal object I, at this moment, held in my grasp.

When I'd told the team what I intended to do, Val and Lore had jumped to come with me, but I told them that I was level 10 now and that I should be able to handle myself. They hadn't seemed convinced, but their concerns were put to bed when Arzak said she would come with me. She'd said that she had family to visit in Thistle Fort, that it was a good excuse to go. I didn't know if she was sparing me embarrassment by not saying that she'd be keeping an eye on me, too.

As we traveled, we talked, and I got to know the older orc a good deal better. She spoke about her time after the Slayers disbanded, about her freelance work and how she'd marketed herself. She told me about her family—a clan, really, and one that made little distinction between siblings and third cousins twice removed—and how most of them still lived in the orcish cities. And, most surprising of all, she told me about her passion: knitting.

Arzak produced her latest work in progress as we made camp one night—a long dark purple scarf with circular patterns on it. It wasn't until after she made me inspect it and got my opinion on it that I realized it was for me. "For die to save us," she had explained. "Is cold in Rose Home." Rose Home being what the orcs called Thistle Fort, of course.

The orc tried to get me into knitting, too, and I gave it my best shot, but it was something that I just didn't have the patience for. Arzak explained that it would be good for me to have a craft skill—that it was a good way to level up while we had some downtime—and I pressed on. After watching me getting into a state of knots and strands, however, she sighed, took the knitting needles away from me, and handed me instead a small sewing needle and thread.

I raised an eyebrow. "Sewing?" I asked.

"You want take more damage? Use light armor. You want make light armor? This where you start."

I studied the needle, trying to push the thread through its eye. "You gonna tell Val?"

Arzak didn't respond, only smirking.

Admittedly, I got on a lot better with this particular type of crafting, and soon I was the proud owner of level 1 in a new skill, as well as the relevant ability:

Needlework increased to Level 1!
Base Points Gained: +1 DEX, +1 CHA, +1 Free Point (DEX/CHA)
Ability Unlocked: Stitch
Stitch (Needlework): Create a basic stitch in common fabrics. Ability scales on [CHA].

Was it going to be make-or-break in the midst of fighting a Player? Absolutely not, unless they were particularly into the arts. But was it, long-term, likely to pay off? Well, who's to say? I was proud of it nonetheless.

That didn't mean I didn't also have a few new much more handy abilities, courtesy of all the leveling up I did when I defeated the pyroknight. There were two new ones, each of which I picked to round myself out a little more. If I was going to keep investing in Intelligence, with little Vitality, then I figured it was a good idea to start picking some more defensive abilities.

> **Shrill Perimeter (Worldbending):** Create a perimeter wall of a 20-foot radius, invisible to all but those adept in magicks. If an enemy crosses this perimeter, this spell releases the shriek of a banshee.

I'd tested this one out at Lore's farm to figure out precisely how it worked. My first observation was that it didn't have a continuous drain on my mana while it was active, only taking an initial mana cost, though that amount was fairly hefty. My second observation had been that sheep did *not* constitute an enemy. However, a sheep after you took its food away *did*. What I took from this was that the label *enemy* was defined by their intentions toward you. Finally, I'd learned that the banshee's wail was bloody *loud*, and very likely to piss off Val— this was the best news of the lot.

So that was the defensive ability. As for *Knifework* . . .

> **Mana-Fueled (Worldbending):** *Passive.* Optionally, use mana in place of stamina to activate *Knifework* abilities.

When I'd seen this option, my eyes had actually lit up, I think. I'd been investing in Intelligence all this time, and so Dexterity hadn't had much of a look-in. Now that I could use mana in place of stamina for my *Knifework* attacks, this wasn't a problem at all—I could continue to invest in this stat and use it to power both of my main combat skills. This ability choice had required level 20 in any magick skill to unlock, and so was definitely geared toward hybrid magick and melee builds like myself.

These days, I was feeling like a fully grown adult once more.

Arzak and I parted ways the first morning spent in Thistle Fort, after I told her at least three times that I didn't need her to come with me. When I left, she still wasn't looking all that happy about it, but she did at least let me go. Alone.

I checked. She definitely wasn't following me, though unlike in cities further south, her head didn't stick up over the crowds here, so it was hard to be completely sure.

I held my new purple scarf tight as I pushed through the blizzards rattling through the streets. Well, *I* say blizzards, but I did pass a greengrocer who seemed sincere when they said it was a "nice day."

Pressing on, I found the address that had been given to me by the nice innkeeper at the tavern in which we'd taken board. A small wooden sign with faded lettering squeaked on its hinges as it blew in the wind. I wrenched the door open, pretty much threw myself inside, and slammed it shut behind me. I breathed a sigh of relief as I rid myself of the bracing winds.

An orc looked up from behind the shop counter, a pair of thick glass goggles making her eyes look enormous, a tiny device in her hands. "Woah," she said, looking at me, "big."

I gestured to my face. "Glasses," I said.

"Ah yes." The orc hurriedly pulled the goggles off. "Oh, small now."

I resisted the urge to make a sarcastic comment, though if Val was around, I thought she would have encouraged it. That or mocked me. I shook the last of the snow from my coat and scarf before responding. "You're Lillya, right?" I asked, and my question was answered with a nod. "I was sent to see you about getting some information."

"Oh? Someone send you? Who?" Lillya replied, sitting back in her stool.

"A man in Birrow."

"Old?" the orc asked. "White hair? Small? Read lot of books?"

I nodded.

"Bertram, yes," Lillya said. "How is he?"

Pausing for a moment to work out if there was any way of getting out of having to answer this, I stumbled on my words. "Dead, I'm afraid."

But the orc didn't seem to take this news poorly. "Mm," she said. "Sound like him. What he send you for?"

I pulled the metal octahedron from my pocket, the one that had saved my life not once, but twice, by this point, and I placed it on the counter.

"May I?" the orc asked, gesturing to the artifact.

I nodded. "That's what I'm here for."

The goggles went straight back on the orc's eyes and she studied the artifact carefully, turning it over gently in her hands. "Hmm," she said. "Mmm. You use this?" Lillya placed the Sisyphus Artifact gently in my outstretched hand.

"Twice," I replied, against my better instinct.

The orc froze for a moment, studying me, then nodded. It took me a second to realize that she was *identifying* me. "You do not say Player," Lillya said.

I blinked. "No. Why would I?"

"Because only Players use Sisyphus Artifact."

I couldn't help but laugh. "No, no, I'm not a Player. Trust me, if you knew all I'd been through."

"Mmm. In blood, then. How well did you know parents?"

"I knew my dad well, but—"

"And mother?" Lillya asked.

"I . . ." I started, stifling a gulp. My absent mother. The adventurer that my father had only met twice—once on the night they . . . well, you know, and the other on the night I turned up on his doorstep. "No, no, she couldn't have been—"

"Is only way," Lillya said, reaching below the counter to pick up a gold amulet. "You know what this is?"

I blinked, still struggling with the revelation of who—or *what*—my mother might have been. When I finally looked down at the piece of jewelry, it took me a moment to recognize the symbol on it—a golden sun with a line through it.

"I am member of ancient order," Lillya said. "One that stretch from the Isle of Old Ways to Badlands. The Cult of Ascendency, they say. You know us?"

"I . . . I . . ." I found myself saying, stumbling backward.

"We live to serve blood of Players. We live to serve *you*."

I stared the orc down for a moment, searching desperately for signs that she was joking, that this was a prank, that this terrible revelation simply couldn't be. But it rang true; the pyroknight had been surprised to see that I could use the artifact. Why would he be surprised, unless . . .

"How I serve?" Lillya asked.

The only answer I could give was to turn and run.

Tana

Tana watched on as her associates squeezed the last bit of health from the mercenary. The orc—Lev, his name had been—had given up all he'd known about Jacob, confirming Tana's belief that the pyroknight had sought to betray them. It had taken hours—the orc deserved credit—but in the end there had been no secrets left to uncover. Only at that point had Tana told her interrogators to let the orc die.

The head of the Council stared at the dead mercenary, now drooping from the bindings on the rack, taking in the sight of what she had done. She took no relish in the deaths she'd caused. In fact, if they'd been able to seize their victories without hurting a single soul, Tana would have jumped at the opportunity. But the reality was that some people had to die in order for the Council to succeed. With every death, Tana felt herself grow more and more numb to the guilt, and she wasn't sure she liked how this was changing her.

Finally, Tana tore her eyes away from the body, turning away and heading up the stairs, out of the dungeons of Castle Ryse. As she traveled through the twisting corridors of the fortress, a young woman suddenly appeared at her side.

"My Lady, the Council await—"

Tana rid herself of the assistant with the flick of her hand, not wasting so much as a breath on someone who was little more than a peasant risen above her station. If Tana were to interrogate why those sorts irritated her so, she might have realized that it was because she had begun her journey at that station—that it was a memory of her distant past. But she shook her head, ridding herself of those thoughts before they could plague her once more.

When she burst into the Council's meeting chamber, she found that all but two of the seats were already occupied. Of the Council's members, some wore enchanted hoods that obscured their features, while others displayed their faces with pride. It was the latter with whom Tana felt more affinity; those who weren't too cowardly to own their actions. But she couldn't speak this aloud, for she needed the lot of them.

"Council is in session," she said as she entered the chamber, taking one of the two unoccupied seats—the one at the center of the round table, rather than the one near the end of a wing. Silence fell across the room, punctured only by the screech of the chair leg against the stone floor as Tana sat, and all eyes were upon her.

Tana paused for a moment before speaking. Not because she needed to think, but because she needed to reiterate that she led this secret contingent; she would speak when she was ready, and not before.

"You will notice that the rumors are indeed true; we are down to eleven."

A gentle murmur passed over the table.

"But I don't wish any of you to worry about Jacob's departure. He was the weakest of us, of course, but there is another reason we should not be concerned."

She waited for questions at this point, but none came; she had trained her Council well.

"I have just finished speaking with one of Jacob's associates, who reinforced that which Niamh"—Tana spared a nod for the woman sitting two places to her right—"suspected all along. He was indeed seeking to betray us."

The murmuring was louder this time, punctuated by a man at the end of the table—a hood obscuring their identity—asking, "And is this what we can expect from the Council? Backstabbing and betrayal?"

Tana met the man's eyes, or where the man's eyes would have been. "I assure you, Jacob was the exception, not the rule. The weakest of us in more ways than one, perhaps. He did not believe in the grand plan, that which we have all put great pains into pushing forward. He wished to take our life forces as his own."

"How?" the mysterious man asked.

"The Sisyphus Artifact," Niamh replied. Her spies had been busy.

Tana allowed Niamh another nod. The woman didn't smile externally, but Tana knew that she had the woman well under her thumb—she would feel great pride at such recognition from her. "Indeed. That which we thought a myth is indeed a reality. Our ancestors—the original Architects themselves—were not flawless. There were oversights. We, of anyone, know that to be true. But we have a problem no longer; the man is dead."

The leader of the Council intentionally left out the part that the man hadn't died at her hand; it would not do for the rest of the Council to know that the locals were fighting back.

"In Jacob's place, I am putting Niamh in charge of our efforts in the Gentle Tundras. Though Jacob did indeed set the groundwork for our plan in this region, his focus lately has . . . drifted. Niamh will see to it that our schemes catch up with the planned timeline."

Niamh stood up from her seat, nodding to the Council as though she had heard this news already; it suited her for the rest of the Council to believe that she was held in Tana's private confidence. "We are behind schedule," the woman said. "Of that, there is no doubt. But I believe with a little coin in the right hands, and a little more pressure from our hired bandits, we can resolve this in no time."

"And the Golden Canal?" another member of the Council asked—one wearing a golden amulet bearing the sigil of a sun split in two. Yusef, his name was, though few in this room knew his identity, for he kept his face disguised by the hood of his pale orange robe.

"We will complete the project in due course, I assure you," Tana said. "We have people soothing the diplomatic relations with the elves. After all, Amira needs us to succeed just as much as we do, does she not? She has suitable motivation."

"Power and fortune represents the carrot," the leader of the cult continued. "Perhaps we might also try the stick."

A murmuring passed over the Council, and Tana held out a hand to beg their silence. The noise ceased instantly. "In due time, perhaps. For now, our efforts are working. Let's not risk changing that."

Once the Council dissolved, Tana grabbed Niamh by the arm, leading her away into one of the back rooms. From the look in the young woman's eyes, she was wondering what Tana might need from her—but just which of the rumors about Tana did she believe?

"There is another matter," Tana told the young woman. "One which I am trusting to you, and you alone—the others must not learn the truth."

Niamh remained quiet, waiting for Tana to continue. She was loyal, this one.

"Jacob's death was not our doing. While you are in the Tundras, if you hear anything that might identify the culprit . . ."

"I will bring it to you," the woman responded with a nod.

"No need," Tana replied. "I already have so much to oversee. Just handle it yourself, will you?"

Niamh smiled. "It would be my pleasure."

About the Author

O. S. Marrow is a progression fantasy author with a particular interest in the philosophical and metaphysical. His passion for writing started at a very young age, as he scribbled down fan fiction inspired by his favorite books (none of which should ever see the light of day). Marrow currently lives in London, United Kingdom, and is often seen staring out of his study window, searching for the perfect next word.